"Aren't you wearing the uniform of a challenger?" the guy asked, looking every bit as bewildered as I felt.

Uh-oh. It was the shirt. It seemed this red shirt with the black diagonal stripes was only worn by challengers. Whoever *they* were. I could only hope that challengers were cool people whom everyone loved and nobody ever gave a hard time to.

Yeah, right.

Before I could ask the guy anything else, I heard a tortured scream come from across the noisy room. A quick look told me that unlike the guy who was playing the shoot-out game, the player who was running through the 3-D maze wasn't having as much luck. GAME OVER flashed in big blue letters on his screen. The player had fallen to his knees. He truly looked beaten. His head hung and he was breathing hard. No doubt he had given the game his all, only to lose. I wondered if the reaction of a loser was going to be as dramatic as that of a winner.

I wasn't prepared for the answer.

Read what critics and fans have to

"The nonstop plot developments keep the many pages turning and readers wanting more."

—*School Library Journal*, on *The Lost City of Faar*

"A talented world builder, MacHale creates endlessly fascinating landscapes and unique alien characters. . . . The series is shaping up to be a solid addition to the fantasy genre and will keep readers not only busy but also content until the next Harry Potter appears."

—*Voice of Youth Advocates*, on *The Lost City of Faar*

"A fast pace, suspenseful plotting, and cliff-hanger chapter endings . . . nonstop action, snappy dialogue, pop-culture references, and lots of historical trivia."

—*School Library Journal*, on *The Never War*

"MacHale's inventiveness makes this book the best entry in the series so far . . . remarkable insight."

—*Voice of Youth Advocates*, on *The Never War*

"Pendragon rules!"—Java

"PLEASE KEEP THEM COMING!!!! And if you need somebody to pre-read your books like I believe you said your nephew and wife do, I'd be right there to do it. THEY ARE THAT GOOD!!!"—Joshua

❖ ❖ ❖

say about the Pendragon series:

"I am insanely in love with the Pendragon books. I think that they are even better than the Harry Potter books."—Monique

"I absolutely LOVE your Pendragon books. My two best friends also love them, and whenever I get the next one they fight over who gets to read it first!"—Elisabeth

"Forget the Wands and Rings!! Pendragon all the Way!!"
—A Fan

"I'm pretty sure that I no longer have nails, as I was constantly biting them as I read the fourth Pendragon adventure."—Dan

"Pendragon is the best book series of all time."—Dark

"Nothing compares. I can't read another book without thinking 'Pendragon is better than this.' "—Kelly

"The Pendragon books will blow you away like no other books you have ever read."—Karen

"This series just pulls you into a world filled with suspense, treachery, and danger. Five stars easily; it deserves ten!!!"
—Greg

"Man, I gotta tell ya—these books are fantastic!"—Adam

❖ ❖ ❖

PENDRAGON

JOURNAL OF AN ADVENTURE THROUGH TIME AND SPACE

PENDRAGON

JOURNAL OF AN ADVENTURE THROUGH TIME AND SPACE

Book Seven:

The Quillan Games

D. J. MacHale

Aladdin

New York   London   Toronto   Sydney

ALADDIN
An imprint of Simon & Schuster Children's Publishing Division
1230 Avenue of the Americas, New York, NY 10020
Copyright © 2006 by D. J. MacHale
All rights reserved, including the right of reproduction
in whole or in part in any form.
ALADDIN and related logo are registered
trademarks of Simon & Schuster, Inc.
Also available in a SIMON & SCHUSTER BOOKS FOR YOUNG READERS
hardcover edition.
For information about special discounts for bulk purchases, please contact
Simon & Schuster Special Sales at 1-866-506-1949 or business@simonandschuster.com.
The Simon & Schuster Speakers Bureau can bring authors to your live event. For more
information or to book an event, contact the Simon & Schuster Speakers Bureau
at 1-866-248-3049 or visit our website at www.simonspeakers.com.
Designed by Debra Sfetsios
The text of this book was set in Apollo MT.
Manufactured in the United States of America
First Aladdin Paperbacks edition December 2007
4 6 8 10 9 7 5
The Library of Congress has cataloged the hardcover edition as follows:
MacHale, D. J.
The Quillan games / by D. J. MacHale.—1st S&S ed.
p. cm. —(Pendragon ; bk. 7)
Summary: With more questions than answers about Saint Dane, Bobby travels to the
territory of Quillan and is forced to play games where only the winner survives.
[1. Adventures and adventurers—Fiction. 2. Diaries—Fiction. 3. Fantasy.]
I. Title. II. Series: MacHale, D. J. Pendragon ; bk. 7.
PZ7.M177535Qui 2006
[Fic]
2005029902
ISBN 978-1-4169-1423-5 (hc)
ISBN 978-0-689-86913-6 (pbk)
0211 OFF

For my sister Kathie,
who loves to play games and tell great stories

A great big greeting to everyone in Halla.

The flume beckons. It's time to jump in for another trip. For those of you new to the story, welcome. For everyone who has followed Bobby's adventure from the beginning, the next pieces of the puzzle are here for you. Many questions will be answered in these pages. Of course, just as many will be raised. That's the way it works in Halla when you're trying to keep pace with a demon who loves to confound and torment. I'm not talking about Saint Dane, I'm talking about me. Muhahahahahaha!

As always I want to send out a great big thanks to all you readers who have been loyally following the story. From Canada to China to Australia and all points in between, more and more people are stepping into the flume. I especially have to thank all readers who have been sending me mail to discuss the story. One of the favorite parts of my day is sitting down to read about your thoughts and answer your questions. Or should I say, answer *some* of your questions. Everybody knows I don't like to be a spoiler and give away secrets. That would be cheating.

As with all my books, I'd like to thank some of the many people who help bring them to you. The wonderful folks at Simon & Schuster have been great supporters from the beginning. Rick Richter, Ellen Krieger, Jenn Zatorski, Kelly Stidham, and so many others are hugely responsible for keeping the Pendragon story rolling. My editor, Julia Richardson, has once again been a great help in getting the best possible story out of my sometimes muddled brain. If you think these stories have lots of twists and turns that are sometimes tricky to follow, try writing them! Thank you, Julia. Victor Lee has created one of my favorite covers with this book. It's great to see each of his individual covers, but also to see them all together. It's visual proof of how far we've all come. Heidi Hellmich did an amazing job of copyediting this book. When you jump around through time and space, it's tough keeping all those tenses straight, but Heidi has managed to do it yet again. Amazing. Of course I have to thank my continuing band of acolytes: Richard Curtis, Peter Nelson and his team, and Danny Baror. They are all responsible for worrying about the many details of the book business that make my head hurt. Thank you, guys. My wife, Evangeline, is my constant source of support and encouragement. Without her calming assurances, I'd probably be throwing out more work than I keep and these books would take years to write! Finally, my daughter, Keaton, has provided me with one of the most satisfying experiences I think a writer can have. She wasn't even born when the adventure began and the first few books were published. Now, at two and a half years old, when we walk through a bookstore she'll point to the Pendragon shelf and exclaim: "Daddy's book!" It does my heart proud. Of course she then blows right past them and heads straight for the Dr. Seuss section, but that's another story. These are only a few of the people who have helped bring Bobby Pendragon's story to you, and I sincerely thank all of them.

Okay. Are we done here? Are we ready? When last we were with Bobby, he had received a mysterious invitation that brought him to the territory of Quillan; Mark had saved Courtney's life, though she lay near death in a hospital on Second Earth; and Andy Mitchell had performed a most curious and impossible deed. With all that has happened and all that is still to come, there's one question that must now be asked:

Do you like to play games?

Hobey ho, let's go.
—D. J. MacHale

QUILLAN

I like to play games.

Always have. It doesn't matter if it's a simple game of checkers or something more brainy, like chess. I like board games like Stratego or Risk, and pretty much every team sport that exists. I like playing computer games and card games and charades and Scrabble, and when I was a kid, I was known to play a killer game of red rover. I like to win, too. Doesn't everybody? But I'm not one of those guys who has to win constantly or I get all cranky. Why bother? When I lose, I'll be upset for about half a second, then move on. For me, playing a game is all about the fun of the contest and seeing the best player win, whoever that may be.

At least that's the way I *used* to think.

What I found here on the territory of Quillan is that games are a very big part of the culture. All kinds of games. So given the fact that I like games so much, you'd think hanging out here would be pretty cool, right?

Wrong. Really, really wrong. Games are about being challenged and plotting and developing skills and finding strategy and having fun. That's all true on Quillan . . . except for the fun part. There's nothing fun about what goes on here. On this territory games are deadly serious. When you play on Quillan, you had better win, because the price of defeat is too high. I've seen what happens when people lose. It's not pretty. Or fun. I'm only beginning to learn about this new and strange territory, but there's one thing that's already been seared into my brain: Whatever happens, don't lose. It's as simple as that. *Do not lose.* Better advice would be to not play at all, but that doesn't seem to be an option here on Quillan. When you live here, you play.

You win, or you pay.

As ominous as that sounds, I've got to accept it because I know these games will somehow factor into the battle against Saint Dane. He's here. This is the next territory he's after. It doesn't take a genius to figure that out. He sent me a big-old invitation. I already told you about that in my last journal. But there's more—something I didn't write last time. You see, another Traveler was here before me. I'm not talking about the Traveler from Quillan. I mean someone from another territory. I don't want to tell you much more about it until I reach that point in this journal. My story should play out on these pages as it happened. The way I saw it. But I will say this much: I'm angry. Angrier than I've ever been since becoming a Traveler. If Saint Dane thinks challenging me to playing games is the best way to bring down Quillan, he's in for a big surprise. He picked the wrong battleground, because I like to play games. I'm good. And I'm mad. Bring it on.

Mark, Courtney, the last time I wrote to you guys was from a fairytale-like castle here on Quillan. There was way more I wanted to write in that journal, but I didn't think I had the time to get it all down. Besides, the information I gave you in my last journal was pretty intense all by itself. I needed to write all of that down while it was still fresh in my memory. I'm not sure why I was so worried. There's no chance I could ever forget what happened during my last few minutes on Zadaa. No matter how many different ways I look at it, or try to understand it, or search for a reasonable explanation for what happened, I keep coming back to the same undeniable fact:

Loor was killed, and she came back from the dead.

No, let me rephrase that: I think I helped Loor come back from the dead. If I live to be a hundred, I can't imagine a single day going by without reliving what happened in that cave deep below the sands of Xhaxhu. I know I already wrote about this, but I can't get it out of my head. Those few minutes keep coming back to me like a movie that only gets so far before it automatically rewinds and plays again. Of course, the outcome never changes. Saint Dane murdered Loor. I saw it. He blasted out of the flume and drove a sword straight through her heart. She didn't have time to react, let alone defend herself. He killed her in cold blood. Though she was gone, I didn't get the chance to grieve, because I wanted revenge. What followed was a fight to the death between me and the demon Traveler. Or so I thought. The thing is, I beat him. I fought him like a crazed madman because, well, I was a crazed madman. I guess seeing someone you love murdered in cold blood would send anybody off the deep end.

Saint Dane and I fought as if we both knew only one of us was getting out of that tunnel alive. It was a vicious, violent battle that could have gone either way. But in the end he made a fatal mistake. He thought he had won, and charged in for the kill. I grabbed the very sword that he had used to kill Loor and swept it into place. My aim was perfect. Instead of finishing me off, he drove himself into the weapon. To the hilt, just as he had driven the sword into Loor moments before. I won. Saint Dane was dead. The nightmare was over. But my victory didn't last long. His body transformed into a black mist that floated away from the sword and re-formed at the mouth of the flume. I looked up to see the demon standing there calmly, not looking any worse for wear. He stood there in his original form, standing well over six feet tall, wearing that dark Asian-looking suit. The lightning-bolt red scars on his bald head seemed to pulse with blood. It was the only sign that he had exerted himself at all. But what I couldn't stop looking at, as usual, were his blue-white eyes. They locked on me and held me tight, taking away what little breath I had left. We stayed that way for a long moment, staring, waiting for the other to make a move. But the fight was over. He gave me a cold, knowing smile as if to say everything had happened exactly as he had planned.

"I see you are capable of rage," he said cockily. "I will remember that."

"How could you . . . ?" I gasped in shock.

"Didn't Press tell you how futile it would be to try to kill me?" he said with a smirk. He kept his eyes on me and shouted into the flume, *"Quillan!"*

The flume came to life. I didn't have the strength, or the will, to stop him. Even if I had, I wouldn't have known how.

"Zadaa has been such an amusing diversion," the demon said. "In spite of what you may think, Pendragon, this isn't over. I can lick my wounds and move on." He glanced down at Loor's lifeless body and added, "The question is, can you?"

The light from the flume enveloped the monster. He took a step back and was gone. As the light disappeared, I could hear his maniacal laugh fading away.

Have I told you how much I hate that guy?

When I turned to Loor, I saw that I was too late. She was dead. I'm no doctor, but it didn't take one to know that she was gone. Blood was everywhere. She wasn't breathing. She had no heartbeat. I stared down at her, not believing that it was true.

It was only the night before that I had told her I loved her by trying to give her a kiss. But she turned away. I was crushed. It had taken every bit of courage I had to admit I had such strong feelings for her, but with that one small gesture she let me know that it was not meant to be.

She told me, though, that she had deep feelings for me too. She said, "We are on a mission, Pendragon. No group of people have ever been given such a monumental responsibility. We must prevail. We must stop Saint Dane. That is our quest. We are warriors. We will fight together again. We cannot allow emotions to cloud our judgment in any way. That is why I cannot be with you."

It hurt to hear that, but she was right. We would fight together again. Letting our emotions get in the way of that, even in a small way, would be a mistake. Whatever feelings we had for each other would have to be put aside until the time was right. Or so I thought at the time. The next day I watched as Saint Dane killed her. As I sat there in that cavern, with my hand over her mortal wound, a million thoughts and feelings rushed through me. None were good. I had lost my friend. She was not only someone I loved, but my best ally in the battle against Saint Dane. The gut-wrenching realization began to settle in that the time for us would never be right, because she was gone. I found myself wishing with every ounce of my being that it wasn't true.

And she woke up. Simple as that, she opened her eyes. Her wound was gone too. Like it had never been there. But it *had been* there. I swear. The drying blood on her black leather armor was proof of that. It was un-freaking-believable. Since that moment I've tried to make sense of what happened. But how can you make sense of the impossible?

Sorry for repeating all of that, but as hard as it is for me to understand what actually happened in that cave, it's almost as troubling to wonder what it might mean for the future. My future. Up until then a few things had happened with the Travelers that made me think we aren't exactly, oh, how should I put it? Normal. I had been injured pretty badly on Zadaa, and healed faster than seemed possible. The same happened with Alder from Denduron. He was hit in the chest with a steel arrow that should have killed him. But his wound healed quickly, and he recovered so fast it was like it had never happened. But healing quickly and coming back from the dead are two different things. Still, it's not like we Travelers can't die. We can. If we were invincible, then Uncle Press, Seegen, Spader's dad, Osa, and Kasha would still be around. It's not like we can't be hurt, either. I've taken the lumps and felt the pain to prove it.

But I've seen three Travelers take mortal wounds . . . and live to tell the tale. Loor, Alder, and Saint Dane. I hate to put my friends in the same category as that monster, but after all, he is a Traveler too. On the other hand, Saint Dane is capable of doing some things that the rest of us can't. I can't transform myself into other people. Believe me, I tried. Once. I felt pretty stupid afterward too. How do you "will" yourself to become somebody else? I closed my eyes, concentrated my thoughts, and said to myself: *Become Johnny Depp.* Nothing happened. Maybe I should have been more specific and thought: *Become Johnny Depp in* Charlie and the Chocolate Factory *as opposed to Johnny Depp in* Pirates of the Caribbean. It all seemed so silly. Especially since nothing happened. I didn't even bother trying to think: *I want to become black smoke and drift across the room.* If I couldn't become Johnny Depp, no way was I turning to smoke. Bottom line is, Saint Dane may be a Traveler, but he's operating on a whole nother level than we are.

Still, both he and Loor came back from the dead. There

was no getting around that. I wondered if it was possible that I had something to do with Loor's recovery. But I was with Uncle Press when he died. Same with Kasha. Neither of them came back. When I try to relive each of those final, horrible moments, the only thing I can think of that was different with Loor was that it happened so quickly, and I was so totally stunned that I didn't allow myself to believe it was real. It sounds crazy, but it was like I wouldn't accept her death. I didn't want to let it happen . . . and it didn't. She woke up. I know, impossible, right? But it's true.

I suppose I shouldn't be so upset about it. The ability for a Traveler to "will" another Traveler into staying alive is a pretty good thing. To be honest, it gives me a lot more confidence in our battle against Saint Dane. Not that I want to try it out again. No way. Testing death is not high on my "to do" list. As nifty as that might be, the idea leads me to some truly disturbing thoughts. I've always questioned the reasons that I was chosen to be a Traveler. I don't think you'll find a more normal guy than me. But after this whole healing/coming back from the dead thing, I'm beginning to wonder just how normal we Travelers really are. Uncle Press said that my mom and dad weren't my real parents, but he never told me who my real parents are. That starts me thinking. Where exactly did I come from? Knowing that my family disappeared along with every scrap of evidence that any of us ever existed defies every law of nature, yet it happened. It seems as if all the Travelers have had similar experiences. Each of us was raised on our own territory, yet none of us has a history to show for it.

I guess the overriding feeling I'm left with is sadness. Ever since I left home, my goal had been to get back to my normal life. It was the single biggest driving factor in everything I'd done since stepping into the flume for the first time.

I'm not thinking that way anymore.

This is tough to admit, but I'm beginning to wonder if I truly belong on Second Earth. I miss you guys more than I can say, but my family is gone. It's as if some grand cosmic entity highlighted everything to do with Bobby Pendragon, and hit the delete key. What would I say if people asked me where I came from? What would I say? "Well, I grew up in Stony Brook, Connecticut, but my entire history was wiped out, and my family disappeared right after I left through a flume to battle a demon who was trying to crush all of existence. Pass the salt." I don't think so.

I don't say this to make you guys feel sorry for me. Just the opposite. These journals are about writing down all that happens to me as a Traveler, so that when this cosmic battle with Saint Dane is over, there will be a record. And for the record, I'm fine. But there's nothing more important to me than finding the truth. About me, about my family, and about Saint Dane. I have to stop this guy. Not only for the sake of Halla, but for me, too. I have absolute faith that once he is stopped for good, the journey will lead me to the truth. That goal is what keeps me going. I'm going to try to not question so much, keep my head down, and get it done. Getting it done means stopping Saint Dane. That's why I'm on Quillan.

I wrote to you in my last journal how, shortly after Loor rejoined the living, she and I stood at the flume while it activated and deposited a brightly colored square box in front of us. It had red and yellow stripes and was tied up with a big red bow. Hanging from the ribbon was a yellow tag with the word PENDRAGON written in fancy red lettering. Loor unfolded the tag and we saw that written inside were the words: "With my compliments. S.D." Right. Saint Dane. (It was either that or South Dakota, but that didn't make any sense.) I didn't know what to make of the box. The demon had just murdered Loor, had fought me to the death, was killed and had come back to life, and now he was sending me a birthday gift. And it wasn't even my birthday. Compared to that, maybe getting a present from South Dakota wouldn't have been so odd. Welcome to my twisted world. Fearing that something nasty would be inside, I squinted when I pulled off the top. What jumped out was nasty indeed. At least to me. You remember, right? Springing out was a jack-in-the-box clown. It was a scary-looking thing with a hideous smile and a court jester's hat. In fact, pretty much all clowns are scary-looking to me. I hate clowns. I wondered if Saint Dane knew that. The clown laughed with some recorded cackle as it bobbled on the spring. It sounded familiar. Swell.

At the bottom of the box was a blue envelope with the word PENDRAGON on it. I quickly opened it to find a single sheet of bright yellow paper with fancy red lettering. It was an invitation that read:

Riggedy riggedy white
Come and spend the night
We'll play some games
Some wild, some tame
Cause if you will, you might

Your hosts on Quillan,
Veego and LaBerge

Veego and LaBerge. I had no idea what that meant. I had no idea what any of it meant, but one thing was very clear: The next stop for me was Quillan. Alone. Loor wanted to come, but I needed to learn what Quillan was going to hold before deciding which Traveler could best help me there.

Besides, Loor had just come back from the dead. She needed the rest. At least I thought she did. What did I know? I'd never seen anybody come back from the dead before. So I reluctantly left Loor at the mouth of the flume on Zadaa, stepped into the tunnel, and shouted, *"Quillan."*

And that's where my latest adventure began. . . .

QUILLAN

The flume.

As impossible an experience as flying through time and space may be, it has become the only time when I can totally relax. There are no surprises, nobody lurking around the corner waiting to pounce, no Saint Dane. I hope it stays that way. Once I announce the territory where I'm headed and get swept into the crystal tunnel of light and music, I can relax. I think back to that very first flume ride from Second Earth to Denduron and how flat-out terrified I was. Now I'm at peace. It's almost like a flume ride recharges my batteries. I do think there's a whole lot more to these magical tunnels than simply being highways across the cosmos, though. There has to be some kind of intelligence at work here. How else would the flumes know where to send us? More importantly, how else would they know *when* to send us? We always arrive where we need to be, when we need to be there. Even if there are two gates on a territory, we always end up at the gate where we need to be. I'm sure that when I learn the truth about the Travelers and Halla and Saint Dane, I'll also learn all about the flumes and how they can do what they do. Until then, I'll accept the flume rides as being my little vacation away from reality while speeding me to my next destination.

Still, there is one thing that haunts me about the flumes. Ever since Saint Dane won the battle for Veelox, I've been seeing strange, ghostly images floating through the starfield beyond the crystal walls as I travel through the cosmos. The black sky full of sparkling stars is now littered with near-transparent living pictures of people and things that exist on the various territories. I've seen the *Hindenburg* from First Earth, along with Jinx Olsen's flying seaplane. I've seen the white-skinned Novans of Denduron marching in line, and underwater speeders from Cloral being chased by bloated spinney fish. Batu warriors from Zadaa have floated alongside zenzen horses from Eelong. I've seen immense Lifelight pyramids from Veelox and even small animals that look like cats from Second Earth. Many things I don't recognize. I've seen swarms of people holding spears in the air, cheering for something or other. I've seen stiff-looking muscular men, running quickly, with stern faces and sharp jaws. I wouldn't want to get in their way. I've even seen some clown faces, laughing maniacally. I hate clowns. Have I mentioned that?

There are thousands upon thousands more images that I won't bother to describe, because I think you get the idea. Many I recognize, but just as many I don't. They are ghosts from all the territories, floating together in the sea of space. That's why it makes me uneasy. We all know that elements from the territories are not supposed to be mixed. We've learned that the hard way over and over. Yet here in space, or wherever it is, the images of all the territories are jumbled together. It's not like they are interacting or anything. It's more like I'm watching movies projected all over the place.

But seeing these images right next to one another makes me realize just how different each of the territories is. They all have their own histories and their own destinies. That can't change. Mixing them would be like throwing random numbers into a perfect equation. The result won't be the same. I think that's what would happen to the territories if the cultures were mingled. None of the territories would be the same and that could be disastrous.

Which is exactly what Saint Dane wants. He's played fast and loose with the rules about mixing elements between territories, and I'm beginning to realize why. The more he can throw a territory off balance, the easier it will be for him to send it all crashing into chaos. I believe he's not only working to push the turning point of each territory toward disaster, but he's helping his cause by mixing them together as well. What does that all mean to me besides making my stomach twist? Nothing, except that it's all the more reason he must be stopped. As I was speeding through the flume toward Quillan, I couldn't help but wonder if those images floating in space were there as a warning, or evidence that the worst had already begun and the walls between the territories were beginning to crumble.

It was the first flume trip that I didn't enjoy.

I didn't have time to sweat about it for long, though. I heard the jumble of sweet musical notes that always accompany me on a flume ride begin to grow louder and more complex. This familiar song signaled that I was nearing the end of my trip. I took my focus away from the images in space and looked ahead. A bright light shone at the end of the tunnel. I was about to arrive on Quillan. The time for theorizing was over. The show was about to begin.

As the cushion of light gently deposited me on my feet, every sense instantly went on alert. I stood there for a second to get my bearings. It was dark, but that could have been because I had just been sailing along in a shower of light. I needed a few seconds for my eyes to adjust. I waited with my knees bent, ready to jump at the first sign of trouble. After only a few seconds I heard an odd noise. It sounded like chattering. I'm not sure how else to describe it. There was a series of high-pitched clicking noises coming from somewhere off to my right. They didn't sound dangerous or aggressive. Just . . . odd. I strained to hear, but it stopped. Silence. All I heard was the faint echoing of the musical notes as they receded into the depths of the flume. I didn't move. I didn't want to step into something stupid. I waited a solid minute, but the noise didn't come back. Whatever it was, it was gone.

Looking around, I saw nothing but black. Swell. I would have given anything for a flashlight . . . assuming they had flashlights on Quillan. Another minute passed, and I figured I wasn't doing any good standing in the dark, so I took a tentative step forward and . . . *smack!* I walked right into a wall. Head first. Ouch. I took a quick step back, feeling more stupid than hurt. I reached out, more carefully this time, and eased forward until my hand touched the wall. At least I thought it was a wall. It sure felt like one. It was hard. It was flat. It stretched out to either side of me. You know . . . wall. The space between the opening to the flume and this wall seemed to be only a couple of feet. It was the smallest gate area yet. Of course, I knew there had to be a way out, the trick was finding it. I took a few steps back into the flume to get some perspective. I stood there for a few seconds until, slowly, I began to make out cracks in the wall. Actually, they looked more like seams. The lines were straight, crossing one another, forming a grid pattern with two-foot squares. I didn't see this at first because I was so close to the wall and my eyes hadn't adjusted to the dark. The light coming through was very faint. But it was there. I knew there had to be a way out, so I slowly scanned the wall, looking for anything that might be a doorway, or a window, or a hole. I didn't care. I was starting to get claustrophobic.

I heard the clicking sounds again. This time to my left. I shot a look that way to see . . . nothing. But there was no mistake. Something was there. I had no way of knowing how far off in each direction this wall stretched. The seams disappeared off to either side. It's not like they ended abruptly, they just kind of faded out into the dark. This wall could have gone on for miles for all I knew.

The chattering stopped. Whatever it was, was creeping me out. I wanted out of there. Out of desperation I walked up to the wall, put my hand on it, and started pushing. I reached up over my head and pushed on one of the squares that was marked off by the seam of light. It didn't budge. I moved my hand down, pushing on the square below it. Nothing happened. My thinking was that maybe one of these squares was also a doorway of some kind and . . .

It didn't take me long to find it. The fifth square pushed out. One side was on a hinge. Instantly light flooded in. I glanced back to the flume to see the big, round mouth of the rocky tunnel. I looked off to the sides to see if I could catch a glimpse of whatever it was that was doing all the clicking, but my pupils had already contracted because of the light. All I saw was pitch black. The mystery would have to wait. The door was about at my waist and just large enough for me to enter. I put one leg through, then ducked down and put my head through, and finally I dragged my other leg behind.

I was out! Great. But where was I? I turned around to see that the wall I had come through was made of cement, or stucco. Whatever it was, it was definitely man-made. That answered one of my questions. Wherever the flume was, it wasn't in some natural cave or tunnel. It was in a building. I suppose the hinge on the door should have been a tip-off too. Duh. The face of the wall was covered with what looked like a grid of metal. That accounted for the pattern of squares I'd seen inside. It looked to me like some kind of support to keep the wall secure. It was one of the sections of this grid that was actually the gate to the flume. I was about to close the hatch behind me, when I realized I needed a way to figure out which of these squares was the gate once it was closed. They all looked the same. Of course, I needn't have worried. They *didn't* all look the same. I saw a small star burned into the upper right corner of the open panel. It was no bigger than a quarter, but it was there. It was the mark that showed this was a gate to the flume. I knew how to get back. I closed the two-foot square secret door, then quickly opened it again, just to make sure I wasn't locking myself out. If I had to get to the flume fast, I didn't want to have to monkey with a temperamental door. After closing it again, I put my back to the wall to get my first look at Quillan.

I found myself in a huge room that looked to be a storage facility. Wooden crates of all sizes were stacked everywhere. The ceiling was about forty feet high. The walls to either side were so far off I couldn't tell how big the room really was. The words "airplane hangar" came to mind. I could now see that the grid on the wall behind me must have had a couple of thousand squares in it . . . with exactly *one* that led to the flume. It was a brilliant place for it, like hiding a needle in a haystack . . . made of needles. I just hoped I could find my way back to the haystack and find that particular needle. Light came from glowing strips in the ceiling. I couldn't tell if they were electric lights or openings to the outside. The light they gave off wasn't bright. The whole place was kind of gloomy. But there was enough light for me to get the overall feeling of the place. There looked to be thousands upon thousands of containers of all sizes. Some were as small as a shoe box, others were big enough to hold a car. There was no way to tell what any of them contained, other than the black series of numbers that was painted on each. From looking around I came to my first conclusion about Quillan. It wasn't a primitive society. They had manufacturing and construction and enough advanced technology to create a huge indoor space.

There looked to be a thick coating of dust on all the crates, which told me this was a place for deep, long-term storage. Who knew how long these crates and boxes of whatever had been there? Good thing, too. Having a flume in a heavy-traffic area wasn't a good idea. This place was ancient, and probably forgotten. The word "tomb" came to mind, which conjured a whole nother image of what might be in those containers. I had to shake that idea, quick.

The containers were arranged in such a way that there were twisting alleyways between them that led deeper into the room. Or out of the room. I had no idea which way was which. I could have been near the exit, or on the far side from it, or anywhere in between. I was going to have to make my way through this labyrinth and hope it didn't take a year to find the exit. Getting back was going to be another matter. I looked at my Traveler ring to make sure the stone was sparkling the way it does when I get near a flume. I knew I would have to trust the ring to get me back to this spot, and this tiny hole in the wall.

I was about to take a step to begin my search for the exit when I realized something important. I was still wearing the white tunic of a Rokador from the territory of Zadaa. I had no idea what they wore on Quillan, but the odds were long that they'd have the same white pajama-looking clothes as I had on. Usually acolytes leave clothes for the Travelers at the flumes. But I didn't see any here. Then again, I didn't see much of anything because it was pitch dark. I went back to the square in the wall with the star, pulled it open, and peered through. After a few moments my eyes adjusted, and I saw what I was looking for.

On the ground was a pile of clothing. Perfect. I climbed back inside and picked up the clothes that were left for me, or any other Traveler who paid a visit. I first picked up a long-sleeved, bright red shirt. There were no buttons or zippers. No collar either. It was like a long-sleeved T-shirt, but the material was heavier and a little bit stretchy. The only design was a series of five black stripes that ran diagonally across the front from the left shoulder down to the right side of the waist. It reminded me a little bit of a rugby shirt. There was also a pair of pants. Simple, black, made from the same stretchy material. I was psyched when I saw the shoes. They were like my running shoes from Second Earth. They were black and didn't look fancy, but they definitely looked comfortable. On my travels I had worn leather sandals and rotten rags and leather dress shoes and swim boots and pretty much anything else that was designed specifically to be uncomfortable. Here, I couldn't wait to get them on. I quickly took off my Rokador clothes and slipped into the local attire. I kept on my boxers. That's where I drew the line. If the future of all humanity was going to be decided on whether or not I wore boxers from Second Earth, there was no hope of saving it. The clothes fit perfectly, as usual. Even the sneakers. For the first time in forever I actually liked wearing my clothes.

I then noticed there was something else on the floor. It looked like a silver bracelet. It was a thick oval ring with a single groove etched deeply all the way around. It wasn't fancy or anything. Nor did it look like it had any function. It was kind of clunky and felt heavier than it looked. But I figured if it was at the flume with the local clothing, I was meant to have it. So I jammed it in the back pocket of my new pants, along with the paper that had the strange rhyming invitation from Veego and LaBerge.

That's when I heard the chattering again. Whatever was making the sound, this time there were more of them. Many more. The clicking and crunching sounds grew. I waited a second, expecting the sound to disappear again. It didn't. Whatever it was, their numbers were growing. I slowly turned around. What I saw shouldn't have surprised me. I don't know why I didn't think of it right away, but I didn't. Bad move. What I saw in the darkness on the far side of the flume were dozens of tiny little eyes peering at me. That's all I saw. The eyes. Yellow eyes.

Quig eyes.

My adrenaline spiked. A nanosecond later I was in the air, head first, diving for the square doorway out of the gate. I sailed through the opening, hit the ground, rolled, then popped back up and turned to see if I was being followed. I stared at the opened door, waiting for something to come out. It didn't. That's because it was already out. I felt a little tickle on my shoulder. Before I could react, something bit me. Hard.

"Owwww!"

I threw myself against a tall crate, hoping to crush whatever had attacked me. I slammed my shoulder, but I didn't care. I wanted whatever had chomped me to be gone. I heard a crunching sound, and a squeal. Throwing myself away from the crate, I looked down as the vicious little hitchhiker fell to the ground.

It was a spider. A big spider. No, a HUGE spider. It looked like a tarantula on steroids. The beastie had to be the size of a kitten, but there was nothing cute or cuddly about it. Its thick body and multiple legs were bloodred; it had pincers in front that snapped like an angry lobster's, and its head was so black that its yellow quig eyes looked as if they were glowing. I wasn't sure if it had snagged me with one of its pincers or bitten me with its mouth. Either way, I hoped it wasn't poisonous, or I would be done before I even got started on Quillan.

When I slammed the quig-spider into the crate, I rattled it, but didn't kill it. The thing was on its back with its legs scrambling in the air. I was about to go over and step on it, when it suddenly flipped back onto its feet, and looked at me. I swear, guys, this little monster looked at me. It had intelligence. But as vicious as this little beastie looked, there was worse news.

It wasn't alone.

I heard the scratching sound again and shot a look toward the hatch to the flume. What I saw made my stomach drop. Out came hundreds, no, thousands of the little quig monsters. They cascaded out of the hatchway and down onto the floor like a living, evil waterfall. I could hear their sharp little claws clicking against the cement floor like nails. Sharp nails.

Was I scared? What do you think? But as I watched those vicious little beasties stream out of the gate, I actually had a fleeting thought that snuck through the terror: I was in the right place. Saint Dane had brought quigs to the flume. This territory was hot. Things were going to happen. But it wasn't more than a flash of a thought that was immediately replaced by another.

These monsters were coming for me. It was time to be someplace else.

QUILLAN

I'm not afraid of spiders.

A lot of people are terrified of the little critters, but I never understood that. They're bugs. They're tiny. Even if they bite you, which is rare, it's not all that painful. What's to be scared of?

On Quillan, plenty. At least at the flume, anyway. These quig-charged little monsters weren't anything like the spiders on Second Earth. They were the size of small hams and bit like angry dogs. If that weren't bad enough, there must have been eight-freakin'-thousand of them, all with one thing on their evil little minds: Get Bobby Pendragon.

I was now officially afraid of spiders.

I did the first thing that any brave Traveler would do under the circumstances: I turned and ran like hell. But I had no idea where to go. I was caught in a maze of wooden crates. My only thought was to weave my way through and find the door out of that musty old tomb of a warehouse. The crates were stacked up all over the place, some towering almost to the forty-foot-high ceiling. Whatever they were storing in there, there was a lot of it. I didn't turn around to see if the spiders were following. I didn't need to. I could hear them. Thousands of little spider claws clattered against the cement floor as they scrambled to get me. They all gave off this odd high-pitched squeak that sounded like a juiced-up war cry. A single one of these would sound creepy. Multiplied by many thousands made the hair go up on the back of my neck. They were fast, too. It was hard to outrun them. Worse, I couldn't break into a full-on sprint because the aisles were so narrow and windy. Every so often I'd hit an intersection and make a quick decision which way to go. Left, right, left, left. I had no idea where I was going, but it didn't matter so long as it was away from that attacking army of bugs.

I didn't know how long I could stay ahead of them. My fear was that I'd hit a dead end and be trapped. Quigs took different forms on each territory, but the vicious killing machines that Saint Dane created to guard the flumes all had one thing in common: They were bloodthirsty. Remember the quig-bears on Denduron? The smell of blood made them eat their own. The quig-sharks on Cloral nearly tore themselves apart to get under the rock overhang where Uncle Press and I were hiding in fear. At least I was hiding in fear. Uncle Press was pretty cool about the whole thing, if I remember. But whatever. Bottom line was, here on Quillan I didn't want to get trapped in a dead end with these yellow-eyed fiends.

I hoped that if I got far enough away from the gate, the quigs would lose interest. A quick look over my shoulder told me I was wrong. If anything, there were more of them rolling toward me like a dark, demonic wave. I looked around to get my bearings and realized I was in the middle of a sea of crates, with no exit to be seen. Anywhere. I was getting tired, fast, and I was no closer to escape than when I started. But stopping wasn't an option.

I made one turn and pulled up short when I saw that up ahead of me a swarm of spiders had rounded the corner and were charging right for me. These weren't mindless bugs; the little creeps were using tactics! I saw more proof of that when I realized that they were being led by a single spider. At least I thought it was in the lead. It's not like it was carrying a big flag and shouting "Charge!" or anything. But it was obviously bigger than the rest. It had more red in it, and its yellow eyes were bigger too. The multitude fanned out behind it as if this big fatty were the point of an arrow. This was no cute group of insects from some animated Pixar movie where the boss bug shouted out clever wisecracks. No, when this bad boy opened its mouth, it would be to rip into flesh. My flesh.

I wheeled to run the other way, but froze when I saw that the rest of the sea of spiders was behind me. They had split up and circled me. Smart bugs. Good for them. Bad for me. I was trapped. The only way I could go was up. I was next to a stack of wooden crates that towered a few feet over my head. I leaped straight up, grabbed the top of the crate, and pulled myself up. It's amazing what adrenaline will do. In seconds I was throwing my leg up over the top and looking back down to see the two groups of spiders converge. I was safely out of harm's way . . .

For about ten seconds. The two groups of bugs joined together and, without missing a beat, began climbing up the side of the wooden crate toward me, with the not-so-itsy-bitsy spider in the lead. I quickly rolled onto my feet and ran. I was on a whole new playing field. Looking forward, I saw that I was on top of a sea of crates that rose up on multiple levels. I couldn't run there. One wrong step and I'd fall to the floor, break my leg, and become bug chow. No, I had to be careful. It was more about leaping from crate to crate than actually running. No sooner did I get to the end of one big crate than I'd have to climb up to another, or jump down a level. This didn't seem to bother the spiders, though. They reached the tops of the crates and swarmed forward, rolling over the terrain like a creeping shadow. They were definitely going to catch me unless I thought of something, fast.

I bounded across one crate and had to stop short, or I would have fallen down into an aisle that stretched out to either side. I looked back to see the spiders were nearly on me. Their screeching grew louder, as if they knew the end was near. Or the beginning, if you were talking about their lunch. I had no choice but to leap across the chasm between the crates. I took a few steps back, held my breath, sprinted for the end, and leaped through space.

I made it to the far side with a few feet to spare. Again, thank you, adrenaline. I soon got more good news. Bugs couldn't jump. At least they couldn't jump far enough to make it across the aisle. The bugs had to climb down one side of the wall of crates, scramble across the floor, then crawl back up on the other side of the aisle. My side. I was kind of hoping they wouldn't make it across at all, but the extra time it took for them to go down and across and up gave me the chance to get some distance from them. I jogged forward, looking for more aisles to leap across and get even farther away. I leaped across one, two, three more aisles. With each crossing my confidence grew. I was buying enough time to find my way out of this not-so-fun house. As I traveled farther away from the bugs, their squeaking and chattering grew faint. I figured I had survived yet another brush with Saint Dane's quigs without a scratch.

I was wrong.

I decided to leap across one more aisle to make sure the bugs were far enough back that I could climb down and find the exit. But when I launched myself across and landed on the crate on the far side, the top edge cracked under my weight. If I had been prepared, I probably could have landed safely. But I was getting cocky. I should have jumped farther. Oops. The surprise was what got me. The wood of the crate must have been old and rotten, because before I realized what was happening, I crashed down to the floor in a shower of splinters and dust. I must have conked my head, because I was knocked loopy. All I remember of those few moments was the dust and debris raining down on me from the fractured crate. I didn't know if I was hurt or stunned or simply confused. I remember sitting there for a while, though I'm not sure for how long. It could have been a few seconds, or more than a few minutes. What finally snapped me back to reality were the familiar sounds.

Screech. Chatter.

The bugs were back.

I was in no shape to get up and start running. I was too dizzy for that. But I still had enough sense to realize they would be on me any second. I looked around for something to defend myself with. At my back was the splintered crate. It was made from long slats of inch-thick wood. The one side had cracked open and I was able to yank off a long piece of wood. It was about four feet long and a few inches wide. More importantly, it was solid. I tested it against my knee. The rotten boards must have all been on top. This side piece was intact. It wasn't exactly a wooden stave like the one Loor had taught me to use on Zadaa, but it would have to do.

I got weakly to my feet, with my eyes looking up at the top of the crate I had just fallen from. If the bugs were coming, they'd come from there. I gripped the rough piece of wood, turned my body sideways to make a smaller target as

Loor had instructed, and lifted my weapon. I was ready . . . or at least as ready as I was able to get.

So were the spiders. They attacked by flinging themselves from the edge of the crate above. These devilish bugs couldn't jump up, but they could definitely jump down. I briefly thought how it was incredible that these bugs could be so focused. So smart. There was definitely intelligence going on here. They were smarter than any quig I had faced so far. The thought quickly flashed through my head that all the inhabitants of Quillan might be bugs, like the cat klees of Eelong. But that gruesome thought only distracted me from my mission, which was to survive. If I was going to have to fight a race of intelligent, vicious bug people, the battle for Quillan was under way.

They came at me, flying through the air, screaming. I batted them with my makeshift wood-plank weapon, knocking them away like, well, like bugs. These guys may have been smart, but they weren't very strong. The first bug I hit screamed and flew back across the aisle. It smashed against a crate on the far side, and fell to the ground. It looked dead. Of course, I wasn't going to go and check its pulse. I had a few thousand other things to deal with at the time. But seeing this gave me hope. These spiders were fragile. They had the numbers, but I had the power. The question was, would I burn out before they ran out of reinforcements?

They flew at me from above; I swatted at them quickly. *Whap! Crack!* It was like high-speed batting practice. Good thing I knew how to switch-hit. It wasn't much different from fending off Loor's attacks when we sparred in the training camp of Mooraj. I was on fire. The dizziness was long gone. Thanks again, adrenaline. I cracked the attacking bugs as fast as they came at me, sending them crashing against the hard wooden crates.

But the bugs weren't done. They were leaping in ones and twos. That's how I was able to smack them all away. I feared that once they realized my defenses were limited, they'd send more than a few at a time and I'd be in trouble.

"Ouch!" I felt something bite my leg. I didn't need to look down. I knew that a spider had made it to the floor and was on my ankle. I shook it off, only to feel another stinging bite on my other ankle. I knew I couldn't stand my ground anymore. There were too many of them. I had to get out. While still swinging away at the leaping kamikaze bugs, I started to back out of that aisle. The bugs countered. I could see them above me, gathering on top of the crates across the aisle, getting into a new position to attack. As I backed off, I could feel the bodies of the beaten spiders crack under my feet. If I weren't so charged up, I probably would have been grossed out. But that was the least of my worries. I was losing. I had to retreat.

With one last swing of my wooden plank, I knocked another spider into next week, then turned and ran. I rounded the corner of another aisle, hoping to see a straightaway where I could turn on the jets and sprint out of there. What I saw was the straightaway I hoped for . . . but it was filled with more spiders. At the front of the pack (do spiders come in packs?) was the fatboy. Its bright yellow eyes were trained on me. It was a showdown. No, worse. It was over. I had nothing left. The big spider reared back on its legs, like a cat ready to pounce . . . and charged. The others were right behind it, screaming and scrambling.

I couldn't go back. I couldn't go forward. All I could do was climb again. I looked up and saw that the crates here were stacked just as high but were smaller in size. The top crates were about two-feet square. I got an idea that sprang from pure desperation. I jumped up and hooked my finger on top of one of the smaller crates. But rather than pull myself up . . .

I pulled the crate down. It was heavy, but I wasn't about to let that stop me. For what I wanted to do, heavy was good, and timing was everything. I pulled the crate down so hard I felt the muscles of my arms burn. But it toppled. The spiders were nearly on me. I dove out of the way. The crate came down and smashed on the cement floor . . . right on top of the fat leader. I heard it scream. It sounded almost human. But I didn't have time to be grossed out. I hoped this move would buy me the few seconds I needed to escape, so I jumped onto the broken crate and launched myself up to where it had been. I was about to continue my escape across the carton tops, when I glanced back to see something impossible: The spiders were retreating. Fast. I stopped to watch as the wave of black little demons slipped back like the receding tide. They kept chattering and screeching, but there screams sounded more scared than angry. It was like the queen bee of a hive had been destroyed, and none of the other bees had a clue what to do, so they scattered. Psych! I didn't even mean to crush the fat little monster. All I wanted was a few extra seconds to escape. But hey, I'd rather be lucky than good anytime. I sat on a crate to catch my breath, and watched the spiders disappear to who-knows-where. I didn't care. All that mattered was that they weren't after me anymore.

Once I was sure they were gone, I jumped back down to the floor. I'm not sure why I did what I did next. I guess it was out of some morbid curiosity. But I moved to pull the broken carton off the lead spider. I wanted to get my first close look at a quig. Most every time I saw a quig in the past, whether it was a bear on Denduron or a snake on Zadaa or a dog on Second Earth, I was usually running too fast to get a good look at it. But now I had the chance to see one up close. Saint Dane created these things somehow; I thought that by taking a closer look, it might give me some clue as to how he was able to make these mutants appear at the gates to do his bidding. Or maybe I just wanted to make sure it was dead and not waiting for me to relax so it could call its buddies back. Either way, I wanted to see it.

As I began to pull away the wooden crate, I saw that one side of the container had almost completely broken off. My curiosity shifted to the box. I wanted to know what was being stored in this monster tomb of a warehouse. I yanked the side off the rest of the way to reveal . . . a stack of plates. I'm serious. Plain old white plates like you'd see in a diner or something. I picked one up to confirm that there was nothing special about it. Somebody had packed away about a dozen white boring plates. The one thing that was of any interest at all was the logo printed on the back of the plate. In simple black one-inch letters was a single word: BLOK. That's all. BLOK. A quick check showed me that all the plates had this same word printed on their backs. This meant exactly nothing to me, so I put the plate back and reached over to pull the crate off my victim.

When I heaved the crate over, I instantly realized two things. One was that this particular itsy-bitsy spider was not going to be chasing me anymore. It was definitely dead. Though as I stared at it, I wasn't sure if "dead" was the right word, because this quig was never alive. Not in the true sense, anyway. That was the second thing I learned. The weight of the carton had smashed open its body and spread it all over the floor. But it wasn't disgusting or anything. That's because the remains of old spidey weren't organic. That's right. The outside was fur covered and looked every bit like a very real, very big spider. But the insides were a different matter. My little nemesis was mechanical. Instead of blood and guts, I was looking at a pile of high-tech computer-driven machine parts.

It was a robot.

The works weren't like any kind of machinery I had ever seen. It was actually fairly simple. You'd think that with such a sophisticated piece of machinery there would be thousands of little gears and joints and rotors, but there were surprisingly few. All I saw was a squished metallic spider skeleton, along with something that looked like a computer core. I figured the technology would have to be pretty advanced to get that simple spider skeleton to run, turn, jump, bite . . . and think. That was the scariest part. They could think.

Staring at the mess of smashed metal, I realized that Quillan was a territory with technology that was so advanced, they were able to create lifelike self-powered robots. I could only hope they weren't all going to be chasing me.

I did a quick cleanup of the broken crate and the crushed robot-quig-spider. I didn't think anybody would be wandering by, but just in case, I wanted to hide any evidence that I had been there. I kicked the debris into a corner between a couple of large crates, making sure I swept up every last remnant of mechanical-gut stuff. After I was satisfied that the mess was hidden, I set out to find my way out of there. It was time to see what other surprises lay in wait for me on Quillan.

QUILLAN

Which was worse: A territory populated by spiders? Or one controlled entirely by robots? I wasn't thrilled by either option. All I knew for certain was that whatever this territory held, I wouldn't learn about it hanging around in a dusty old warehouse full of dinner plates. I needed to get out and find the Traveler from Quillan. That was key. The Traveler would have answers. That is, of course, unless the Traveler was a robot. Or a spider. Sheesh.

After cleaning up the metal spider guts, I climbed up onto a crate to take another look around at the vast space. In the distance I saw the far wall with the grid that hid the gate to the flume. I figured the exit wasn't back that way, so I turned in the opposite direction and began my search for the way out. It wasn't long before I realized I had made the right choice. I didn't find an exit right away, but I did hear something. I'm glad to report that it wasn't the chattering of more mechanical spiders. It was music. The sound was far off and faint, but it was definitely music. Music to me meant civilization, so I kept heading toward the sound. As I drew closer to the wall that was directly opposite from the wall that hid the flume, the music grew louder. It was muffled, but I heard enough to realize it was an odd tune. I couldn't make out what the instruments were, but they sounded electronic. The music itself was a kind of upbeat, new age, happy, haunting, never ending melody that went nowhere. It was kind of creepy-strange, like no music I had ever heard before. I didn't hate it, but I didn't think I'd be downloading the MP3 file either. The music had energy, like it was setting a happy mood. Maybe I was overthinking it, but the music seemed to be almost . . . hypnotic.

A few minutes later I hit the wall on the far side. Scanning both ways, I quickly found a doorway. It was just that simple. It was a double-wide door, which made sense because it would have to be big enough to get the bigger crates through. Before leaving, I took a look back onto the monster space of the warehouse. It was a great place to hide a flume. There must have been a quarter of a mile between this wall and the wall with the gate. It was so loaded with stuff, I couldn't imagine anybody going all the way to the far side to find anything. It was like the gate and the flume were hidden in plain sight, with no chance of actually being seen. I took a quick check of my bearings to remember which direction to go when I came back, then spun, and pushed open the wide doors to Quillan.

I found myself in a dark room with no windows. No big surprise. This warehouse had to have been underground in order for the flume tunnel to be behind the far wall. The question was, how far underground was I? And where was the music coming from? When my eyes adjusted, I saw that there were several vehicles in the room that looked like forklifts. These would be the lifts they used to move the crates in and out of the warehouse. (Whoever "they" were.) I ran my finger along the seat of one vehicle, leaving a line in the thick dust. These machines hadn't been used in a long time. Either that, or Quillan was so covered in dust that people had to wear filters over their mouths. Unless they were robots of course. Or spiders.

Scanning the room again, I saw an open metal staircase along the side wall that zigzagged upward. I jogged around a couple of the forklifts, hit the stairs, and tentatively climbed. With each step the strange music grew louder. My anxiety grew right along with it. I'd been through this before, many times. I was leaving the secret, underground place that held a flume to step into the real world of a territory. All my speculation, all my preconceived notions, all my wonder as to what I would find, would soon be gone. It's an exciting feeling . . . and terrifying. I'll never get used to it. I climbed quite a few stairs. If I was headed for the surface, I figured I would have to climb at least as high as the ceiling of the warehouse I had just left. Finally, as my legs began to burn, I got to the top. There was nothing out of the ordinary to see, just a double door. This one was much smaller than the one leading into the warehouse. It was definitely a people door. Or a spider door for big spiders.

I had to get over that.

I pushed the door open and boldly walked through. The music was now very loud. I was getting close to the source. The doors opened up into a long corridor. Looking either way, I didn't see a single person. Or robot. Or spider, I'm happy to report. I had made my way into Quillan without being noticed. It was time to find out what made this territory tick. I wasn't sure which way to go because the music was coming from everywhere. There must have been speakers hidden in the walls. It looked as if there might be a door farther down to my right, so that's the way I went. I walked about twenty yards and came upon a single door with a metallic doorknob. I felt sure that beyond these doors would lie the answers to some of my questions. Either that or it would bring me into a broom closet, and I'd have to keep looking. There was only one way to find out.

When I opened the door, I was instantly hit with a wave of music. Man, it was loud. I understood immediately how I was able to hear it so far down below in the warehouse. I can't say that what I saw beyond that door was the last thing I expected to see. It wasn't. It was lower down the list than that. In fact, it wasn't even on the list. This was my first look at the real Quillan, and it made no sense.

I was standing on the edge of a giant, loud, exciting . . . arcade full of games.

Imagine the most elaborate, noisy high-tech video arcade you've ever been in, and then multiply that by about a hundred. This place was stupid-big. Hundreds of computer games lined the walls and formed aisles everywhere. I guess it's dumb for me to say I'd never seen games like that before, being that I was on a new territory. But I never had. The overall setup wasn't that much different from a Second Earth arcade, though. Some games were contained in big boxlike structures with colorful designs on the sides. Others were giant video screens that loomed over the gaming floor. I saw one game that looked to be a battle challenge, with the player shooting it out with the computer-generated image of an opponent on a giant screen in front of him. Another looked like a maze where the player stood on a platform, running in place while negotiating turns that he saw on his own big screen. It was all way more sophisticated than anything from Second Earth. All the games had some version of flashing colored lights to get the customers' attention and entice them to play. The weird electronic music added a feeling of excitement and fantasy. The arcade was on three levels. I was on the bottom and could look up to see two more balconies full of games.

Sorry for sounding like a kid here, but this was the most awesome arcade I had ever seen. No, that I could ever *imagine*. If this existed on Second Earth, it would clean up. It was gaming nirvana.

Oddly though, it wasn't very crowded. Most of the excitement and noise came from the games themselves, and the music. A quick guesstimate told me that there might have been about thirty people hanging around. That wasn't a lot for such a huge arcade. On Second Earth this place would be packed. Only a few people were actually playing. Others watched. Once I got used to the environment, I could take a closer look at the people. I wandered through the games, observing the people. First, I'm happy to say that they weren't spiders. Check that one off the list of scary possibilities. They looked every bit as human as I did, which meant they probably weren't robots, either. Things were looking up. There looked to be a mix of different races, too. Some had dark skin with blond hair, others were fairly pale with darker hair. I saw heavyset people, and older guys, and . . . I guess there's no need to keep describing the specifics. Bottom line was that the people of Quillan looked every bit as normal and diverse as the people of Second Earth.

As normal as this appeared, I did notice some things that struck me as odd. For one thing, there were no kids. You'd think the place would be a kid magnet. There were women and men, some old, some older. But no kids. I noticed the clothing they wore was kind of, I don't know, boring. There wasn't a whole lot of style going on. Not that I'm the best judge of that, but when you see a bunch of people together in the same place, you'd expect to see a big range of clothing styles. Not there. Everyone wore some kind of variation of pants and plain shirts. Some wore jackets. Some tucked their shirts in, others didn't. There wasn't much difference in style between the men and women, either. I didn't see any dresses or skirts. I don't mean to say they all wore the exact same thing. They didn't. There was some variation in color, but the clothing all tended to edge toward the darker side, with muted shades of green and blue. There was lots of gray, too. But nothing bright or lively or patterned. And many of the pants were just plain black. Their shoes didn't jump out at me either. They mostly appeared to be plain and black. I wasn't sure what conclusion to draw from this, other than that the people of Quillan had absolutely no sense of style or fashion. I suppose there are worse things to say. They could have been mutant spider robots.

I wasn't worried about being the youngest person there, but I was self-conscious about my clothes. The long-sleeved, bright red shirt with the diagonal black stripes was kind of radical for this dull crowd. But there was nothing I could do about it. I had to trust that whoever put the clothes at the flume knew what they were doing.

As I made my way through the arcade, there was something else that I started to realize. This was a bright and colorful place full of games. I'd been to plenty of arcades before, and I always felt that there was as much energy coming from the people as from the loud games. But here on Quillan, nobody seemed to be having any fun. Just the opposite. The people playing the games were focused. Seriously focused. There was no laughter, no screams of surprise or disappointment, no victory cries. These people were playing with serious intensity. They may have been running through an electronic maze, or testing their reflexes, or dodging video bullets, but they were all doing it with such concentration that it didn't seem to be any fun at all.

The same went for the people who were watching. They looked about as excited as they would be watching chess, which for me is about as thrilling as watching trees grow. There were only a few games actually being played, and each one had a small group of spectators who were watching with the same intensity as the players. There were no shouts of encouragement or taunting or advice being shouted out. I guess the best word to describe the whole atmosphere was "tense."

There is one other thing I need to point out. Remember the silver bracelet I picked up at the flume and stuck in my back pocket? Several of the people had similar ones. They wore them on their left arms, just above the biceps. All the people playing the games had them, and some of the spectators. It added one more curious touch to the already bizarre scene.

"Yayyyyy!" came an excited scream from the other side of the arcade.

Finally! A sign of life! I jogged over to see the guy who was playing the 3-D shoot-out game. Apparently he had won. (The words YOU WIN! flashing in red on the giant screen were a dead giveaway. Duh.) Unlike the other zombielike players, this guy was over-the-moon thrilled. A woman hugged him as if he had just won the zillion-dollar lottery. I think they were crying. Others gathered around, clapping and smiling. They were totally psyched that this guy had won. What was up with this? It was a freakin' video game! I remember breaking the record on a snowboard simulator at the theater on the bottom of the Ave at home. Remember that game? Is it still there? I'm embarrassed to say how many quarters it took me just to see my initials at the top spot. And I did it, finally. But I didn't go all nuts like this. I was happy, but give me a break.

"What are you doing here?" came a voice from behind me.

I spun quickly to see a concerned-looking little bald guy staring at me. He wore a frown that crinkled his forehead. Was I not supposed to be there? Was this arcade off-limits to the general public? Maybe you had to be a member to get in, and I was definitely not a member. I had to play this very carefully.

"Uhh . . . ," I said. "Are you talking to me?"

"Of course I'm talking to you!" the little guy whined. "What are you doing here?"

"Just hanging around," I said casually. Okay, maybe that wasn't the slickest comeback, but I had no idea where this guy was going.

"Just hanging around?" he parroted with surprise. "Challengers don't just hang around. Are you here to train?"

Challengers? Train?

"Yes," I said, though I had no idea what I was agreeing to. Obviously this guy thought I was somebody else. I figured it wasn't a good idea to tell him otherwise. "Yeah, I'm training," I bluffed. "Lots of training. Right here. Yessir."

The guy lunged at me and grabbed both my arms. It happened so fast I had no time to react. He looked me square in the eye. He was shorter than I am, so he had to look up to do it. He wasn't angry, he wasn't scared. I know this may sound weird, but the look I saw in the guy's eyes was . . . desperation.

"What's your event?" he whispered, as if not wanting anybody else to hear. "How good are you? Honestly. I've never seen you before. What are your chances? Tell me, please. I won't share it with a soul."

The guy was weirding me out. He definitely had me mistaken for somebody else. Stranger still, he was asking me questions that he desperately wanted answers to. No, it was like he *needed* the answers. I debated about making something up to calm him, but that felt wrong. He wanted answers so badly that I didn't want to say something that might upset him even more. I was absolutely, totally frozen.

"Daddy!" came a shout from across the arcade. It was a little kid's voice. Both the bald guy and I looked to see a little girl running through the arcade with a huge smile. I was glad for the distraction. The little blond girl sprinted past some games with her arms wide open. She ran up to the guy who had just won the game and flung herself into his arms. The guy hugged her as if he hadn't seen her in years. The woman who had been so happy for him joined in. I'm guessing she was the mommy. The three of them stood there for a long moment, hugging one another tightly while the spectators applauded. I figured the guy must have won something big. At least it had to be bigger than simply getting top score. But nobody official-looking came up with his winnings, or even to shake his hand. There didn't seem to be any prize at all. I watched as the family walked off, followed by the others, who all shared happy knowing looks.

"Thank goodness," the bald little guy said. I thought I saw a tear in his eye.

I took a chance and asked, "So what's the big deal about beating that game?"

The bald guy snapped me a look as if I had just asked the most idiotic question in the history of idiotic questions. He still held on to my arms, which, to be honest, was making me nervous. The guy had a hell of a grip. I didn't know if that was because he was strong, or driven by insanity. He looked at me in wonder, as if trying to find the right words to answer such a stupid question. He looked to my left arm and asked, "Where's your loop?"

"My what?" he asked.

"Your loop!" he said, looking at my upper arm. "Do you

know how much trouble you can get in for taking that off?"
His face lit up as if he'd just gotten a brilliant idea. He asked,
"Is that why you're here? Did you learn something?"

He kept asking questions and I kept not having answers.
He let go of my arm and held his own arm out toward me. He
had one of those silver bands above his biceps. "Tell me what
you know," he demanded. "Please."

I realized that this silver band must have been the "loop"
he was talking about. I reached into my back pocket and
pulled out the one that had been at the flume. The guy's eyes
went wide. He quickly grabbed the loop and looked around
as if he feared being seen.

"Are you insane?" he seethed. "Don't flash that around."

Before I knew what was happening, he grabbed the loop,
then took my hand and shoved it through.

"Hey," I protested, and tried to pull away. It was too late.
He shoved the round bracelet all the way up to my biceps.
Instantly I felt it tighten around my arm, as if it were alive. I
tried to pull it back down, but it wouldn't move. It rested just
above my biceps and clung there.

"Why did you do that?" I shouted.

"I helped you, now you help me" was his answer. "What
are your chances? Be honest. It doesn't matter to you if I
know, does it?"

"Chances for what?" I asked while trying to pull the loop
down my arm. It wouldn't move. The harder I pulled, the
tighter it squeezed. It felt like there were a thousand tiny
needles inside, keeping it in place. I was frightened, and
more than a little creeped out. What was this diabolical loop?
How could it know that I was trying to pull it off so it knew
to cling tighter? And why didn't it want to get pulled off in
the first place? Could it think like the robot-quig-spiders
back at the gate? Things were happening a little too fast.

"Get it off!" I shouted to the bald guy.

His answer? He laughed. "I just did you a favor!" he said. "If you were seen without that loop, you'd never see another challenge."

Before I could ask what the hell he meant by that, I felt the loop tighten on my arm again—on its own. Remember the groove I described that was etched in the circle? It was glowing bright purple. A thin, bright light circled the band that was squeezing the heck out of my arm.

"What's with that?" I asked nervously.

"What do you mean?" he asked dismissively. "That's what happens when a loop activates."

"Activates?" I shouted. "I don't want anything on me 'activating'!"

"I don't understand," the guy said genuinely. "You're a challenger. All challengers wear the loop."

"What do you mean, I'm 'a challenger'?" I snapped. "What makes you say that?" I had decided to give up being coy. I needed answers. The pulsing, glowing, grabbing ring on my arm was making that all too obvious.

"Aren't you wearing the uniform of a challenger?" the guy asked, looking every bit as bewildered as I felt.

Uh-oh. It was the shirt. It seemed this red shirt with the black diagonal stripes was only worn by challengers. Whoever *they* were. I could only hope that challengers were cool people whom everyone loved and nobody ever gave a hard time to.

Yeah, right.

Before I could ask the guy anything else, I heard a tortured scream come from across the noisy room. A quick look told me that unlike the guy who was playing the shoot-out game, the player who was running through the 3-D maze wasn't having as much luck. GAME OVER flashed in big blue letters on his screen. The player had fallen to his knees. He truly looked beaten. His head hung and he was breathing hard. No doubt he had given the game his all, only to lose. I wondered if the reaction of a loser was going to be as dramatic as that of a winner.

I wasn't prepared for the answer.

This guy had a crowd around him as well, but rather than console him, they slowly backed away. It was weird, as if they just got word that the guy had the plague. They all had dark, pained expressions. Nobody so much as threw him a casual, "Too bad, dude. Try again." They were taking this loss very seriously. One person did break from the crowd. She ran up to the guy and hugged him. The guy didn't move. I saw that her eyes were screwed shut and her lips pursed, as if she were holding back a scream. The two stayed that way for a few moments while the others continued to move away. That's when the loop around this guy's arm began to glow. Unlike my loop that had given off a bright purple glow, his loop glowed yellow. The woman saw this, gave the guy one last squeeze and a kiss on the top of his head, then turned and ran. Seriously. She ran away. By this time the other spectators had blended back into the arcade, disappearing among the other people. Some pretended to be playing games, others were gone entirely. It was like the guy who lost had suddenly developed leprosy.

I heard a *crash* come from somewhere. It sounded like a door being thrown open. It made the bald guy next to me jump.

"Dados," he whispered softly, almost reverently.

I gave the guy a quick look and asked, "What's a dado?"

He scoffed, as if he didn't believe for a second I didn't know. "Now aren't you glad I put your loop back on?" he asked smugly. The next thing I heard was footsteps. It sounded like quick marching, as if a parade were about to pass through. This seemed to snap the guy who'd lost the game back to life. He looked around quickly. His eyes were wide and scared. I didn't know if he was looking for help, or trying to see where the marchers were coming from, or choosing the best escape route. Or all three. He ran . . .

The wrong way. He took only a few steps before he ran right into the arms of two uniformed men who were headed his way. They grabbed him, held his arms, and without breaking stride kept on moving. The guy struggled to break away, but it was no use. They had him and weren't letting go.

"This was my first try!" he complained nervously. "I'm allowed two tries, aren't I? I thought those were the rules? If I'm wrong, I'm sorry, but I know I'm supposed to get two tries."

Obviously he was wrong. Or the uniformed guys didn't care. They kept marching him away. The guy was near panic. It was incredible. He lost at a video game, and by losing, some police-looking guys called "dados" came to take him away. It really didn't make sense. What kind of games do you lose, and then get dragged away by the police? These dado guys weren't fooling around, either. They were both big. I'm guessing they stood about six-foot-four. They had broad shoulders and wore shiny gold helmets. Their uniforms were dark green and looked like they'd just come from the cleaners. That's how tight and pressed they were. Each guy had a round patch on his upper arm that was bright yellow, with a logo that looked like a "B." On their hips they each had a shiny black holster that held a golden pistol that seemed to be made of the same material as their helmets.

As scary as all this looked, there was one more thing about these guys that told me you didn't want to mess with them. It was their faces. I don't know how else to describe this except to write that their faces were big. And square. They almost looked like cartoon bad guys, with sharp jaw-lines and deep-set eyes. They had no expression. Even as they carted off a guy who was yelling and squirming to get loose. Their faces remained stone blank. They didn't give instructions. They didn't tell the guy to calm down. They definitely didn't say where they were going. They simply kept moving.

The guy didn't have a chance.

They dragged him past two more police guys who were standing on either side of the aisle. They had entered from two different directions to surround their quarry. When the loser guy was dragged past these two other uniforms, I saw that the two new guys were standing stock still, their hands behind their backs, surveying the crowd. Nobody else in the arcade made eye contact with them. It seemed pretty clear to me that they were afraid of these police dudes. Heck, I would be too if I lost at a pinball game and my punishment was to get dragged off by a couple of Terminator-looking guys. I now understood why all the players were so intent on their games. Losing wasn't a good thing.

The two sentries followed the others. One of them took one last look around the arcade, scanning the room, until his gaze came to rest . . . on me. The two of us made eye contact. I felt a chill. This may sound weird, but it was like I was star-ing into the eyes of a doll. A big, living doll.

"What's he looking at me for?" I asked the bald guy. "I wasn't even playing." I looked to the bald guy for an answer, but he was gone. I was alone. I snapped a look back to the doll-man-police-dado-whatever that was suddenly so inter-ested in me, and my knees went week. He and his pal had changed their minds. They stopped following the others . . .

And came after me.

QUILLAN

I've been a Traveler for a couple of years now. I've learned more about time, the universe, and everything in it than I ever thought possible while growing up in sleepy little Stony Brook. Above all else I've learned a very important rule that I try to live by:

When big, scary-looking guys chase you, run.

I wanted to know who these dado police were. I wanted to know why winning and losing at these video games was so important. I wanted to know what "challengers" were, and why I was given a shirt that marked me as one. I wanted to know what this eerie "loop" thing was that wouldn't let go of my arm. There was a whole lot I needed to know about Quillan, but I wasn't going to find out by letting myself get dragged off to who-knows-where by a couple of Frankenstein-looking thugs. It had to be on my terms. So I took off.

Trouble was, I had no idea where I was going. The arcade was big and loud, but it wasn't very crowded. I couldn't lose myself among the people. Especially since I was wearing a bright-freakin'-red shirt that made me stand out like a tomato in a bowl of blueberries. My best shot was to get out of the arcade. At least that was my hope. I had no idea what I would find outside, either. We could have been in the middle of a desert. But I knew that if I stayed inside I'd be caught for sure. Outside was better. Or so I hoped.

I dodged around a couple of game machines, ducked low, reversed my direction, and walked calmly the other way. I didn't want to draw attention to myself and alert the goons who were chasing me. It didn't work. It was the red shirt. Many of the people in the arcade ran up to me, and with the same look of desperation that the bald guy had, they pawed at me while asking, "When do you compete? How good are you? What is your event? Please, tell me!"

I gave up trying to be inconspicuous and took off running. I glanced back to see if the dado dudes were following. They were. Their dead doll eyes were locked on me as they stormed their way through the arcade. People had to get out of their way or risk getting run down. Who were these guys? At least my misdirection bought me a little space. I had a few seconds to find the exit before they'd catch up. But the main floor of the arcade was huge and I had no idea which way was out. All I could do was run, and hope. I blasted through the rows of machines like a running back dodging tacklers. The strange electronic music offered an odd accompaniment to the chase. As I ran along, people would see me and start applauding, as if I were running a race. I wanted to shout out "Shhhh!" but figured that would have been a waste of breath. It was clear that I wasn't going to make a quiet exit; all I could hope to do was make a fast one. But after running for about a minute, snaking through the arcade to ditch the dados, I still hadn't found the exit.

The thought hit me that there might not be any exits, and

that Quillan was all one giant arcade. I'm not sure if that would be a dream come true . . . or a nightmare. Right then it felt more like a nightmare. I was getting a stitch in my side and had to stop to catch my breath. I ducked behind a tall game and gulped air. That's when I saw it. It was nothing more than a thin shaft of white light on the floor, but it stood out amid the brightly colored flashing strobes. Daylight. I knew I had to be near a door. Or a window. It didn't matter, whatever it was, I was going through it. I ran for the light, and after ducking past two more rows of games, I saw it: double glass doors leading to the outside and safety.

I was only a few yards from . . . what? I wasn't sure. But I had to get there. As I ran for freedom, I saw something else that I knew would help my escape. Next to the door was a long row of hooks with jackets hanging on them. My first thought was that these people were pretty trusting to leave their jackets where anybody could steal them. My second thought was that I had to steal one. I'm not a thief, but this was an emergency. If I was going to blend into this territory, I couldn't go around wearing a uniform that made me stick out like some kind of rock star. So I swiped one of the hanging jackets that looked to be my size, though the fit really didn't matter. All it had to do was cover up the red shirt. Note to self: Return the jacket if you get the chance. Like I said, I'm not a thief. But this was an emergency.

As I put the jacket on, still headed for the door, I glanced back into the arcade. The police thugs were gaining fast. I had to get outside and get lost as quickly as possible. While still jamming my arms through the sleeves of the jacket, I backed into the door, banged it open, and spun outside.

I found myself on the sidewalk of a busy city, jammed with people. That was good. I could blend in here, no problem. I quickly pulled the jacket around me to hide any sign of the telltale red "challenger" shirt, and walked quickly through the crowd to get as far away from that arcade, and the dados, as I could. I kept my head down and moved as fast as possible without knocking anybody over. That wasn't easy. The sidewalk was pretty crowded. Mark, remember when we'd take the train into New York City and walk up Fifth Avenue to go to Central Park? Remember how crowded it always was, with hundreds of people all going one place or another? I always wondered why people didn't keep bumping into one another. Well, that's pretty much what it was like. I was in the center of a very busy downtown of a very busy city, but I didn't take the time to stop and look around until I was sure I had lost my pursuers. It wasn't until I had made a couple of turns, crossed a few streets, and finally turned onto a wide boulevard that I felt sure I had ditched them. I slowed down. My heart stopped racing. I had escaped. But to where? It was time to take a look and see what a city on Quillan was all about.

Tall gray buildings loomed above me. Some were like skyscrapers that would rival anything you could find in the big cities on Second Earth; others were smaller. But by smaller I'm talking twenty to thirty stories high. The buildings themselves didn't have much personality. Whoever designed them must have been the same guy who designed the drab clothing. There wasn't a lot of imagination going on there. The buildings were big and gray and, well, boring. The windows were spaced out in uniform rows, floor after floor. Looking across the wide street and up and down the boulevard, I saw similar buildings as far as the eye could see. The only variation from building to building was in height. They were all boxy rectangles that reached up to a gray, cloudy sky. I felt that if I closed my eyes and spun around, I wouldn't know which way was which. The sick thought hit me that finding my way to the flume was going to be a challenge. I was standing in the middle of busy foot traffic, so I backed away to the side and stood with my back to one of these big gray buildings to get a better look at what was happening on eye level.

The street was packed with traffic. They had cars, kind of like on Second Earth. I'm sure you can guess what I'm going to say about them. Yep. Boring. They all had the same basic shape, which was rounded front to back. They were kind of like VW Beetles, but not as interesting-looking. Some were black, some silver. That's it. There were two-wheeled motor scooters as well. The people on those were able to move a little faster because there weren't as many, and they could slide between the cars. I guess it was kind of like those busy Asian cities at home, where there's so much traffic, many people ride motor scooters. It looked as if riding a scooter was the way to go because the cars were getting nowhere fast.

All the vehicles were pretty quiet, I'm happy to say, because the street was choked with them. They must have been electric powered, because I couldn't hear any engine sounds. They were all moving in the same direction, slowly. Nobody seemed too angry about it. I didn't hear any car horns or frustrated shouts. There were signal lights at the corners, but rather than the round red and green lights we're used to, a single, narrow blue light stretched above the roadway from sidewalk to sidewalk. When the light was lit, the traffic could move. When it went dark, the traffic stopped. I couldn't tell much difference between moving and stopped, but that's how it worked.

It was the same with the pedestrians. Like the people in the arcade, everyone was dressed in simple, drab clothing. But unlike the arcade, which was next to empty, there were loads of people on the street. People walked on the sidewalk in front of me, slowly but relentlessly. Those moving to my right were closer to the building, those moving to my left were closer to the street. I didn't see much interaction. Everyone was in their own little gray world, thinking about whatever they were thinking about, going wherever they were going. The looks on their faces were blank. Maybe not as blank as those dado guys, but definitely spacey. I didn't see anyone laughing, or angry, or even talking. This was a busy, crowded city, yet it was eerily quiet.

On the ground level of the buildings were stores. Each with its own entrance. But unlike stores on Second Earth that used names to try to catch your attention, the signs above the doors here on Quillan all used the exact same typeface. The silver metallic letters were about eight inches high and mounted on a shiny black background. Stranger still, they didn't show the name of the store, all they said was exactly what you could buy there. I'm serious. I saw a sign that said FOOD. Another said HEALTH CARE. I saw signs that said CLOTH-ING, HOUSING, DOCUMENTS, EMPLOYMENT, CHILD CARE, and even one that said LIGHT. I'm not exactly sure what they sold there. Lightbulbs maybe? Every single store had the exact same kind of sign, no matter what they were selling. The lettering looked oddly familiar. It took me a minute to realize the style of the print was the same as I'd seen on the back of that plate that was being stored in the vast belowground warehouse. These signs looked the same as the one word on the back of those plates: BLOK.

I've painted a pretty bleak picture of this city. It was uni-form, it was drab, it was dull. The best thing I can say is that it all seemed to function smoothly. It was like the workings of a fine-tuned clock where everything fit into place and oper-ated the exact right way.

There was one more thing I haven't mentioned yet. I was saving this for last because it was the single most interesting thing I saw. Erected on the roofs of the smaller buildings were billboards that looked like giant plasma TV screens. I'd say there was one on every block. They looked to be about twenty feet across by ten feet high. No matter where you stood, you could catch sight of one. Each of these screens had the exact same thing playing on it. For the longest time I saw nothing but colorful, animated patterns. Intricate 3-D geometric shapes danced and bounced and morphed into one another in a hypnotic dance. Along the bottom was a running crawl like you would see on those TV news channels at home. It gave information about the day, like the time—"17:2:07." I thought that must be the time because it kept going up. The weather—"Clouds all day, followed by a chilly night with possible rain." I also saw what looked like game results, but I had no idea who was playing or what the game was— "Pimbay d. Weej 14–2, Linnta d. Hammaba 103–100."

Every so often the animated graphics would give way to the face of a pretty young woman or a handsome man. They were dressed the same as everybody else in the city, only they had small patches on their front pockets like the dado police dudes had on their arms. Each patch had a small "B." These people were like TV newscasters who would speak right to the camera with a pleasant, soothing voice.

"There is a program of music this evening," one announcer said, his voice booming through the city. "Please set your digits to the blue location at precisely nineteen-zero-fifty-six. Have the best day ever." Then the bright, lively patterns would return for a few moments. Followed by another announcer who came on to say, "Drivers are needed for dislocation work. If you are working in sections four-four-two-seven through nine-seven-five-two, please report during the next work period. Have the best day ever."

It went on and on like that. Every thirty seconds or so an announcer would come on to give some kind of report or announcement and end it by saying: "Have the best day ever." I expected a little yellow smiley face to pop on at the end. I hate little yellow smiley faces. Almost as much as I hate clowns.

The people walking along the street barely gave notice to the animated billboards. I didn't know why. I couldn't take my eyes off them. Not that they were all that exciting, but there was nothing else to look at! The city was so . . . gray. These billboards were the only sign of life. Okay, they were creepy, too, because it felt as if the people were being spoon-fed information by some grander force. But it was kind of cool looking down the long, straight street to see hundreds of the big TVs lined up for as far as I could see. It was like looking at a mirror, with another mirror to your back. You know how that makes it seem like you can see to infinity? Well, that's kind of the impression I got by looking down the street at these colorful TVs. If not for them, it would have seemed like a city populated by zombies. It was pretty depressing, but who was I to judge? Maybe these people were happy to be living this way.

Tweeeeeee!

A shrill whistle blast shattered the calm. Without thinking, I ducked back into the doorway of a store that sold soap. Across the street and a block to my right, I saw two big dado dudes run out from an alley, headed for the street, toward me. My first thought was *How did they find me*? I was about to turn and run when I realized that I didn't have to worry. I wasn't the quarry. Directly down the sidewalk to my right was a young guy running to get away from the dados. He looked terrified as he desperately tried to get through the people on the sidewalk. I figured he must have been a thief or something, because the dados definitely looked like police, with their gold helmets and dark green uniforms. Nobody would give the guy a break and get out of his way. Nor did they try to stop him. It was like he wasn't even there. Even when he banged into a woman, nearly knocking her down. She didn't say a word. All she did was put her head down and continue walking as if nothing had happened. It was like these people were brain-dead! On the other hand, about a half block behind him the people in the street parted to allow the dados a clear path. I didn't know if the people wanted the dados to catch the guy, or if they were just being smart, because if they didn't move, they'd probably get bowled over. It looked like it would be only a matter of time before the dados caught the fugitive.

When the guy ran by me, I saw that the loop on his arm was glowing yellow, just like the guy who'd gotten carted off inside the arcade. I wondered if the big crime this guy had committed was that he had lost a game. As he ran by, I saw the panic on his face. He was breathing hard and sweating. It wasn't just because he was tired either. No way. This guy was scared. I felt bad for him, but then again, maybe he really was a thief and deserved to get caught. Either way, it wasn't my business. The guy continued past me, dodging pedestrians. I looked back to the chasing dados, who would soon pass by. I stepped back into the shadow of the doorway. I didn't want them to give up on the scared guy and pick on somebody who wasn't moving so fast. Me. Everyone parted to let them pass. I crouched down, but peeked out from between two people to get a better look at these dado guys. I actually thought they looked strangely familiar, but couldn't imagine where I might have seen these thugs before. Still, there was something about them that I recognized.

It was at that moment that a woman riding a motor scooter shot off the street, headed for the sidewalk. She jumped the curb, shouting: "Look out! The throttle is jammed!" She was out of control. People dove out of the way. The woman maneuvered the bike into the space the pedestrians had cleared for the dados to run through. You guessed it, there was a collision coming.

"Help!" she shouted, and turned the motor scooter toward the running dados.

"Clear the way!" shouted one of the dados. His voice made me shudder. It didn't sound human. It was low and gravely and monotone, like he was some kind of, yes, I'll say it, like he was some kind of robot. Could it be? Were these dados actually robotic? His warning came too late. The woman saw the dados headed toward her. She screamed, and bailed off the bike. The bike fell on its side and skidded right toward the sprinting dados. They didn't have time to dodge it. The woman couldn't have hit them any more perfectly if she had been aiming. They were running side by side, and the careening bike hit them both at the ankles. They tumbled simultaneously, like circus performers. They hit the ground, rolled, and got tangled up in each other. It was a jumble of arms and legs and would have been kind of funny if the whole scene weren't so intense.

The woman tucked and rolled a few times. I wanted to run out to see if she was okay, but I had to keep a low profile. I wasn't on Quillan to get involved in minor disputes. I had bigger game to worry about, so to speak. So I stayed back and observed. The woman looked dazed as she sat up. Oddly, nobody else went to help her. If anything, all the pedestrians backed off even farther. There was now a wide circular clearing on the sidewalk, with two crumpled dados, a trashed motor scooter, and a dazed woman in the center. The woman looked pretty young. I'd say she was in her twenties. That was good. If she'd been really old, she probably would have been hurt by the fall. As it was, she looked to have only skinned her elbows. She sat on the sidewalk, looking as if she were trying to clear her head.

A few feet from her the dados were getting their act together as well. They both surveyed the scene. I truly don't think they knew what hit them, until they saw the bike and the dazed woman. One of them jumped to his feet and looked in the direction that their quarry had gone. He started to go after him again, but the other grabbed his arm to stop him.

"He will not get far," the second dado said in that same eerie, low robotic voice. The two turned their attention to the woman who had allowed the guy to get away. Both took a step toward her. They didn't look like they were worried about her well-being. They looked angry.

"What is your sequence?" the first dado demanded.

The woman looked up and was about to answer, when another guy suddenly pushed his way through the crowd and into the circle.

"Hey!" he shouted angrily at the woman. "What is wrong with you?" He looked even angrier than the dados. It was a guy with graying hair who could have been the woman's father. "I lend you my scoot and this is what you do? Drive like a crazy person?"

The woman didn't answer. She seemed too dazed. The guy didn't stop to help her. He went right to the scooter, or "scoot" as he called it, and picked it up. "If this is damaged, it'll come out of your pay!"

One of the dados grabbed him by the wrist and said, "Do you know this woman? She has obstructed a pursuit."

The guy cowered a bit. He may have been steamed, but it was clear he didn't want to mess with a dado.

"Sure I know her," he said. "She works for me. But not for long if she keeps acting so recklessly." He then turned to the woman and barked, "Get back to the store now!"

"I—I'm sorry," she stammered, and started to get up. "I lost control. It was the throttle—"

"I don't want to hear it," the guy snarled. "Go!" The guy smiled at the dado and said, "Forgive me. She won't be driving a scoot again anytime soon. At least not one of mine!" Without waiting for a response, he started to wheel the scooter away.

The dados looked from the guy to the woman, as if they weren't sure what to do. Finally one of them said to the other, "Come. We must continue the pursuit." Without another word the two dados took off running after their quarry.

The excitement was over. The crowd started to move along again. I didn't. I kept my eye on the woman and the man. Something didn't feel right. What happened was an accident, sure, but it all seemed to happen a bit too perfectly. The woman on the bike hit the sidewalk at the exact right time to nail the dados. Was it intentional? Who knew? Maybe it was a total accident. But one thing definitely happened because of it. The guy the dados were chasing got away.

There was one other thing that made me think there was something more going on. It happened a moment before the crowd filled up the sidewalk once again. The woman got to her feet, brushed herself off, and looked to the older guy. I followed her gaze. The older guy was looking back at her. His anger seemed gone. That's when it happened. He reached up and clasped his hand over his left biceps. It was an odd move. I quickly shot a look back to the woman in time to see her do the exact same thing. Her expression didn't change; all she did was clasp her right hand over her left biceps. It was fast. By the time I looked back to the guy, he had been swallowed by the crowd.

I stood there for a moment, trying to figure out what I had just seen. Maybe I was reading too much into it, but it sure seemed as if these two people had given each other a silent signal. I couldn't begin to guess what it meant, but there was no question, the accident allowed the running guy to get away, and the older guy made sure the woman didn't get in trouble for it. It all happened so fast, the dados didn't know what hit them. I couldn't help but feel that I had witnessed something important.

I didn't have much time to think about it. There suddenly came a huge fanfare from the overhead screens. It was much more dramatic than anything I had heard up until then. It was an electronic trumpet tune that called everyone's attention to the screens. Everyone stopped and looked up at them. Literally. Everyone. All at the same time. This was way different from when the other announcements were made. The people barely paid attention to those. But not now. I felt an excited buzz travel through the crowd. People came alive. They exchanged looks. They chattered to one another. All the way up and down this crowded street, you could feel the electricity. Cars stopped, which wasn't that big a deal because they weren't going anywhere anyway, but the drivers got out of their vehicles to look up at the screens. Whatever was going to happen, they were excited about it. Thousands of people were suddenly all staring up, in anticipation of . . . what?

Naturally I looked up too. The screens were all blank for a few more seconds as the fanfare built. Finally, as the music reached a crescendo, a single word appeared in a shower of light and drama.

BLOK.

There it was again. Blok. What the heck was it? The way it appeared on-screen with such a flourish, you'd think people would cheer, as if their favorite wrestling champion had just been announced. They didn't. They continued to look up with anticipation, but there was no cheering. The inspirational music continued, and a man's voice was heard.

"The competition is about to begin," the voice said, teasing the crowd. He sounded excited, almost giddy, as if this news were as exciting to him as he was trying to make it for the crowd. I guess it worked, because I could feel a buzz growing. The people of Quillan were getting psyched up. "We are in midquad, which can only mean one thing!"

Suddenly everyone in the crowd shouted out: "TATO!"

Yikes! The roar was deafening. They all shouted out the word and began to applaud and cheer. It was like the fuse had reached the dynamite and the crowd had exploded. Whatever "Tato" was, the crowd thought it was pretty good. The word TATO flashed on-screen, which made them cheer again. I couldn't imagine what was so incredibly great about this "Tato" thing that it could finally inject some life into this listless world.

The man's excited voice continued over the roar, louder, so it could be heard: "Place your bets, the time is near; the greatest games on Quillan are here!" He sang this out like a singsong children's rhyme. The people responded with a cheer and applause. I didn't. Rhymes. I had heard a rhyme recently. Where was that? Why did this give me an uneasy feeling? I couldn't remember.

On the screen the word TATO dissolved in a brilliant flash of orange. What was left was a close-up of the announcer. The guy had a big toothy smile. His hair was long and blond and totally wild like he had stuck his finger in a toaster. He was an older guy, in his forties maybe. Whatever age he was, he was way too old to be acting so crazy. He reminded me of one of those nutty guys in cheesy TV commercials who try to sell you kitchen stuff, or used cars. Or report the weather. His eyes were wild and always moving. Above all, he looked like he was having a great time. The people responded.

"We are proud, so very proud, to bring you the greaaaaatest Tato match in history!" He was whipping the crowd into a frenzy. The shot on-screen widened out to include another person. A woman. She was as still and intense as the guy was animated and nutty. She stared out at the world with an unwavering glare. Her hair was dark and slicked back so severely, it almost looked like she was bald. Her features were sharp, like a fox's. Whoever she was, she meant business.

"The match will begin in moments," she said clearly but with no emotion. "Wagering must be completed by the tone. Do not dally. If you plan to wager, the time is now."

What an odd couple these two made. The hyperactive nutty guy who looked like he was auditioning for a kids' TV show, and the intense, glaring woman who was everybody's nightmare of a strict teacher. Who were these two?

The nutty guy gave me the answer. He sang out another rhyme that went, "The time is now; let's have some fun; we're ready for the show. Our games aren't tame; you know our names, your friends LaBerge and Veego."

I remembered where I saw the rhyme.

LaBerge and Veego. Veego and LaBerge. These were the guys who sent me that odd rhyming invitation to come to Quillan. I pulled the thick paper out of my back pocket and read it one more time:

> *Riggedy riggedy white*
> *Come and spend the night*
> *We'll play some games*
> *Some wild, some tame*
> *Cause if you will, you might*

More importantly, this invitation was in a box that was sent to me through the flume by Saint Dane. Somehow these two wack jobs on the video screen were tied in with the demon Traveler. I needed to know who they were, and what they were all about. My hunt for Saint Dane had officially begun.

Veego said, "LaBerge and I feel this will be an exciting, well-played Tato. Not since the famous match of twelve-oh-six have there been two competitors who are so closely matched." (She pronounced LaBerge like la-bearj. It sounded French, but there was no such thing as "French" on Quillan. As far as I knew.)

"They are entering the Tato dome now!" LaBerge announced. "Last chance for betting. The action is about to begin!"

The screen flashed white. Veego and LaBerge disappeared and were replaced by an overhead shot of what looked to be a sports court of some kind. It was a big platform in the shape of an octagon, about fifteen yards across. There was a red logo in the center that said TATO in the familiar block letters. Or should I call them "blok" letters? I saw five black round domes spaced evenly in a circle on the floor of the court, near the edges. Each looked to be a couple of feet in diameter and about a foot high in the center—like shiny bumps on the floor. They appeared to be made out of dark glass. Finally, there were two squares across from each other that were nothing more than marks on the floor of the court. I guess it goes without saying that this didn't look like any kind of court I had ever seen.

"Announcing!" came LaBerge's voice. Music started to

build. The excitement was growing. "He is undefeated in six Tato matches and is looking to set the new, unheard-of record of seven straight wins. Citizens of Rune and all Quillan, we present to you, everyone's favorite . . . Challenger Green!"

The crowd cheered. A chant of "Green, Green, Green" went up from most of the people gathered on the street. I watched as the contestant stepped up onto the platform and stood in one of the squares. Challenger Green was a guy who looked about my age with long, wavy red hair that fell below his shoulders. He was a big light-skinned guy who looked very much like an athlete. But what I zeroed in on was his shirt. It was bright green with five diagonal black stripes . . . just like the red shirt I was wearing. Things were starting to come clear. The bald guy at the arcade had called me a "challenger." He must have thought I was one of the guys who competed at this Tato thing.

It was not a realization that made me particularly happy.

What I saw next made me even less happy.

Veego announced, "Competing against Challenger Green is a newcomer. Though he has never entered the Tato dome, he has so impressed the judges that he has been fast-tracked into this very special match. If Challenger Green is to break the record, it will have to be against the most promising challenger to have ever stepped into the Tato dome. Introducing for the first time here in Rune or anywhere else on Quillan, today's worthy adversary . . . Challenger Yellow!"

Rune. What was Rune? Before I had the chance to think too much about it, the guy called "Challenger Yellow" stepped onto the octagon wearing, you guessed it, a yellow jersey with black diagonal stripes. I guess that meant I was Challenger Red. Lucky me. I wondered why exactly these challenger clothes were left for me at the flume. I would much rather have had something bland and inconspicuous, so that

I could blend into the territory. I made the decision to ditch this shirt and find some boring old Quillan clothes as soon as possible.

I could see why Challenger Yellow was considered to be a strong competitor. He was taller than Challenger Green by at least a head. He was dark skinned, though not as dark as if he were a Batu from Zadaa, like Loor. He moved gracefully, with little wasted movement. I guess "fluid" was the best way to describe him. He was thin, but not skinny. He definitely had some muscle, but with very little body fat. He looked like the kind of guy you'd see competing in the Olympic long jump or something. These two guys were very much opposites. One was tall and lanky, the other broad and strong. I had no idea which was better for this game called "Tato."

While the two challengers limbered up on opposite sides of the octagon, the big screen showed them in close-up. First it was Challenger Green. He looked confident and relaxed. He didn't look even the slightest bit concerned about Challenger Yellow dethroning him. He was the champion and fully expected to remain so. I wondered if Challenger Yellow stood a chance. To be honest, I didn't care much either way. I had no idea what I was watching and had absolutely no stake in it. That is, until the big screen showed a close-up of Challenger Yellow. I stared up at the huge screen, not believing what I was seeing. I blinked. There had to be some mistake. It was impossible.

Challenger Yellow had his arms folded across his chest. He looked nervous. I could see it in his eyes. He stared at Challenger Green, watching his opponent carefully. I could only guess what was going through his mind, probably a lot of things, but it didn't seem like one of them was confidence. Challenger Green already had the edge in the mind game department. But that wasn't what shocked me. I looked down the long city street at all the giant screens that projected the image of Challenger Yellow. I don't know why, but I kept looking at screen after screen, expecting to see something different. No, *hoping* to see something different. That was idiotic, because it was all the same image, shown again and again and again. There was no mistake. The image was big enough for me to make it out clearly.

Challenger Yellow wore a ring. It was heavy and silver with a gray stone in the center.

It was the ring of a Traveler.

QUILLAN

No mistake. It was a Traveler ring. I had found the Traveler from Quillan. Sort of. He was an athlete. A challenger. I needed to get to him, but knew nothing about this match or Veego and LaBerge or, well, anything else. I needed answers, but looking at these mesmerized people of Quillan wasn't going to do me any good. I turned to the guy next to me and asked, "Where is this match happening? Where is the Tato dome?"

The guy looked at me like I was nuts. I guess I must have sounded a little off, seeing as none of the other multiple thousand people were doing anything other than staring up at the screen. Or maybe it was just a dumb question because everybody knew where the Tato dome was. I didn't care if the guy thought I was loopy or not. I got right in his face and repeated with more force, "Where is this match happening?"

The guy took a step back. I scared him.

"In the garden," he said with a frown. "Where else would it be?"

"What garden?" I shouted. "Where is this garden?"

The guy backed away from me like I was dangerous. Who knows? Maybe I was. I know for sure I was starting to panic. Throw in a little confusion for good measure. Never forget the confusion. I had found the Traveler from Quillan, my one and only ally here on this strange new territory. But I had no idea how to get to him. I looked up at the screen, trying to find any clue that would tell me where they were. It looked as if the octagon were surrounded by dense forest. Wherever this "garden" was, it definitely wasn't anywhere near this gray city. All I could see in every direction were tall, ugly sky-scrapers. I decided that as soon as the match was over, I'd find somebody who could tell me where this garden was or, better yet, take me there. I had to smile. I wasn't going to be alone much longer. It was a good feeling . . .

That didn't last very long.

I suddenly had a rooting interest in this contest. The crowd wasn't impressed with Challenger Yellow. There was some cheering and applause for him, but nothing compared to the champion. That guy was cheered like he was the heavyweight champion of the world. He stood inside one of the squares on the floor of the platform, arms at his sides, glaring at Challenger Yellow. He looked calm. Challenger Yellow didn't. There was no doubt, he was in trouble.

Each of the challengers held something in his hand that looked like a short steel club. The word "weapon" sprang to mind. I would have been much happier if they'd had a ball. Or a Frisbee. Or anything else that said "game," as opposed to a lethal-looking club that could break bones.

A loud, steady tone sounded, and everyone became quiet.

"The betting is closed," boomed Veego's voice.

As the two challengers faced each other from across the

octagon, the platform began to lift up into the air. At the same time the crowd joined in with a loud, sustained chorus that sounded like they were chanting: "Taaaaaaaaaaaa. . . ." The platform rose higher and higher, revealing a single heavy post underneath. The two challengers didn't move. I didn't blame them. The platform was getting pretty high. One slip and they'd go over the edge. I hoped they weren't afraid of heights. At least, I hoped Challenger Yellow wasn't afraid of heights.

"Taaaaaaaaa . . .," droned the crowd.

The platform continued higher. I'm guessing it rose four stories before it finally stopped. Whatever it was those guys were going to do on that platform, they had to be careful. It was a long way down. My fear rose along with that platform. This had gone beyond being just a game. The Traveler was in *real* trouble. He wasn't in danger only of losing some sort of Quillan game, he was in danger of getting killed.

"Taaaaaaa . . .," continued the crowd. They started to applaud. The beginning of the match was near. You could feel it.

LaBerge's voice rang out above the din, "Four, three, two, one!"

The crowd screamed in unison, "TAAAAAAAA . . . TO!"

The bout was on. The challengers crouched down and circled each other. I had no idea what the point of this contest was, but I didn't think these guys were about to play hopscotch. It felt like there was going to be violence.

Challenger Yellow made the first move. I cringed. If there was one thing I'd learned about fighting, it was never to make the first move. He dove at Challenger Green, trying to knock his legs out from under him. Green saw it coming. He casually jumped into the air and over a flailing Yellow. I had the sick feeling that the winner of this contest was the one who stayed on the platform. That would have been fine if it were still on the ground, but up there in the stratosphere the drop would be deadly. Leaving the platform meant leaving life.

Yellow quickly jumped back to his feet and spun around, ready for an attack from Green. I was right. He was agile. Question was, was agility enough to win a game of Tato?

Green casually walked away from him. He was too cool to attack. Smart guy. Yellow crouched down and circled the octagon. Green mirrored his move. I didn't like this. The Traveler was trying to set the tempo, but it didn't seem like he knew what he was doing. Green looked to me like a sly cat, waiting patiently in the bushes for a dumb mouse to stumble by. Yellow's size made him look athletic, but he was tense and squirrelly.

The crowd shouted encouragement. Most of the people seemed to be rooting for Challenger Green, probably because he was the favorite. But I heard a handful of people cheering for Challenger Yellow. I would have been one of them, if I weren't so terrified for him. Yellow lunged at Green, taking a swing with the steel rod in his hand. Green blocked the shot easily, then rammed his own steel rod into Yellow's exposed gut.

Ouch. Yeah, it was violent. I cringed as if I had taken the shot myself. The crowd cheered. Yellow backed away quickly. I think his whole plan was to try to get in a lucky punch. That was a mistake. Green looked too smart for that. At this rate, I figured, it was only a matter of time before Yellow made a dumb mistake and Green took him out. The thought made me sick.

The Traveler then made a move I didn't expect, or understand at first. He backed away to the far side of the octagon. For a second I thought he was going to back off into oblivion. With his eyes trained on Green, he knelt down next to one of the round black domes on the floor of the octagon. He raised his hand with the steel club and brought it down hard onto the dome's surface. The black dome shattered like glass. The crowd let out a collective gasp, as if they couldn't believe he had done that. Some people were horrified. Others laughed.

Yellow shot a quick glance into the broken dome. It seemed like what he saw in there disappointed him. His shoulders fell slightly. He shook it off, reached down into the wrecked dome, and pulled out . . . a whip! But that wasn't the only surprise. When Yellow stood up, the platform was no longer stable. It swayed a bit, teetering to one side. It wasn't a huge difference, but it made me wonder what would happen if more of those domes were broken. Would the platform become even more rickety?

Yellow switched the steel rod into his left hand and grabbed the handle of the whip with his right. He gave it a menacing crack. Yes! He knew how to use it. Green tensed up. Now that Yellow was armed, the odds had gotten a little closer. The Traveler stalked Green, his whip at the ready. I saw the platform tilt ever so slightly. He had to be careful. Yellow faked a whip crack. Green flinched. Yellow was quickly gaining confidence. He smiled. My confidence grew too. I wanted him to finish off Challenger Green and get the heck off that platform. After that I would find him, to learn what was happening on Quillan.

Green kept his cool. Now that his opponent had a second weapon, he was more guarded, but he wasn't in a panic. Yellow took a step closer to him. The platform tilted that way. Yellow wound up and faked another whip crack. Green flinched—and Yellow struck. He quickly flipped out the tip of the whip toward his opponent. The whip slashed across Green's arm. Green didn't back off in the slightest or even show pain. Instead he quickly grabbed the end of the whip and spun it around his arm, effectively tying up the loose end. Yellow yanked on the handle; Green yanked back. Unless the Traveler let go of the handle, he and Green were now attached by either end of the whip.

I heard disgusted shouts of "No!" and "Amateur!" from the crowd. Most applauded with delight.

It was a standoff. The two contestants stood no more than six feet apart, waiting for the other to make a move.

It was Green. He knelt down and smashed his steel rod down onto another black dome, shattering it.

"What is he doing?" somebody shouted with dismay.

The platform instantly became more unstable. It started tilting back and forth with every weight shift. If any more domes were cracked, and the tilting got worse, both these guys would be going down. Green dropped the steel rod and quickly scooped something out from inside the broken dome. It looked like a boomerang. I was beginning to understand this match. The domes held weapons, but getting them came at a cost, because smashing the domes made the platform unstable. The challengers had a choice to fight it out without extra weapons, or risk making the platform dangerous by breaking the domes. I guess that wrinkle evened out the match. The weaker contestant could go for the weapons because it was the only chance he had. At first the weaker challenger was Challenger Yellow, the Traveler. Now it was Challenger Green.

The two circled. Yellow held the whip taut. The other end was still wrapped around Green's arm. Green held it tight with one hand and grasped the boomerang with the other. He faked a throw at Yellow. Yellow flinched. Green didn't throw. The Traveler was in a bad spot. If he let go of the whip, Green could haul it in and have two weapons. If he held on, he was in point-blank range of the boomerang. Green could easily whip it at his head.

The platform wobbled. My palms were sweating and my mouth was dry. I couldn't imagine losing another Traveler.

Challenger Green made a strange move. He quickly unwrapped the end of the whip and let Yellow draw it back. The crowd gasped. No kidding. Have you ever heard thousands of people all gasp at the same time? Neither had I, until then. Green had just given Yellow the weapon. I figured the only question now was, which weapon was more effective? The boomerang or the whip? Yellow stepped back quickly, coiling the whip, ready to attack. I didn't understand why Green had given it up.

Green faked a throw of the boomerang. The Traveler flinched. But Green didn't throw it. Instead he dropped to his knees and smashed another dome with one end of his weapon. The glass shattered. Instantly the platform tilted dramatically. This was it. Somebody was going to fall. The crowd went deadly silent. They sensed the end was near. But for which challenger?

A moment later I saw Green's plan. Yellow was near the center of the octagon, far away from any edge, but he wasn't safe. He was losing his balance. The platform was teetering so steeply, there was no way he could stay on his feet for long. He looked like a sailor trying to stay upright on the deck of a ship in thirty-foot waves.

Challenger Green saw that his opponent was in trouble. He threw away the boomerang and dropped down to his belly. At the same time he reached out and grabbed the lip of the dome he had just broken. With one quick move he threw his legs out toward the edge of the platform. His sudden weight shift made the platform tilt down dramatically to that side.

I now realized, with horror, that he knew exactly what he was doing. He was making the platform impossible to stand on, while having the smarts to hold on to something solid. That's why he broke the dome. He didn't want the weapon. He wanted to make the platform completely unstable, while creating a handhold for himself.

The platform tipped over. Yellow fell to the floor.

"No!" I shouted out, as if that would help. Others were shouting too. They all knew the end was near. But none of them cared as much as I did. None of these people knew that the person who was about to die was working to stop a mad demon from destroying all time and space. To them he was Challenger Yellow, a nameless victim of their champion. To me he was a fellow Traveler . . . who was seconds away from death.

Yellow slid toward the edge of the platform. He let go of the whip and the steel baton so his hands were free to find something to grab on to. He needn't have bothered. There was nothing to grab. Yellow flipped onto his belly, clawing at the floor with his fingers. He dug his toes in, desperately trying to halt his slide. I didn't want to watch, but I had to. It would be a dishonor to him if I didn't.

He didn't scream, he didn't show fear. He fought to the end. Mercifully, it came quickly. Challenger Yellow slid to the end of the platform and disappeared over the edge.

I had been on Quillan for less than an hour and we had already lost another Traveler.

QUILLAN

The screens up and down the street turned white and the words TATO CHAMPION—CHALLENGER GREEN! flashed in glowing red letters. Most of the crowd went crazy with cheering and hugging and car-horn honking. Their champion had won. It was like New Year's Eve in Times Square.

I stood in the center of the swirling craziness, feeling very alone and very stunned. Another Traveler was dead. How could this have happened? Who was he and why had he played that deadly game? I didn't even know the poor guy's name! I knew I would find those answers. I had to. But I also knew that when I did, it wouldn't change the fact that he was dead. I had the faint hope that, like Loor, he could beat death. After all, Travelers weren't like normal people, right? But that was a fleeting thought. Travelers *did* die. Something had happened between Loor and me in that cavern on Zadaa. She was dead, and she came back. But that was different. I was there with her. Whatever bizarro cosmic power we Travelers had, it was stronger when we were together. Here on Quillan,

Challenger Yellow was alone. He had fallen from a four-story-high platform. Nobody could survive that.

Saint Dane was clawing his way back into the battle for Halla. Or maybe he was never out of it. Was he just toying with us? Was the battle for each territory secondary to his overall plan of conquest? It sure seemed like it. As I stood there on that busy, lonely street, I made myself a promise. I would avenge the deaths of the Travelers. All of them. I didn't know when. I didn't know how. I was certain that Saint Dane somehow played a role in Challenger Yellow's death, and for that I would make him suffer. It couldn't be as simple as killing him. I'd already discovered that couldn't be done. Besides, I'm not the killing type. Something else had to be done. Something significant. Saint Dane would pay for what he had done to Challenger Yellow, and so many others.

But first I had to find him.

Music echoed through the canyons created by the towering buildings. The crowd continued to celebrate. Most of them, anyway. I wondered how many people had actually bet on the outcome. Glancing around at the crowd, I saw that a disturbing number of "loops" on people's arms were glowing yellow. Could it be? Could that many people have actually bet on the outcome of this death contest . . . and picked the loser? I'm sorry to say the answer was, yes. No sooner did the loops begin to glow, than I heard a far-off siren. Followed by another, and another. The panicked look on the faces of the losers told me all I needed to know. If what had happened in the arcade was any indication, the sirens meant one thing:

The dados were coming for the losers.

The people with the flashing armbands scattered. Some jumped out of their cars and started to run. The people celebrating didn't do anything to help them, or show any concern. They were too busy being happy. Or relieved. Or, in many cases, oblivious. A moment later I saw three dados on motorbikes charging along the sidewalk. They must have been inside the buildings, waiting for the Tato match to end. Waiting to begin the round-up. People scattered to give them room. One woman with a flashing yellow armband ran into the store behind me. A dado shot up on his motorbike, jumped off, and was right after her. She didn't stand a chance. More dados swarmed into the crowd, rounding up people with flashing loops. Some people fought the dados, refusing to be taken. Others seemed resigned and went quietly. It didn't matter either way. The dados would not be denied. They grabbed their quarry and quickly hauled them off. Their victims were every sort of person you could imagine. Older men, young women, middle-aged people . . . at least there were no kids. That's one consolation. This all led me to a really disturbing question: Why were so many people gambling? And what exactly were they betting so that as soon as they lost, the thugs came to get them? Did the people running the contests automatically assume they weren't going to pay? It made me wonder how big their bets were.

A moment later the woman who'd ducked into the store was dragged out by the dado, fighting against the much bigger guy. "I have children," she whined. "I had no choice. Please. I have resources. I can make amends."

The dados didn't care. They simply carted her off roughly to . . . who knows where? I imagined there was some central place where everybody who lost a bet had to go to pay up. The real question was, why? Who was collecting these bets and why did they have an army of scary robotlike guys to round up the losers? The whole scene was disturbing for all sorts of reasons.

I kept to the shadows, observing. I didn't want to get in the way or be involved. What I really needed to do was find the two nut jobs from the video screen. Veego and LaBerge. Whatever Saint Dane was doing on Quillan, it was obvious that Veego and LaBerge had something to do with it. Since they seemed to be the people who staged the contests, and I was given the uniform of a challenger, the pieces of the puzzle were coming together in a way that made me a little nervous. Would I eventually end up high on that platform, fighting for my life the way the Traveler from Quillan did? The thought made me want to find my way down to the warehouse basement, dump these challenger clothes, and get the hell off Quillan. But that's not the way it was meant to be. I needed to be here and face whatever Saint Dane had set up for me. That's the way it worked in the life of Bobby Pendragon, lead Traveler.

"Do not move," came a stern, gravelly voice that had the unmistakable growl of a dado. I really, really hoped he wasn't talking to me. Slowly I turned to see . . .

He was talking to me. Swell.

Two dados stood side by side. I wasn't sure if they were the same goons that had chased me out of the arcade. It didn't matter. One of them had his golden pistol out. It was aimed at me.

"You talking to me?" I asked innocently. "I didn't bet on the contest, see?" I took off my jacket to show them that my loop wasn't flashing yellow. It was flashing purple. I had forgotten. Oops. What the heck did purple mean?

"Challengers must never enter the city without an escort," the second dado said. "Come with us."

I wasn't going with them. No way. I needed to be on my own to find Saint Dane. Besides, I didn't want to be the next one on that platform and risk facing the same fate as Challenger Yellow. I pulled my jacket the rest of the way off and took a step toward the dados.

"Okay," I said casually. "But first let me do this—"

Without warning I shoved the jacket into the face of the dado with the gun. At the same time I ducked down, spun my leg, and swept the legs out from under the second dado. He slammed into the dado with the gun, knocking him off balance, making him fire his gun. The sound it made wasn't a *crack* like you'd hear from a gun on Second Earth. It was more like a short, sharp discharge of energy that gave off a hollow echo. *Fum.* I had no idea what kind of ammunition it fired. I didn't want to know. I needed to get away. Before they could get their balance back, I took off into the crowd.

The chase was back on.

QUILLAN

I'd been on the run from the moment I hit Quillan. How long had it been since I landed? An hour? At that rate I was going to drop from exhaustion before anything actually happened. Still, I couldn't imagine anything good coming from getting nabbed by a dado, so I bolted.

I made the quick decision not to run down the crowded street. I was afraid the pedestrians would get in my way, and step aside for the dados. So I made a flash decision and ducked into the store with the sign FOOD over the door, hoping there would be a back exit. If not, I'd be trapped, but at least this way I felt I had a chance.

The store was like no other grocery store I'd ever seen. There were long aisles like at home, but rather than seeing an array of different products, everything in this store came in similar rectangular containers. They were different sizes and colors, but they all fit squarely on one another like Legos. I didn't stop to browse, obviously, but as I ran by I saw that the labels were marked simply VEGETABLE and MEAT. Not exactly tantalizing. One said TRIBBUN, whatever the heck *that* was. My Traveler brain always translated the local language for me, unless it was something unique to that territory that didn't have a similar word in English that I would know. Whatever tribbun was, it couldn't be found on Second Earth. Just as well. It didn't sound so hot. I also saw that there was the same word printed on each label above the contents. BLOK. There it was again. Blok. Over and over.

As I sprinted down one of the long aisles filled with multi-colored containers, I heard the door smash open behind me. I didn't have to turn around to know the dados were right on my tail.

"On the ground!" shouted one of the dados in that low, robotic voice. Instantly every one of the people in the store moved to the side of the aisle and knelt down to let the dados by. It was scary to see how these people were so obedient. Were they afraid of the dados? From what I'd seen so far, I didn't blame them. I was too. I turned quickly into another aisle and kept running. My only hope was that there would be an exit on the far side of the store. I saw a counter ahead of me where people were paying for their purchases. At least that's what they usually did. Right then they were ducked down and cowering, because somebody was being chased. Me. I was relieved to see a doorway behind the counter. Without hesitation I ran for the counter, vaulted over it, and landed next to a very frightened-looking store clerk. I made quick eye contact. He was scared, no question, but as soon as he saw me, he whispered, "Good luck."

Those words said a lot. He had no idea who I was, or why I was running from the dados. But that one brief comment from a very scared guy told me that they weren't rooting for the dados. At least as far as this frightened guy was concerned, the dados weren't the good guys.

Fum!

A container that was on a shelf near my head exploded. Somebody screamed. It might have been me. Everything had just gotten a little more serious. I was no longer being chased; I was being hunted. I dove through the door behind the counter, desperate to get anything in between me and those goons. I found myself behind the counter of another store. Of course I couldn't see the sign outside, but I could guess what it said. I had just come out of a store called "Food" to enter a store called "Drink." There were long aisles in here as well, only they were all stacked with row after row of rounded canisters of different colored liquid. As I sprinted down an aisle, I glanced quickly to see that the labels on each had the same word: BLOK. Blok was everywhere . . . on plates, on food and drink products, even on the giant screens outside. Sooner or later I needed to find out what Blok was.

But not just then.

Fum! Fum!

Two canisters of bright blue "drink" exploded next to my head, splashing me. I didn't stop, but jammed for a door that looked as if it led back outside. Going into these stores had turned out to be a bad idea. I figured that at least outside, with so many people, there'd be less chance of them shooting at me for fear of hitting an innocent bystander. Innocent bystander? I was an innocent bystander too! What was I guilty of? Nothing! But nobody told the dados that. Nope. No bystanding for me, innocent or not. I was on the run. So I hit the door and crashed back out onto the street, knocking into a few people along the way.

"Sorry!" I shouted, but the people didn't care. They continued on their way, heads down, as if nothing had happened. All I could do was keep on moving and try to find a place to hide. I crossed over a street, running low, hoping that they wouldn't see me. It slowed me down, but it wasn't like I could break into a full-on sprint anyway. It was way too crowded for that.

I reached the next intersection and saw something that gave me hope. Walking ahead of me was the older, gray-haired guy who had chewed out that woman for crashing the motorbike into the dados. He was walking his scoot along the sidewalk. I had to trust my instinct. I felt like there was something going on with that guy. If I was right, and he had helped that other guy escape from the dados, I had to hope he would do the same for me.

I looked back to see that the dados had run out of the store and were scanning the crowded sidewalk. I had a short window. I ran forward until I got ahead of the guy. He was walking with his head down, just like everybody else. I ran past him, then turned around, and walked backward.

"Hey," I said breathlessly. "I need help."

The guy looked up quickly. I saw the surprise in his eyes. I didn't know if it was because a crazy guy had just jumped out of nowhere asking him for help, or because I was wearing a challenger shirt. Or both. He didn't stop walking.

"How can I help you?" he said softly, with a touch of confusion.

His calm voice didn't fit with the surprise that he showed. The guy was very cool.

"They're after me," I said, glancing back toward the dados. "I didn't do anything. I didn't bet on the match, but they're shooting at me."

The guy glanced back toward the dados, then to me. He said, "I'm surprised to see a challenger on the street."

There wasn't time for discussion. The dados were almost on us. If I didn't get through to this guy, fast, I'd be done. I took a chance and grabbed my left biceps with my right hand—the same signal I'd seen him exchange with the woman who drove the motor scooter into the dados. I didn't know if the guy would react, or keep walking as if it meant nothing to him.

"Get on," he said, suddenly all business.

Yes! The guy threw his leg over the motor scooter. I hopped on to the back as he kicked the engine to life. It hummed with a soft whine that didn't speak to the true power of this bike, for when he hit the throttle, we took off. Fast.

"Hang on," he commanded, and made a hard right, turning into traffic. The instant he made the turn, I heard the familiar sound of shots being fired.

Fum. Fum. Fum.

So much for the dados not wanting to hurt innocent bystanders. A guy to the right of me was knocked off his feet. Another woman was hit, and spun around but was able to stay upright. I was horrified. Were people dying around me? Why were these dados so desperate that they were willing to shoot innocent people to get me? Did life mean so little to them? Or was I that important? If I was going to find the answers, I first had to stay alive. My fate was in the hands of this mysterious old guy and his scoot.

The guy may have been old, but he knew how to handle the motorbike. He drove us across traffic, weaving back and forth, threading between the slow-moving cars. I didn't dare look back, for fear of throwing us off balance. We hit the far sidewalk, bounced up over the curb, and turned into the flow of pedestrians. People had to dodge out of our way, but this guy didn't care. He drove the bike quickly and dangerously. For a moment I flashed back to riding behind Uncle Press on his motorcycle as he took me from home to my first rendezvous with the flume. It felt like a lifetime ago. Or six.

The guy made a hard right, turning into a narrow alley between buildings. We reached the end of the building, where he skidded us into another hard right and an even smaller alley. He seemed to know exactly where he was going. I had made the right call. He wound us through a few more turns until we were in a place of twisted streets, hidden deep within the cavern of buildings, where no people were walking. I was ready for him to stop because I didn't think the dados had any chance of following that wacked route, but he kept pressing forward. I didn't say a word. This was his show.

Finally he made an abrupt turn that nearly threw me off the bike. We side-slid a few feet, then shot inside a garage door. Once in, he hit the brakes so hard I thought I was going to fly over his head. Before we came to a full stop, the garage door was already closing. The door hadn't hit the floor before the guy pulled himself off the bike and turned to me. His eyes weren't so calm anymore. I didn't blame him. That was a pretty wild ride.

"Who are you?" he demanded.

Uh-oh. He had just risked his life to save me and now he wanted answers.

"Uhhh . . ." was all I could get out. Nice answer, huh? I had been too worried about getting away from the dados to think up a plausible story.

"How did you escape?" he asked. "No challenger has ever escaped."

"I, uh, you see, funny thing." I chuckled, trying to sound casual. "I'm not a challenger. This isn't my shirt."

"And I suppose that isn't your loop?" he asked with suspicion. I glanced at the silver bracelet around my arm. It was still blinking purple. I looked to the guy, sheepish. He reminded me of my father. He was about my size, with short brown hair that was going gray. At that moment it actually *felt* like I was being scolded by a doubting parent. I tried to pull the loop off, but again, it clung to my arm.

"It's *not* my loop," I said. "I found these clothes and—"

"Who is that?" came a woman's voice. I looked deeper into the dark garage to see someone approaching. She took a few steps toward us, stepping into the light that came in through an overhead window. I immediately recognized her as the woman who skidded the motorbike into the dados, allowing the terrified guy to escape. She had short dark hair that was kind of spiked up. The collar of her dark shirt was turned up. That little bit of style made the drab outfit look suddenly . . . cool.

"An escaped challenger," the old guy answered. "He was being chased by dados and asked for my help."

"So you brought him here?" the woman said, angry, as if it were a totally stupid thing to do. When she had crashed the bike, the old guy acted all superior, like he was an angry boss. Now the roles were reversed. She seemed to be the one in charge. It confirmed my suspicion that the whole incident on the street had been staged to help that guy escape.

"He won't stay long," the older guy argued. "I knew it was safe here."

"But why here?" the woman shot back. "Of all places! What if they're looking for Mr. Pop?"

"Who's Mr. Pop?" I asked without thinking.

They both shot me a quick look. Oops. Wrong question to ask. I should have known better. The woman stared me down and took a step closer. I didn't turn away.

"He knew the gesture," the man said, as if defending himself. "I had to respond."

Right. The gesture. The hand grabbing the biceps. I had the feeling that if I knew enough to give that gesture, I should have known who Mr. Pop was.

"How did you get away?" the woman asked without taking her eyes off me.

It was time to start making things up. Why not? I had nothing to lose. I hoped.

"Okay, okay," I said. "This is what happened. I got my loop off—"

"That's impossible," the woman said.

"Can we be sure?" the man added. "Maybe he did."

"Or maybe he's a spy," the woman snarled.

Uh-oh. I had to get her off that track fast. "I'm no spy," I declared. "I got my loop off; that's how I escaped. But once I was out, I didn't want to stand out so I put it back on." I had no idea what I was talking about, but the woman nodded as if I were making some sense. I'm glad she was getting this, because I was totally winging it. I thought of trying to persuade them by using whatever Traveler abilities I had to influence people's thinking, but these two seemed too strong for that. That only worked for me when people weren't thinking clearly to begin with. These guys were very much in control, and cool. But I had to do something. I took a very big chance and added, "All I wanted was to see Mr. Pop."

The woman's eyes widened as if I had just asked to see the Wizard of Oz. She glanced at the man. He shrugged. She looked to me and said, "I'm sure you would. But do you realize how foolish it was for you to put the loop back on?"

No, actually, I didn't.

"I didn't think I had a choice," I answered. I wondered how long I could keep this double-talk up before they realized I had no idea what I was saying.

"Maybe not," the man said. "But that's exactly why you have to leave. Now."

"Why's that?" I asked.

"Are you a fool, or just ignorant?" the woman asked.

I felt like a little of both.

The man added, "Don't you realize they can track you with that loop?"

Uh-oh.

Crash! We all jumped in surprise as a vehicle smashed down the garage door. The large metal door slid to the side and slammed to the floor, revealing a dark truck that hit it like a battering ram.

"You're on your own!" the woman shouted. "Good luck!" She took off into the depths of the garage. The guy was right after her. I made the mistake of looking back at the invader truck. Jumping out of both front doors were dados with their guns already drawn. They were taking aim. I turned to run and heard the *fum* of a gun going off.

This time they didn't miss.

I was hit square in the back. The force was so hard, it snapped my head back. I had never been shot before. I didn't know what it was supposed to feel like, but I never imagined this. The wind was knocked out of me as if I had been hit with a baseball bat. There was a tingling, numb feeling that started where I was hit and instantly spread to my arms and my legs. It was like I had been stung with a massive electrical current, not that I know what that's like either. I'm just guessing. The sensation spread up my spine and wrapped around my head. I had the vague knowledge that my cheek was on the floor. A moment later everything went black and I was gone.

QUILLAN

Half-awake. Half-asleep. I hate that feeling. I didn't know if what was happening was real or a dream. I had to force myself to focus. I was lying down and vaguely aware of a rocking sensation. That meant I was moving. Was I on a boat? A train? The flume? There was absolute silence, so no clue there. I sensed light flashing across my face. That also added to my feeling of movement. Man, what a vulnerable feeling. I had to concentrate what little energy I had and get conscious. I have to admit, part of me wanted to go back to sleep. Then again, part of me also wanted to be home in bed on Second Earth watching TV. But since neither of those two options seemed practical, I had to get vertical.

As more of my brain cells started to function, I realized a very important truth. I wasn't dead. I remembered being shot from behind, and losing consciousness, but I wasn't feeling any pain like from a bullet. Of course, the idea also occurred to me that maybe I *was* dead and was actually being transported to the next life. But that thought went away when I willed my eyes to open and saw tall buildings flashing by outside. I figured that either there were tall gray buildings in the next life, or I was still on Quillan. Odds were that I was still on Quillan.

I soon discovered that I was lying down flat in the backseat of a really big car. I say it was really big because it was wide enough for me to be stretched out fully on the bench seat, with room to spare. Looking up, I realized that I was seeing the buildings through the rear window. My body felt numb. You know when your arm falls asleep and you have to rub it to get the circulation back? Well, my whole body felt like it was asleep, like I was paralyzed. There was a moment of panic when I feared I really was paralyzed. But I focused and forced my hand to move, then my other hand. Reality was flooding back. I was alive. I could move. What I needed was to jump-start my brain.

I figured that the dado must have shot me with some kind of tranquilizer. That was the good news. Bad news was that I had finally run out of luck. They got me. That fear was confirmed when I was able to sit up. In the front seat were two dados. They could have been the guys who were chasing me, or not. It didn't matter. They both kept their eyes on the street, looking dead ahead. I wondered if these guys really could be robots. If that wasn't strange enough, if it was true, then it meant a machine was driving another machine . . . and I was along for the ride. I hoped they didn't have a short circuit or anything. I didn't want their electrodes to fart and end up driving us all into a wall.

"Hey," I said dreamily.

They didn't turn around. That was okay. I was still trying to get my brain to work. And my mouth, too, for that matter.

"You two guys robots, or what?" I asked. What the heck? Why not cut to the chase? They didn't respond. We were driving quickly along city streets. Traffic was lighter, and the driver weaved us in and out kind of dangerously. I guess he wasn't afraid of being pulled over by a cop, seeing as he probably *was* a cop. "Where are we going?" Still no answer, big surprise. "How about a tour of the city?" No response. "Anyone ever tell you how truly ugly you guys are?" They never took their eyes off the street.

I decided to stop asking questions that weren't going to be answered and concentrate on getting my act together. Wherever they were taking me, and whatever we would find, I needed to be ready for it. So I sat back in the seat and watched out the window. The city here didn't look much different from the area near the arcade. Though as I said, it wasn't as busy. I had a quick moment of panic wondering how long I had been out and how far we had driven. At some point I was going to have to find my way back to the flume. As of this second I had no idea where I was, or how to begin finding my way back through this endless, boring city. I felt a slight tug of panic, but fought it off. I learned a long time ago that I should only worry about things I had control over. I had to trust that someway, somehow, I'd find the flume.

We traveled for a few more minutes, turning onto streets that didn't look any different from the ones we had come off of. I tried to keep track of where we were going, but it was impossible. Everything looked the same. That is, until we made the final turn. What I saw in front of us was so out of character with the rest of the city, I think I actually gasped. The two dados turned around to look at me. Swell. They wouldn't answer any direct questions, but a little thing like a gasp got their attention.

"Are you all right?" the driver asked, as if concerned that my gasp meant I was having a heart attack or something.

"Yeah," I said, and pointed ahead of us. "What is that?"

The two dados turned forward, ignoring me again. I guess if there was any communicating going on, it had to be on their terms. I didn't care anymore. I was way more interested in what was in front of the car.

Looming before us was a huge golden gate. It was awesome, with elaborate carvings and detailed sculptures. The design wasn't anything specific. If anything, it reminded me of the 3-D graphics that scrolled across the giant overhead screens throughout the city. Very modern, but still elegant. It was in the center of a tall white stone wall that had to be thirty feet high. It was definitely too high to climb over, but not so high that I couldn't see what was beyond it.

Trees.

Yup. Over the wall and through the detail of the gate, I saw green parkland. I instantly thought of the Tato match where Challenger Yellow was killed. The Traveler from Quillan. There were tall trees all around the platform. What did that guy call the place? The garden. Right. The garden. My hope rose that I was being taken to the spot where the Traveler was killed. The car slowed as we approached, and the gates slowly opened. We were going inside! It was like moving into an entirely new world. We were leaving a gray, soulless city and entering a thick forest. The only sign inside that things might not be as different as all that was the two dados who stood inside the gate. Guards.

"Is this the garden?" I asked the dado driver, forgetting for a second that he wouldn't be answering. He didn't. I shut up. We followed a winding road through dense forest. It was paved, and wide enough for two cars to pass. The forest itself reminded me of the woods back home. It must have been summer on Quillan, because the leaves were big and green. In places the trees were so close together it looked as dark as night. Every so often the forest opened up onto large rolling meadows with multicolored wildflowers dotting the green grass. I saw a few birds, but none that looked any different from those on Second Earth.

What was most amazing about this forest was that it was here at all. We drove along for about fifteen minutes, which meant it was huge. I didn't know if this was a forest surrounded by city, or a city surrounded by forest. Or maybe city ended and forest began. Or forest ended and . . . never mind. You get the idea. No matter the case, it was odd to go from a gray concrete-covered city to forested wilderness. Of course, this wasn't truly wilderness. There was a paved road, with a destination. I saw it over the treetops in the distance. At first I thought it was another huge tree that loomed above the others. Then I thought it might be some kind of radio tower. The thought hit me that we had reached the far side of this forest and were about to come out to the city again. We rounded a bend, the trees opened up, and the mystery was solved.

It was a castle.

I did a double take, that's how stunned I was by seeing something so whimsical on a territory that was pretty much devoid of character. The structure was huge. There were several soaring towers with pointed spires and circular battlements. There were so many levels and balconies that I imagined the inhabitants needed a map to get around the place. Though I had no idea who the inhabitants were. Bright yellow flags with purple stripes flew from every spire, snapping in the breeze. The color of the castle itself was a pale pink. In a word, it was dazzling.

We had to drive another few minutes to actually get to the castle, that's how massive it was. As we approached, I saw that a wide water-filled moat ringed the giant structure. The waterway looked more like decoration than protection. The whole place was immaculate, as if they had a thousand gardeners working night and day. (Again, whoever "they" were.) But I didn't see anyone working. I didn't see anyone at all. That felt odd, but who was I to say what was odd and what wasn't on Quillan? As we drew closer, I saw that the front entrance was a giant wooden door. You guessed it, it lowered and became a bridge that spanned the moat. We didn't even have to slow down. It was as if they knew we were coming. They. I really wanted to know who "they" were. The car drove onto the wooden drawbridge and rattled across the boards, and we rolled into a vast, open courtyard around which the castle was built. There were fountains everywhere and hedges that were carved to look like animals. I didn't recognize any of the sculptures, though. Either they were abstract designs, or there were some pretty odd-looking animals on Quillan. My vote went for the abstract designs. I didn't want to run across any twisted-looking animals.

The car rolled to a stop at the bottom of marble stairs that led up to wooden doors ornately trimmed with gold. The car had barely come to a stop when these doors opened. Somebody was coming out to greet us. I hoped I was about to find out who "they" were. Whoever "they" were, "they" had gone through a lot of trouble to get me here. I felt pretty sure that once I found out who "they" were, "they" would tell me why these goons had chased me down like a criminal and shot me. The doors opened wide, and "they" stepped out onto the top of the stairs.

"Welcome, my friend, welcome!" shouted a jovial man wearing what looked like a long red and black bathrobe. I recognized him instantly. "LaBerge is my name, though I'm sure you already know that. Everyone does, of course. Please, let me shake your hand."

Yeah, it was LaBerge. The guy from the video screen who

ran the Tato contest. The guy who sent me the invitation. He looked even nuttier in person. His blond hair was a mass of long, tight curls that bounced when he walked. His eyes were alive with excitement, or insanity. I wasn't sure which. He opened the car door and I tentatively got out.

"I trust your trip was a pleasant one," he said sincerely, holding out his hand to shake mine.

I didn't shake his hand. I didn't know this guy, but I didn't like him. Not only was he making my life miserable, he had something to do with the death of a Traveler. What was to like?

"They shot me" was all I said.

LaBerge frowned, leaned into the rear door, and barked angrily at the dados, "Cretins! Go away!"

The dado hit the gas, or whatever it was that made those cars go. The car shot forward so fast that LaBerge had to pull himself out quickly or he would have been dragged along. I wouldn't have minded seeing that. LaBerge glared at the departing car as it sped out of the gateway, then collected himself and turned to me with a smile.

"I don't like having those vulgarians anywhere near me, but they are useful. Now," he said brightly. "Let's get you settled."

The guy was playing the part of a flamboyant, charming host. I wasn't having any part of it. He turned to scurry back up the stairs. I didn't move.

He said, "I'm sure you will be comfortable in the—" He saw that I wasn't following him, and turned back to me. "Is there something wrong, my friend?"

"I'm not your friend," I said flatly. "I don't know who you are, and I definitely don't know why you had those thugs hunt me down to bring me here."

LaBerge looked confused. He walked back down the steps

toward me, saying, "Didn't you get our invitation?"

I reached into my back pocket and pulled out the paper that had come in the gift box that Saint Dane sent through the flume to Zadaa.

"Yeah, I got it," I said.

"Then why did you run from the dados?" he asked.

"Because I don't jump when Saint Dane snaps his fingers."

LaBerge looked at me quizzically. "Who?" he asked.

I realized that Saint Dane probably didn't call himself that here. He must have taken on some other identity that fit into this territory. Finding out what that identity was and what his plans were for Quillan were the real reasons I was there.

I said, "Who told you to send me this invitation?"

LaBerge took the invitation from me and looked at it. "'Riggedy, riggedy white,'" he said, reading. He chuckled and added, "Has quite a ring to it, no?"

"No," I said.

The smile fell from LaBerge's face.

"Oh," he said, sounding hurt. "I think it's quite melodic."

"Who told you to send me that?" I asked again, more emphatically. I took a step toward him to emphasize the point. LaBerge took a step back. I intimidated him. Good.

"I never divulge my sources, young man," he said. "That would be bad for business."

"Business?" I said, backing the guy off. "I don't care about your business; I don't care about you. I want to know what I'm doing here!"

"I thought that would be obvious," LaBerge said nervously. "You're about to be treated like royalty!"

Huh? Royalty. I didn't know what I expected the guy to say, but it wasn't that.

"LaBerge! Why haven't you brought our guest inside?" came a stern voice from above.

I shot a look up the stairs to the doorway into the castle and saw a tall thin woman wearing a purple jumpsuit that was so dark it looked almost black. She stood flagpole straight with her arms at her sides, staring at me. Unblinking. It was Veego, the woman from the video screen.

LaBerge said, "Challenger Red is concerned as to why we asked him here. I'm trying to explain how—"

"I'm not a challenger," I said to the woman.

"No," she said. "You are not."

Good, at least somebody was listening to me.

She added, "But you will be."

Oh. Swell. I took a step up toward the woman, looking her right in the eye. I wanted her to know I was as serious as she was. I have to admit, she gave me the creeps. We stared each other down for a moment, then she twisted her lips into a crooked smile.

"Yes?" she asked.

I took a shot and said, "Saint Dane?"

She gave me a strange look and said, "I beg your pardon?"

Either she wasn't Saint Dane in disguise, or the demon was playing it very cool. My guess was that it wasn't Saint Dane.

"You should be honored," she continued. "Your life is about to change in ways you could never imagine."

Hah! Obviously she had no idea who I really was. I had to make a decision. I was there to find out how Saint Dane was trying to destroy the territory. He definitely sent me that invitation through the flume, which meant he wanted me at that castle with those two oddballs. Was it a trap? Probably. The question was, should I play along and learn what I could, or take off and start from scratch? As scary as it was to go along with what Saint Dane wanted, I didn't know what else to do. I didn't know anybody here, the Traveler from Quillan was dead, and I had a freakin' loop stuck on my arm that would lead those dado dummies to me again anyway.

"All right," I said. "What do you want me to do?"

The woman smiled. But it wasn't a happy smile. It was a smile of smug victory. I hated that.

"Wonderful!" exclaimed LaBerge as he bounded up the stairs next to me. "Let's get you settled first. You are going to love this!"

Somehow I doubted that.

Veego entered the door first. I followed her, and LaBerge followed me. I felt as if I were about to enter the lion's den. With a quick breath and a shrug that was totally for my own benefit, I stepped through the doorway . . .

Into a spectacular entrance hall. The ceiling soared up several stories. Light came in through massive stained-glass windows near the arched ceiling. The scenes in these windows reminded me of a church, but I didn't think they depicted anything religious. Instead they showed scenes of people playing games. There were elaborate images of people running, or throwing balls, or wrestling. I happened to notice that all the competitors wore brightly colored long-sleeved shirts with diagonal stripes across the front. This entryway was like a cathedral dedicated to the "challengers," as they called them. Believe me, it didn't make me feel special. It made me a little nauseous.

The place wasn't some old, musty castle from the Dark Ages. (Assuming Quillan had Dark Ages, that is.) Just the opposite. This place looked as if it had just been built. The floor was marble, with elaborate mosaic patterns. It was so clean, it looked like I could eat off it. (I hate that saying. Why would anyone even consider eating off a floor? No matter how clean it was.) There was a wide, curved staircase of stone that led up to a balcony high overhead. Colorful flags hung down from every level, making the place feel like it was decked out for a festival. Several hallways on the ground floor led off to other parts of the castle. I tried to memorize the layout. I feared it would be easy to get turned around and lost in this mammoth palace.

"Nice place you have here," I said casually. Big understatement. "Who does it belong to?"

"Why, it belongs to us of course!" LaBerge said quickly, as if insulted. "Who else would it—"

"LaBerge!" Veego chastised. She was treating him like an annoying kid. He *was* annoying. But she was scary. I wasn't sure which was worse. "Challenger Red has never been here," she said slowly, as if he were too stupid to understand. "He is our guest and must be treated with respect."

"I wasn't being disrespectful!" LaBerge argued. "I simply thought that since we are who we are, it would follow that our living arrangement was suitable to our position and—"

"But I don't know who you are," I interrupted.

LaBerge looked stunned. He grabbed his chest like he was having a surprise heart attack. "Don't you watch the games?" he asked.

"No," I said. "I'm not from around here."

"What difference does that make?" LaBerge shot back. "Everyone knows who we are and—"

"LaBerge!" Veego snapped again. "Didn't you hear what I said?"

LaBerge didn't argue this time. He looked down like a pouting scolded child.

I said, "You two married or what?"

Both LaBerge and Veego burst out laughing.

"Married?" LaBerge chuckled. "No, we're business partners, and very successful I might add, as anyone can tell simply by looking around."

I had to give him that. If these two lived in this incredible castle in the forest, they had to be doing really well at whatever it was they did.

"What is it exactly that you do?" I asked.

"What?" LaBerge blurted out, more shocked than before. "We're famous! How could you not know—"

"Enough questions," Veego said, cutting him off again. "There will be time for that at the evening meal." She turned to me and said, "You will be our guest, won't you?"

"This is your show," I said. "You tell me."

She gave me that smile again that said, "Yes, I will tell you . . . and you'll do exactly as I say." Or maybe I was reading too much into it. But I knew I was going to have to be very careful with Veego. I didn't know what to think of LaBerge. He was kind of a goof. But Veego—she could be trouble.

"Fourteen!" Veego called out.

I had no idea what that meant, so I stood there looking stupid. A moment later a guy appeared on the curved staircase.

"Yes?" he said formally. Fourteen wasn't a number, it was the name of a guy. Or the name of this guy was a number. Or . . . something. He couldn't have been more than five feet tall. He was dressed totally in white, with a long-sleeved shirt, white pants, white gloves, and white shoes. Hanging around his neck was a wide two-colored necktie. One side was bright purple, the other bright yellow. Those two colors were everywhere. They must have been the signature colors of Veego and LaBerge. The other thing about this little guy that stood out was that he was totally bald. We're talking cueball shiny. It made it hard to figure out how old he was. I couldn't tell from his voice, either. He could have been anywhere from twenty to forty years old. He walked up to us, stopped, and bowed.

"At your command," he said formally.

"Please bring Challenger Red to his room," Veego said. "He'll be joining us for the evening meal."

"Very good," Fourteen said, and motioned for me to walk to the stairs.

I looked at Veego, who said, "You've had a busy day. Take some time to rest. Fourteen will come get you before the meal."

I didn't know what to do. I had been kidnapped. There's no other way to put it. They were being nice to me, but so what? I was kidnapped! They kept calling me Challenger Red, like one of those guys who battled to the death in that Tato match. And just to confuse things further, LaBerge said I was there to be treated like royalty. None of this added up. The only thing I had to keep in mind was that the real reason I was there, the only reason that mattered, was because Saint Dane sent me an invitation. There was no mistaking that. I was there to stop Saint Dane. If I was going to find him, I had to play along. At least for a little while.

"You're going to love the meal this evening!" LaBerge said giddily.

I looked to him and said, "Just as long as there's no tribbun." I had no idea what tribbun was, other than a label on some food at the food store. I just wanted to mess with the guy. LaBerge's eyes went wide.

"Tribbun!" he exclaimed. "Tribbun is delicious!"

"Yeah, well, I hate it," I said.

"Well," he said in a huff. "We'll have to take it off the menu." He turned and stormed off. I know, it was a dumb thing to do, but it made me feel as if I had a tiny bit of control.

"This way, please," Fourteen said.

"Enjoy your rest," said Veego.

"I will, " I replied, and went for the stairs. Before climbing, I glanced back to see that Veego hadn't moved. She was watching me. It was a creepy feeling, like she was sizing me up.

"Take a right at the top of the stairs," Fourteen said. He was following me closely.

"What's your real name?" I asked. "Mine's Bobby."

"My name is Fourteen," he replied.

"No, it's not, " I shot back. "And my name isn't Red. You don't name people numbers or colors."

"Whatever you say, sir," Fourteen said.

"Who do you hang out with?" I asked jokingly. "Thirteen and Fifteen?"

I chuckled. He didn't.

"Yes, I do" was his answer.

Oh.

The guy wasn't about to joke with me. I'll bet he was afraid of what Veego might do to him. I decided not to give him a hard time. Reaching the top of the stairs, he directed me down a long, wide corridor that had closed wooden doors every few feet.

"What's behind those doors?" I asked.

"This is where some of the challengers live," he replied.

I noticed that each door had a different colored rectangular plate on it. White, black, orange, blue. It was like the challenger dorm. We must have walked fifty yards down the long hallway before stopping at a door with a red rectangle. Fourteen opened the door and said, "This is where you will be staying."

I stepped past him into the room that I described to you in my last journal. It was like something out of a little kid's imagination. A *twisted* little kid. It was a big room, with plenty of area to walk around. The walls were purple and yellow striped, no big surprise. The ceiling was covered with balloons of all colors. The bed was in the very middle. It seemed to be floating in space. The blanket on it was yellow, the pillows purple. There was a desk that looked like a giant hand, palm up. As ridiculous as all that sounds, the worst part was the extra decorations. There were shelves everywhere that were loaded with dolls. Clown dolls. I hate clowns. Have I mentioned that? In my opinion there are two kinds of people: those who fear and hate clowns . . . and clowns.

"I'm not staying here," I said to Fourteen.

"Is this room not to your liking?" he asked.

"Are you kidding?" I shot back. "It's full of clowns! Who decorates a room with clowns?"

"That would be LaBerge," he answered.

Figured.

"Well, I'm not staying here," I said.

"I am sorry, sir," he replied calmly. "There are no other rooms."

I was going to argue, but decided that I wasn't going to be staying very long anyway, so I'd deal with the clowns. At least I'd *try* to deal with the clowns. I hate clowns. I wasn't so fond of Quillan, either.

This is where I'm going to end this journal and send it off. I'm lucky they left me alone long enough to write two whole journals and get you guys up to speed. Of course, now my hand is cramped from having written so much, but I'll live.

I feel as if I'm getting close to Saint Dane, if only because I've met Veego and LaBerge. The invitation may have come from them, but it was delivered by Saint Dane. There's a connection between them. It's my job to find it. The first step is to figure out why Veego and LaBerge want me here. If they plan on treating me like royalty, well, that would be cool. But I'm no idiot. I'm afraid they're going to want something from me and I've got a pretty good idea what it is. They think I'm a challenger, which has to mean they want me to compete. I can't help but think Saint Dane has set this whole thing up, which means *he* wants me to compete. I can only hope that I'll be able to duck that long enough to figure out what the demon has planned for Quillan. It's going to be a dangerous tightrope. I need to be here to learn more, but if I stay, I may have to compete.

I wonder if the Traveler from Quillan followed the same steps I did. Did he get an invitation too? Did Saint Dane send an invitation to *all* the Travelers? Is this how it's going to end? Will our battle with Saint Dane come down to a series of deadly games on this twisted territory? If Saint Dane summoned the Travelers here, I have no doubt that each and every one of us would come. For the first time I'm actually happy that Gunny and Spader are trapped on Eelong.

As I sit here in this creepy room, I'm feeling very alone. There's no one to bounce ideas off and challenge my thinking. Nobody I can trust. For whatever reason, I was made the lead Traveler, but that doesn't mean I don't need help. Or friendship. It doesn't bother me when I'm running around, but when I'm alone like this, my mind wanders. It isn't fun. At times like this the fight against Saint Dane seems so overwhelming, all I want to do is chuck it all and go home. But that makes me remember that I don't have a home anymore. My past has been erased. I don't belong on Second Earth. I'm not sure I ever did. So where *do* I belong?

Yikes, I've got to get a grip. Feeling sorry for myself doesn't help anything. I want to get some sleep so I can stop worrying, but I'm worrying so much I can't get to sleep. Don't worry, I don't feel this way all the time, only when things slow down. I need these breaks to recharge my batteries and write journals. But to be honest, I dread the downtime, because that's when I realize how truly alone I am.

It's okay. I'm fine. I just needed to get that off my chest.

I'll add one more thing before I sign off. Before leaving my room, Fourteen said, "I'll come for you when the meal is ready."

"Whatever," I said. He backed out as I took another look around the room, and saw all those creepy clown eyes staring back at me. "Hey," I said, stopping him.

"Yes?"

"Are you sure there aren't any other rooms?"

"Very sure," he said. "But there will probably be another opening after the next tournament."

At first I was encouraged. I wanted to be away from the clowns in the worst way. But then the weight of his words sank in.

"Who had this room before me?" I asked.

"That was Challenger Yellow," he answered. "He won't be returning. Enjoy your rest."

He closed the door, leaving me feeling more alone than ever. Challenger Yellow was the Traveler from Quillan. He didn't survive the fall. Challengers died.

I was a challenger.

I hadn't even found Saint Dane yet.

And so we go.

I miss you guys.

END JOURNAL #24

❂ SECOND EARTH ❂

Courtney Chetwynde was coming home.

Spending nearly two months in a hospital had been torture for her. In more ways than one. But she knew she couldn't rush things. Broken bones took time to heal. So did a broken spirit. She would never be able to shake the memories of what happened to her the night of the accident. That was good. She didn't want to shake them. She wanted to remember every last detail. She had been riding her bike on a lonely country road when a car ran her off the side of a steep embankment. The fall was brutal. It broke four ribs, and her left arm in two places. Her left leg was broken so badly that they had to put four pins in to help it set properly. She even got a concussion. But as horrible as those injuries were, they weren't life threatening. The real problem came with the internal injuries. She needed surgery to repair tears in so many places that Courtney would stop listening whenever a doctor discussed how bad off she was. She didn't want to hear it. In the two months since the accident, not a day went by without some doctor saying, "You're lucky to be alive."

Courtney didn't feel very lucky. If she were lucky, she wouldn't have been nearly killed. If she were lucky, she never would have gone to summer school and met a guy named Whitney Wilcox. If she were lucky, she wouldn't have thought he was cute and developed a major crush on him. If she were lucky, she wouldn't have been riding her bike to meet him when she got run off the road. If she were lucky, she would have realized there really was no such person as Whitney Wilcox. He was an illusion. A lie. As she lay crumbled in the woods on the side of the road that horrible night, just before she lost consciousness, she saw that the person driving the car that hit her was none other than Whitney Wilcox. The guy she was growing to like. The guy she thought might become the boyfriend that Bobby Pendragon wasn't able to be.

The guy who turned out to be Saint Dane.

The demon had tried to kill her. He had looked down on her broken body from the road above and said, "I give, and I take away. You people of Second Earth are so easily controlled. I was hoping this would be more of a challenge, but alas. It was not meant to be." The demon had then transformed himself from the image of Whitney Wilcox into a huge black bird that flew away into the night, leaving her to die.

But Courtney didn't cooperate. Thanks to Mark Dimond. Good old Mark. She managed to get a call out to him on her cell phone. All she was able to say before passing out was, "He's here." It was all she needed to say. Mark knew what she meant. He knew she was in trouble. Mark came screaming up to Massachusetts, where Courtney was going to summer school, and found her near death on the side of the road. Mark saved her life. It was the one thing that didn't surprise Courtney about the whole nasty experience. She knew that if there was anyone she could always count on, it was Mark.

What *did* surprise her was that Mark was helped by a guy who had been his archenemy since they were little kids. Andy Mitchell. Mitchell gave Mark a ride from their home in

Connecticut up to the Berkshires on a moment's notice. (Mark didn't have his driver's license.) If not for Andy, Mark wouldn't have made it in time. That was a strange and somewhat unsettling thought. Courtney knew that if not for Andy Mitchell's help, she'd be dead.

As grateful as she was, it was an odd feeling, because Andy Mitchell had been nothing more than an obnoxious bully for as long as she could remember. He took particular pains to harass Mark. Poor nerdy Mark. Bully bait. But it had recently come out that as idiotic as Andy Mitchell was, he was very gifted at math. So gifted that he was asked to join Mark's elite science club at school. Sci-Clops. Courtney knew that Mark hated the idea of his beloved club being invaded by the un-beloved Andy Mitchell. But even Mark had to admit that Mitchell was special. Better still, after he joined Sci-Clops, Mitchell stopped harassing Mark. The two seemed to have found common ground and made peace.

But that didn't make it any less strange for Courtney to see the two of them standing, together, at the foot of her bed in the intensive care unit after she came out of surgery. After that horrible day, Courtney often asked Mark how they could suddenly be so tight.

"You know he's a turd," Courtney would say.

Mark would always laugh and say something like, "He used to be, but I'm really getting to know the guy and he's okay. And he's, like, a genius, too!"

"Andy Mitchell? Genius?" Courtney would reply. "That's like saying you found a cockroach that can do algebra."

But Mark didn't back down. If there was anyone who deserved to hate Andy Mitchell, it was Mark. Bullies always went after the insecure, brainy types. Mark was the perfect target. Andy had harassed him for years. So Courtney figured that if Mark could forgive him, who was she to hold a grudge?

Especially since he helped save her life. Courtney decided to be less judgmental, no matter how big a slug Mitchell was. Or used to be.

After the accident Mark would often take the train from their home in Connecticut up to Massachusetts to visit Courtney in the hospital and keep her company while she went through therapy. Courtney looked forward to those visits. Being stuck in a hospital three hours from home was not a fun way to pass the time. The doctors didn't want her to travel until she had completely healed, so she spent week after boring week sitting in her room watching daytime TV. She started getting hooked on soap operas, which embarrassed her. Courtney didn't think of herself as someone who would be interested in such goofy TV. But it wasn't like she had a whole lot of choices. Talk shows were boring and she was too old for cartoons. So she got wrapped up in the make-believe lives of some fakey TV characters. When it got to the point where the nurses would come in and ask her, "What happened to so and so?" or "Who's cheating on who?" and Courtney actually knew the answers, she decided it was time to stop watching. She didn't want to be working so hard to heal her body, while letting her brain turn to pudding.

Eventually they moved her out of the regular hospital and into a wing that was all about rehabilitation. It was a welcome relief, but a grueling experience. When the cast came off her leg, Courtney had to learn how to walk again. The pain was incredible, but the physical therapists didn't cut her any slack. She didn't want them to either. She told them to push her. She'd remind them, "If I complain, push harder."

That was Courtney. She had always been driven, but the recent turn of events in her life had given her new purpose. It was hard for her to think back on the chain of circumstances that led to her being in the hospital, but she forced herself to. She wanted to remember it all, if only to learn from the ordeal. It was a difficult journey that had begun long before the accident.

Months before, she discovered that she and Mark had made the ultimate mistake by traveling through the flume to Eelong. As much as they had done an amazing job and helped Bobby save a territory, she later learned that by using the flumes, she and Mark had caused the death of a Traveler. Only Travelers were supposed to use the flumes, and by using it themselves they had weakened the tunnels through time and space so badly that the flume on Eelong had collapsed. When it crumbled, it trapped Spader and Gunny, and killed Kasha. The horrible truth was that by trying to help Bobby, they actually had helped Saint Dane in his quest to control Halla. What she thought was her greatest victory turned out to be a tragic failure.

The realization crushed Courtney, who was already going through a tough time at home and at school. Growing up, Courtney had always been the best at everything. Especially at sports. But when she hit high school, she found that others were as good as she was. Some better. Courtney was *not* used to losing. She wasn't even used to trying that hard. She didn't handle the pressure well, which felt like yet another failure. She always defined herself by her abilities on the field. Losing that made her feel worthless and depressed. She barely spoke with her parents. It was becoming unbearable to be Courtney, or to be around her. The many weeks lying in a hospital bed gave her time to think back on that difficult period and try to figure out why things had gone so wrong. She was disappointed in her inability to compete, of course, but she realized that what bothered her even more was the fact that she handled it so badly. Being good at sports was one thing. Having the strength to deal with life challenges was a whole nother ballgame, so to speak. A more important one. Courtney realized she didn't have the strength to deal with either, and it depressed her.

The months of healing and introspection finally allowed her to admit that the reason she was so quick to jump to Eelong was because she wanted to prove something to herself. Of course she wanted to help Bobby, but she also desperately needed to restore her self-confidence. She wanted to win at something in the worst way. It almost worked, too. That is, until she realized how much damage she and Mark had done by traveling. When the truth came out, she fell into a total depression. It was so bad she couldn't get out of bed. Her schoolwork was sent home or she would have flunked tenth grade. As it was, she was barely able to concentrate long enough to do the absolute minimum, and she barely squeaked into the eleventh grade.

It was a difficult time, but beneath it all Courtney was still a fighter, and committed herself to a new challenge. She wanted to put her life back together. She knew that to face the world again, she was first going to have to face herself. To that end she convinced her parents to send her away to summer school. She figured that six weeks on her own, with people who didn't know her and who had no expectations, would be the perfect way to get back on her feet. She was right. Courtney slowly began to feel like herself again.

It bothered her that she left Mark alone to deal with Bobby's journals, but she wisely realized that if she was going to have any hope of being useful to Bobby as an acolyte, she was going to have to get her life back together. Mark understood and supported her decision. It was all working out beautifully.

Until she met Whitney Wilcox.

Saint Dane had come to Second Earth and set her up for a fall. Literally. He took great trouble in getting her to trust him, and to like him, only to pull the rug out and try to kill her. Courtney spent hours trying to figure out why he'd done this. Was he just being evil for evil's sake? Was he trying to prove something to Bobby? Worst of all, was this somehow part of his overall plan to target Second Earth in his quest to control Halla?

Courtney and Mark began discussing these questions on his very first visit to the hospital after the accident. Courtney's parents would pay for Mark to take the train, and stay in a motel so he wouldn't have to make the trip up and back in one day. They couldn't be there all the time because of their jobs and knew that having visitors helped Courtney. They had no idea that Mark was there not only to be a supportive friend, but to discuss the future of all existence.

On one visit in early autumn, Mark brought all of Bobby's journals that detailed his adventure on Zadaa. Courtney read them in one straight shot. Mark wanted Courtney to know all that was happening with Bobby, but he dreaded her finding out that Bobby had fallen in love with Loor. It was Bobby and Courtney who were supposed to be together. That was the way it was meant to be. They had kissed, and not just a dumb make-out kind of kiss. It was real. They truly loved each other. Mark could barely breathe as he waited for Courtney to read the part where Bobby admitted he had such strong feelings for Loor.

But when Courtney reached that section in the journal, she looked to Mark calmly and said, "I saw that coming."

"You did?" Mark said, surprised.

"You didn't?" was Courtney's response. "C'mon, Mark. Things have changed a little, don't you think? I mean, we aren't the same people we were in junior high."

"Well, I suppose," Mark said sadly. "We're getting older."

"Yeah," Courtney said quickly. "And we're dealing with a powerful demon who's trying to throw all time and space into chaos. Let's not forget that little detail."

"Right," Mark said. "That too."

"I love Bobby," Courtney said. "And I know he loves me, too. But it's not right for us now. Who knows? Maybe someday . . ."

Courtney's voice trailed off. She didn't want to speculate on anything. There was too much to deal with in the present. "I'm okay with it, Mark," she said sincerely. "Really."

Mark nodded.

"Besides," she added. "Loor doesn't want to be with him for the same reason. Things are too weird right now. But they won't be forever." She gave Mark a sly smile and said, "This isn't over."

Mark smiled too. Courtney was starting to sound more like Courtney every day. After reading the journals the two of them walked slowly around the grounds of the hospital. The leaves were starting to turn and the sky was the kind of deep blue that only comes with autumn. Courtney used a walker to keep weight off her leg. It was difficult for her to move. Her left arm was still mending, and she was incredibly stiff. Mark let her set the pace, which was odd for him, because usually he was the one who had to work to keep up with Courtney. Courtney was strong. She had the body of an athlete. The doctors told her she would heal and be back to her old self before she knew it. Her goal was to dump the walker before she got back to school, and be ready for spring soccer. She was right on schedule, though she was going to miss the beginning of their junior year at Davis Gregory High. The plan was for her to get assignments sent to her so she could keep up, then if all went well, she would be back in regular classes by Thanksgiving. Everyone felt confident that she could meet that timetable. Courtney wasn't just confident. To her, it was a lock.

Both Courtney and Mark knew that as bad a time as Courtney was having on Second Earth, Bobby was still out there chasing Saint Dane and they were still acolytes. They had to get back with the program. Bobby had written some disturbing things in his last journals that had to be faced.

"I'll just say it," Mark announced boldly. "Are you as freaked as I am that Bobby brought Loor back from the dead?"

"I don't know," Courtney said with a smile. "How freaked are you?"

Mark didn't laugh.

Courtney said, "I don't think Bobby brought her back from the dead."

"But—"

"Let me finish," Courtney said quickly. "Yeah, maybe he had something to do with it, but I don't think it was all about him. I think it has to do with the Travelers in general."

"What do you mean?"

"Let's stop kidding ourselves, Mark," Courtney continued. "I know we grew up with Bobby and played with him when we were kids and pretty much had the same life he did until he took off with his uncle Press, but after all that's happened, I think it's pretty obvious that the Travelers aren't normal. This fast-healing thing is only part of it. Why is it that they're able to go through the flumes and everything is fine, but when we go through, they tear apart?"

Mark didn't answer. He kept looking at the ground, weighing Courtney's words.

She continued, "And how is it that when Bobby left home, every trace that he ever existed disappeared right along with him, including his family? And the house he grew up in? And every record, document, and photograph? Even his dog disappeared! I know we've been living with that for a couple of years now, but we've got to face it, there's some force at work here that we know nothing about. Things don't just disappear. At least not if you go by the rules of how things work here on good old Second Earth. You know that better than anybody. You're the scientist. Whatever Bobby Pendragon is all about, I don't think it has anything to do with the reality we know. He said it himself in his journal, he's not so sure he even *belongs* on Second Earth." Courtney took a breath and then said, "I'm not so sure he belongs here either."

Mark shot Courtney a look. "You really *have* been thinking."

"Yeah, well, it's not like I have a whole lot to do," she fired back. "I'm not really sure how to say this, but I don't think the Travelers are human."

"Are you serious?" Mark asked.

"What other explanation is there?" Courtney said. "None of them know who their real parents are. Sure, they were raised by people from their home territories, but then they were all told that their parents weren't their biological parents. So who *were* their biological parents? I think if we ever find that out, we'll know why they're able to heal like they do."

"And come back from the dead," Mark said.

"Exactly. That's not something humans can do, last time I checked."

"What about Press and Osa and the others who died?"

"I don't know," Courtney said. "But Press said Bobby and the others were the last generation of Travelers. Maybe they had to die to give way to Bobby's generation."

"Okay," Mark said. "So Bobby and the Travelers are operating under a different set of rules than the rest of us. Any idea who made up those rules?"

"That's the big question," Courtney said firmly. "When we find that out, we'll unravel this whole thing."

Mark let that sink in, then said softly, "Do you really think Bobby isn't human?"

"C'mon!" Courtney snapped. "Tell me you haven't been thinking the same thing!"

Mark nodded reluctantly.

"Of course you have," she said. "I didn't say I'm not weirded out by the idea, but what else can we think?"

Mark said, "So how does Saint Dane fit in?"

Courtney frowned and said softly, "I don't know. But his powers are greater than all of them. He's definitely part of the equation, but I can't figure out how. All I've got are a bunch of theories. I'm short on real answers."

They walked a bit more in silence, then Courtney said, "Do you remember what I said to you at the hospital right after the accident?"

"Every word," Mark answered. "You said you were done hiding and feeling sorry for yourself. The exact thing you said was: Mark, I want that bastard."

"He's here, Mark," Courtney said. "Saint Dane is on Second Earth. I don't know why he came after me, but I think he's starting to work whatever evil he's got planned for our home. We've been worried about this from the beginning, and now it's happening."

"I was kind of hoping that by saving First Earth, the Travelers had saved Second and Third Earths, too," Mark said.

"You're dreaming," Courtney said, scoffing. "We always knew the battle would come here. There are only ten territories. The turning point for six of them has already passed. Saint Dane is running out of options."

Courtney saw that Mark was rubbing his palms on the legs of his pants. She knew why. Her palms were sweating too.

"So what do we do?" Mark asked. "Tell Bobby?"

"Yeah, I think so," Courtney said. "And I want you to know something. What I said before, I meant. I don't know how, I don't know when, but I want to hurt Saint Dane the way he hurt me."

"Be careful," Mark said. "Don't let your emotions get you. Look what it did to Spader."

"Don't worry about me," Courtney said. "I'm mad, but I'm using it. With every exercise I do, every time I feel the burn, I focus on him. He doesn't know it, but he's helping me get better. Mentally and physically. He may have wanted to kill me to get me out of the way, but he only made me more focused. I'm coming back, Mark. And when Bobby comes home, we're going to beat him . . . together."

Mark nodded, though Courtney thought he looked a little green.

Seven weeks to the day after the accident, Courtney was released from the hospital. Mr. and Mrs. Chetwynde were there for the occasion, of course. Mark drove up with them. He told Courtney he wanted to see her leave the hospital in person. He said he hoped that Saint Dane would be there too, somewhere, just so he could see how badly he had failed and how strong they were. There was a little party thrown by the nurses. They brought in a cake, and they all kidded Courtney by saying how they were going to lose touch with their favorite soap operas because they wouldn't have Courtney to fill them in anymore. Courtney laughed. She didn't think it was funny, but she laughed to be polite.

Many of the doctors who treated her were there too. They all told Courtney how proud they were of her, and how she deserved all the credit for her recovery. Courtney appreciated their kind words. She was going to miss the doctors. They had saved her life. But as tearful as the occasion was, she wanted out of there. She wanted to go home.

When the party was over, everyone stood outside the front entrance of the small hospital. A long walkway led from the door to the street. Mr. Chetwynde pulled their Volvo station wagon to the bottom of the walkway, ready to bring his daughter home. He and Mrs. Chetwynde stood by the car and looked up at the two rows of nurses, doctors, and hospital staff that lined either side of the walk, waiting for her. The glass doors opened. Mark pushed Courtney outside in a wheelchair. Immediately the two rows of people applauded and cheered. But they hadn't seen anything yet.

Courtney smiled and stood up. Mark handed her the metal walker that she had relied on for the past few weeks of therapy. He had attached a small horn with a black bulb on the end that blared out "Aooooga!" when Courtney squeezed it. He told her she needed it so she wouldn't run anybody over. Courtney grasped the walker, moved it around in front of her, looked up at the cheering crowd, smiled . . . and tossed the walker away. The doctors and nurses went nuts. Mrs. Chetwynde let out a small worried gasp and moved toward Courtney, but Mr. Chetwynde stopped her.

"Let her do it," he said.

Courtney was tentative, and stiff, but for the first time in seven weeks, she walked on her own. She walked stiffly past the cheering nurses, most of whom were crying happy tears for her. Even some of the doctors sniffled. Mark walked behind her, ready to jump in if she faltered.

She didn't. Not even a little. Courtney Chetwynde had her wheels back.

Mark whispered, "You okay?"

Courtney gritted her teeth in a smile and whispered back, "I'm dyin', but it feels great."

"You look great," Mark said.

Courtney made it all the way to the car, where her father helped her into the front seat. Mark and Mrs. Chetwynde hopped in back. With a final wave to the hospital staff, Courtney left Derby Falls, headed for home.

The ride was a very long three hours. Courtney wasn't used to sitting up for so long, let alone on the hard seat of a car. Their Volvo was many years old, and to Courtney the seat felt like it was carved out of rock. She didn't complain though. She was too happy to be going home. They arrived back in Stony Brook before dinnertime. Mrs. Chetwynde asked Mark if he'd like to stay and eat.

"C'mon," Courtney said. "Let's keep the party going."

Mark called his mom to say he wouldn't be home for dinner, and helped bring Courtney's luggage into the house. The first thing Courtney did when she got inside was call out, "Winston! C'mon, Winnie."

Instantly Courtney's cat came running. Winston was a short-haired tortoiseshell, and in Courtney's opinion, more dog than cat. Winston jumped into Courtney's arms, purring like a lawn mower. Courtney buried her face in the kitty's belly.

"Hmmm, I missed you, purr-face!" Courtney said.

She walked slowly through the house, looking around like she hadn't been there in months. Which she hadn't.

"Hasn't changed a bit," she declared. "Same furniture, same smells, same crummy old computer that we all have to fight over." She said this last while pointing to an old monitor that was on a table in the living room. Mark noted that it looked to be about five years old, which in computer years is ten lifetimes.

"You know, Dad," Courtney said. "If I'm going to be home-schooled for a couple of months, I'm not going to be able to sit on that hard chair down here, in front of that archaic old bucket of bolts you call a computer. I think we're going to have to—"

Courtney stopped short when she saw that her father had lifted up a cardboard box from behind the couch that, by the look of the markings on it, contained a brand-new laptop.

"Wow," Mark said. "That just came out!"

Mr. Chetwynde said, "And if Mark is impressed, I think you better be too, young lady."

Courtney broke out in a smile and hugged her dad.

"I love you, Daddy," she said.

"Welcome home, baby," Mr. Chetwynde said.

It was at that exact moment, the moment when everything felt right again . . . that Mark's ring began to twitch. He quickly clasped his hand over it and ran around behind Mr. Chetwynde so Courtney could see him.

"Uhh," Mark said. "C-Courtney? Wh-Where's the bath-room?"

Courtney said, "Same place it's always been. Over by the—" She stopped short when she saw the look in Mark's eyes. He held up his ring so Courtney could see that the gray stone had gone crystal and was starting to fire out light.

"Use mine upstairs," she said quickly. "Bring my bags up with you, okay?"

"Y-Yeah, no problem," Mark stammered. He ran for the entryway to the house, nearly tripping over Courtney's bags. He grabbed one and stumbled for the stairs. He was about to turn up, when Mrs. Chetwynde appeared from around the other side of the stairs. Mark instantly turned his back to her, shielding the glowing ring.

"Need some help?" she asked sweetly.

"N-No, I got it!" Mark said quickly as he tripped up the stairs.

Mrs. Chetwynde shrugged and turned back toward the kitchen to start dinner. Mark made it up the stairs, hurried down the hallway to the last door on the left, which he knew was Courtney's room, and dove inside. He had long ago gotten over the rush of actually stepping into a girl's bedroom. Life had gone way beyond that. He dropped Courtney's bag on the floor, closed the door, took off the ring, and put it on the floor. The ring had already begun to expand. It quickly grew to the size of a Frisbee, with flashing light spewing from the center and the familiar jumble of musical notes that Mark knew meant he was about to receive a delivery from another territory.

He had long ago gotten over the rush of seeing this, too.

It took only a few moments for the event to be over. The lights disappeared, the music ended, and the ring returned to normal. Sitting on the rug next to it was a journal. Like the journal before it, the rolled-up pages were bright yellow and tied with a purple ribbon. Mark stared at it on the floor. He may have gotten used to the ring opening up a pathway to the territories and depositing Bobby's journals, but there was no way to be prepared for the news a journal would bring.

"Mail's in," Courtney said. She had made it to her room and poked her head inside the door. "Just like old times."

Mark picked up the yellow pages. "Looks like it's from Quillan," he announced.

"The circus clown territory," Courtney added. "I have no idea what's up with that twisted place."

"I think we're about to find out," Mark said. "Should we read it here? Now?"

Courtney entered the room, closed the door behind her, limped over to Mark, and grabbed the roll of pages. "I've been out of the loop for too long," she said while pulling off the ribbon and unrolling the pages. "No way I'm going to wait."

Mark smiled. They were together again. They had always read Bobby's journals out loud to each other, except for when Courtney was hurting so bad. This felt good, for all sorts of reasons.

"You want me to start?" Courtney asked.

"Absolutely," Mark said with a smile as he sat down on the bed.

Courtney hobbled over to the cushy easy chair that her father had moved up to her room, and settled in. She looked at the pages, ready to read.

"Courtney?" Mark said.

"Yeah?"

"Welcome back."

Courtney smiled and began to read, "'Journal number twenty-four. Quillan. I like to play games. Always have. . . .'"

"Dinner's ready!" called Mrs. Chetwynde from downstairs.
Courtney had already finished reading Bobby's journal aloud.
She and Mark were busy sitting there, not moving, staring at
each other, trying to digest the news from Bobby's latest entry.
Courtney broke the silence first.

"He sounds bad," she said.

"Can you blame him?" Mark asked. "He's only got the biggest
responsibility in the history of all time on his shoulders."

"I wish there was something we could do to let him know
he's not alone," Courtney lamented.

"But he *is* alone," Mark said soberly.

Courtney looked out the window. She wanted to cry.
Bobby was doing an incredible job battling Saint Dane. It
hurt to hear that in spite of all his success, he was feeling
so sad and lonely. It wasn't fair. It almost made her wish
that when Bobby and Loor were together, that Loor had
kissed him.

Almost.

Mark added, "And now he's even more alone, because the
Traveler from Quillan is dead."

"It's a weird feeling," Courtney added glumly. "It's like hearing a relative died that you never met."

"Really," Mark said soberly. "I-I can't believe another Traveler is gone."

"And Bobby's just getting started on Quillan!" Courtney shouted out. "He's being set up for something, I know it."

"I think so too," Mark said. He jumped up and started pacing nervously. "Why else would Saint Dane have sent him that invitation? And what about the loop and the challenger clothes at the flume? Saint Dane must have put them there."

"Really," Courtney said. "And those two weird people, Veego and LaBerge. They had something to do with putting on that fight. Bobby's being lured into that Toto competition."

"Tato," Mark corrected.

"Whatever," Courtney snapped. "Bobby walked into a trap."

"What else can he do?" Mark argued. "If he wants to find out what's happening on Quillan, he's got to be right where he is. Where Saint Dane asked him to be."

Courtney took a deep breath. She knew Mark was right. But it didn't make her any less anxious about it. "I guess," she said, pouting. "I hate getting the story in short doses, and I hate even worse not being able to help him."

"Yeah, well, that's the deal," Mark said.

Courtney tapped her foot on the floor. Her good foot. She was full of nervous energy. "There's something I don't understand," she finally said. "Why doesn't Saint Dane just kill him?"

"What?" Mark shouted in surprise.

"Don't get all squishy," Courtney countered. "It's a legitimate question. With all of Saint Dane's powers, you'd think he'd just swat Bobby down and be done with him. The same with the other Travelers. He's had plenty of chances. I mean, if he spent all that time trying to get rid of me, you'd think he'd at least give it a shot."

Mark stopped pacing and sat back in the chair. "I have to admit, I've wondered that myself."

Courtney said, "You think maybe it's because they can't be killed? Like with Loor."

"But they *can* be killed!" Mark shot back. "There's a whole roster of dead Travelers as proof, and it's getting longer."

"Then what about Loor?" Courtney asked. "She was dead and then she wasn't."

"I don't know," Mark said, shaking his head. "Maybe it's like Bobby said. It might have something to do with the power they have when they're together. Bobby was there for Loor, and she survived. The Traveler from Quillan was alone, and now he's gone."

"So . . . could that be it?" Courtney asked nervously. "Is it finally happening? Is Saint Dane luring the Travelers to Quillan, separately, to kill them off one by one?"

The two shared a nervous look. The thought of a systematic Traveler execution was a grim one.

"Is this the Travelers' last stand?" Courtney asked, surprised by her own conclusion.

Mark jumped up and paced again. "No!" He shouted. "N-No way. It can't be that simple." He was forming the ideas as he spoke. "I've studied every word of Bobby's journals. I know everything that's happened to him since he left home, and I see a pattern."

"Which is . . . ?"

"Saint Dane likes to play," Mark answered. "He lures Bobby to a territory and gives him just enough information to get him thinking."

"But the clues usually send him in the wrong direction," Courtney pointed out.

"I think that's part of it," Mark said. "Saint Dane challenges Bobby. He forces him to make tough choices. Bobby never has a clear path."

"So what's the point?" Courtney asked impatiently. "Why does Saint Dane give Bobby any shot at all?"

Mark answered, "Because I think for Saint Dane, it's more than just trying to tip a territory toward chaos. I think he wants to beat Bobby. No, I think he *needs* to beat Bobby. If he didn't, why would he bother dealing with Bobby at all?"

"Because Bobby *forces* him to deal," Courtney said. "He's all over Saint Dane."

"Yeah, Bobby and the Travelers keep messing up his plans, but Saint Dane keeps giving him opportunities. I don't think anything that happens is by coincidence. I think Saint Dane has orchestrated everything, and part of it is to go head-to-head with Bobby whenever he can."

"Even when he lost his cool and beat Bobby up on Zadaa?" Courtney asked. "And tried to kill Loor?"

"Especially then," Mark answered. "Did he really lose his cool? Or was it just one more strand in the web he's weaving to mess with Bobby and keep him off balance?"

"You're making my head hurt," Courtney said. "And thanks for nothing because it's the only body part I've got left that doesn't ache."

"Sorry," Mark said.

Courtney asked, "So you think Saint Dane cares more about messing with Bobby than about ruling Halla?"

"No," Mark said. "Just the opposite. I believe that for Saint Dane, the road to Halla goes through Bobby. Until Bobby is defeated, he can never truly win. Just killing off the Travelers won't be good enough for him. Everything he does has a bigger purpose."

"Including setting up the Traveler from Quillan to die?" Courtney asked.

"Yeah, it's sick, but that's what I think," Mark said with confidence.

Courtney glanced at the yellow pages of Bobby's journal

from Quillan. "You make it sound like it's all one big game," she said.

"It kind of feels that way," Mark said. "With very big stakes."

Courtney looked out the window again and said, "The more we learn, the less sense it makes."

"I'll make it even more confusing," Mark said. "If I'm right about all this, then the really big question is, why? If this is all some big cosmic game, who made up the rules? What's the point? Why is Bobby so important? What is Saint Dane trying to prove? And—"

"And who's he trying to prove it to?" Courtney finished Mark's thought.

"Exactly," Mark said. "There's nothing in Bobby's journals that gives me a clue, other than what Gunny said—"

"Right," Courtney interrupted. "He thinks that somebody out there chose the Travelers."

"Yeah, but he doesn't know who it might be and neither does Bobby. Which means all he can do is keep playing the game and hope for the best."

"Courtney! Mark!" Mr. Chetwynde called from downstairs. "Dinner's getting cold."

"Coming!" Courtney shouted.

"So what do we do?" Mark asked.

"What do you mean?" Courtney shot back. "It's not like we can jump into a flume and hop over to Quillan to tell him our theory."

"No, I mean about you. Saint Dane nearly killed you. We both agreed that Bobby should know."

Courtney stood up. "I changed my mind," she said with finality.

"But—"

"It doesn't matter anyway. Even if we wanted to tell him, how could we? We don't know if the Traveler from Quillan had an acolyte. Who would we send the message to?"

"We could send it to one of the other acolytes, like Saangi, and she could tell Loor and—"

"And Loor would go to Quillan and do what? Tell Bobby that he's gotta get home because Saint Dane is messing with poor Courtney? What if that's exactly what Saint Dane wants? I've had a lot of time to wonder about why he came after me, and all I can come up with is that he wants Bobby to run home to protect me."

"Yeah, I thought about that too," Mark agreed.

"Look," Courtney said. "We can't travel to another territory, that's a fact. We're stuck here. But you know what? That's a good thing. Saint Dane is going to come after Second Earth. What he did to me might be part of his plan for this territory, or maybe he was just trying to distract Bobby. We don't know. But the fact remains, Second Earth is in play. It's not our job to go to other territories and interfere. Our job is to help Bobby protect Second Earth. I say we hold off on telling him anything about what's happened until the turning point on Quillan passes, no matter which way it goes. The battle isn't on Second Earth right now; it's on Quillan. That's where Bobby belongs, and it would be wrong for us to distract him."

Mark nodded.

"Now let's eat, I'm starving," Courtney said, and walked stiffly for the door. Conversation over.

The dinner that Mark shared with the Chetwyndes was a lot of fun, in spite of all that was bothering Mark and Courtney. They did their best to put their concerns about Bobby aside and focus on the celebration to welcome Courtney home. It was a warm, wonderful time. The tension between Courtney and her parents that existed before she left for summer school had evaporated. Courtney realized that her brush with death went a long way toward putting her priorities in order. Not being the best girl on the soccer team suddenly seemed trivial. Her parents were just happy that she was alive. Courtney kind of liked that fact too. If Saint Dane had accomplished anything, it was to bring Courtney and her family back together.

For Mark and Courtney there was an added reason to celebrate: They had survived Saint Dane's plot to hurt Courtney. Courtney's body may have been worse for wear, but their resolve was stronger than ever . . . and their confidence. It truly was a time to celebrate, in spite of the sad and scary news from Quillan.

Mark and Courtney decided to go about their lives as normally as possible, which meant Mark started his junior year at Davis Gregory High, and Courtney continued the grueling process of physical therapy. Both knew they had to stay aware, in case Saint Dane made another appearance, though neither knew exactly how to do that, or what to look for. Of course they were wary of strangers or anyone new who came into their lives. Courtney wasn't about to let another Whitney Wilcox weasel his way into her confidence. At least not until Saint Dane was done for good.

Mark brought Bobby's latest journal to the National Bank of Stony Brook, where all of Bobby's journals were kept in a safe-deposit box. Every day he would check the newspaper and the online news services, searching for any hint of something that might lead to a turning point on Second Earth that Saint Dane could exploit. After a week of sleepless nights spent online, he realized it was futile, because *everything* seemed like it could lead to a turning point. There was no shortage of stories about strife in other countries as well as at home. There were countless reports of terrorism and border disputes and sickness and crime and any number of things that Mark could easily imagine blossoming into a full-blown turning point. It was making him crazy. He began to realize that even if he ran across the right information, he'd never recognize it and make the connection to Saint Dane. He had to accept the fact that he'd never come across an item on Yahoo! that read: STRANGER APPEARS OUT OF NOWHERE TO OFFER PROSPERITY BUT REALLY PLANS DISASTER. Short of that, he knew he was spinning his wheels, so he reluctantly gave up doing research.

Courtney's mom dropped her off every day at the High Point Rehabilitation Center, where she spent a solid two hours being tortured. She worked right alongside many elderly people with various problems. One man had suffered a stroke and had to learn to use his legs again. Courtney found herself being a cheerleader and coach for the guy, encouraging him to keep trying. She also helped a young boy who had injured his hand so badly, he had trouble holding a fork to eat. Courtney sat by him, telling him jokes and getting him to focus. Many times the older man was nearly in tears out of frustration, but Courtney was able to get him to think ahead to where he would soon be, as opposed to dwelling on where he'd been. In the few weeks that Courtney was there, she saw great improvement in both the old man and the kid. The therapists told her she played a big part in their recovery, which made Courtney feel great.

Her own recovery went very well. Most of the patients there would have to be coaxed and cajoled into exercising, since exercise usually meant pain and frustration. With Courtney it was the opposite. The therapists had to caution her to back off, for fear she'd hurt herself again. The term "back off" was not in Courtney's vocabulary. She had a deadline. She wanted to play soccer that spring. But more than that, she was driven by her hatred of Saint Dane, and what he'd done to her. It fueled her and it healed her.

The investigation continued in Derby Falls as to who the stranger named Whitney Wilcox was, who showed up at Courtney's summer school, pretended to be a student, nearly killed Courtney, and then vanished. Courtney spoke many times with the local detectives and with school officials, answering the same questions over and over again. But it was all for show, because she knew they were wasting their time. They'd never find the guy. At one point she wanted to blurt out, "Look, Whitney Wilcox was actually a demon named Saint Dane who is trying to crush all of humanity, and the reason he tried to kill me is because my friend Bobby Pendragon is off in another time and territory trying to stop him, and I think he wanted to get Bobby to come home and protect me. Does that clear things up for you now? Have a nice day."

She didn't say that.

Instead she bit her tongue, answered their questions as truthfully as possible, and secretly felt sorry for them because it was such a total waste of their energy.

By the time November rolled around, Courtney was itching to get back to school. Up until then she had been getting her assignments brought to the house. Her parents even hired a tutor to help her with math. (Courtney wasn't big on math.) Her grades rebounded from the disaster of the year before, and after the first quarter she was back on the honor roll. As great as that felt, Courtney was still frustrated. She wanted to get back to normal, and normal meant going to school.

The final step was to get a clean bill of health from her doctors. The bones in her leg and arm were healing nicely. She could get around, though she still used a cane as a precaution. What the doctors were more concerned about was that she had recovered enough from her internal injuries to resume a normal, busy, tiring life. It was the week before Thanksgiving when Courtney had the examination she had been aiming for. She walked into the doctor's office, sat on the crunchy paper that covered his exam table, and announced, "Just so you guys know, the Monday after Thanksgiving, I'm going back to school."

The doctor raised an eyebrow and smiled. After asking a

number of questions as to how she was holding up, examining her, ordering a few blood tests, and then checking over her chart, the doctor called Courtney and her mom into his office to say, "Congratulations. You are good to go."

If there ever was a Thanksgiving when Courtney felt she had a lot to give thanks for, it was this one. Her life was back on track. She still had some pain and stiffness, especially after the weather turned cold, but Courtney was confident that in time any residual effect from the crash would be gone. She did feel a little nervous about going back to school though. She hadn't been there since the previous spring. She knew there would be questions as to where she had been. Mark told her how there were all sorts of rumors flying around school. Kids were saying how she'd had a total nervous breakdown and had to be committed to an insane asylum and spent the last few months strapped into a straitjacket in a padded hospital room. That made Courtney laugh, because of course none of it was true, except for the breakdown part, but secretly she was nervous about what she would tell people. Courtney prided herself on being strong, so it was embarrassing for her to admit that during the previous semester, she'd had trouble coping.

It wasn't like she could tell the truth about what had put her over the edge either. She couldn't say how she and Mark had traveled to Eelong and caused the death of one Traveler and trapped two others. That wouldn't fly, unless she really wanted to be put in a straitjacket and a padded hospital room.

Courtney wasn't used to admitting fault, or weakness, so the worry about how to explain her absence to the kids at school caused her more anxiety than just about anything else. Eventually she came up with a story that was partially true. She decided to be honest. Sort of. She would boldly say how she was under a lot of stress and was having trouble dealing with it. So rather than forcing it and alienating all her friends, which would have only made things worse, she chose to take a time-out. Courtney wanted to show strength in discussing her weakness. Then, she decided, she would immediately tell people about how she was nearly killed up in Massachusetts. She knew that story would be way more interesting than the one about her being depressed, and hoped the kids would soon forget about why she was gone in the first place. With that plan in place, Courtney felt she was ready to reenter her life.

The day after Thanksgiving, before she returned to school, Courtney got a call from Mark, who seemed all sorts of excited.

"I've got to show you something," he said. "Can I come over?"

"Is it—"

"No," Mark said quickly. "No new mail. It's something we've been working on."

"We?"

"Yeah," Mark said. "Is it okay if I bring Andy Mitchell over too?"

Courtney hesitated, then said, "You know I'm still not used to you hanging out with that roach."

Mark laughed. "I know. But things are different."

"Fine," Courtney said. "Just make sure he takes a shower first. And washes his hair. The guy's disgusting. That hair always looks like the Crisco fairy just paid him a visit."

"I'm not going to tell him that," Mark said.

"And there's no smoking in my house," Courtney said. "And deodorant is good. So is a toothbrush."

"Can I bring him over or not?" Mark asked impatiently.

"Yes," Courtney said. "I'm just giving you a hard time. But make sure he takes his shoes off before he comes in. No, wait, I don't want to smell his socks. He can leave his shoes on."

"Good-bye, Courtney," Mark said with a laugh. "We'll be there in an hour."

Right on time, Courtney's doorbell rang. She opened the door to see Mark and Andy standing there. Her first thought was, *He didn't wash his hair.* But she didn't say anything. She didn't want to embarrass Mark.

Courtney thought the two guys made an odd pair. Mark was shorter than Andy, with black hair that wasn't so much long as it was curly and unruly. It always looked like he had been in a windstorm, even after he got a haircut. They were the same age, but Andy looked much older. *Or maybe*, Courtney thought, *Mark still looks like a little kid.* Andy had the red blotches from a bad bout with acne, which didn't do much for his overall appearance. Courtney always thought that if he washed his face and hair a little more often, he might not have had to deal with so many skin problems. His dirty-blond hair always looked stringy and wet. He wasn't a handsome guy either. Where Mark was cute in a kind of little-boy way, Andy looked like an older kid who had already seen too much of life.

"Hi!" Mark said brightly.

"Hey, Chetwynde, how you feeling?" Andy asked.

"Great," Courtney said. "Steal any good books lately?"

"Courtney!" Mark chastised.

Andy shook his head and snorted. Courtney wanted to gag.

"You're hysterical, Chetwynde," Mitchell said. "Anybody ever tell you that?'

"Sorry," Courtney said. She meant it too. "Old habits. C'mon in."

She led the boys into the house and to the kitchen.

"You guys want some leftover pumpkin pie?" Courtney asked.

"Sure!" Mark chirped.

"Did you make it?" Mitchell asked.

"Are you kidding?" Courtney answered. "No!"

"Then I'll have some," Mitchell said.

Courtney glared at him, and got the pie out of the refrigerator. Mark and Andy sat down at the high counter across from her.

"So what's going on?" Courtney asked.

Mark could barely contain his excitement. "The project Andy and I are working on got accepted for the eastern regional science exposition! Isn't that awesome?"

"Uh, yeah," Courtney said, though it didn't sound like she meant it.

"Geez, Chetwynde," Mitchell said. "Try to contain your joy."

"I'm sorry," Courtney said. "That was rude. I just don't know anything about it."

"It's leading up to the single biggest high school science competition of the year is all!" Mark explained. "The regionals are next week in Orlando. If we win our class, we go to the nationals in January!"

"Wow," Courtney said. "That *is* pretty good." This time she meant it.

"Pretty good?" Mitchell said. "It's freaking awesome. You're looking at a couple of geniuses."

Courtney stopped and looked at them. Neither looked like a genius, but then again, she didn't know what geniuses were supposed to look like. She could accept that Mark had the goods, but she still couldn't get her head around the fact that Andy Mitchell could spell his own name let alone create something that would be honored by a national committee. She decided not to challenge them, for Mark's sake. She put their pieces of pie down on the counter and said, "So what's the big project?"

Mark smiled and said, "That's why we're here. Nobody outside of the club at school and the judging committee has seen it. We wanted you to be the first civilian to get a look."

"Mark wanted you to be the first," Andy corrected.

Courtney let the dig pass. Mark reached into his backpack while Andy picked up the piece of pie with his hands and bit off half. He could barely close his mouth to chew. Courtney stared at him in wonder. She held out a fork.

"This works too," she said flatly.

"Nah, I'm good," Andy said through the mouthful of gooey pie.

Mark pulled a small metal box out of his backpack. He opened it and reached inside, saying, "This is so revolutionary, Mr. Pike at Sci-Clops thinks we should get it patented."

"Enough buildup, what is it?" Courtney demanded.

Mark took something out of the metal box and placed it down on the counter. It was a round dull-gray object about the size of a golf ball. It wasn't perfectly round. It had facets and bumps, as if it were made of clay. To Courtney it looked like . . .

"Silly Putty," she said. "This is your big revolutionary invention?"

Mark and Andy exchanged knowing smiles.

Mark said, "We call it 'Forge.'"

"Because . . . ?"

"Watch," Mark said. He leaned in close to the object and said, "Activate."

The thing didn't move.

Courtney looked at the two guys curiously and asked, "Did it activate?"

"Yup," Andy said.

Courtney nodded. "Nice," she said, unimpressed. "Dull, but nice."

Mark said, "The mechanics are fairly rudimentary, nothing big there. The skin is something Andy's been working on for a while now. My contribution is the brain that drives it."

"Wow," Courtney said sarcastically. "No wonder you're going to Orlando! Be sure to say hi to Mickey and Goofy for me. Especially Goofy."

Andy said, "You just don't get it, do you?"

"What's to get?" Courtney said quickly.

Mark leaned down to the object and said in a firm, clear voice: "Cube!"

The object began to writhe. It looked to Courtney like the center was full of worms that had all decided to shift at the same time. She heard a faint metallic clattering sound. Five seconds later the object had changed itself from a ball into a cube. Courtney stared at it, wide eyed. Andy gave Mark a smug look. Mark beamed.

"Still think we should be hanging with Goofy?" Andy asked.

"That's incredible!" Courtney shouted. All traces of sarcasm were gone. "How did it do that?"

Mark leaned down and said, "Pyramid!"

As before, "Forge" moved and squirmed and transformed itself into a pyramid. Courtney couldn't take her eyes off it. Then it was Andy's turn. He leaned down and said, "Sphere."

The object bumped and shook, and in moments it was back to ball shape. Still wide eyed, Courtney leaned down to the sphere and said, "Orlando Bloom!"

The object didn't move.

"What's that supposed to mean?" Andy asked.

Courtney shrugged and answered, "I figured if it could turn into anything, it might as well be something interesting."

"Courtney!" Mark said, chastising.

"Hey, I said we were geniuses, not magical," Andy said defensively.

"I'm kidding," Courtney said quickly. "This is awesome. How does it work?"

Mark answered, "Like I said, the skin is something Andy's been working on for a long time. It pulls into any shape and it's almost indestructible. I programmed the voice-activated device and built the arms inside that form the shapes. It's pretty rudimentary, but there are a lot of moving parts. That's why it only becomes three different shapes."

"Oh," Courtney said. "No Orlando Bloom?"

"Not today," Mark said. "But who knows? The idea of Forge technology is to create products that can become a variety of different shapes."

Andy said, "So instead of having a whole toolbox full of wrenches, you have only one that can mold itself into whatever size you need. Or into any other tool you need."

Mark added, "Or imagine a road that won't crack when it expands and contracts with the weather. Forge technology would make roadways breathe, so that you'd never have to repair them."

Andy said, "Or you can have a chair for your little kid that grows along with him. Or a football helmet. One size fits all."

"Imagine a car that can be reduced to a third of its size when you get out," Mark said excitedly. "Think of the space saving!"

"The idea is to take things that are solid and make them flexible," Andy said proudly.

"It's all about options," Mark added.

"But no Orlando Bloom?" Courtney asked.

Mark and Andy looked at her blankly.

"It's a joke," Courtney said flatly. "Is all that really possible?"

Mark shrugged and said, "Not now, but who knows where this might lead? The whole thing works with a watch battery!"

Andy picked up the Forge object and threw it on the floor. It bounced up like a Super Ball. He caught it and announced, "It bounces pretty good too!"

Courtney took the Forge object from Andy and stared at it. "I don't know what I'm more amazed at," she said. "The technology, or the idea that the two of you came up with it."

Andy said, "What you really mean is you can't believe I had anything to do with it."

"Well, yeah," Courtney admitted.

"I don't know what our competition is," Mark announced proudly, "but I can't imagine anybody beating this."

Courtney looked to Mark, then to Andy and said, "Neither can I. This is amazing. I am totally impressed."

Mark beamed. Andy shrugged.

Mark put the Forge object back in its case, and they finished their pie. As they ate, Mark excitedly went into the details about how he and his mother and father were flying down with Andy to Orlando the following Wednesday and the competition was the day after. Andy didn't say much of anything. He wasn't the best at making conversation. Before it was time to go, Mark hit the bathroom, leaving Courtney and Andy alone in the kitchen. Courtney watched Mitchell as he wiped his plate with his finger and licked the pumpkin remnants off. She had to force back the urge to retch.

"So," Andy said. "Things ain't turning out the way you thought, are they?"

"Give me a break," Courtney shot back. "You've been a jerk your whole life. You expect me to believe you suddenly turned into a great guy?"

"I don't care what you believe," Andy said. "I'm not a great guy. I'm not a bad guy. I'm just me. What can I say?"

"You can say that you won't do anything to mess things up for Mark," she said sternly. "He *is* a great guy, and if you do anything stupid, you're going to have to deal with me."

"Oooh," Andy said with mock fear. "I'm quakin'!"

"Just don't be a jerk, all right?"

Andy stood up and said, "I might be a jerk, but if it wasn't for me, you'd still be lying in a ditch up there in the mountains."

This stopped Courtney. For a moment she had slipped back into remembering the old Andy Mitchell. The Andy Mitchell that was the scourge of grade school.

"You're right," she said softly. "I'm sorry. I owe you."

"No you don't," Andy said. "Just try to be a little more, I don't know, open-minded. All right?"

Courtney didn't say anything. She knew he was right, but it killed her to admit it.

Mark came bouncing back into the room saying, "So? You coming back to school on Monday?"

"Absolutely," Courtney said. "The return of Courtney."

"Whoa! Stand back!" Mitchell said jokingly. They all laughed.

When the guys left, Courtney was left feeling off balance. She was happy for Mark and proud that he was going to the regional competition. She was even legitimately impressed with their Forge thing. It was Andy Mitchell that made her feel odd. Having him turn out to be an incredibly smart, good guy didn't fit the way she thought the world was supposed to work. As much as it was a good thing, it just felt weird. As she cleaned up the pie plates, she decided that the only problem with Andy was her. She realized she was being rigid. People change. People grow up. They mature. She knew that. Who was she to say that Andy Mitchell couldn't be one of those people? If Mark accepted him, then why couldn't she?

Courtney promised herself that she would stop judging Andy Mitchell by the old rules, and look at him the way Mark did. Besides, she thought, she's got her own problems to deal with. On Monday she was going back to school.

◐ SECOND EARTH ◐

(CONTINUED)

It felt like the first day of school for Courtney because in many ways, it was. It was strange and exciting and scary and overwhelming all at the same time. In a word, it was excellent. Her mom had dropped her off and asked if she wanted help to get inside. Courtney's answer was a stern "You've got to be kidding" look. Mrs. Chetwynde shrugged, gave her daughter a kiss on the cheek, and watched as she walked slowly back to school for the first time in seven months.

When Courtney stepped into the school, it reminded her of when she stepped into the flume. It was like entering a strange and scary new dimension where she didn't know exactly what to expect. She knew she could handle the physical part. She'd worked too hard on her therapy to worry about that. She also knew that classes would be fine. She looked forward to being back with a real live teacher. What made her nervous was facing her friends. She had no idea how they would treat her.

What happened was . . . things couldn't have been better.

Courtney was totally relieved to find that nobody pressed her on the details of what had happened the year before. They all wanted to know about the accident, and how she was feeling, but when it came to the question of why she'd left school in the first place, her friends were cool. It wasn't like they were avoiding the issue. Just the opposite. They would bring it up, but would say things like, "Glad you're back to your old self." And, "We missed you." And, "If you ever want to talk, I'm here for you." Even some of her rivals from the soccer team went out of their way to wish her well and say they hoped she'd get back up to speed as soon as possible. They told her that since a whole senior class had graduated, they needed her in a bad way. It blew Courtney away. She never expected to be treated so nicely. It wasn't like anybody felt sorry for her either. They seemed to respect that she was having a tough time, and genuinely wanted her back to her old self. Nobody judged her, or made fun, or snickered behind her back. What she'd feared was that her friends were going to act like kids and not know what to say. What she found instead was that they, like Andy Mitchell, were growing up. It made her realize just how long she had been gone. It made her a little sad, but she couldn't have wished for a better homecoming. Or schoolcoming. It felt to Courtney like the whole nightmarish experience made her stronger. At one point she had to chuckle when she thought that she had Saint Dane to thank for getting her head back on straight. *If he only knew,* she thought.

Courtney didn't see Mark for those first few days. They didn't share any classes. They didn't share any friends, either. Other than Bobby. She wanted to see him though, if only to show him that she was almost back to normal. By Wednesday she still hadn't seen him, and knew that he was leaving for Orlando that evening. So rather than go home after school, she had her mom drop her off at Mark's house to say hi and wish him good luck at the competition.

What she ran into instead was . . . disaster.

She rang the doorbell. There was no answer at first. She

was about to leave when the door was suddenly thrown open. Mrs. Dimond stood there, looking stressed.

"Courtney!" she exclaimed. "You look so good!" Mrs. Dimond threw her arms around Courtney and gave her a big hug. "But I can't talk now, we're in the middle of a crisis."

"What's going on?" Courtney asked.

"Don't ask," she said. "No, go ask Mark. He's in the living room with Andy Mitchell." Mrs. Dimond leaned into Courtney and whispered, "Is that guy a little, I don't know, greasy?"

Courtney chuckled and said, "No, he's a *lot* greasy."

"Good," Mrs. Dimond said. "I'm glad I'm not the only one who thinks so. Go talk to them."

Mrs. Dimond left her and hurried up the stairs. Courtney saw that at the foot of the stairs were all their suitcases, packed and ready to go. She walked into the living room to see Mark sitting on the sofa looking nervous, while Andy paced.

"Hey, ready to go?" Courtney asked.

Mitchell looked up, spotted Courtney, and his shoulders fell. "Don't you go giving me a hard time," he said anxiously. "I'm having a bad enough day as it is."

"Why? What's going on?" Courtney asked as she sat in an easy chair. She needed to sit down. Though she was feeling better, the three days she'd spent at school had taken a lot out of her.

Mark said, "The sprinkler in Andy's uncle's florist shop just exploded."

"It didn't explode," Andy said. "He must have been smokin'. I know that guy. He set it off. Idiot."

"Whatever," Mark said. "Andy came over, we were all set to leave, and then he got the call."

"Five minutes from a clean getaway," Andy lamented.

Mark added, " His uncle says the place is a wreck."

"There was a flood and it blew out the heat," Andy said

angrily. "Just his luck the weather turned frigid last night. The place is turning into a skating rink."

"So what does that mean for you?" Courtney asked.

"Oh, not much," Andy answered sarcastically. "Only that I can't go to Orlando! Months of work, all for nothin'. Unbelievable!"

"Why can't you go?" Courtney asked.

"Because I gotta help him clean up the mess!" Andy cried. "He just took delivery of all his Christmas flowers. If we don't get them out of there and over to his house like, right now, they'll die and his whole season will be gone, which means I'm out of a job. I gotta go there right now and get to work."

"It's not fair," Mark said. "We've worked so hard for this."

"Is there a later flight?" Courtney asked.

"Yeah, but there's too much work to do," Andy said, sounding defeated. "I'd never get it done and make it down to the airport in time."

Mark said, "I told you I'd stay and help. With extra help you might still make the later flight."

"Or I might not, and then you'd be stuck too," Andy said.

Mr. Dimond entered the room holding a piece of paper. "I just called the airline," he announced, referring to the paper. "Good news, bad news. There's a later flight tonight, and one first thing in the morning. If worse comes to worst, you can make the flight tomorrow and still be at the convention center in time for the presentation."

"Seriously?" Andy asked, gaining hope. "What's the bad news?"

"It'll cost two hundred bucks a ticket to make the change" was the answer.

"Ouch," Mark said. "That's a lot of cash."

"Eight hundred bucks for all of you," Courtney pointed out.

"I can do the math," Mitchell snapped.

"Here's my suggestion," Mr. Dimond said. "Mrs. Dimond and I will go down on the flight as scheduled. We're there to chaperone, but it's a vacation for us too. I'd just as soon not miss any of it. Sorry, Andy."

"No problem," Andy said.

"But if Mark wants to stay, he can help you clean up the shop and maybe you can both make it to the airport for the later flight. If not, I can book you on the flight tomorrow and you'll come down then. How does that sound?"

"Fine," Andy said. "Except for the part about the extra two hundred bucks to change my ticket. I ain't got that kind of cash. If I did I wouldn't be working for my idiot uncle."

"I'll spring for it," Mr. Dimond said. "For both of you."

"Are you serious?" Andy said.

"Really, Dad?" Mark asked.

"Hey, how often do I get to see a couple of geniuses change the world?" Mr. Dimond said. "What do you say?"

Andy looked at Mark. Mark shrugged and said, "Let's go save some flowers!"

Courtney said, "I'd help but I barely have enough energy to get out of this chair."

Andy ran over to Mr. Dimond and shook his hand. "Thank you, man. Seriously. I don't know what to say."

"Say you'll hurry up," Mr. Dimond said, laughing.

"Dad, you are the best," Mark said.

"Don't tell him that," Mrs. Dimond said as she entered the living room. "It'll go right to his head, and I won't be able to live with him."

"Thank you, both," Andy said. "C'mon, Chetwynde, we'll drop you at home."

Courtney pulled herself out of the chair and said, "Well, glad I came by to solve the dilemma."

"Yeah, you're swell," Andy said sarcastically. "Let's go."

He ran out. Mark gave his mom and dad a quick hug and said, "See you in Florida. You guys are awesome." He ran after Andy; Courtney was right behind.

They all headed for Andy's ancient station wagon. Since Andy used it to transport flowers, the backseat was down. That meant all three had to sit in front on the bench seat. Andy jumped behind the wheel. Courtney looked to Mark and said, "You're not going to make me sit next to him, are you?"

Mark laughed and jumped in first. Courtney didn't live far from Mark, so the drive only took a few minutes. Andy pulled the car up to the curb in front of her house, skidding to a stop.

"Okay, out!" he shouted. "We ain't got a whole lot of time."

Mark said, "Wait, I gotta use Courtney's bathroom."

"What?" Mitchell exclaimed. "We just left your house a minute ago!"

"Wh-What can I say," Mark said. "When you g-gotta go . . ."

Mark's words caught Courtney by surprise. Why was he stuttering? Mark only stuttered when he got nervous. She opened the door, pulled her stiff body out of the car, and headed up the walkway to her house. Mark was right after her.

"Make it quick!" Andy shouted. "We got a plane to catch!"

Mark hurried up behind Courtney, took her by the arm, and hurried her toward the house.

"Geez," Courtney said. "He's right. Why didn't you go back at your house?"

Mark didn't stop. "Just hurry," he said.

He pulled her quickly toward the door. Courtney pulled her keys out and could see that Mark was nervously hopping from one foot to the other.

"You gonna make it?" she asked, chuckling.

"Just open the door," Mark ordered.

Courtney wasn't used to Mark giving orders like that. Something was wrong, and it wasn't that he had to go to the bathroom. When she got the door open, Mark jumped past her and inside.

"Close the door!" he shouted.

She did. "What is wrong with you?" she demanded.

Mark pulled his right hand out of his coat pocket.

"This!" he shouted.

His ring had come to life. Bobby's next journal was about to arrive.

"You're not gonna make that plane later tonight," Courtney said, breathless.

"No," Mark said. "We'll fly tomorrow."

No sooner had Mark finished saying that than the entryway to Courtney's house came alive with light from the expanding ring. Mark and Courtney already had their eyes shielded.

"Courtney?" came a familiar voice. It was Courtney's mother.

"Uh-oh," Mark said. He quickly took off his jacket and threw it over the growing ring just as Mrs. Chetwynde entered.

"Oh, hi, Mark!" she said cheerily. "Congratulations, I heard all about your, uh, your science thing."

"Thanks, M-Mrs. Chetwynde," Mark stammered nervously.

Both he and Courtney stepped onto Mark's coat, pressing the edges down into the rug so no light would shine out.

"What is that strange sound?" Mrs. Chetwynde asked.

Mark and Courtney knew it was the strange music that always accompanied a delivery through the ring.

Courtney said, "That's part of Mark's project. They're experimenting with sound, too."

Mrs. Chetwynde looked at the jacket they were standing on and frowned. "It's in the jacket?"

"Uh-huh," Courtney said.

"The jacket you're standing on," Mrs. Chetwynde added.

"Uh, yeah, we didn't want to track dirt onto the rug," Courtney said, thinking fast.

"Since when?"

Courtney could feel the ring shrinking under her foot. The music ended too.

"Hey! Dimond!" Andy Mitchell called from outside. He was pressing his face against the small window next to the front door.

Mrs. Chetwynde saw him and jumped in surprise. "Oh!" she exclaimed. "Who is that person?"

Mark took the opportunity to scoop up the jacket, along with the ring and the pages that had just arrived.

"He's my partner in the project," Mark explained.

Courtney said, "He won't bite, he only looks scary. You know how those genius types are."

Mrs. Chetwynde shook her head in dismay and walked out of the room. "If you say so," she said with confusion. "Good luck, Mark."

"Thanks, Mrs. Chetwynde!"

"Come on!" Andy Mitchell yelled. "My uncle's waitin'!"

Mark held up his finger to Andy as if to say, "One second!" He pulled Courtney away from the window, into the living room, out of Andy's sight. From under his jacket he pulled out a thick brown envelope. Bobby's latest journal.

"What happened to the yellow pages with the purple ribbon?" Courtney asked.

Mark ripped open the envelope quickly and looked inside. "It's a journal all right," he announced. "Maybe he wrote it from another territory."

"You're not going with Mitchell now, are you?" Courtney asked. "We've gotta read!"

"I can't blow him off," he said. "What would I tell him?"

"Who cares! You don't owe that jerk anything. After all he's done to you? Mark, it's a journal from Bobby!"

"He's not a jerk anymore; he's my partner," Mark said seriously.

Courtney backed down, saying, "Yeah, you're right. I'm sorry. But you're not gonna take that plane tonight!"

"No," Mark said. "I'll help move the flowers, then come back here right after. I'll just have to make sure it takes long enough so we miss the night flight."

"Do you realize how hard it's going to be for me not to read this?" Courtney said.

Mark gave her a stern look. Courtney smiled and said, "Don't worry. I'll wait for you."

Mark put his ring back on his finger, pulled on his jacket, and headed for the front door. "I'll be back as soon as I can. Put the journal someplace safe."

He was about to leave, then he turned and walked back to Courtney. He held her by the arms and said, "I am really glad you're back."

The two hugged. They had forged such a strong bond over the last few years that if Courtney were asked, she would have to say that as strange as it might seem, her very best friend in the world was Mark Dimond.

Mark felt the same way.

They hugged for a second more, then without another word, he was gone. Courtney looked at the envelope. She hadn't thought about it until that second, but it was the first time she'd been entrusted with one of Bobby's journals. Usually that was Mark's job. Now she was the one who had to have the patience to wait, knowing that the next chapter in Bobby's adventure was right there. She sat down and felt the paper envelope, wanting to pull the pages out and start reading. She almost did, too. But she stopped herself. It was always Mark who had to wait for her. She now knew just how hard that was.

She took the envelope and brought it up to her room, carefully placing it under her pillow for safekeeping. She had no idea why she did that. It wasn't like the underside of her pillow was any safer than her desk, or her dresser. But she felt as if she needed to treat the pages with special care. It also helped to get the journal out of her sight, because she feared her willpower would crack and she'd read.

She went downstairs and had dinner with her parents, then did her homework in the dining room. Her mother asked her why she wasn't working in her room as she usually did. Courtney said it was because she was tired of being alone. It was the truth, she *was* tired of being alone. It was one of the great things about going back to school. After being in self-imposed exile, and then being hurt for so long, she loved being around people again. But if Courtney were being totally honest, she'd admit it was also because she didn't trust herself alone with Bobby's journal. She was afraid that if it were in her reach, she'd go for it. So rather than be tempted, she did her homework downstairs. When she finished, she sat with her dad to watch some TV. But her mind wasn't on the news-magazine they watched. It was on the treasure under her pillow upstairs.

Courtney checked her watch. Mark had been gone for over five hours. How long did it take to clean up a couple of flowers? Another half hour went by. Still no Mark. Courtney couldn't take it anymore. She went into the kitchen and called his cell phone. All she got was Mark's message. As far as she knew, she was the only one who ever left a message on Mark's cell phone. Her message this time was short and to the point, "Where are you? It's after ten! Call me!"

Mark didn't call her. Ten turned into ten thirty and then eleven. Where was he? Could he have taken the night flight to Orlando after all? *No*, she thought, *he would have called*. This wasn't like Mark.

Finally, at eleven thirty, Courtney broke. She convinced herself that Mark wasn't coming back that night, and was angry with him for not calling. In her mind that justified her taking a peek at Bobby's pages.

"I'm going upstairs, Dad," she said. "There's a chance Mark Dimond might come by tonight; he was supposed to help me with calculus."

"Tonight?" Mr. Chetwynde said with surprise. "Isn't it a little late to study on a school night?"

"Yeah, I don't think he'll come, but don't be surprised if he does. Mark is an odd one."

Mr. Chetwynde would never question anything that Mark Dimond did. He had saved his daughter's life. Whatever Mark did was okay with him, no matter how odd.

"Good night, sweetheart," Mr. Chetwynde called.

"G'night, Dad."

Courtney hurried up the stairs, rushed into her bedroom, closed the door, and locked it. She stared at her pillow. She was torn between curiosity and guilt. Curiosity won. She jumped on her bed, jammed her hand under the pillow, and pulled out the envelope.

He'll understand, Courtney thought.

From out of the envelope she pulled a thick stack of small gray pages. It was notepaper, with each sheet around five-by-seven inches. Each sheet was filled on both sides with Bobby's familiar handwriting. She was about to read when she noticed one more thing about the pages. Printed on the bottom right hand corner of each page, in small square letters, was a single word.

BLOK.

"Blok," she said to herself out loud. "I hope he's figured out what that means, because it's making me crazy."

Courtney's head went to Quillan. She knew Mark would understand. It was time to read.

QUILLAN

I've been kidnapped. Again.

Abducted, captured, taken prisoner, whatever. I'm not really sure what to call it. All I know is, I was grabbed, tied up, driven somewhere, and thrown into a dank, wet cellar. It's cold in here. It smells like rotten fish.

At least there aren't any clowns.

What I don't know is, why. My kidnappers can't be looking for ransom. Who would pay it? They're not treating me badly, other than sticking me in this tuna-smelling dungeon. They gave me food, and even some blank paper when I asked for it. That's what I'm writing this journal on. I truly don't know how much danger I'm in. Nobody will tell me anything. All I know for sure is that I'm trapped in this cell. And that it stinks. The only thing I can do is wait, and write down all that's happened to me since I finished my last journal.

There is one more odd twist to this mess that I should mention. My kidnappers all wore dark masks, so I don't know who any of them are, except for one. One of my kidnappers is a Traveler. Yes, a Traveler. You'd think that would make me feel better, but after all that's happened on Quillan, it doesn't.

I don't mean to sound paranoid but, well, I'm paranoid. After you read about what's been going on, I think you'll understand why. That's the reason I want to write now. If things turn sour and these guys are looking to hurt me, I want a record of everything that led to my being here. But don't worry, if they try to hurt me, they're in for a big surprise. They picked on the wrong guy.

I finished my last journal a long time ago. I don't know how they measure time here on Quillan, but my internal Second Earth clock tells me it was at least a couple of weeks since I finished Journal #24. When last I wrote, I was in that circuslike room in the fairytale castle that belonged to Veego and LaBerge. Writing both those journals so close together really fried me. I suppose being chased, bitten, chased, chased, and shot in the back with a tranquilizer gun had a little to do with it too. I lay down on the floating platform bed that was in the center of that odd room and closed my eyes to get some rest. As exhausted as I was, I couldn't keep my eyes shut. My mind was racing in too many directions. I kept thinking about Challenger Yellow, and the Tato match, and why the challenger clothes were left for me at the flume, and the robot-spiders and . . . well, everything. It didn't help that there were hundreds of clown-doll eyes staring down at me either. I kept thinking that LaBerge had to be some kind of freak to decorate a room like a clown carnival. Okay, I was also thinking that these dolls were going to come to life and tickle me to death or something, but that's embarrassing to admit.

I told you how much I hate clowns, right?

After tossing around for I don't know how long, I gave up and paced the room. This had gone on long enough. I wanted to know what was in store for me. Was I a prisoner? Was I a guest? Who were Veego and LaBerge and what did they want with me? The waiting and wondering were making me nuts! I was tired of playing it their way. I wanted answers. So I walked over to the door and was all set to bang on it and start screaming for that Fourteen guy to come get me, when I had a thought. I reached down and tried the doorknob. It was open! I had assumed that once I was put in that room that I was locked in. What an idiot. I could have left anytime I wanted. Oops. I felt stupid and curious at the same time. Why didn't they lock me in? Could I leave? Maybe I really was just a guest. With more questions now than before, I opened the door and stepped into the corridor.

I was surprised to see that a sign had been erected outside my door. It was a yellow card, about a foot square, with purple handwriting. It sat on a three-legged easel and was positioned so it would be seen as soon as I came out. How long had it been there? The sign read: CHALLENGER RED GOT OUT OF BED. Under the writing was an arrow that pointed to the right. Not knowing what else to do, I turned right and walked down the hallway. What kind of game were they playing? I walked to the end of the hallway to find another hallway that stretched out to either side. Dangling from a string that hung down from the ceiling was another sign. It read: AND WENT TO TAKE A LOOK. Beneath this writing was an arrow that pointed left. I followed the instructions and made the turn. This hallway stretched for almost as far as I could see. Man, the castle was huge! About twenty yards farther along, another yellow sign dangled from the ceiling. It read: HE SAW A DOOR AND WENT TO EXPLORE. The arrow here pointed left again. I turned to see that, sure enough, there was a double-wide door right there, with another sign on it. I had the feeling that I was getting near the end of this mysterious treasure hunt. As big as the door was, the writing on this sign was so small I couldn't see it from even a few steps away. I had to walk right up to the door and lean in so close that my nose nearly touched it. In tiny letters the sign read: AND PLAYED A GAME CALLED HOOK.

Hook? I said to myself. *What's Hook?*

Instantly the door spun open. Yes, I said "spun." The door twisted on a center axis, like a revolving door. I was so surprised, I didn't have time to react and got swept inside. What kind of wicked fun house was this? I got thrown inside a room that was pitch dark. Limbo dark. My every sense went instantly on alert. I crouched down and closed my eyes, trying to feel if anyone or any*thing* was in there with me. I wasn't scared. I had been there before. It was like the ordeal that Loor and Alder put me through on Zadaa. I knew how to fight in the dark. Only back on Zadaa, it was for training. This was for real. I didn't move. Whatever was going to happen, I was ready.

I heard a bright chime sound. In the distance a white light appeared in the shape of a door. Because the room was so dark, I had no sense of depth and couldn't tell how far away it was. It could have been a small rectangle only a few feet away, or a large door on the far side of a long room. It seemed suspended in space, glowing brightly, beckoning me. I didn't move. There was way too much mystery between here and there. A moment later another chime sounded, and a lighted number appeared over the rectangle: 70. Huh?

There was another chime. I was relieved to see a series of spotlights kick on and illuminate the room. Some were in the ceiling, casting sharp patterns of light to the floor; others were in the floor, pointing straight up. There must have been a hundred lights shooting beams in both directions. The room was big. Really big. The ceiling must have been twenty feet high. It was a long, narrow space that I realized ran the same length of the hallway where my clown room was. I could now see that the rectangle with the number 70 above it was indeed a door. I guessed it was fifty yards from me. Fifty long yards. As much as the spotlights gave me a sense of the room, they also created dark areas in between the brilliant light from their beams. Danger could be hiding in dark areas.

A bell rang. I jumped. Do you blame me? I looked at the number to see a countdown had begun: 70 . . . 69 . . . 68 . . . With each tick there was a little *blip* sound. Swell. There was a time limit. But for what? What was I supposed to do? Go for the door? What if I didn't go? What if the blipping number reached zero and I was still crouched on the floor next to the revolving door? What would happen to me? Would I have to go back into that clown room without supper? And if this was some kind of game, why was it called "Hook"?

The answer to that last question came a moment later, and it hurt.

I felt a sharp, stinging pain across my back and shoulders. A second later I was spun around like an unraveling yo-yo. The force came so fast and so hard I lost my balance and crashed down on my shoulder. I popped right up and spun around to see who had attacked me.

I was face-to-face with a dado. He stood with his legs apart over one of the up-facing spotlights. The bright light shining up on him from below made him look even more imposing. He was well over six feet tall, with wide shoulders and strong arms that looked ready to burst the seams of his sleeves. He wore the same dark uniform as the other dados I'd seen, but he didn't wear a helmet or a gun. His weapon was a six-foot-long curved stick with a ball on the end. I guessed that was the "Hook." It looked semirigid, like it was made out of soft plastic. It wasn't as long as a whip, but he used it like one. I knew it had to be what he had slashed me with. It wasn't a lethal weapon, but if he knew how to use it, he could control me.

I had no doubt he knew how to use it.

More frightening than anything was his face. It was like a mask, with a big sharp jaw and eyes that had no life. He was bald, too. It was at that moment that I finally remembered where I had seen dados before. I'm not talking about the arcade, or the city street. I mean in the flume. Remember the floating images I described? One of those images was of tall muscular guys running. Dados. They looked imposing then, and even more so in person.

The number blipped down: 64 . . . 63 . . . 62 . . .

I jumped for the revolving door I had just come through. I didn't want to play this game, no matter what it was. I hit the door hard. It didn't budge. Why was I not surprised? If I wanted to get out of there, I was going to have to get past Franken-dado and run to the far side. Without a second more of hesitation, I sprinted for the rectangle of light. I figured if I was fast enough, I might catch this goon by surprise and beat him there before he hooked me again.

I was wrong. No sooner did I take off running, than the number blipped down to 60. The number over the door flashed red and a harsh horn sounded. That wasn't the problem. That was the warning. When the horn sounded, several silver cylinders the size of telephone poles drove down from the ceiling, slamming into the floor like demonic pile drivers. I barely missed getting crushed by one, as they hammered the floor so hard the vibration almost knocked me off my feet.

Yikes! This room was a minefield! The cylinders quickly retracted into the ceiling. I had no doubt they'd be back. Before I had the chance to think, I felt the stinging slap of the hook around my ankles. The dado pulled and I was on my butt, feet in the air. What kind of game was this? I didn't know the rules or have any way to defend myself. It was clear to me that my job was to get through that door on the far side before the number ran down, and before I got crushed by a giant cylinder. It was the dado's job to stop me. . . . 57 . . . 56 . . . 55 . . .

I rolled to the side wall. I wasn't about to fight the dado. Though he had a weapon and outweighed me by a good fifty pounds, I was way more worried about the crushing cylinders. . . . 54 . . . 53 . . . 52 . . .

I rolled until I hit the wall, hoping that the cylinders were more toward the center of the room. My plan was to hug the wall as I made my way to the far side.

Bad plan . . . 51 . . . 50 . . .

The number flashed red, the horn sounded. But the cylinders didn't come crashing down. Instead another set shot up from the floor. I was directly on top of one. The cylinder lifted me into the air! I had to quickly roll off or it would have driven me through the ceiling. I hit the floor awkwardly and was lucky not to have broken or twisted anything. The silver cylinders continued up until they slammed into the ceiling, then quickly retracted. On the floor the dado was waiting for me. He whipped the hook around my neck and pulled hard, choking me. I pulled back, but that only made the hook pull tighter. In desperation I spun in the opposite direction and unwound myself. The cylinders had all retracted into the floor, and I lay there, gasping for breath. . . . 44 . . . 43 . . . 42 . . .

The cylinders came out every ten seconds. I looked around for the dado but didn't see him. After every attack he'd hide back in the shadows and give the crushing cylinders their turn to hurt me. He'd played this game before. I hadn't. . . . 41 . . . 40 . . .

The horn sounded as the cylinders from the ceiling crashed down again. I couldn't tell exactly where they were, so I had no way of knowing where to jump to get out of the way. A descending cylinder grazed my shoulder. Too close. They slammed into the floor, the building shook, and they retracted. I looked to the far doorway to see I hadn't gotten much closer. I had ten blips of the clock before the next cylinders would pile into the room. I figured if I sprinted for it, I'd make it.

The dado must have sensed this. I wondered if he had done this enough times to know what to expect from his victims. I had barely started to run when I felt the sting of his hook around my waist. He didn't pull me down this time, all he did was yank me a few feet and keep me there. I was still upright. What was he doing? I pulled away, but he held me tight. . . . 34 . . . 33 . . . 32 . . . 31 . . . 30 . . .

Blaring horn. The cylinders came down. I was directly under one. The dado had positioned me to be crushed. I had nowhere to go but directly at the dado. I leaped at him and felt the falling cylinder brush my back. I hit the big guy square in the chest. He barely moved. It was like running into a tree. The guy lifted me up like a doll and heaved me across the floor. I slammed into one of the cylinders—they hadn't retracted into the ceiling yet—spun around, but kept my balance and had the presence of mind to keep running toward the door of light. . . . 27 . . . 26 . . . 25 . . .

The horn blared. What was this? Only five seconds apart now? As the numbers got closer to zero, the pace increased. Worse, as the cylinders shot up toward the ceiling from below, I dodged one, only to see that the overhead cylinders were shooting down at the same time. They were now coming from both directions. My options just got cut in half. One wrong step and I'd be cut in half too. I looked up and down as the cylinders retracted, and learned something valuable. They were each right next to one of the spotlights. I guess I didn't realize this at first because everything had happened so fast. But now that I understood the program, it was obvious. I knew where *not* to be when the cylinders released. I had to position myself directly in between the lights. Good plan, except that the dado had other plans.

Ooof! I had been standing in one spot too long. I was a target. The dado threw a cross-body block at me. I felt like I'd gotten hit with a bus. The shot knocked me off my feet. I rolled . . . 22 . . . 21 . . . *horn.*

The cylinders shot up and down. I was lying right over one. It hit me in the side, lifting me up. I rolled off and quickly scrambled to get between the lights, as all around me the cylinders blasted the floor and the ceiling. I was trapped in some infernal piston engine. There was no time for finesse; I had to get to the far side. I didn't even want to imagine what would happen if I let the number roll down to zero. Before the cylinders had fully retracted, I started running again.

Horn.

No! It wasn't even five seconds this time. The cylinders shot up and down. It was random now too. The bottom cylinders charged up and a second later the top cylinders hammered down. I was twenty yards from the rectangle of light, but it felt like a mile. I turned back to see where the dado was. He was coming for me, cautiously but steadily. He seemed to know the pattern of the cylinders. He'd jump forward and stand still as cylinders shot up and down around him. Then jump forward again and wait as the cylinders shot by. He knew exactly what he was doing, and he wasn't in any hurry. . . . 18 . . . 17 . . . 16 . . .

I knew that if I started for the door again, he'd attack. If I had any hope of beating this game, and surviving, I'd have to do something drastic.

I attacked the dado.

I guess nobody had ever done that before, because the dado wasn't ready. I lunged for him and grabbed the front of his shirt. I moved so fast and was so close that he couldn't use his hook on me. I held on to his shirt and threw myself backward, pulling him toward me. It must have been a complete surprise because this guy was so big, if he had been ready, it would have been like trying to pull down a tree. But he came with me. As I fell back I jammed my foot into his chest. He tried to pull back but it was too late. I was in control. Gravity helped. I rolled onto my back, thrust my leg into him, and pulled the guy over my head. He was heavy, but I had physics on my side. I flipped him butt-over-head. He slammed the ground hard on his back. At that instant a cylinder came blasting down from the ceiling. The dado had landed in the wrong place. For me it was the exact right place.

The cylinder crushed his leg. I heard it before I saw it. The crunching sound was unmistakable. It took me a second to register that in spite of the fact that his leg had just been crushed, he didn't scream out. He barely even reacted. A quick look at my fallen enemy showed why.

His leg was severed above the knee. Gross, right? Not exactly. There was no blood, no shattered bone, no gore. Jutting from the injury was a tangle of damaged metal, not unlike what I'd seen with the crushed spider near the flume. Any doubt I had before was gone. It was official. The dados were robots.

And he wasn't done. The guy pulled off the remains of his shattered leg, threw it away, and got up. . . . 12 . . . 11 . . . 10 . . .

Robot or no, there was no way he'd catch me on one leg, so I bolted for the door. The cylinders were flying up and down randomly. I ran, dodged, stopped, jumped, and wove my way toward the door, barely skirting the pumping cylinders. An inch one way or the other and I'd have been hamburger. The clock ticked down to five seconds. I waited for the last cylinder between me and the door to retract . . . and leaped into the rectangle of light.

I hit a revolving door like the one I had come through on the far side. The door spun; I fell through and landed, still in one piece. I stayed on my knees for a second, trying to catch my breath and stop my heart from racing. I didn't even look up for fear I had landed in another game.

"Bravo, Challenger Red!" came a familiar voice.

Yet another voice said harshly, "You nearly failed."

The first voice scoffed and said, "I never doubted him!"

I took a deep breath and looked to see what I now had to deal with. I was in another large, narrow room, though much smaller than the last. It was brightly lit by daylight streaming in through overhead windows. Yellow and purple flags lined the walls near the high ceiling. On the ground was a long wooden table surrounded by high-backed wooden chairs. It was a medieval-looking banquet hall, complete with huge tapestries on the walls that depicted competitors playing various games. The table was loaded with silver platters full of food and tall silver tankards with drink.

Seated on either end of the long table, kicking back and casually sipping drinks, were Veego and LaBerge.

Veego looked at me coolly and said, "You took much longer than others with fewer qualifications."

LaBerge was quick to say, "Don't listen to her! You were stupendous! Let me be the first to say that you are now officially a challenger." He held up a silver goblet as a toast.

"And what if I'd failed your test?" I asked.

LaBerge looked down at his plate. Veego smiled and said, "You'd be dead of course. Now please, join us. I'm sure you've built up a healthy appetite."

She was wrong. Whatever appetite I'd had was long gone.

QVILLAN

I was ticked. I think that nearly getting crunched would make anybody a little testy. I jumped to my feet and strode for LaBerge. I would have gone for Veego, but she gave me the creeps. The guy saw me coming and his eyes grew wide. He plunked down his goblet, splashing green liquid across the table, and pushed himself back into his chair.

"Don't be foolish!" he said nervously. "The test is over! You passed!"

I grabbed the guy by the front of his robe and pulled him up to me. I don't normally do stuff like that. It's way too bold for me. But after having just barely escaped being turned into paste by those cylinders, I had had enough. If I had any hope of controlling my own future here, I needed to show some backbone. Besides, I knew this wheezy LaBerge guy wouldn't fight back.

"Look," I seethed. "I am not a challenger, and I will not play your sadistic games." I stared him right in the eye to show how serious I was. The guy kept glancing away and licking his lips. Wimp.

"I understand your f-feelings, dear boy," he stuttered. "But I'm afraid you don't have a choice."

As if on cue, two dados appeared from behind his chair. They loomed over me, staring me down with those dead eyes. I had officially been out-intimidated. LaBerge gave me a smug smile. I let him go and backed away. No way I was messing with those robo dudes. Even if I wasn't exhausted, two-on-one wasn't fair. I'm not so sure one-on-one was fair either.

"What do you mean I don't have a choice?" I asked, trying to sound like I was still being aggressive, which I wasn't.

Veego stood and walked toward the dados. "Leave," she commanded.

They obeyed instantly. The two robots took a few stiff steps backward, but stayed within striking distance.

"I said leave!" Veego said more forcefully. "This is our guest. There won't be any more trouble."

The dados backed away and left through a doorway, though I was pretty sure they were standing right outside, waiting to see if there really was going to be any more trouble or not. Sneaky robots. Note to self: No more macho stuff in front of the dados.

Veego stood by LaBerge, but didn't look at him as she spat out with disdain, "Get hold of yourself, ninny."

I got the feeling that Veego didn't think much of LaBerge either. They looked about the same age, but she treated the guy like an annoying little son. Though my mom never talked to me like that. Then again, I wasn't annoying. Usually. LaBerge straightened his robe and took a drink of the green stuff that was left in his goblet, trying to calm his nerves. Veego, on the other hand, was all sorts of calm. I had the feeling that if I had gone after her instead of LaBerge, she would have stayed just as cool. Veego worried me.

"I'm getting too old for this," LaBerge grumbled.

"You can go home anytime you wish," Veego shot back.

Interesting. These guys may have been partners, but they didn't exactly get along. I had to remember that. I figured it might come in useful.

Veego smiled at me, though it looked like it might make her face crack. "You must forgive us," she said. "We know you are not from the city of Rune, or you would know of us and our enterprise."

"That's just silly," LaBerge chirped in. "Everyone knows who we are, no matter where they're from."

"I don't," I said flatly.

LaBerge snapped a look at me. I didn't know if it was disbelief, or if he was hurt that I didn't know who he was.

"Where *are* you from?" he asked.

Uh-oh. Not a good time to start telling the truth. But I didn't know enough about Quillan to make something up. "You kidnapped me, stuck me in a room full of creepy clown dolls, then threw me into some game that nearly got me killed. I think it's my turn to ask some questions."

LaBerge shot a questioning look to Veego. She didn't flinch. He looked back to me and said, "You are very, very wrong, Challenger Red. Those dolls aren't creepy at all!"

"Oh, be quiet!" Veego snapped at him. "If he doesn't understand why he's here, then it will benefit us all to explain." She gestured to the long banquet table and said, "Please, join us. We will answer all your questions."

I was torn. I needed to know who these two were and what their connection to Saint Dane was, but on the other hand, they had a hand in killing the Traveler from Quillan. Part of me wanted to grab them and throw them both into the monstrous piston room I had just come through. But that wouldn't get me any closer to Saint Dane. I needed to suck it up and play it their way.

"All right," I said. "Where should I sit?"

"In the place of honor of course!" LaBerge said happily, as if we were suddenly buddies. "It's where all the new challengers sit when they first arrive!" He gestured to a high-backed chair that was at the center of the table. I walked over to the chair, glared at LaBerge, then sat in another chair that was closer to the end. I don't know why I did that. Probably just to annoy the guy. He stood there for a second, sniffed, then walked quickly back to his chair at one end of the table.

"Suit yourself!" he said in a huff.

As soon as I sat down, a servant appeared as if from nowhere. It was the same small bald guy in white with the two-tone tie who had shown me to my room. He placed a silver plate and some utensils down in front of me.

"Thanks, Fourteen," I said.

LaBerge chuckled and said, "That's Thirteen."

I looked at the bald servant. He looked exactly like Fourteen. Either he was a twin or . . .

"Is he a dado?" I asked Veego.

Veego took her place at the other end of the table.

"They are quite useful, don't you think?" Veego answered. "They always do what they are told and—"

"And they don't ask questions," LaBerge said with a smug smirk.

I decided to let it go. I still hadn't gotten my mind around the fact that Quillan was loaded with lifelike robots. From what I had seen so far, they were used as servants and policemen. And spiders. Don't forget the spiders.

"Are any of the challengers dados?" I asked.

LaBerge burst out laughing. Even Veego chuckled. I was glad I was amusing them.

"Of course not!" LaBerge said. "Where would our reputations be if we pitted programmable dados against each other? There's no challenge in that, or drama."

"So you two stage the Tato matches?" I asked.

"Among others," Veego said. "Tato is one of our more popular contests. But there are so many unique games. The most popular on Quillan, if I may be so boastful. No others put on games that are as entertaining, and successful, as ours. You'll see."

I didn't want to see.

"I invent the games," LaBerge said proudly. "All of them. Big and small."

He reached into his robe and pulled out a small handheld toy. It looked like the wooden handle of a jump rope, with a button on one end. He held it upright and pressed the button. Instantly there was a whistling *tweeee* sound and a spinning red propeller flew up and out of the end of the handle. It rose into the air for about five feet, then ran out of energy and gently fluttered back down. LaBerge watched it intently, then expertly caught it in the hollow end of the launcher, where it settled back with a *click*. He looked at me and smiled like a proud kid who had just accomplished the impossible.

"Don't you just love playing Runkle?" he asked.

"Never heard of it," I said flatly.

LaBerge's eyes went wide. "How can you not know Runkle?" he shouted. "Every child on Quillan has a Runkle!"

"Sorry, must have missed it," I said.

LaBerge dropped the toy on the table and took a drink from his goblet. "You are an odd one, Challenger Red," he said, pouting.

"Ignore him," Veego said to me. "He may seem like a

buffoon, but he is quite brilliant. One must have a bit of the child in them to concoct such unique games."

"Unique games where people get killed," I added, staring right at Veego.

She stared back at me and said, "We provide a service. We didn't create the demand."

We held eye contact for a moment. Man, she was cold.

"If he comes up with the games, what's your job?" I asked.

"I'm the more practical side of this partnership," she said. "Where LaBerge imagines the games, I make them real. Part of that is to find able contestants, which is why you are here, Challenger Red."

"So it was your idea to bring me here?" I asked.

Before she could answer, three more identical servant dados entered with trays of food. They placed the trays in front of each of us and backed away. I saw fruit and slices of meat and some orange gnarly-looking vegetables that could have been squash, or carrots, or potatoes, or anything else. LaBerge picked up one of these twisted veggies from his plate, took a big crunchy bite, and said haughtily, "I, on the other hand, *love* tribbun."

That answered *that* question. The thought crossed my mind that this food might be poisoned, but I had to eat. I needed to keep up my strength and there was no telling when I'd get another chance. Besides, I figured if they wanted me to compete in their games, they weren't going to kill me. At least not yet. I took a bite of the tribbun, and I'm surprised to say that it was actually pretty good. It was crunchy like a carrot, but had the sweet flavor of a melon. Actually, all the food was pretty good. I didn't realize how hungry I was until I started eating. I emptied my plate quickly, and Fourteen was right there to heap on more food. Or maybe it was Thirteen. Or Twelve. Sheesh.

"You see?" Veego said. "Challengers are treated very well."

"Until they have to die," I said.

"You keep saying that!" LaBerge shouted. "Don't you understand? We offer you a better life! You know what it is like out there. It's a harsh, miserable existence. Here, the challengers are pampered and fed like they never could be on the outside. Here you have music and art and servants at your disposal. Can you imagine how wonderful that is? And yes, all right, every so often we ask that you compete in our games. And there is some risk. But is that so much to ask in return for living the life of a king?"

"Well . . . yes," I said. "I told you, I'm not playing your games."

LaBerge smacked his hand on the table and shouted, "You will!"

"Sit down!" Veego barked.

"He is making me very upset!" LaBerge yelled back at her.

"Get used to it," I said cockily.

LaBerge shot me an angry look. Before he could say anything, a door opened on the far side of the room. I glanced up, expecting to see Twelve, or Thirteen or Fifteen-and-a-Half or whatever, or possibly another dado cop charging in to see what all the shouting was about. It was none of these. Hurrying in with an armload of papers was a young woman. She was wearing an outfit similar to Veego's. It was deep blue, with long pants and sleeves, and a jacket of the same color that came to her waist. Her clothes weren't all that different from what the people wore outside in the city, but looked a bit more stylish. Or better made. Or something. Maybe it was the way they fit her, like the outfit was perfectly tailored. Yes, that's the best way I can describe the outfit, and the woman, for that matter. Perfectly tailored. There wasn't a wrinkle in sight. She had straight brown hair that was combed and parted on the side, and fell to just below her ears. Not one hair was out of place. She was pretty, too. Her eyes were big and brown and, I'm not quite sure how else to describe this, but they were . . . alive. Unlike most of the other people I had seen out there in the city of Rune, this woman looked like she had some spark. If I were to guess, I'd say she was a couple of years older than me. Maybe eighteen? Or nineteen? I'm not even sure how old I am anymore! She entered the room and walked quickly toward us. She seemed to be on a mission.

"Veego, LaBerge," she said in a quick, professional way. "Good afternoon. I have the budget estimates from the trustees."

She walked quickly past LaBerge without giving him a second look. This woman was all business. She didn't have time for that goof. She didn't notice me, either. She went right to the brains of the operation. Veego. She stood over the woman and held out the stack of white pages.

"I trust these will meet with your approval," she said.

Wow, how stiff could you get? Veego looked up at her for a long moment without speaking. The woman looked kind of awkward standing there because Veego didn't take the pages.

"Can't you see we are in the middle of our meal?" Veego finally said. She may have sounded calm, but her voice was cold. "You come into my home, unannounced, uninvited, and proceed to annoy us with your personal concerns. Have you no manners?"

The woman blinked. Her efficient, professional appearance was shaken. "I—I apologize," she said nervously. "I was told that getting these to you was triple important. I should have known you were—"

Veego grabbed the papers out of her hand. "Oh, be quiet!" she spat at the woman. Veego looked through the pages, and the woman backed away.

"Don't move!" Veego ordered.

The woman froze. I felt sorry for her. She was totally intimidated. I can't say that I blamed her. While Veego scanned the pages and LaBerge played with his Runkle toy, the woman stood there, looking uncomfortable. I watched as her eyes wandered around the room. When she finally saw me, she gasped and jumped back with such surprise you'd think I had shouted "Boo!"

Veego didn't look up from the papers as she said, "Miss Winter, this is our new Challenger Red. Challenger Red, this is Nevva Winter."

Nevva Winter. Interesting name. She opened her mouth as if to say something to me, but no words came out. That was weird. I knew the term "speechless," but had never actually seen it happen.

"Hi," I said.

She didn't say anything. She didn't close her mouth either.

LaBerge said in a singsong voice, "Nevva, Nevva, works all day, but doesn't have the time to play."

"Close your mouth, Miss Winter," Veego said without looking at her.

Nevva Winter blinked. Seeing me had really thrown her for some reason. "I—I knew that the new challenger was due, but I didn't expect it to be so soon," she said, trying to put her efficient face back on. "In fact, he's mentioned on page four of the file I brought and—"

Veego tossed the pages into the air.

"Unacceptable," she declared.

The pages fluttered to the floor, spreading everywhere. LaBerge laughed and clapped. Idiot. Nevva Winter tried to catch the floating pages but only managed to grab a few before they hit the ground.

"Please, Veego!" she implored. "They're in a specific order—"

"We have increased profits by twenty percent for each of the last seventeen quads," Veego hissed through clenched teeth. "Those are unheard-of numbers, and if your panel of ignorant keepers doesn't recognize that, LaBerge and I would be all too happy to return home and let any of our substandard competitors take on the challenge of following in our immensely successful footsteps."

Nevva Winter quickly scooped up the pages and pushed them together, trying not to wrinkle them. It looked like she was trying to put them in order at the same time.

"Yes!" LaBerge added. "Let's see how their precious profits look without us!"

"That appears to be a possibility," Nevva Winter said.

"Huh?" LaBerge grunted in surprise.

While Nevva Winter gathered the papers, she said, "Maintaining this operation has proven to be very costly. I'm afraid that the trustees are trying to find some way to justify continuing their relationship with you."

"What?" LaBerge shouted in horror. His bravura was gone. "They're going to throw us out of our castle?"

Veego slowly got to her feet and stood over Nevva Winter.

"Was that a threat, Miss Winter?" she said in about as cold a tone as I'd ever heard.

Nevva Winter shoved the last paper onto the stack and got to her feet. She was so nervous she wouldn't even look Veego in the eye. "I'm only telling you what the trustees have been discussing," Miss Winter said, her voice cracking. "I'm only their assistant. I don't make policy. But I can tell you that for every trustee who supports you, another thinks you should be doing better."

"That's impossible!" LaBerge shouted. "How can we do better than perfect?"

Nevva Winter looked right at Veego for the first time. Though she was knee-knocking-nervous, she didn't blink. "I'm only passing along the information," she said. "Perhaps you should talk to the trustees yourself."

Veego stared at her for a moment, then backed away and walked toward me. "This gaming operation has been run longer and more successfully than any other on Quillan," she said. It seemed like she was holding back anger. "That's because I know what I'm doing. I have the experience, I have the resources, I have the games, and most of all, I know talent. I would very much like to meet with the trustees. Maybe then I can ask them why they have decided to interfere by telling me who to use in my competitions."

"They aren't trying to interfere——," Nevva Winter said.

"But they are!" Veego shot back. "The trustees want the games to be competitive, yet they force me to use challengers who are unprepared. You saw the last Tato match. It was a travesty. Challenger Yellow was no match for Challenger Green. He wasn't ready, yet the trustees forced me to use him!"

Challenger Yellow. She was talking about the Traveler from Quillan . . . a guy I never met and still didn't know the name of. I fought back the urge to jump up and scream, "Why did you kill a Traveler?" But that wouldn't have helped anything. I bit my lip, grabbed the chair, and did all I could to keep from exploding. That got even tougher when Veego put her hand on my shoulder. My skin crawled.

"And now they've sent me a new challenger," she said. "Challenger Red. Did you know he was almost killed in our Hook gauntlet? Hmmm? He nearly failed the simplest of tests. Children have done better. Now your trustees expect me to stage the next Grand X with him?"

She was getting worked up. So was I. What was the Grand

X? More importantly, how did these trustee people know about me? Who were they?

"Please tell your oh-so-wise employers something," Veego continued. "I will not damage our reputation by presenting an inferior product."

"No one is asking you to—"

"If they want me to play Challenger Red, I will. But he must first prove himself in a more challenging test." She nodded to LaBerge.

LaBerge clapped his hands together like a giddy child and ran to the side wall of the banquet room, where a giant tapestry hung. He grabbed a velvet rope that dangled from the ceiling and turned back to me, saying, "You should be honored. Challengers don't usually enter the Tock arena until much later in their training."

I looked to Veego and asked, "What is this?"

Veego returned to her place at the head of the table. "You have come highly praised for your abilities, Challenger Red," she said. "I, for one, have yet to see why."

"Who praised me?" I asked.

Veego didn't answer. She didn't have to. I was pretty sure of the answer. I smelled Saint Dane in this mess.

"Veego, please, this isn't necessary," Nevva Winter said nervously. "Challenger Red will be given adequate time to prepare for the Grand X."

"Who will guarantee me that?" Veego snarled at her. "You? I'm sorry, but I don't believe you and I don't believe the trustees. I'm left with no choice. He will either prove himself worthy right here and now, or die trying."

Uh-oh.

LaBerge yanked on the velvet rope. The tapestry pulled up toward the ceiling like a retracting window shade. Behind it, a large entryway was revealed, beyond which was another playing arena. Standing in the center of the arena were three guys wearing different color jerseys. Challengers Blue, White and Black. They each held long metal rods about seven feet long. Weapons. I was about to play another game, and this time I wasn't going to be up against a mindless dado.

"Please, Veego, " Nevva Winter begged. "This is totally irregular."

"What if I don't want to play?" I asked.

"Nothing would make me happier," Veego said. "It would prove to the trustees that you are unworthy, and you would be executed."

Oh.

"And what happens if I play and lose?" I asked.

Veego smiled and said, "That would also make me happy, because the situation would be resolved."

"You don't want to lose at Tock," Nevva Winter cautioned me.

That sounded ominous. I was beginning to think that making Veego happy meant making me dead. Not a lot of choices. Like I wrote to you guys before, on Quillan you play. You win, or you pay.

It looked like Challenger Red was about to make his debut.

QUILLAN

"I thought I passed the test," I said to Veego. "Why are you putting me through this?"

"Because I don't like being told how to run my business," Veego answered with a snarl. "I don't know why the trustees are forcing me to use you in the competitions. Their meddling will be the ruin of my games."

"And mine!" LaBerge threw in.

"So you want me to get beaten before I can ruin your games?" I asked. "Is that it?"

"Perhaps," Veego said. "Then again, I'm not one to miss an opportunity. If it turns out that you actually have some ability, this little diversion will start to build some excitement around you."

"Uhhh . . . what does that mean?" I asked.

"If you're going to compete, I want the betting to be strong. That won't happen unless the people love you . . . or hate you."

"So how are you going to do that?" I asked.

Veego gave me one of her icy smiles and gestured for me to enter the arena. "Let's find out."

"Veego," Nevva Winter protested. "This game hasn't been scheduled. It goes against every protocol I can think of that—"

"Then stop thinking, Miss Winter," Veego said coldly.

A million questions flashed through my head. Who were the trustees? I guessed that in some way they were the bosses of Veego and LaBerge, but what kind of business were they running that had to do with these deadly games? Whatever it was, Saint Dane was somehow involved. He had to be. Who else would know about me?

The answer to that mystery was going to have to wait. I first had to survive this latest challenge that Veego was throwing at me.

"This way, Challenger Red," LaBerge said while gesturing into the arena.

I thought about running away, but the two dados that suddenly appeared behind me ended that idea. I was trapped. I stood up from my chair and walked toward the arena entrance. Nevva Winter stood with her arms folded tightly in front of her. She seemed genuinely nervous about what was going to happen. Join the club. I wasn't sure if she was worried about me, or about what her bosses would say if something bad happened to me.

I stopped right in front of her and asked, "Can you stop this?"

Her gaze darted around like she didn't want to make eye contact. "I—I'm sorry," she said. "I didn't mean for this to happen."

"Yeah, tell me about it," I said. "You owe me."

What the heck? I thought I'd throw a little guilt on her. If she hadn't shown up, I probably wouldn't have been headed for another showdown. Maybe if she felt responsible, I might be able to get help from her later. If there *was* a later for me, that is.

"This is so exciting!" LaBerge squealed. The guy really was annoying.

As I walked, I tried to subtly stretch my muscles. I had no idea what to expect inside that arena, but I needed to be ready. I stepped through the portal into what looked like a big gym. It was at least a couple of times larger than the double-gym back at Davis Gregory High, so that made it about the size of four basketball courts. The black floor felt like firm rubber that sprang back a little when pressed. Looking up, I saw that the ceiling soared up many stories. There looked to be a jumble of apparatus up there that would probably be lowered when needed, just like in a gym. High up on one wall I saw a big black screen that was very much like the screens on top of the buildings out in the city. But this screen didn't show any images or geometric patterns. Instead there was a slew of brightly colored numbers in vertical columns. I had no idea what any of it meant, other than the two words that were above the columns of numbers: CHALLENGER RED.

"What's all that?" I asked Veego.

"That shows us how the wagering is running for the match," she answered. "With some contests, challengers compete against each other and wagers can be placed on either. With Tock, wagers are placed on a single challenger to either win or lose."

"You mean all the people out there are going to bet on me?" I asked, stunned.

"No," she said.

That was a relief.

"Most will be wagering *against* you."

Oh. Great.

The three other challengers stood inside a large circle marked on the floor; it looked to be about twenty yards in diameter. The challengers were spaced evenly apart from one another and about five yards inside the edge of the circle. Each stood in a square outline on the floor, holding one of those long metal weapons. Halfway between each challenger was a pedestal that rose about five feet in the air. On each was a purple and yellow flag. These pedestals and the challengers formed a circle within a circle.

"So how does this game work?" I asked Veego.

"Very simple!" LaBerge answered. He bounded into the circle of challengers. In the very center of the ring was another circle on the floor. This one was about three feet in diameter. LaBerge jumped inside this tiny circle and said, "You begin here, in the dead center. When the counter starts—" He looked up to the wall opposite the betting scoreboard, where I saw another, smaller screen. On cue, the number "120" appeared. "You'll have a hundred and twenty clicks to gather each of the flags and return them here to the center. Couldn't be simpler!" To demonstrate, he ran to one of the pedestals, grabbed a flag, and ran back to the center circle.

He was right. It couldn't be simpler. But I didn't think for a second that it was going to be that easy. The three challengers with the weapons pretty much confirmed that. I didn't think they were there as cheerleaders. Blue, White, and Black. There was nothing unique about them, though they did look to be in pretty good shape. They all seemed to be roughly my age, maybe a little older. There was nothing about them that screamed out: "Highly trained, awesome competitor." That was good. Maybe this would be a level playing field after all. Or playing court. Or gym. Or whatever the heck it was.

The one thing that stood out about them was their attitude. The three of them stood straight, like soldiers, looking straight ahead, showing no emotion. These guys definitely had their game faces on.

"What about them?" I asked.

LaBerge lifted his hand into the air and said, "The challengers are what make Tock interesting."

Yeah, I figured that.

While LaBerge stood with his hand in the air, I saw something being lowered from the ceiling. There were three large silver balls on the ends of ropes. Each was about the size of a beach ball and they were tied together. The cluster descended toward LaBerge, who reached up and untied them. Instantly the balls swung free. The ropes they dangled from seemed positioned roughly above the outline of the circle, so the balls swung outward. All three swung right toward a challenger. They each put their metal weapons down on the ground and grabbed the ball that came their way.

"They will try to stop you, of course," LaBerge explained. "They will swing the Tock rocks to try and knock you off balance. I should warn you, they're heavy. Getting hit . . . hurts."

Big surprise.

"Of course, the other challengers aren't allowed to step outside their squares," LaBerge said. "That wouldn't be fair.

"Wouldn't want to be unfair," I said sarcastically.

As I looked at the setup, I had a feeling of déjà vu. This game looked somehow familiar, but I couldn't remember why. There was no way I had seen anything like this on Second Earth, but still, I felt as if I'd seen it before. I didn't spend much time wondering about it. I had other things to sweat about. Getting hit with a swinging ball didn't seem like that big of a deal though. Even if I got knocked down a few times, the worst that would happen is I'd be black and blue. It would be like playing dodgeball at home, only the balls would be a little harder and I had to be better at dodging. How bad could it be?

LaBerge explained exactly how bad it could be.

"Oh, one other teensy little thing," he said. "It would be in your best interest to gather the flags quickly. For after sixty clicks . . ." He made a gesture to nobody in particular. All three challengers let go of the silver balls and let them swing free. Good thing because a moment later I heard a sharp sound, like a knife being sharpened. Or three knives. My stomach dropped when I saw that the silver balls had changed. A ring appeared around each one that made it look like the planet Saturn. The ring stood out from its orb by about six inches all the way around. "Razor sharp," LaBerge explained. I then heard a steady *hummm* sound. The circular blades began to spin. The Tock rocks had transformed into buzz saws. "Quite effective for cutting off limbs . . . and other body parts."

Gulp.

LaBerge continued, "Once the blades appear, the challengers use those metal rods to control the Tock rocks. Wouldn't want them to lose an arm. This game isn't about them; it's about you."

"You're a sick guy, you know that?" I said to LaBerge.

He chuckled. "The blades make for an interesting contest."

Interesting contest? I could think of a few other words to describe it. LaBerge made another gesture. The blades stopped spinning and retracted into the silver balls. The three challengers each retrieved one and they went back to their positions. I wondered who was controlling all this apparatus. Probably some behind-the-scenes dados.

"So what happens if I duck these things for the full time and don't get all the flags?" I asked.

Veego walked up next to me and said, "You'll start over, only the second time around, the blades will be out from the start. You'll keep playing until you get all the flags . . . or bleed to death."

I hated Quillan.

Glancing back, I saw Nevva Winter standing in the entrance to this gym-from-hell. She gave me a slight helpless shrug. It looked as if she genuinely felt sorry for me. Not that it did me a lot of good.

"Let's begin!" Veego announced.

She cleared her throat and strode to the center of the ring. LaBerge quickly returned the flag to its pedestal and joined her. With a wave of her hand, the lights went out. We were in pitch darkness. Music blasted from unseen speakers. It was the same kind of upbeat thumping music I'd heard before they played the Tato match. The show had begun. A moment later multicolored strobe lights swept the arena. The other challengers didn't move. They kept looking straight ahead. Sixty ticks. That's when the blades would come out. I needed to get those flags in sixty clicks of that clock. How long was a click? A second? Two seconds? A half second? Whatever it was, after sixty of them I'd be deli meat.

A spotlight hit Veego and LaBerge.

"Click click click . . . ," LaBerge sang. "It's time to make your pick. Eyes on the clock, watch for the rock, it's time to play some Tock!"

His rhymes were getting old.

"Good evening to the citizens here in Rune and across all of Quillan," Veego announced like a circus ringmaster. "Tonight we present you with a unique event. A new challenger has joined us, and has requested that he be given the chance to compete in the games immediately."

Liar.

"LaBerge and I are only too happy to accommodate him, and bring the contest to you in this special presentation! We have high hopes for this challenger, though as of yet he is untested. Will he survive the dangers of Tock? Or is he simply another pretender who will fall to the blades?"

Man, she really knew how to sell it. Or sell me.

"Of course, wagering on an unknown is a risk, but if the new challenger succeeds in gathering all the flags, a full wager will provide you with enough nutrition to feed you *and* another citizen of your choice for the unheard-of time span of four quads!"

What? These people were gambling for food? How long was a quad? A day? A week? A year? The time frame didn't matter as much as the payoff. How bad were things on Quillan if people had to gamble for food?

"Of course," LaBerge added, "you don't have to make a full wager. Perhaps you think the challenger will retrieve only one flag. Or two. Or run out of time and need to try a second time. Or perhaps you feel he will lose an arm! There are so many ways to wager, but you must hurry because the match will soon begin."

This was just wrong.

"Introducing," Veego said, "for the first time in the city of Rune, or anywhere else on Quillan, our new competitor. Will he last? Will he fail? Will he move on to become a force to be cheered? Or die here before his career begins?"

Good questions.

"It is my pleasure," Veego said, raising her voice, "to present to you, the new . . . *Challenger Red*!"

The music pumped hotter as I was hit with a spotlight. I

had all I could do not to shield my eyes from the light. That would have made me look like an idiot. Not that I should have cared. It was an odd feeling. I didn't see the cameras, but I assumed that our images were being transmitted all over Quillan, just like the match that killed the Traveler from Quillan. But here in this lonely gym there were no crowds. There was no cheering. There was music, but that was about it. I wondered if Saint Dane was watching.

I walked slowly into the ring, toward Veego and LaBerge. The numbers on the overhead scoreboard started flashing. It looked like a computer screen, with numbers rising and falling quickly. I had no idea how the betting was going. Did people get a look at me and think I had a chance? Or did they think I was pitiful and would soon be swimming in my own blood? Truth be told, I didn't care what anybody thought. I wasn't fighting for food, I was fighting for survival. Veego and LaBerge glanced up at the flashing numbers. They frowned and gave each other knowing looks.

"What?" I asked.

"You're not inspiring confidence," Veego answered. "The betting is running twenty to one against you."

Great. Everybody thought I would soon be hamburger.

"Good luck," Veego said, and strode off.

"Have fun with it," LaBerge said, and clapped me on the shoulder.

Fun? You say that to somebody before a basketball game, not a date with three swinging guillotines. LaBerge hopped out of the ring. I was left alone. The strobe lights kept flashing and the spotlights swept the floor. It was unnerving. Every time I got hit with a light, I was momentarily blinded.

"When do the lights stop?" I asked.

"They don't!" LaBerge called back. "It's all part of the fun."

Right. More fun.

Above me the numbers on the board continued to move. I didn't know how long they were going to wait until closing the betting. I took the time to look around and formulate a strategy. An idea hit me that seemed too good to be true. I looked up and judged how far those killer pendulum balls would swing outside the circle, and guesstimated that it wouldn't be all that far. Nobody told me I couldn't leave the circle. I figured that all I had to do was run outside beyond the swing of those balls, then duck back inside to grab each flag. Could it be that easy?

No, it couldn't. A second after I formulated this plan, I heard a slow, steady *hummmm* sound. The wide circle we were standing in wasn't a painted line on the floor after all. It was the top edge of a metal cage! The cage rose up out of the floor until it became a circular steel curtain all around us. No wonder they didn't bother telling me I couldn't leave the circle.

"Anything else you haven't told me?" I called out.

"No, that's about it." LaBerge chuckled. "Are you ready?"

"No," I shouted back.

The numbers on the overhead board froze and flashed red.

"The wagering is complete," Veego announced. "The Tock match will now begin!"

The strobes and spotlights flashed faster and brighter. I looked around, trying to figure out where the other challengers were. I saw them standing in their squares, holding their lethal silver pendulums, ready to pummel me.

LaBerge shouted out: "Four . . . three . . . two . . . one . . . TOCK!"

A horn sounded. The number started clicking down from 120. I had no way of knowing how much time I had before it hit 60 and I'd start losing blood. Or body parts. I dove to the ground in the general direction of one of the pedestals. I did a somersault, bounced back to my feet, lunged at the flag . . . and got knocked into next week. One of the silver balls hit me like a speeding car. LaBerge had understated it. This didn't hurt, this was just . . . brutal. The ball hit me so hard in the side, I feared it broke a rib. Or three. The shot knocked me off my feet so fast and so hard that I rolled into the steel cage, slamming it almost as violently as the ball had slammed me. It was a good thing the ball hadn't hit me in the head.

I lay at the base of the steel cage, trying to get some air back into my lungs. I was in a spot where the steel balls couldn't reach. That was good. But the clock was ticking down. Fast. Lying there wasn't an option. Looking out, all three challengers had their Tock balls at the ready, waiting for me to make a move. I quickly rolled toward the closest pedestal, but a challenger expertly swung his ball out on an arc. It rounded the pedestal just as I stood up to grab the flag. I almost didn't see it because of the flashing strobes, but at the last second I sensed a shadow sailing for my head and I hit the ground. I felt the air move as the ball whistled over my head, barely missing me. I quickly stood up, thinking I'd have a few seconds in between shots. I was wrong. A second ball swung at me from the other direction. It hit me square on the spine, snapping my head back and sending me sprawling. All I could do was log-roll back to the base of the steel cage.

I was already hurting and the match had barely started. Those challengers were absolute experts in aiming those pendulums. I didn't stand a chance. A quick look up showed that the clock had already ticked down to 105. I knew that if I didn't come up with some kind of plan, I'd be done.

It's amazing how clear my thinking becomes in times of intense stress. It's happened to me before. I don't know if it's adrenaline or fear or blood flow or whatever. But when the pressure is at its worst, I think the most clearly. It also helps that in situations like this there's no time to debate options. It's about going with instinct. That ability has saved my life many times. I looked at the challengers who were ready to bean me again. I looked at the clock. I looked at the whole arena. The answer came to me. I knew how to beat the game. At least, I knew what my only chance was. I wished I had thought of it sooner. When the blades came out spinning, my plan would be done. There wasn't time to question it. I had to go with my gut.

I crawled back for the pedestal with the flag, knowing that a silver ball would soon come sailing my way. The only question was, from where? This time I didn't focus on the pedestal, I focused on the Tock balls. Sure enough, I saw a deadly shadow sailing my way. I quickly judged the direction it was coming from and the speed it was traveling. Timing would be everything. Just as the ball was about to hit me, rather than ducking out of the way, I took a quick step back . . . and grabbed the ball. I had to hold on for all I was worth, because the thing was heavy and moving fast. But I would not be denied. The ball pulled me across the floor, dragging my feet. I needed to control it and keep it away from the other challengers. I didn't try to stop the ball so much as change its trajectory by pushing my feet off the floor.

I looked up at the clock: 74 . . . 73 . . .

I got control of the ball just as another ball came swinging toward me. I ducked and it flew past. I grabbed hold of the large Tock rock and looked for the nearest flag. I didn't swing the ball at the flag or at the other challengers. I ran with it and launched myself into the air like I was on a tire swing. The ball swung out, lifting me into the air moving directly toward the flag. I reached out and grabbed it as I swung by. Yes! I had one.

The clock was down to 70. Ten clicks to go. The momentum of my swing brought me up past the pedestal. I reached the end of the arc, and my feet hit the metal cage. I bent my knees, glanced back to see where another flag was, and pushed off in the direction of my next target. I straddled the rope and sat on the steel ball. I leaned out, desperate to control the arc and continue on toward the next flag as . . . *clang!*

Another ball hit my ball from behind, rattling my teeth. It nearly knocked me off, too. I managed to stay on, but I was nowhere near another flag. I had to stop, quickly jump off, aim myself, and sprint forward while holding the rope and the first flag. I dodged one more swinging ball and launched forward, rising back into the air. I had to hold the rope and the flag with one hand and reach out as far as possible, but I grabbed the second flag—67 . . . 66 . . . 65 . . .

The other challengers picked up their metal rods in anticipation of the blades whining to life. I swung past the pedestal and spun around, looking for the last flag. I sat on the ball with my legs dangling down . . . right where the blade would appear in a matter of seconds. I hoped that LaBerge was accurate about when they would come out. If they came out early . . .

When I reached the top of the arc and started back down, I realized that I was not headed in the right direction. No amount of pulling or weight shifting was going to get me there. There wasn't enough time for me to make another swing either. . . . 63 . . . 62 . . .

I swung down toward the center of the circle, along with the other two Tock rocks. I instinctively realized there was going to be a three-way collision, with me in the middle of it! The only thing I could do was bail. I flipped off the swinging ball seconds before the three collided. I hit the floor and tuck-rolled in what I hoped was the direction of the final flag . . . 60.

An instant before the balls crashed, I heard the piercing sound of the razor blades spinning to life. The three balls collided. The blades smashed into one another first, sending a shower of sparks and torn metal everywhere. I saw one of the challengers duck in fear. All around me bits of twisted metal from the splintered blades whizzed by. But I was not about to stop. I rolled one more time, misjudged where I was, and slammed into something hard. Ouch. But the pain was a small price to pay, for I realized I had smashed into the pedestal that held the third flag. I leaped up, grabbed the final flag, then crawled all the way back toward the center of the circle. The Tock rocks were swinging free. No way the other challengers were going to try to control them, even with the metal rods. They bounced off one another, headed in random directions with pieces of broken blade flying around like mad bees. I kept low, hoping I didn't get this far only to be stabbed by a random piece of hot metal.

When I reached the center, I slammed all three flags into the circle. A loud horn sounded and the lights of the arena came on. The strobe lights stopped flashing, the music ended. The whizzing sound of the spinning broken blades stopped, and the Tock rocks retracted back into the ceiling. Finally, the steel cage that had trapped me in this little circle of hell sank back into the floor. It was over. I lay there exhausted, the winner. Or maybe I should say, the survivor. My cheek was on the ground, right next to a big chunk of shattered blade that was stuck into the floor. I was beat, though I think it was more about coming down from the adrenaline rush than about being tired from the physical exertion. I couldn't even feel the bruises. That would come once I calmed down. I got up on my elbow and looked around to see blade splinters everywhere, along with one of the Tock rocks that had been severed from its rope.

The scoreboard flashed with red letters saying: WINNER—CHALLENGER RED! I liked the idea that a few daring people had bet on me and they'd be able to have food for a while. At least that would give some meaning to this whole idiotic event. The other challengers were okay, though Challenger White had a gash on his arm and was bleeding. I assumed that came from a flying chunk of blade. The guy stood up, and for the first time he looked at me. I expected to get the cold, hard stare of an injured enemy who was looking forward to a rematch. That's not what I got. Instead the guy nodded. It was a slight gesture, but I felt the acknowledgment that we were both in the same tough situation. Looking at the other two as they walked away, I saw them give me the same nod. Up until then I'd thought of them as nameless enemies whose job it was to beat me, which by the rules of that game meant they were supposed to kill me. I didn't think of them as anything more human that robot dados. What I realized at that moment was that we were all challengers, and all in the same boat. They probably didn't want to be fighting any more than I did.

The first person who came to me, I was surprised to see, was Nevva Winter. She ran into the circle and knelt down in front of me.

"Are you all right?" she asked, sounding concerned yet relieved.

"Sure," I said. "You still owe me."

"Yes, I do," she said. "But I knew you'd win."

"You did?" I asked. "How's that?"

Nevva Winter took a quick look to see that LaBerge and Veego weren't paying attention to us. The two were in some kind of heated discussion about . . . who cares. She reached up to her chest and put her hand between the buttons of her shirt.

"Because I expected nothing less . . ."

She pulled out a dark beaded necklace that hung around her neck, hidden by the shirt. Dangling from it was a ring.

"From the lead Traveler."

It was a Traveler ring.

QUILLAN

Things were happening a little too fast. I hadn't even caught my breath after having nearly been sliced into sushi, when Nevva Winter revealed to me that she had a Traveler ring. Seeing it gave me such a jolt, I think my brain momentarily froze. What was the deal? Had she taken it from Challenger Yellow after he died in the Tato match? I figured she must have, because how else would she have gotten it? Unless maybe it was her own ring, and she was the Traveler's acolyte. Or could it be that Challenger Yellow was an acolyte, and Nevva Winter was the Traveler from Quillan? Or maybe it was none of the above. Remember what I wrote before about how great I was at handling myself under pressure? Forget it. I was stunned into a semicoma.

Luckily, Nevva Winter was cooler than I was. She looked over her shoulder to see that Veego and LaBerge were headed our way. "Meet me later, in the octagon," she whispered.

"The what?" I asked in confusion. I must have sounded like an idiot, because at that moment, I was an idiot.

"Congratulations!" LaBerge said. "No other challenger in the history of Tock was able to figure out how to beat the game so quickly. And believe me, dozens have tried. We've lost many a challenger to the blades. Bravo!"

He tried to help me to my feet, but I yanked my arm away. Veego joined us and stood looking at me with her arms folded, appraising me with that superior little smirk.

"What?" I asked angrily. "Wasn't I good enough for you?"

"Oh, no," she said. "I am quite impressed. Apparently you have had some training. We don't often get challengers with that much . . . experience."

"Gee, wow," I said sarcastically. "My day is complete."

Veego kept her eyes on me but spoke to Nevva. "Miss Winter, please inform the trustees that I intend to meet their increased profit demands this quad. And be sure to thank them for bringing such a talented challenger to our attention. Challenger Red is going to become a valuable member of the Blok family."

Blok. There was that name again.

"Thank you, Veego," Nevva said politely. "I'm sure the trustees will be very pleased to hear of your enthusiasm." She held out the stack of pages that she'd brought in earlier and said, "Now, if you would be so kind as to initial these pages I'll file them with the—"

"Don't push it," Veego snapped harshly. "Unless you'd like to try your luck at a game of Tock yourself."

Nevva stiffened, cleared her throat, and pulled the papers back. "Thank you, no, " she said formally. "I'll report back to the trustees right away."

"You do that," Veego said as if she couldn't care less.

"Thank you for your time, and for the, uh, demonstration," Nevva Winter added.

"The pleasure was all ours!" LaBerge chirped.

Nevva Winter looked at me and said, "Congratulations, Challenger Red. I will be following your career with great interest." She looked directly at me and opened her eyes a touch wider. It was a subtle signal that acknowledged that we would talk later. She pulled the pile of papers in tight and strode quickly for the exit. I can't tell you how badly I wanted to go with her, no matter where she was going. Any place would have been better than the castle. I was at the mercy of two sadistic psychopaths who got their kicks from making up games where people died. I needed somebody on my side. I needed help.

"Are you done torturing me?" I asked Veego, trying to sound as tired as I felt. "If I've got to play another one of your stupid games, you might as well just kill me now."

"We would do no such thing! Not now!" Veego said cheerily. At least it sounded like she was being cheery. I couldn't tell with her. "Your value has just increased dramatically. Another few matches like that and you *will* be ready to compete in the Grand X!"

"What exactly is a Grand X?" I asked. I didn't care anymore if I didn't sound like I came from that territory. I was too burned out to care about anything except lying down and getting some rest.

Veego and LaBerge gave each other a surprised look. I guess pretty much everybody knew about the Grand X. Everybody but me, that is.

"You're tired," LaBerge said. "Let Fourteen take you to your room."

"No!" I snapped. "I'm not sleeping in that clown room again."

"You don't have to," Veego said. "As we told you, the challengers are treated like royalty during their stay with us. Now that you've proven your value, you will be put in much more suitable accommodations."

"I *like* the clown room!" LaBerge said, sounding hurt.

"Then *you* sleep in it," I said. I saw that Fourteen was standing at the entrance to the arena. I walked away from Veego and LaBerge without saying another word and went right up to the dado. "Are you sure you're Fourteen?" I asked. "You wouldn't really be Thirteen and trying to mess with me, would you?"

Fourteen didn't crack a smile. Robots didn't have much of a sense of humor. "C'mon, robo boy," I said. "Let's get out of here." I walked past him, out of the gym, and back into the banquet hall.

"Get some rest!" LaBerge called. "Big day tomorrow! It will be the best day ever!"

I ignored him. As I passed the banquet table, I grabbed a few of those tribbun things. Who knew when I would eat again? I crunched them down quickly. Fourteen caught up with me and led me on a twisting route through the castle. I could see through the windows that night had fallen. That was good. I needed sleep in the worst way. We climbed the stairs back to the second story, but didn't head toward the corridor with the clown room, I'm happy to report.

"Isn't that where the challengers stay?" I asked.

Fourteen spoke in a monotone voice, though it wasn't as low and gravelly as the dado cops. Fourteen sounded more human. "Only when they first arrive," he answered. "As their value increases, they are given more comfortable accommodations."

I'm calling Fourteen "he." Can a robot actually be a he? Or a she? He looked like a he, but it was a machine. The question didn't bother me enough to want to go the next step and ask to check his parts. Machine or not, that wouldn't have been cool.

"What about Challenger Yellow?" I asked. "Did you know him?"

"I did," Fourteen answered.

"What was his deal?" I asked, hoping to find some clue as to why both he and I ended up as challengers. I figured the answer might point me toward Saint Dane.

"His deal?" Fourteen asked.

"Yeah, how did he end up here? As a challenger, I mean."

"I am not involved with the decisions that are made concerning the challengers," he answered. "I have to believe that he came here the same way all the challengers do."

"And how's that?" I asked. "Did he get an invitation?"

"I do not understand that question. An invitation implies there is some choice. None of the challengers are here by choice. I do not believe that anyone would accept an invitation to play the games."

Except for me of course. But I didn't feel like explaining that to him.

"None of the challengers are here because they want to be?" I asked. "LaBerge and Veego said it's a great life. Better than on the outside."

Fourteen looked at me blankly. Of course, it was probably the only look he had. "I am but a dado," he answered. "I do not have the same concerns as you. But I do not believe a citizen would choose to be here, no matter how comfortable it may be, knowing the high price for that comfort."

"I know, it's dangerous. But some do well, right?" I asked. "I mean, aren't there champions that hang around for a while and then, I don't know, retire or something?"

Fourteen stopped walking. I think that was his way of showing confusion, dado style. "I regret to inform you of this, Challenger Red," he said. "Challengers die. They all die. The only question is how long it can be avoided. This is your room."

He stopped in front of a door that already had the sign CHALLENGER RED on it. I stood there, letting his last comment sink in.

"They all die?" I finally asked. "Every last one?"

Fourteen didn't answer. He didn't have to.

"Good night, Challenger Red," he said. "I hope you have a restful evening."

Restful evening? After having a death sentence dropped on you? Nighty night! Sleep tight! Yeah, right.

"Oh, hey, do you know where the octagon is?" I asked.

"Yes. It is a small garden across the courtyard from the front entrance to the castle," he answered.

Wow, that was easy.

"Thanks," I said. "Good night." I started to open the door when—

"Remudi," Fourteen said.

"Huh?" I said, thinking I didn't understand him.

"Remudi," Fourteen repeated. "I believe that was the given name of Challenger Yellow."

Remudi. The name meant nothing and everything to me.

"He appeared to be a talented combatant," Fourteen added. "Yet he was oddly gentle. I cannot say that of all the challengers."

I nodded. I knew what he meant. There were a few other Travelers who fit that description.

"Remudi," I repeated out loud. I had a name for the face.

Fourteen added, "I do not know many of the challengers' given names. We are instructed to call them by their titles. But he was somehow different. Much like . . . you."

The robot sensed that there was something different about us. About the Travelers. I was beginning to think that this dado dude actually had some feelings. Was that possible? I mean, aren't robots dispassionate machines? Like walking toasters? At least that's the way it worked in sci-fi stories. I couldn't know for sure, because before coming to Quillan I hadn't run into any real robots.

"Did you like Remudi?" I asked.

"Like is not something I am familiar with, though I understand it," he said. "I regret that he died."

"What happened to his body?" I asked.

"He was cremated," Fourteen said. "The ashes were scattered. That is always the way it is done."

I nodded. Another Traveler turned to ashes.

"If you need anything, no matter what, touch the call light inside your door," Fourteen said. "I am assigned to you and will make your stay here as comfortable as I possibly can. Would you like me to bring you food, or drink?"

"No, I'm fine," I said. "I just want to sleep."

"Very well. Good night, Challenger Red."

"Pendragon," I said. "My name is Pendragon."

"Pendragon," Fourteen echoed, as if trying it on for size. He nodded and left.

I was about to enter the room, when I stopped and took a look around. The corridor was wide, with large windows that looked out onto a starry sky. Thick ornate carpets ran the length of the hall, with various sculptures and elaborate lamps lining both walls. It was strange. I was being held captive. If I followed in the footsteps of the other challengers, I would die. This place may have looked like a fancy hotel, but it was death row. Yet my door wasn't locked. I had to believe that if I tried to leave the castle, I'd have a couple of dados on my butt firing their nasty little golden tranquilizer guns, but could I go wherever I wanted inside? As badly as I wanted to lie down and sleep for a week, my job wasn't to be a good little challenger and rest up so I could put on a good show for the zookeepers. My job was to find Saint Dane. To do that, I first needed to find Nevva Winter.

I watched as Fourteen walked to the end of the long corridor and disappeared around a corner. I actually liked that bald little robot guy. Mostly because he said some nice things about the Traveler Remudi. But he also treated me like a human instead of a commodity. Still, he worked for Veego and LaBerge. I didn't want to trust him and have it come back to bite me in the butt.

I walked in the opposite direction from the one Fourteen was going. The idea was to find my way down to the courtyard without running into one of those dado goons. Or a Veego or LaBerge goon, for that matter. I quietly crept along the dimly lit hallway, tuned for any sign of life.

I turned down another corridor and heard faint far-off sounds. I stopped and listened for a moment, and was surprised to realize that what I was hearing sounded like a party. It was muffled, but I definitely heard music. People were talking loudly and laughing. Not that a party is all that strange, but in this twisted death-house castle, the idea of people partying it up didn't compute. I followed the sound. It grew louder as I got closer. It was definitely a party. I figured it was probably LaBerge getting crazy, which for him wouldn't be a big stretch. Though I didn't want to know what kind of people that guy would party with. Probably clowns. Who else would hang with that loser? The thought made my skin crawl.

I approached an open doorway and cautiously took a peek inside. It wasn't LaBerge and a bunch of clowns, I'm happy to say. It was a full-fledged, raucous party of . . . challengers. The room looked to be a dining hall. It had long wooden tables and heavy padded chairs. There were plants and paintings and lamps that cast a warm, pleasant glow to the place. The table was heaped with food and drink. It was a feast! Servant dados scurried around, making sure that plates stayed loaded with steaming delicacies and that tankards remained filled with drink. All the servants looked exactly like Fourteen. You'd think they would at least have them wear numbers to tell them apart.

None of what I just described was as interesting as the challengers themselves. There were about twenty of them, all young, all in great shape. They weren't all guys, either. There were just as many girls. I knew they were challengers because most wore their striped jerseys. But many had the jerseys off and wore T-shirts of the same color. They were laughing and telling stories, and clapping one another on the back and talking too loud and basically having a great time. One guy took a goblet of something and dumped it on the head of another guy. Everybody cheered and whooped like it was a frat party.

The music came from a band that was set up in the far corner. It was made up of more Fourteen clones. Dados. They played a weird tune that was kind of like rock, but had a haunting, loopy undertone. Their instruments were electronic keyboards. The band stood up and played like a regular house band, but it looked like they were standing at computers. Even the drum guy was on a computer. He was good, too. They played a dance tune with a driving beat. They may have been robots, but they could play! Yes, there was dancing. It didn't look like any couples were together, it was more like a mosh of gyrating, sweating bodies. They were having a blast.

I didn't get it at first. How could these guys be partying like high school kids when they were in such a bad way? I even recognized the three guys who'd tried to behead me in that gruesome game of Tock. They were dancing and shouting like everybody else. The only sign that they were any worse for wear was the blood stain on the sleeve of Challenger White.

One of the challengers leaped off the dance floor, jumped up onto the table, and held up a goblet, shouting, "To Mr. Pop!"

Everyone screamed in approval, raising their goblets and toasting. A chant started: "Pop, Pop, Pop, Pop . . ." They stomped on the tables and clapped their hands. The chanting reached a crescendo, everyone cheered, and the party continued.

Mr. Pop. Who was he? To the challengers he was obviously some kind of hero. Was he a challenger himself? No, that couldn't be, because he wasn't here, he was out in the city somewhere, hidden. The people who rescued me from the police dados were trying to protect him. The idea that I might have led the dados to Mr. Pop's secret hiding place was horrifying to them. Whoever he was, he was being protected by people who weren't on the same side as the dados, which meant they weren't on the same side as Veego and LaBerge and this mysterious Blok that was run by a group of trustees. Confused? Yeah, me too. I really hoped that Nevva Winter would clear things up . . . right after she cleared up who the heck she was. Sheesh.

As I stood there watching the fun, the party began to make sense. These guys were under a death sentence. None of them knew how much longer they'd be around. My guess was that they needed to relieve some of the stress and enjoy what little time they had left. It felt like a victory party. Maybe they were rejoicing in the fact that three challengers made it back alive from the Tock game. Four if you counted me. On the other hand, there wasn't a whole lot of grieving going on because a challenger *had* just died. Challenger Yellow. Remudi. Maybe it was because he wasn't around long enough for anybody to get to know him. Or maybe it was because they were so used to death, grieving wasn't a part of the equation.

Veego and LaBerge said the challengers were treated like royalty. Judging from this party, they definitely were given the chance to have some fun. These guys were taking advantage of every second of life they had, for none of them knew how long they had left.

I wasn't in the mood for partying. I had other business. I was about to move on, when something caught my eye. A lone challenger sat at the table. He wasn't dancing, he wasn't laughing or telling stories. He sat alone at the end of the table . . . looking at me. He was the only one in the room who even knew I was there.

I caught my breath. Why did I know this guy? It took only a second to remember. Challenger Green. The champion. The record breaker. The guy who killed Remudi. Challenger Green stared at me and lifted his goblet, as if in a toast for my eyes only. In that moment it all came clear to me. I was being set up. Whatever the Grand X was, if it was as big a deal as they said it was, it would have to involve their champion. Challenger Green. If I was going to be part of it, it meant I would be competing against this guy. He was the all-time doo-da big cheese that nobody could beat. How could I possibly stand a chance against him?

I guess I should have been scared, but you know what? I wasn't. Just the opposite. The realization actually gave me a feeling of hope. I was going to go up against the guy who killed a Traveler. I would get the chance to avenge his death. I gave the guy a small salute. He drank from his goblet, and I continued on. I knew we would be seeing each other again.

As I made my way cautiously down toward the courtyard, I found that the castle was strangely empty. Once I left the blowout challenger party, everything became eerily quiet. I wondered where Veego and LaBerge lived, but wasn't curious enough to try to find out. It was tough enough finding my way through the dozens of twisted corridors and intersections to make it down to the courtyard. It was slow going, because I didn't want to risk being caught. Finding Nevva was too important. So I kept to the shadows and tried to be quiet.

Finally, after twenty minutes of wrong turns and dead ends, I found a side door that led outside to the courtyard. The next part was tricky. I got my bearings by looking out on the wide space and finding the front door, where I had first entered the castle. Looking directly across from that door, I saw a wide archway that seemed to lead into a small garden. According to Fourteen that was the octagon. The trick was to get across the wide open space without being seen. I stayed along one wall, moving quickly, holding my breath. I'm not sure why I held my breath. It didn't make me invisible. It just seemed like the thing to do. Thirty seconds later I ducked through the archway and into the octagon.

It was a pretty garden that was ringed by, you guessed it, an eight-sided wall. Three of the sections were the outer walls of the castle. The other five were built out from the castle and rose up too high to think about climbing over. It was maybe thirty yards across in all directions . . . big enough to hide in the trees and bushes. There were lots of flowers, a brook, small flowering trees, and some stone benches. It was the kind of place where you'd see old people hanging out to feed the ducks. The sky was full of stars that were so bright they provided plenty of light to see all this. I wondered briefly if one of them might be Second Earth. I had a quick feeling of homesickness, and forced myself to change gears. I didn't need to be feeling sorry for myself right then.

Nevva said to meet her there "later." When was later? An hour? Three hours? A quad? A click? I found a small bench nestled between two flowering bushes, and settled in for I didn't know how long to wait for her.

"Hello, Pendragon," came a voice. "Thank you for coming so quickly."

I whipped around to see Nevva standing behind the bench. Phew. "Later" meant now. Good thing. I didn't like the idea of sitting on a hard bench for long. I was too beat.

"I can't stay long," she said. "I wouldn't know how to explain to Veego and LaBerge why I'm still here."

Nevva came across as somebody who was überefficient and buttoned up. I wouldn't be surprised if she had "to do" lists. I was never like that. I'm more of a "wing it" kind of guy.

"You are everything Press said you would be," she said.

"You knew my uncle?" I asked. It still surprised me to hear how Uncle Press had covered all the territories before I even knew I was a Traveler. Man, I missed him.

"Of course," Nevva answered. "He came to Quillan a long time ago to tell me of my true destiny, and to give me this." She pulled out the ring that dangled from her dark beaded necklace. When she spoke it was quickly and precisely. She seemed to know exactly what was going on. I, on the other hand, was floundering.

"Your true destiny," I repeated. "What exactly *is* your true destiny? Who are you?"

"I'm the Traveler from Quillan of course," she said as if she didn't understand how I didn't know that.

I stared at her for a long moment. I think my brain went back into the deep-freeze again. Nevva was the Traveler from Quillan. Then who was Remudi? Here I was looking for answers, and everything she said only led to more questions.

She continued, "I've been receiving journals from acolytes all over Halla, detailing your encounters with Saint Dane."

"Acolytes send you journals?" I asked dumbly, trying to keep my head above water and make sense of all this.

"Yes," she said. "Many share information, though I have

yet to hear from your acolytes, Mark Dimond and Courtney Chetwynde."

"I don't think they know they're supposed to be writing," I said.

Are you guys writing journals? Are you communicating with other acolytes? I have no idea.

"I haven't chosen an acolyte myself yet," she said. "I simply haven't had time. In fact, I may not choose one. I can operate more efficiently on my own."

"Whoa, wait wait, slow down," I said. "If you're the Traveler from Quillan, wasn't Remudi your acolyte? He had a ring, didn't he?"

Nevva frowned. "That should never have happened. I tried to stop him from competing, but I have no power. You saw how Veego and LaBerge treat me. I am only an assistant to the trustees. Remudi was a brave and talented soldier, but he wasn't ready to compete. I'm heartsick that we've lost another Traveler. Perhaps if he'd had more time . . ."

"What?" I shouted. "You just said that *you're* the Traveler from Quillan! Was Remudi the Traveler before you?"

"No," Nevva snapped. She sounded irked that I didn't know the whole story, but she softened quickly. I think she finally realized that there was no way I could know the whole story. "I'm sorry," she said. "I thought you knew."

"Knew *what*?" I insisted.

"Remudi was the Traveler from Ibara," she said.

For the third time that day I stared at Nevva Winter as my brain left to go on vacation somewhere. She had just dumped a truckload of information on me that I wasn't even close to expecting.

"Ibara?" I croaked. "That's another territory?"

"Well, of course," Nevva said with surprise. It was if I had just said, "United States? Is that a country?"

"How did a Traveler from another territory end up here on Quillan?" I asked. "No, how did a Traveler from another territory end up *dead* here on Quillan?"

Before Nevva could answer, we heard a car pull into the courtyard. Nevva grabbed me and pulled me down into the bushes.

"Remudi is the least of it," she whispered hurriedly. "There is so much to tell. You need to see it all. Quickly."

Yeah, no kidding.

"Who is Mr. Pop?" I asked. I couldn't get the questions out fast enough. "And who are the trustees? And what is Blok?"

I heard voices coming from the courtyard. It sounded like Veego. She was barking orders to somebody.

"Tomorrow," she said. "You will learn it all tomorrow. That's why I needed to see you tonight, to give you this." She handed me a small silver clip that looked like a thick staple.

"And this is . . . ?"

"A blocking diode," she explained. "Keep it with you, but don't let anyone know you have it. And don't use it unless it's absolutely necessary. You can only use it once. After that they'll know you have it."

"O . . . kay," I said skeptically. "It would help a little if I knew what it did."

"Clip it onto your loop," she said. "It blocks the signal. They won't be able to track you."

Oh. Cool.

"I'd rather just take the loop off," I said.

"No," she said. "They'll know if it's off."

"How come you don't have one?" I asked.

"Because I don't wager," she answered. "And I'm not a challenger."

I heard the sound of dado voices outside. More were arriving.

"I have to go," Nevva said. "Don't lose that; it might save your life."

She didn't have to tell me that twice. Nevva moved to leave, but I grabbed her arm.

"You can't leave!" I said. "I have to know what's going on! A Traveler is dead!"

"You will," she said. "It would take too long to explain now, and if I'm caught, two more might join him."

I couldn't argue with that.

"All right," I said with resignation. "Let's hope I don't get killed before then."

"You won't be," she said. "Just do as they say and you will be fine."

Nevva started away again, and I said, "Wait, you gotta tell me one thing. Have you found Saint Dane? Why did he leave these challenger clothes at the flume?"

"He didn't," Nevva said. "I did."

With that, she was gone.

QUILLAN

I know I've said this before, but I've never felt so alone. Another Traveler had died and I never even got the chance to meet him. Whatever the territory of Ibara was, it no longer had a Traveler. Unless, of course, there was somebody who was going to take Remudi's place, but I had no way of knowing that. I couldn't stress about it, because I had my hands full here on Quillan, and the one person who could help me make sense of it all, Nevva Winter, was beyond my reach because I was trapped inside that twisted castle and forced to play idiotic, deadly games.

Worse, it was Nevva who set me up to play these games in the first place by leaving challenger clothes for me at the flume! Why did she do that? I had assumed it was Saint Dane's doing because seeing me getting beat up was just the kind of thing he liked doing. But another Traveler? She was supposed to be on my side! Why did she put me in this spot? Could the answer be that she was an idiot? No, that didn't fly. If there was one thing I could tell about Nevva Winter, she was smart. And efficient. She wouldn't have made a dumb mistake like that. There was more to it than that. Nevva promised that my questions would be answered the next day. There was only one problem with that.

She didn't come back the next day. Or the day after that. I kept waiting for her to show up and get me the heck out of there, but she didn't. What was she doing? What had happened? It was making me nuts. I was still as much in the dark about how Quillan worked as when I arrived, and the one person who could help me understand, the Traveler from this territory, had abandoned me.

At least I can say that while I was stuck there, I was comfortable. Veego and LaBerge weren't kidding. I was treated like royalty. The food was great; my new room was big, comfy, and clown free; I had the run of the castle and even had a servant, Fourteen. He was always there to get me anything I wanted. Short of freedom, that is. Doesn't sound too horrible, does it?

Well, it was. I felt as though at any moment I'd get thrown into another one of their wicked games. Like with that Hook game, I feared that whenever I turned a corner or walked by a closed door, I'd be rudely sucked in and my life would be on the line. It's not a good way to live. The challenger party I saw was making all sorts of sense to me. They were blowing off steam and believe me, no matter how sweet the place was, steam built up. It was like being on death row, not knowing when the executioner would come knocking at your door.

I guess it shouldn't have felt all that odd to me. In many ways it was exactly how I'd been living my life for nearly three years. Ever since I left home with Uncle Press, I've had to live with the fact that any moment might be my last. Usually there's so much going on that I don't think about it, which is a good thing. I'd have gone out of my mind long ago.

But hanging around that castle, bored, wondering where Nevva was, and waiting for something to happen—man, it was slowly driving me insane. Bored and scared aren't a good combination. When you're bored, your mind wanders. I ended up worrying about things that I normally try not to stress about. I guess on the top of the list was the constant question of how I ended up here. I'm not talking about Quillan. I mean the whole Traveler gig in general. Why me? How come I was the lucky one who got to be the lead Traveler and match wits with Saint Dane? I'm not proud to admit this, but lately when my mind goes there, I get angry. Where before I'd been confused, frustrated, and scared, I now had to add anger to that list. I'm not even sure who to be angry at, which makes me even angrier! Who put me in this spot? Uncle Press? He definitely started me on the journey, but was it his choice to make me the lead Traveler? Or was he just following orders? That's the big question. Who started this whole thing? Gunny's theory is that there's some big cheese out there who selected the Travelers and is running the show. I guess that's possible, but I have no idea who it might be or how it could work.

I've wondered about all this for a long time, of course, but like I said, lately the thought has been making me mad. Sure, I know that stopping Saint Dane is huge. There's no question. But who the hell is he? How did he get those powers? Where is he from? Since it's my job to stop him, I think I deserve some answers. Right? Am I being unreasonable? I put my life in danger every day, but nobody has explained any of these things to me. I think that's just wrong, and it's starting to piss me off.

What if I decided to give up? I could do it, you know. I could jump into the flume, head home to Second Earth, and never look back. I could start a new life. I've learned enough about getting along to do that. What would happen if I did? If I'm really as important as everybody seems to think, then maybe I'd force somebody's hand so they'd have to step up and give me some answers. I've thought a lot about doing that. I'm beginning to think that maybe it's time to start playing a little hardball and force the issue.

Those are the kinds of thoughts that bounced around in my head while I was hanging out in that castle waiting for . . . something. The more I thought about them, the more worked up I would get, and I'd have to calm myself down and focus on reality. As much as I'd like to, I can't go home. Saint Dane cannot be left to do whatever he wants, no matter how unfair it is to me or how angry I get. The only thing I can do is not let it get to me. Being angry doesn't help. It only makes me feel bad. I have to put those feelings aside, now and forever. That was the way it was meant to be, whether I like it or not.

Thanks for letting me vent, by the way.

To keep my mind off things while I waited for Nevva to come back, I spent a lot of time working out. That's a great way to burn off energy . . . and anger. I'd go for runs through the dense forest around the castle. A few times I got as far as the high wall that surrounded the place. But whenever I got too close, a couple of those goon dados would appear from out of nowhere and stare at me as if to say, "Don't even think about it, red boy."

The castle had a pretty cool gym, too. I worked out with free-weights and did stretching and even worked out on a couple of odd machines where the base moved and rubber arms swung at you. It was a device to help build agility and reflexes. It was fun, once I got the hang of it and stopped getting thwacked in the head, that is. I was in pretty good shape too, I'm proud to say. The training that Loor and Alder gave me on Zadaa had stuck. No, better, I built on it. I don't mean to sound cocky, but I was getting pretty confident in my abilities as a warrior. That sounds so weird to say. Warrior. I'm still Bobby, and if I had the choice, I'd never raise a weapon again. But I know as long as I am a Traveler, I have to. Given that, I was pretty confident that I could handle myself in most any situation. Though it was kind of chilling to realize the reason they had all this gym stuff was to keep the challengers in peak physical condition, so they could put on a good show while trying to kill one another. That kind of took the edge off the "fun" part.

I tried to meet the other challengers, but that wasn't easy. They mostly kept to themselves. I'd pass one in the corridor of the castle and try to start a conversation, but they would just nod and keep moving. I guess you'd call it a polite blow off. I asked Fourteen about it. He came for a run with me one day, and I took the opportunity to pump him for some information.

"I don't get the other challengers," I said.

"What do you mean?" Fourteen said. It bugged me that he wasn't short of breath, even after running for a couple of miles. I was pushing it, getting my heart rate up and building a sweat. Fourteen cruised along calmly like he wasn't being stressed at all. Which he wasn't. He was a robot. Duh. Still, it bugged me.

"We're all in this together," I said. "You'd think they'd like to open up a little bit, I mean, if only to complain."

"I cannot say for sure," Fourteen said. "But from what I have heard, they do not wish to know their opponents. They fear it would be difficult if they entered into a friendship with someone they might have to kill."

Oh. I guess that made sense. It was scary, but made sense.

"Where do most of them come from?" I asked. "From the city? What's it called? Rune?"

"Some do," Fourteen answered. "But Veego spreads her net wide in looking for worthy competitors."

"How does she get them to come here if they know it means death?" I asked.

"They do not have a choice," Fourteen said. "Once a candidate is found, dados are sent to retrieve them."

"Retrieve," I repeated. "Like cattle being rounded up for slaughter."

"I do not know what that means," Fourteen said.

"Doesn't matter," I said quickly. "So they come here and train and get chosen for events and as long as they win, they stay alive."

"That describes it," Fourteen said. "We try to make them as comfortable as possible during their final days."

"And what do the challengers get in return?" I asked. "Besides death?"

"Their families are paid a handsome sum when they win," Fourteen answered.

"And if they lose?"

Fourteen hesitated, then he said softly, "Their families are given the ashes."

Life on Quillan was turning out to be cruel.

"So what about the party?" I asked. "If the challengers don't hang out with one another, what about the party I saw the other night?"

"That is an exception," the dado answered. "After a competition there is always a celebration. Like a reward. It is the one time that the challengers socialize with one another, though they never discuss the games. They talk about their former lives and their homes and families, but never about the games. For that very short time they allow themselves to be . . . how would you put it? Normal."

Normal. Yikes. There was nothing normal about how

these challengers were treated. They were expected to perform like trained dogs, put their lives on the line and for what? A couple of bucks for their families? And a party? How wrong is that? I was beginning to get the picture that Quillan was a pretty messed-up place. There were a lot of disturbing puzzle pieces flying around. I needed to start piecing them together.

My run with Fourteen ended up at the place called the "garden." It was on the far side of the wooded compound, surrounded by trees. We jogged into a clearing and I saw a familiar sight: the octagonal platform where the Tato match had been played. The match that killed Remudi. This was the "garden" the guy out in the street told me about.

It was a strangely forlorn place, mostly because nobody was there at the time. I stopped running and stepped onto the platform. It seemed big, but I'm sure it felt much smaller when it was towering high in the air. I tried to imagine what it would be like to be on this tilting platform, desperately trying to keep my balance. I glanced past the platform, wondering where Remudi might have fallen. I know this sounds weird, but even if I hadn't seen the match, I would have known that something tragic had happened to a Traveler there. I don't really know how to describe this; it felt just as weird to me as I'm sure it does to you reading it, but it was like I could sense the loss of life. I know, you're thinking I'm getting all cosmic on you, and maybe I am, but I swear, I felt as if a cold hand had grabbed my heart.

"Why did you bring me here?" I asked Fourteen.

"Forgive me," he said. "This is on the way to the field where a game is being played."

"Then let's go," I said, jumping off the platform. I didn't want to be there anymore and hoped I'd never have to set foot on it again.

The two of us jogged back into the woods, away from the octagon and the cold feeling of death that had settled over me. A few minutes later we came out of the woods to see a big playing field of grass. It could easily have been a football field or a soccer field. There was a game being played that involved not only challengers, but horses.

We quickly climbed up into a tower that was an observation platform. Looking down on the field, I saw two teams of four challengers on horseback. Each team had two girls and two guys. They weren't wearing their personal challenger shirts. Instead they had team colors. A white team and a black team. They still had the familiar diagonal stripes across the front, though. The playing field was about the size of a football field. There were large nets at either end that looked like goals. I saw pretty quickly what the point of the game was. Each of the riders had a long stick with a net on the end. They fought over a soccer-size red ball, trying to scoop it up. They would then pass it to a teammate to throw into the opposing team's net. It was like lacrosse on horseback. Sort of. There was more.

Each team had three more players, but they were on foot. They could run with the ball or kick it like a soccer ball. It was a dangerous position to play. I saw one guy get whacked with a stick. It wasn't an accident. He was running with the ball, and got clocked so hard he dropped the ball and landed on his head. If he hadn't rolled out of the way, he would have been trampled. That didn't look like an accident either. The guy who nearly ran him down was *trying* to get him.

"This is insane," I said to Fourteen.

"The challengers on foot are those who are less gifted," he said in his flat, monotone voice.

"The guys who still live near the clown room?" I asked.

"Yes," Fourteen answered. "They will never compete in the individual challenges. They are expendable."

"So it's okay in this game to run them down?" I asked in horror.

"It is encouraged," he answered. "LaBerge feels it adds to the excitement."

I glanced up above one of the goals to see a scoreboard flashing numbers. This was a game that was being broadcast throughout Quillan. It was hard to watch. Wondering who was going to score wasn't nearly as nail biting as wondering who was going to get hit, or trampled. I couldn't watch. The sounds of the pounding hooves often gave way to sick dull sounds of bodies being pummeled. It was absolutely barbaric . . . and strangely familiar. I felt as if I knew this game, but that made no sense because I definitely never saw anything like it. It was kind of like lacrosse and polo and soccer, but it felt more familiar than that.

I had no idea why, until I asked Fourteen, "What do they call this game?"

"It is called Wippen," he said.

Wippen! I *did* know this game! Wippen was a game they played on the territory of Eelong. The catlike klee would ride on zenzens, which I know you remember were horses with extra leg joints that made them tall and gangly. On foot were the poor gars, the humans, who often didn't survive a game. This was the exact same game that was played on Eelong, right down to the name! But how could that be?

"What do you know about Wippen?" I asked Fourteen. "I mean, is it a traditional game played on Quillan?"

"I do not know," he answered. "You would have to ask LaBerge. He designs the games."

The more I thought about it, the more it didn't make sense that it could be a total coincidence. Maybe it's possible that two games could be developed on two different territories that were exactly alike, but to both be called "Wippen"? That was too much. Yet another confusing twist had been thrown into the soup.

"I don't want to watch," I said to Fourteen, and climbed down the platform.

As we jogged back toward the castle, an idea came to me. "Hey, does this mean there will be a party tonight?" I asked.

"Yes," Fourteen said. "Would you like to attend?"

"Absolutely," I said.

This was going to be my first real chance to interact with the other challengers, other than trying to keep them from killing me in a game, that is. I didn't want to miss it. I ran back to my room, took a shower, and got dressed in a clean Challenger Red uniform. Fourteen brought me a delicious dinner of grilled meat, vegetables, and a tasty, buttery pile of fluff that reminded me of mashed potatoes but, I was told, was mashed tribbun. Who knew I would develop a taste for such an odd fruit? Or vegetable. Or potato? Whatever.

After eating, I lay down and closed my eyes to rest up and think about what to say to the challengers. I needed information about Quillan. It was the only way to piece together what Saint Dane's plan might be for the territory, because Nevva Winter wasn't helping much . . . or at all. I was beginning to worry that something had happened to her. I didn't know what her life was like here on Quillan, other than that she was some kind of lowly assistant to the trustees. Whoever they were. Veego and LaBerge answered to them, so they must have been a powerful bunch. I decided that I'd wait for her until the time came that I had to enter another match. No way I was going to die for the amusement of these losers. If I had to play again, I'd use the blocking diode that Nevva had given me and beat feet out of there.

As usual, all this thinking meant I didn't get much rest before Fourteen came for me. Oh well. As we walked down the corridor toward the party room, I found myself getting butterflies. I felt a little bit like I was going to my first mid-dle-school dance. Only I wasn't nervous about asking some-body to dance with me, I was more concerned about being accepted enough to start learning more about how Quillan worked.

By the time we arrived, the party was already jamming. It was even bigger and rowdier than the party I saw before. Fourteen must have sensed my surprise.

"Nobody died today," he told me. "That makes for a more festive event."

"Thanks, dude," I said. "Don't wait up."

With that, I stepped into the action. I wasn't sure how people would react to me, since I was pretty much a stranger. Turned out, I didn't have to worry. No sooner did I set foot in that room than I was greeted like a long-lost friend.

"Hey! How are you!" "Red!" "Good to see you!" "Whooo!"

It was like going to a party at Courtney's house. Guys were clapping me on the back, girls were hugging me, big smiles were all around. I was handed a silver goblet of that green drink that everybody liked so much. It tasted like warm Gatorade, but what the heck? I liked Gatorade. The same band of Fourteen clones was in the corner playing an upbeat tune. A girl pulled me onto the dance floor, and I was instantly in the middle of a mosh of jumping and bumping. At first I was a little thrown. I really hadn't planned on par-tying, but it was hard to resist. Soon I was dancing for the first time since that Winter Solstice dance back at Stony Brook Junior High. The only difference was that I didn't know any of the tunes. But it didn't matter. It may have been a bizarre situation, but it was fun.

I wasn't the only one given a big welcome either.

Everybody got the same reaction when they showed up. It was like a dam that was holding back all this pent-up emotion had been thrown wide open. In between parties everybody pretended not to know anybody else. But there, we were all best buds. I went with it. Why not? I deserved a little break too. The music was odd, but fun, and I liked to dance. At one point a full-on wet-down fight broke out where everybody threw the green drinks at everybody else. I got soaked and sticky, but didn't care. I had no idea who any of these people were, but in some strange way we were all connected. I tried not to think about how I might be dancing with somebody who I would be asked to fight to the death the next day. It made me understand why they normally avoided one another.

As great as it was, I had to force myself to remember that I wasn't there to have fun. I was on business. I wanted to find out more about these guys and the games of Quillan. I hoped to find out who the mysterious Mr. Pop was, and how he fit into the program. I needed to know everything. I approached a couple of challengers, said hi, and got the same big "Hey! How are you doing!" greeting. I was just as friendly back. But when I tried to get them to talk about themselves, or how they ended up getting captured to be challengers, I always got the same reaction. They gave me a sharp look and said, "Uh-uh." Some didn't even say that much. They just frowned, shook their heads, and moved on. Bottom line? Nobody wanted to talk about anything that was even close to serious.

Once I saw this, the party took on a creepy feeling. I realized that all of the happy greetings and friendly gestures had no basis in anything. Nobody truly knew anybody else there. All they knew was that they were all challengers, faced with the same troubles. I walked around the room and tried to eavesdrop on conversations. I quickly realized that it was all incredibly shallow. Nobody was saying anything that meant anything. It was an outpouring of positive emotion, but with nothing behind it. That's how they were able to welcome me like some long-lost friend. Nobody really knew anybody, but they all went through the motions as if they did. They were all kidding themselves into believing they were among friends. But they weren't. Just the opposite. They may have all been in the same boat, but it was a boat loaded with potential enemies. In order to have fun, they all had to pretend like they cared. That's why they didn't want to talk. If someone said something real, it would break the illusion.

It made me feel incredibly sad. What looked like a celebration was really a desperate attempt to pretend that all was well. I looked around at a sea of broad smiles and wild, laughing eyes. It could have been a scene from a blowout party on Second Earth. It wasn't. It was a funeral. I wanted to be out of there. I backed away and turned for the door, only to come face-to-face with someone I had almost forgotten about.

Challenger Green had arrived. The guy stood there, holding a green drink, staring at me. He didn't have the same wild party look on. He was more in control than that. He was big, too. Bigger than he looked on that screen during the Tato match. The guy stared at me with a knowing smile. It wasn't a broad, false party smile like everyone else wore either. He was like a hungry cat who had stumbled upon a timid mouse. This was the guy who killed a Traveler. I know, it was part of the games. Still, he had killed a Traveler. I wasn't about to put on a show, smile, and clap him on the back with a jovial, "Hey! How's it going!" All I did was stand there, and stare back at him.

"So you're the next big deal," he said.

It surprised me, because this guy actually said something that had relevance.

"That's what they tell me," I said. "It's not like I want to be."

Challenger Green smirked at that comment and said, "Do any of us want to be?" He gulped back his drink and wiped his mouth with his sleeve. His red hair was combed back from his forehead. His skin was pale and freckled. I saw that his hands were big. I'll bet he could palm a basketball, easy. Everything about him was intimidating. He was the main guy. If anybody could help me understand more about how the games worked, it would be him.

"Congratulations," I said. "Breaking that record must have been—"

"Shut up," he snarled.

It came out so fast and so harsh, I think I actually took a step back.

"Don't talk to me," he spat out. "Unless you want it to hurt when I kill you."

He pushed past me and strode into the party.

"Nice to meet you, too!" I said cheerily.

Yikes. The guy was intense. I didn't know if that was the way he was with everybody, or if he singled me out because I was the one being groomed to be in the Grand X. Either way, it was getting painfully clear that if Veego and LaBerge had their way, he and I would be going head-to-head in some game. I started to sweat. I was getting closer to my showdown with the champion, but no closer to finding Saint Dane. Something needed to happen, and it was beginning to look like I was the one who was going to have to make sure it did. I made a snap decision. It was time to take action. I decided to go back to my room, grab the blocking diode, and get the hell out of Dodge. But when I stepped out of the door, Fourteen was waiting for me.

"I'm going back to my room," I said as I walked past him, and strode quickly down the corridor.

Fourteen kept pace with me and said, "I was coming to get you anyway."

"Why?" I said. "I don't have a curfew, do I?"

"No," he answered. "But you need to get a good night's sleep. Tomorrow is going to be a very important day for you."

I didn't like the sound of that.

"Why?" I asked. "Do I have a competition?"

"No," he answered. "Miss Nevva Winter will be here early to bring you into the city."

My heart leaped. "What for?" I asked, trying to contain my emotion.

"You are going to be presented to the trustees of Blok," he announced with about as much fanfare and enthusiasm as a robot could muster, which wasn't much. "It is a very big honor. You must be at your best."

I stopped and looked at Fourteen. "Are you serious?" I asked. "Nevva is bringing me to meet the big bosses?"

"Yes," Fourteen said. "They must be expecting some very exciting things from you."

I laughed.

"Why is that funny?" he asked.

I said, "Because they have no idea how right they are."

The party was over. Or maybe it was just beginning.

QUILLAN

I had a restless night. You know that feeling where you can't get to sleep on Christmas Eve because you're so excited about all the great things that will be waiting for you in the morning?

It wasn't anything like that.

Except for the not being able to sleep part. I was excited, but it wasn't because I couldn't wait to see what amazing things Santa had dropped off for me. I was more worried about finding out what Saint Dane had been cooking up in his diabolical workshop. Everything that had happened since I landed on Quillan kept running through my head. Unfortunately, nothing I thought of got me any closer to figuring out what Saint Dane's plot was. The only hint I had that Saint Dane was even around was the original invitation he'd sent me through the flume from Veego and LaBerge. Though Saint Dane and I were enemies, he had never sent me on a wild-goose chase. Just the opposite. He *wanted* me to follow him. I suppose I should be grateful, but in truth it confused me. If Saint Dane's goal was to tip each territory toward chaos, why did he always let me know where he was headed next?

The only explanation I could come up with isn't a happy one. I've said this before, but with each new adventure I believe more and more that it's true. For Saint Dane it isn't only about tipping the territories toward chaos and ruling Halla. Yeah, I think that's his ultimate goal, but given all that's happened, I believe there's more to it. I think he wants to control Halla all right, but I think he also wants to beat the Travelers . . . and me. Why else would he always let me know where he's going next? He could easily sneak off to a territory and make it that much harder for me to track him. But he doesn't. It's like he wants to make a game out of it. Why is that? We've stopped him on five territories. Obviously we're up to the challenge. Yes, we've paid a steep price and lost many Travelers, but the bottom line is, we're winning. Still, things are never what they appear to be with Saint Dane. He sets the rules. All we can do is react. So even though we've stopped him five times, he's still calling the shots. It makes me wonder. Are we really winning? Or is everything that's happening just one small piece in some grand scheme of Saint Dane's? I want to be happy about our successes, but I can't help but think that in some way, he's playing us.

I have to believe that question will be answered in time, but it doesn't stop me from wondering. That's why I couldn't sleep. I was excited and scared. Excited that I wouldn't have to sit around anymore, and scared because, well, I guess that's obvious. Whatever was going to happen the next day, I had to believe it would bring me closer to Saint Dane.

I finally couldn't take it anymore and got out of bed just before the sun came up. I showered, put on a clean set of Challenger Red clothes, and found that Fourteen had brought breakfast and put it by my bed while I was getting dressed in the bathroom. It was nice of him, but it also kind of creeped me out, like he was watching me and knew exactly what I was doing at every minute.

"Tell me about Blok and the trustees," I asked my robot friend as I ate. "What is Blok? Is it the government? Do the trustees run the city? Or the country? What country is this anyway? Are there more trustees all over Quillan?"

Fourteen put his hand up, signaling for me to stop asking questions.

"We are instructed to see to your comfort," he answered. "And to not answer questions concerning anything that happens beyond the confines of this compound. I am sorry."

"Really?" I said, thinking fast. "But if you want me to be more comfortable, then you'll answer my questions."

Fourteen was in the middle of pouring me a cup of green stuff. He stopped and looked at me. I smiled innocently. For a second I thought my perfect logic had crossed his circuits enough to get him to give me some answers.

"I am a dado, Pendragon," he said. "Not an idiot."

I shrugged and said, "Oh, well, I tried."

Fourteen continued, "There are a few subjects that we are forbidden to discuss. One of them is Blok. If we were to engage the challengers with such talk, we would be taken off line and scrapped."

"Oh, sorry," I said. I took a chance and added, "Are you allowed to talk about Mr. Pop?"

Fourteen didn't respond. If was like he didn't even hear that question. I didn't press.

"When you are finished eating," he said, "I will escort you down to the courtyard. From there you will be taken into the city."

"Any idea what I should expect?" I asked.

I could swear his black eyes softened. I know, he's a

robot. I was probably imagining it. But I felt as if buried somewhere deep in those diodes, there was a heart beating.

"There is no need to worry, Pendragon," he said. "You are being taken to the trustees as a kind of . . . of . . ."

He was looking for the right words. I helped him out by saying, "Show and tell?"

"Yes," he said. "That sounds right. Veego and LaBerge want to show the trustees how valuable they believe you are. It is nothing more than that. You will not be asked to fight again until—"

"Until I come back here." I finished his sentence.

Fourteen nodded.

"Can you tell me what the Grand X is?" I asked.

"Yes," he replied. "As you know, there are games played all the time, but once every two quads there is a tournament that pits the best challengers against each other. It is watched by more citizens than any other contest, because it is always the most exciting and closely challenged."

"Sort of like the Super Bowl of Quillan games," I suggested.

Fourteen gave me a blank look.

"Sorry," I said. "You have no idea what that means."

He continued, "Challenger Green has triumphed at the previous three Grand X's, which has never happened before. Veego and LaBerge have been concerned that they might not find another challenger who has a chance of dethroning him—"

"Because if he always wins, nobody would wager against him," I said.

"That is correct," Fourteen said.

"So Veego and LaBerge want Challenger Green to lose?" I asked.

"I do not know," the robot answered. "But I do know that

it would increase the wagering if there was a chance that Challenger Green might lose."

"That's where I come in," I said with finality.

Fourteen nodded and backed away. "I'll wait for you in the corridor," he said.

Great. I was the guy who was supposed to give the champion a good fight. Did Veego and LaBerge want to dethrone the champion? Or was I supposed to put up a good fight, only to be beaten in the end, kind of like that phony basketball team that always plays the Harlem Globetrotters. And to make it all so perfectly obnoxious, it was a Traveler who put me in this spot! More than ever I wanted to talk to Nevva Winter. She had some explaining to do.

I finished breakfast and went into my bathroom, where I had hidden the blocking diode Nevva had given me. I had no idea if I would need it on this trip, but I couldn't take the chance. The loop on my arm may have been lightweight, but the idea of having something clamped on to my body that monitored my every movement made it feel heavier than it was. For the eight billionth time I tried to slip it off. For the eight billionth time it clamped tighter on to my arm as soon as I applied pressure. It seemed almost alive. I wanted to stick that blocking diode onto it right then, but that would have been stupid. I had to wait for the right time. I had hidden the diode inside an extra bar of soap in my bathroom. So long as nobody wandered in to take a shower, it was the safest and most secret place I could think of. I had to be careful taking it out, because I wasn't sure if I was being watched. So I pretended to wash my hands in the sink, while digging the small clip out of the soap. I casually stuck it in my back pocket, and headed out.

Fourteen was waiting outside my door. We walked quickly down to the ground floor and the front entrance of the castle. Waiting outside for me was a black car that looked exactly like the car that had brought me to the castle originally. I hoped Nevva Winter was inside.

Fourteen said, "Veego and LaBerge have gone ahead. You will meet them at the Blok building. The dados will escort you."

On cue, two police goons stepped out of the front seat and glared at me.

"You're not coming?" I asked Fourteen.

"We service dados do not leave the compound," Fourteen answered. "Do not worry, as long as you do as they say, you won't have trouble with the security dados."

Security dados. That's the first time I heard what those creeps were called. I took a breath and walked down the steps toward the car.

"I'll bring you back something special," I called back to Fourteen.

"Special?" he asked, confused.

"Never mind," I said. "It was a joke." I forgot, dados didn't get jokes. One of the security dados opened the back door for me and stood there, expecting me to get in. A quick glance inside showed me that Nevva wasn't there.

"How 'bout if I drive?" I asked the doll-faced robot.

He didn't react.

"Man, you've gotta lighten up," I said, and sat down in the car. I gave Fourteen a quick wave and saw him wave back an instant before the dado slammed the door on me. I didn't bother to try to see if it was locked. As much as I didn't want to be held prisoner by these sadistic monsters, I needed to be there. I wasn't going to try to escape. Yet.

We drove out of the courtyard, across the wooden bridge, and along the winding road that led through the forest. I had gotten to know the grounds pretty well on my runs. It was a vast green oasis in the center of the gray city. I'd even say it was beautiful, if it weren't for the fact that it was a staging area for games of death.

The elaborate golden gates that led to the city slowly swung open as the car approached. A moment later I once again found myself in the middle of the dark, depressing city of Rune. As we drove through the busy streets, I tried to memorize the route, but it was impossible. Every building looked like every other building. I didn't even see street signs.

"How the heck do you know where you're going?" I called to the dados up front.

They didn't answer. They didn't even turn around. Are you surprised?

"Hey!" I said. "Hit the radio. Let's have some music."

Still no reaction. I decided to stop trying to get a rise out of the security dados.

We drove for around twenty minutes. The only thing interesting to look at were the huge screens on top of the buildings. Each one showed the exact same thing, so it wasn't hard to keep shifting my look from one to the next. What I saw was pretty much the exact same thing as when I arrived. There were moving multicolored geometric shapes, occasionally broken up by a talking head blabbing about the weather or something else just as boring. I was beginning to realize how important the games were to the people of Quillan. From what I could tell, the games were their only source of entertainment.

After we made one last turn, I finally saw something that was out of the ordinary. The long, wide street ended at a building. It was a huge structure that was much bigger than any of the surrounding towers. The thing was massive and dark, as if it were carved from a huge black stone. I didn't have to ask the dado boys what it was. It was all too obvious. Near the top of the building, looming over the street, were shiny silver letters that had to be ten feet high. They reminded me of the silver signs that marked the various stores on street level. I'll give you one guess as to what it said.

Yeah, you're right.

BLOK.

I wasn't sure if I should be impressed, or scared, or excited that I was finally going to get some answers. The car zipped right up to the building and screeched to a stop. A wide set of stairs led up from the sidewalk to the huge front doors of this imposing building. I took a peek out my window and gazed up at the massive structure. Everything I guessed about this Blok thing made me believe that whatever it was, it held a lot of power here on Quillan. This building only confirmed that. Blok = power. Power = control over people's lives. Control over people's lives = Saint Dane. I was getting closer.

My eyes traveled down from the giant silver letters to the top of the stairs, where I saw a welcome sight. Nevva Winter. She stood there looking very efficient, with a clipboard of some kind in the crook of her arm. I had to believe she was waiting for me. At least I hoped she was.

"Now what?" I asked the dado dudes.

Without a word the guy on the passenger side got out of the car and opened my door. I pulled myself out and glanced up at Nevva. She didn't acknowledge me. Fine. I didn't acknowledge her, either. The sidewalks were busy with people, yet as crowded as they were, none walked on the sidewalk in front of the big Blok building. Everybody stayed on the far side of the street, even though walking in front of the building would have been much easier because it wasn't crowded. It was like they feared a plague was on this side of the street.

As big as the building was, nobody exited or entered. The sight gave me a little shiver. What was the deal? Were people afraid of the place?

The driver dado joined his pal and the two looked at me with those blank doll eyes.

"Thanks for the lift, guys," I said. "Wait here for me, okay? I won't be long. Keep the engine running." I started up the stairs. The two dados followed right behind me. I guessed they were making sure I didn't bolt. Just to mess with them, I stopped suddenly. I hoped they would be surprised and stumble or something. They didn't. The instant I stopped, they stopped. I took another step, they took another step. It was like these two were wired to me. I took a step, then quickly whipped around and stared at them. They didn't flinch.

"What are you guys? Robots?" I said.

They didn't react. Oh, well. At least I was amusing myself.

"Challenger Red," Nevva called. "Please hurry. We're running late."

I jogged up the rest of the stairs. She greeted me with a small smile. A very small smile.

"Good morning, Challenger Red," she said formally.

"Where have you been?" I asked, trying to sound as irked as I felt.

Her answer was a quick glance to the dados. I got it. She was saying, "Don't talk in front of the robots."

"We must go right to the trustee chambers," she said. "Veego and LaBerge are already there."

"Sure," I said. "Wouldn't want to keep Pete and Re-Peat waiting."

Nevva started for the front door. I followed. The dados didn't. I figured their job was done once they handed me off to Nevva.

"Bye, kids," I said cheerily to the robots. "Go get your-selves an ice cream, on me."

The dados didn't react. We entered the building through a grand revolving door. Inside was a massive lobby that soared three stories high. On the wall directly in front of us was another huge silver sign that said: BLOK.

"What's with the big signs?" I asked. "Are they afraid they'll forget who they are or something?"

"The trustees like to maintain an impressive presence," Nevva answered without breaking stride.

"Yeah, no kidding," I said. "Are you gonna tell me what's going on?"

Nevva took a quick glance around. I wasn't sure why; there wasn't another person to be seen. The place was huge and empty. Our footsteps echoed back at us.

"Everyone is observed. Always," Nevva said under her breath. She didn't look at me as she spoke, in order to give the illusion we weren't talking. "The meeting here will answer some of your questions. Did you bring the item I gave you?"

"Item?" I didn't understand what she was talking about at first. She gave me a quick, stern look . . . and I remembered. "Oh yeah, right. The item. Yeah, I've got it." She was talking about the blocking diode.

"Good," she said. "You'll need it."

"Want to tell me why?" I asked.

"No," she answered flatly. "I told you, we're being watched."

Okay, I figured it would be best to play it her way. We were on her turf. She was a Traveler. I had to believe she knew what she was doing. She led me to an elevator that was already open, waiting for us. Usually in big buildings like that there's a whole line of elevators. Not there. There was only one. We got in and the door closed instantly. I saw that there were no buttons to push. The elevator rose on its own.

"How does it know where we want to go?" I asked.

"This elevator only goes to the chambers," Nevva answered.

"So anybody could come in here and head on up?" I asked.

"No," she said. "As I have told you now three times, we are being watched."

Oh. Right.

"What's your job here?" I asked. "You can answer that, can't you?"

"I am the special assistant to the trustees of the company," she answered professionally. "I schedule their appointments, handle their correspondence, and generally make sure that their every need is met while they are working."

"Company," I said, my mind spinning. "Working? Blok is a business? I thought it was, like, the government or something."

Nevva chuckled. "Blok is the largest company on Quillan. It is larger than any government on the territory, and far more powerful."

"Wow," I said. "A company that's more powerful than a government. That's . . . scary. What do they do? I mean, what's their business?"

"Blok has many enterprises," she answered. "But above all else, it is a store."

The elevator doors opened and Nevva stepped out. I didn't. Had I heard right? Blok was a store? A store? Like, where you bought stuff? I remembered back to the plates I'd found in that warehouse. They were all marked with the Blok logo. The products on the shelves of the stores had the Blok logo as well. I couldn't get my mind around the concept.

"Please follow me, Challenger Red," Nevva said firmly.

I drifted out of the elevator, trying to make sense of what Nevva had revealed. We were in a bare room that had no furniture and a single door on the far wall across from the elevator. On either side of the door were big Blok logos, no surprise. Nevva hurried over to the door and turned to me.

"Don't ask questions," she said. "Answer only if you are asked directly. This shouldn't take long. Do you understand?"

I said, "Understand? You're kidding, right? I don't understand anything."

Nevva leaned in to me and said softly, "You will."

With a quick wink she opened the door and stood aside for me to enter and meet my future . . . and the future of Quillan.

QUILLAN

It looked like a courtroom. The first thing I saw was a group of people sitting on the far side behind a high, long bench-like desk that faced into the room. The bench was black. Very imposing. I had to believe these were the trustees. There were ten of them. Five men and five women. They were adults, though I couldn't guess how old they were. They sat there wearing the same kind of dark suits that Nevva wore, looking every bit like supreme court judges. They faced an audience that sat in rows. It looked like there were about fifty people in all. They were mostly dressed in the same gray, drab clothing that I saw on the people out in the city.

There was a center aisle that cut through the audience, and a space of about twenty feet between the trustees and the onlookers. In the middle of that space was a small platform with a podium on it. Right now a man stood on this platform, facing the trustees, giving a speech. Nobody else spoke. For as many people as were in the room, it was amazingly quiet.

Nobody fidgeted or coughed. I wasn't even sure if anybody was breathing, that's how still it was. They were all focused on the guy giving the speech.

Before I tuned in to what the guy was saying, I caught some movement off to my right. Looking, I saw LaBerge waving for me to join him. He was in the audience with Veego. He was the only guy dressed in something colorful. It was a suit that was cut like everybody else's, only it was lime green. Clown.

I looked to Nevva. She nodded for me to go, so I left her and made my way toward Veego and LaBerge. My footsteps sounded like thunder in that quiet room. I got a lot of dirty looks. Veego was sitting next to LaBerge and didn't look at me as I sat down next to her. LaBerge gave me a big smile and a thumbs-up. I scowled at him. He shrugged.

I turned my attention to the guy on the platform. He looked nervous as he spoke to the trustees. He kept shifting his weight from foot to foot.

"I need to point out how difficult it has been for the last three quads," he said. "The weather has been unusually warm, so the demand for thermal outerwear has dropped considerably. Combine that with the fact that the last shipment of product we received was far more than we requested—our profit margin has suffered. Now if—"

One of the trustees, a man, interrupted him and said gruffly, "And why exactly did you receive more goods than you knew you could sell?"

The guy on the platform was sweating. I could tell that from as far back as I was sitting. When he spoke, his voice cracked. "Well," he began nervously. "I was told that the manufacturing facility hadn't met its quota and they were, uh, requested to increase their production."

Several of the trustees shared glances. One of the women

said, "And this is what you are blaming your failure on? The fact that a manufacturer was able to step up and fulfill their quota? Is that what you're saying?"

"Uh, no, um," the guy stammered. "I'm very proud of how they were able to meet their requirements. It's just that the need for the product wasn't calculated accurately—"

The first trustee guy said, "You understand that the trustees set the quotas for manufacturing?"

The guy stiffened. It was like a full-body wince. "I do," he said softly.

"Excuse me?" the trustee said, more forcefully. "I didn't hear you."

"Yes, I do," the guy answered. "But—"

"So you're saying that the trustees aren't capable of making a sound decision as to what is best for Blok?"

Oh man, the guy was caught in the middle. It looked like he was supposed to sell a certain amount of jackets or something, but couldn't do it because the trustees told the manufacturer to make too many. It wasn't his fault; it was the fault of the people who told the manufacturer to make too many. The trustees. But they were double-talking the blame back onto him.

"No, I would never question the wisdom of the trustees," the guy said. He was really sweating now. "Of course you know exactly what is best for Blok. All I'm saying is that even in your absolute, unquestionable wisdom, there was no way for anyone to predict the weather and—"

A third member of the trustees said, "The terms of your employment are simple. You are expected to increase sales by 20 percent each quad. You have failed. You are relieved and reassigned to the lower sector."

"No!" the guy shouted in horror. "That isn't fair! It was out of my control!"

The trustees didn't look at him. They were too busy shuffling papers on their big desk. One of them said casually, "Security, please."

The guy lost it. "Listen to me! I have successfully run Blok's outerwear business for thirty quads!" he cried. "I can make up the difference, I know I can!" Two security dados marched up to the platform, grabbed the guy, and dragged him away. It was like he had just been convicted of some horrible crime, and all because he didn't sell enough jackets.

"I worked too hard," the guy shouted as the dados pulled him across the room toward a side door. He now sounded angry. "I've done everything you've asked. More so! I will not go back to the lower sector! I refuse!"

The dados were about to pull the guy out of the room when the first trustee raised his hand and said, "Stop!"

They stopped. Nobody in the room said a word.

"Are you refusing reassignment to the lower sector?" the trustee asked.

The guy's eyes darted back and forth in panic. "No, I didn't mean that," he said, desperately backpedaling. "I'll do whatever I have to. My family needs me. I'll gladly go wherever—"

"Send him to the tarz," the trustee said flatly.

"No!" the guy screamed. "This isn't fair! I have a family!"

For the first time I heard sound coming from the audience. Several people exchanged surprised looks. Some even gasped softly.

I whispered to Veego, "Tarz?"

Veego put a finger to her lips to shush me. Whatever the tarz was, it wasn't good. Looking at Veego gave me another surprise. The woman was normally ice, but at that moment she looked nervous. It wasn't obvious, but I saw it in her eyes. Having that poor guy sent to the tarz, whatever it was, frightened her. Note to self: Avoid the Tarz.

The guy was now in hysterical tears. The trustees didn't care. Nor did the dados. They dragged him out a side door that slammed shut after them. I could hear the guy whimpering for a few seconds until they got him farther away. In moments all was silent again. My mouth was dry. What had just happened? I stole looks at people and saw the same fear in their eyes that I saw in Veego's. How twisted was this? Nevva Winter said that Blok was a store. What kind of store sentenced their people to some horrible fate if they didn't meet a quota? For that matter, what kind of store was run by a group of cold-looking judges who terrified everyone, right down to the people on the street?

As I sat there, trying to make sense of what I had seen, Nevva entered from a door behind the trustees and silently placed papers in front of each. She looked very efficient as she quickly went about her business. She said she was a special assistant . . . whatever that meant. It seemed kind of dull to me. The other Travelers all led interesting lives, beyond the fact that they were Travelers, I mean. Loor was a warrior, Alder a knight. Gunny was the bell captain at a swanky hotel; Spader was an aquaneer; Aja Killian controlled an incredible virtual reality generator. Patrick from Third Earth was a teacher and a librarian at the most incredible library ever. Kasha had battled dinosaurs in the jungle as she foraged for food to feed her city. Each and every Traveler seemed to have an interesting, unique life, except for Nevva.

And I guess me. I was just a regular kid. I went to school; I played sports. End of story. I was thinking that I was the loser of the bunch, until I met Nevva. She was like a slave to these scary people. I could see by the way the trustees ordered her around, barely looking at her, that they had no respect for her. She ran around filling up their glasses with water and taking notes and basically doing simple tasks that these guys couldn't do for themselves. Or wouldn't do. It looked like a thankless job. But then again, she was close to a group that held a lot of power here on Quillan. I couldn't help but think that as bad as the job was, she was in the right place for when Saint Dane made his move.

While Nevva scurried around, attending to the trustees, nobody in the audience said a word. I didn't blame them. If the trustees had the power to banish them to some horrible fate on a whim, their guts must have been twisted with fear. Looking to Veego and LaBerge, I saw that they weren't any different. I already told you how Veego looked scared. Well, if she looked scared, LaBerge looked absolutely nauseous. For a change he wasn't smiling. I saw his lips tremble as if he were going to cry.

"Miss Winter!" one of the trustees barked. "We're behind schedule."

"Forgive me," Nevva said, bowing her head. "It is entirely my fault. We are ready for the next presentation."

Wow, Nevva treated them like royalty. Obnoxious royalty.

"Then why are we still waiting?" a woman trustee barked.

Nevva cleared her throat and announced to the group, "We will now hear the report from the gaming group."

A murmur went through the crowd. I wasn't sure if it was because they were excited about hearing from the gaming group, or just relieved that they weren't the next victims. Veego cleared her throat and stood. LaBerge stood too, but Veego shot him a look and he quickly sat back down. If she was going to make a report to these creeps, she didn't want LaBerge saying something stupid that would get them shipped off to the tarz. Smart move. Veego brushed off the front of her jacket and walked to the podium. She stood straight, like a soldier, but kept her head bowed. It felt like she didn't want to look cocky in front of the trustees. I'm sure that was tough for her because, well, she was cocky. She took her place at the podium and stood with her hands behind her back, waiting for the go-ahead.

"We're waiting," one of the trustees said with an obnoxious growl.

"Thank you," Veego said promptly. "Ladies and Gentlemen, I am proud to be here today and thrilled to present to you a report that I'm sure you will—"

One of the trustees interrupted, "Spare us the theatrics that you are so well known for. What is your response to our request?"

It looked to me like Veego had to stop herself from snapping back at the guy. I didn't think she was used to being treated like a turd, but she was smart enough not to complain. As much as I detested Veego and her gruesome little operation, I felt sorry for her then. Not a lot, but still. Nobody should be treated like that.

"I understand," she said in total control of her emotions. "My partner and I are very aware of and respect the trustees mandate to increase profits by 20 percent each quad. A challenge, I must point out, that we have never missed since taking over the gaming operation."

"Yes, we're all satisfied with your history," one of the woman trustees said. "But it *is* history. With the resources we have provided, we feel as if you should be doing better."

"Better?" shouted LaBerge, jumping to his feet. "How can we do better than perfect?"

The crowd gasped. LaBerge felt the hot eyes of everyone in the room on him, including those of the trustees. He flinched and smiled. "Forgive me," he said meekly. "Pay no attention. I'm a fool."

He sat back down and put his head in his hands. "I'm doomed," he said to himself.

"Please forgive my overzealous partner," Veego said, doing damage control. "It is that very passion that is necessary for the inspiration to create such interesting and successful games."

LaBerge looked up, hopeful. Did the trustees buy that?

"Continue," the woman trustee said.

I could feel LaBerge's relief. He had dodged a bullet that he fired himself.

"Thank you," Veego said. She turned and shot a quick glare at LaBerge that said, "Shut up, idiot." She then continued, "As you know, the success of our games depends on many things: New and provocative contests that will generate excitement for those who wager; a tightly run organization that keeps expenses down; and perhaps most importantly, talented and athletic challengers who will provide us with well-fought games. It truly does not matter who wins, so long as the competitions are close. That is the only way to maximize wagering on both sides, since Blok benefits eithcr way."

However the games worked, Blok profited no matter who won. And from what I saw, lots of people bet on the games. Blok must have been making a small fortune by putting on these games. Or maybe a huge fortune.

The woman trustee said, "Challenger Yellow did not live up to expectations."

She was talking about Remudi. The Traveler. I looked to Nevva, who stood behind the trustees. She looked to the ground.

"We blame ourselves," Veego said. "He was not adequately prepared and should never have been matched with Challenger Green. Perhaps he should have first battled a dado. That was our mistake. You provided us with superior talent, and we failed."

That's not what she said a few days before. She was all sorts of ticked that the trustees told her to put Remudi in the games. I guess she was being politically correct . . . or a weenie. Maybe that's the same thing.

"But I am pleased to announce that we have learned from our mistakes," Veego declared.

She made a motion to Nevva. Nevva pointed a small black remote control at the ceiling. Instantly two big screens lowered on either side of the room. The lights dimmed. Moments later both screens came to life. One showed a challenger running the gauntlet they called "Hook." The challenger was me. It was a replay of my battle with the dado as I ran through the piston-thumping death chamber. While the crowd watched one screen, the other screen flashed numbers.

Veego announced, "As we speak, this game of Hook is being transmitted throughout Quillan. Look at the numbers. After his incredible triumph at Tock, Challenger Red is already a favorite. Citizens are now wagering on him to win."

The trustees weren't watching me run around on screen; their eyes were on the numbers. They looked at one another, nodding. I had no idea what the numbers meant or how the betting was going, but judging from their reactions, they were impressed. I kept my eyes on the numbers too. I didn't feel like reliving that game, even though I knew how it came out. A minute later it was over. I had survived Hook, again. Both screens flashed WINNER—CHALLENGER RED! There was an excited buzz. I guessed the numbers were good.

The lights came back on and the screens retracted into the ceiling. LaBerge was absolutely giddy. He clapped his hands together like an excited little girl.

"Ladies and Gentlemen of Blok," Veego announced with

fanfare. This time the trustees didn't cut her off. "I present to you the challenger who will make the next Grand X the greatest, the most exciting, and the most profitable in the history of Quillan. The new Challenger Red!"

Everyone applauded. LaBerge grabbed my arm and forced me to stand up. Reluctantly I stood, but it was totally awkward. What did they want me to do? Throw my fists in the air and shout, "I am the greatest! Bring on Green!" No way. I felt more like hiding under a chair. I looked around at the audience. They cheered, but not because they were fans. To them I meant money. If I gave them a great Grand X, it would be good for Blok and probably for everybody who worked there. It didn't matter if I won, or died. Veego stood on the platform with her hands on her hips. She had a satisfied look on her face, as if showing off her prized possession. Nevva Winter stood behind the trustees, looking uncomfortable. She gave me a small, nervous smile.

The trustees were sizing me up like a racehorse. To them I was nothing more than a dollar sign. They were too cool to be caught up in the excitement of the moment and break out in applause. Not these guys. I looked at each one in turn. They were a grim-looking bunch. From what I could tell, the course of Quillan was very much guided by these ten people. I needed to learn more about them, and how they'd come to power. And how Blok had come to power, for that matter. I looked at each face. All I got back was cold indifference. That is, until I got to the last person.

It was a man who hadn't been saying anything. Because of that, I hadn't been paying any attention to him. Until then. Where the other nine looked at me with cold dispassion, this guy had a smile. As soon as my eyes locked on his, I felt a cold jolt shoot up my spine. Maybe it was the way he looked at me. Maybe it was the smile. Or maybe his ice blue eyes gave it away. It could have been all those things, but I think I would have known, no matter what. We held eye contact. He reached a finger up to his forehead and gave me a small salute. He didn't have to say the words. I knew what he meant: *Welcome to Quillan, Pendragon.*

The biggest game was on. I had found Saint Dane.

QUILLAN

Before the applause had a chance to die, I felt a firm hand grab my arm. Two dados had appeared next to me and wanted me to go with them. I looked at LaBerge. He shrugged and gave me a confused look. For him, this wasn't part of the plan. For me, I didn't know what that plan was anyway, so nothing surprised me. The dado pulled me into the aisle and pushed me toward the trustees. I looked at Veego, who didn't seem to know what was going on either. The dados gently but firmly shoved me to the front of the clapping audience and toward the same side door that the guy had been dragged out of before. What was happening? A moment before, I was introduced as their big hope of making the Grand X successful. Now I was being hurried out of the room like a criminal. I feared that I would be the next sucker to be shipped off to the tarz.

The applause continued. Nevva Winter leaned over to the woman trustee in the center, speaking quickly. It didn't look like she expected this either. I hoped she was trying to save me.

I looked to Saint Dane sitting at the end of the row of trustees. He had taken the form of a thin needle-nosed guy with slicked-back dark hair. He didn't seem concerned at all, though when was Saint Dane ever concerned about my well-being? He actually winked at me. The dados pushed me out of the room and into a long corridor. The door closed behind us, cutting off the sound of the applause.

"What is going on?" I asked angrily, though I didn't expect an answer.

The dados pushed me down the corridor until we came to another door. One of them opened it and motioned for me to go inside. What else could I do? I stepped inside cautiously. Was this going to be the dreaded tarz that the trustees banished people to? Or was the Grand X going to start right then and there? I was ready for anything . . . and nothing.

I found myself in a big office. I'm serious. It looked like a supermodern, sleek office, like you'd expect an executive at a high-tech computer company to have. The place was decorated entirely in black and silver. There were black leather couches and a silver steel desk. Silver lamps hung from the ceiling and silver sculptures were placed in the corners. The rug was black and the tables were silver. I guess it was supposed to be fancy, but to me it was cold and lifeless. One whole wall was taken up by a window that looked out over the city. I walked toward it and looked out onto the gray sea that was the city of Rune. The screens were all still flashing: WINNER——CHALLENGER RED!

Yay me.

"Congratulations, Challenger Red," came a bemused voice from behind me.

I whipped around to see a man standing inside the door. It was Saint Dane. He was in the form of the trustee from Blok. He had quietly slipped into the room, like a snake. The character he was playing on Quillan was short and thin, with long bony fingers that moved like the tentacles of an octopus. He was the kind of guy you wouldn't look twice at, but if you did, you'd see a mad fire behind his eyes and wish you hadn't.

"What am I doing here?" I asked.

Saint Dane crossed to the desk. I circled the other way, always aware of how dangerous he was.

"Don't be so suspicious, Pendragon," he said with a smirk. "You're in no danger. I simply asked to have a private audience with the new challenger who everyone has such high expectations for. There's nothing sinister going on."

"Nothing sinister?" I said. "This territory is a nightmare! The people here are zombies who have to gamble for food. They bet on games where people die. That's not sinister?"

"No," he answered. "That's free will." He chuckled and sat behind his desk. He put his feet up like he owned the place. If he was a trustee of Blok, I guess he did. "Whatever this territory has become, it is the fault of the people themselves. Doesn't that make you happy?"

"Happy? Because . . . ?"

"Because it's exactly what you're fighting for," Saint Dane said innocently. "To make sure the territories can prosper without being influenced by the likes of me. Isn't that right? Look around, Pendragon. This is what becomes of a territory when man's true nature is left to take its natural course. Congratulations."

"Give me a break," I said. "You expect me to believe you had nothing to do with this?"

Saint Dane stood and strolled toward the huge window. I was glad he didn't transform himself back into his normal image, the tall thin demon with the jagged red scars on his bald head. That would have sent me over the edge.

"As hard as you might find it to believe, it's true," he said.

"I'm simply an interested observer. The people of Quillan have no one but themselves to blame for what they've become."

"I don't believe you, " I said.

Saint Dane looked out over the gray, grim city and said, "Pendragon, you are blind. Or at least you choose not to see what is in front of you. You believe there is good in everyone, and if given the choice, the path to prosperity and peace will always be taken. Well, that simply isn't the case, as I've proved to you time and again, but you refuse to see."

"All I see is you fooling people into thinking you're helping them," I said. "Being tricked into disaster isn't the same as choosing disaster."

"Ahh, but that brings us to Quillan," Saint Dane said while clapping his bony hands together with glee. He enjoyed talking about people's misery. Creep. "The people have found themselves in this dreadful condition for one reason and one reason alone. Greed."

"Greed?" I echoed skeptically. "These people have nothing!"

"It wasn't always like that," Saint Dane said. "At one time Quillan wasn't much different from your Second Earth. It was quite the prosperous territory. Most people lived in comfort, which created the perfect opportunity for an enterprise like Blok."

"What exactly is Blok?" I asked quickly. "A store?"

"Indeed" was his answer. "At least, at its core. Several generations ago a small market opened, right here in the city of Rune. Blok. Their plan for success was simple: They offered products at a lower cost than their competitors. Much lower. It was an innocent business decision. Nothing devious. At first they lost so much money they nearly had to close. But they stayed afloat for one simple reason. People couldn't resist the lure of paying so much less for all the things they wanted. It was as simple as that. So the people of Rune abandoned the other merchants and tripped over themselves to buy their goods from Blok. Little by little the other merchants lost so much business that they had to shut down, which gave Blok even more business. As the competition dwindled, Blok slowly raised their prices, though they continued to keep them much lower than their remaining competitors. Slowly Blok became profitable and powerful. What started as a small store that sold simple items like clothing and furniture grew. Blok began selling food and automobiles, all at such low prices that thrifty consumers couldn't pass up the bargains, which made Blok even more profitable. As their business grew, Blok moved into manufacturing. They not only sold the items, they created them. Their mandate was to manufacture items as simply and cheaply as possible. They didn't care about style or beauty or even quality, they cared about speed. The faster and simpler an item was made, the cheaper it was to sell, and low prices are what lured people to Blok. Eventually they forced other manufacturers out of business because they couldn't create items as quickly or as cheaply as Blok."

Saint Dane told this story with glee, as if it were the most fascinating bedtime story ever. I never thought much about stores and prices and who sold what and why, but I had to admit that the story of Blok was interesting . . . in a scary kind of way.

He continued, "Blok grew. It began buying other companies, folding them into their world. They moved into energy, real estate, banking, and communications. They bought hospitals and began providing medical services. They built their own schools. People followed like hungry sheep because whatever Blok sold, people bought. They simply couldn't resist the prices. Blok lowered their workers wages, which increased their profits even more. They were becoming so huge, and employed so many people, the workers had no choice but to agree to the horrid terms of employment. If they refused, there was always someone ready to take their place, because Blok had become the number one employer on the territory. I think on your territory you would refer to it as 'the only game in town.' Blok eventually moved into entertainment. They made movies and music and artwork, created by people who worked for them, with the prices they set and with their vision in mind."

Saint Dane stepped away from the window and touched a sculpture that was a square piece of steel. There was nothing artistic about it. It was just a boring hunk of steel.

"Needless to say, the art they produced wasn't inspired, but they were able to mass produce it, while at the same time closing down the art galleries and museums, so the only works of art that people saw came from Blok. You see, art makes people think. Blok didn't want people to think. If that happened, they might have realized what was actually happening. After a time the people came to think the art that came from Blok was actually . . . interesting."

What a horrible thought. A company that created all the art in the world in order to keep people from being inspired. It now made sense why the city was so gray and lifeless.

Saint Dane continued, "Blok grew so large that the economy of several small countries became dependent on the business they provided. At first governments welcomed them because Blok promised employment to so many. And not just in manufacturing. Blok needed farmland to grow food and research facilities to create new drugs. Blok swooped into these small countries with the promise of wealth and prosperity, only to become demanding slave masters. Workers were paid measly sums for working long hours—all to meet the demands of their employers. By the time these poor people realized what was happening, it was too late. Blok had destroyed their economy while making everyone dependent on the company. It was brilliant."

Saint Dane gestured out to the gray city beyond the window. "Everything you see has been touched by Blok," he said, almost in awe. "The city of Rune is only one small example. It is not an exaggeration to say that Blok runs the territory. There are governments, yes. They make their laws and have their elections but they wield no real power. Everything is controlled by Blok because Blok controls the money and the minds of the people. They even have their own security force of dados. It's about greed, Pendragon. Blok offered something the people wanted, and they were all too quick to accept. And let's not forget the people who founded Blok. They are quite wealthy. You won't see them living in this wretched city. Oh no. The senior leaders of Blok live in a class by themselves, all over Quillan. And at the top of that pyramid are the trustees. If you think the castle of Veego and LaBerge is opulent, you should see how the trustees live. My name is Mr. Kayto, by the way. He lived on a particularly lush island that's only a short hop from here in my jet." He held out his hands and looked at them as if they belonged to somebody else. "I think I chose my vessel particularly well, don't you?"

It looked as if there'd been a real Mr. Kayto at some point, but Saint Dane stepped in and took over his identity, which meant the real Mr. Kayto was dead.

"People have been fighting wars forever, Pendragon, simply to gain power. The history of each and every territory is written in the blood of those who died trying to fulfill the aspirations of their ambitious leaders. What happened here on Quillan was so much more civilized and far more successful. There were no battles. Not a shot was fired in anger. You won't find military cemeteries crowded with thousands of tombstones. Yet make no mistake, an entire territory has been conquered and the spoils are huge." Saint Dane gave me a twisted smile and added with a chuckle, "And the best part of all is that I had absolutely nothing to do with it."

I stood there, dazed, trying to understand all that he had thrown at me. Was it possible? Could a company grow so huge and powerful that it ruled an entire world?

"How do the games fit into this?" I asked.

"Ahhh! The games!" Saint Dane said with relish. "A particularly interesting sidelight. You see, my boy, greed is an addiction. It's a machine that must constantly be fed. The trustees of Blok saw that their business had grown as large as possible. There was nothing left to conquer, nowhere left to expand. Most importantly, there were no more products to create and exploit in order to increase their own wealth. So they created one."

"The games," I said.

"Exactly! The games provide entertainment for the people and a constant source of revenue for the company. Blok takes a percentage of every bet placed, no matter who wins."

"But people are betting with more than money," I said. "I've seen people carted off after losing a bet."

"Oh, yes," Saint Dane said, laughing. "These people have very little money to wager. Of course that doesn't stop them from gambling. The chance of improving their sorry lives is too tempting. Remember: greed. Though they may not have money to wager, they do have something that is much more valuable—their lives. When people make the ultimate bet, a win means they might have more food for their families. Food grown, processed, and sold by Blok, of course. Or they might win a higher-paying job . . . with Blok. Or a larger home . . . built by Blok. The possibilities are endless."

"What if they lose?" I asked.

"Several things could happen," Saint Dane said. "Usually they are retrieved and sent to an area of Blok where their particular talents are needed. Laboring with little or no pay increases the bottom line for Blok. The losers could be separated from their families for years—in Second Earth terms. Or they could be sent for medical research, or to the tarz."

"What is the tarz?" I asked.

"Tarz is power," he answered. "You might call it electricity. Tarz powers the territory. But it's volatile, much like nuclear power on Second Earth. Cleaning up the waste produced in a tarz factory is the lowest job there is. The good news is no one works in a tarz factory for long, because the waste is poisonous. I understand it is a painful death."

I had to sit down on one of the cold black couches. It was like the weight of what Saint Dane was telling me was pushing me down. He had just described a territory that was a living nightmare. The people of Quillan were zombielike slaves to the greedy people who ran Blok. A store.

Saint Dane added, "I've often seen cases where fathers wager with the lives of their children."

"No!"

"Oh, yes. The lure of the big win is simply too much to resist. Greed, Pendragon."

My thoughts went back to that arcade, where the guy beat the video game and was reunited with a little kid. I wondered if he had bet with the life of that kid. I felt sick to my stomach.

"I'd like to say you've already lost Quillan," Saint Dane said, trying to sound sympathetic. I know he wasn't. "But I'm afraid that isn't entirely true. Quillan never had a chance. The territory will crumble and when it does, I'll be here to help them rebuild. I have wonderful plans. You have to admit that the people here have made a horrible mess of things. Under my guidance Quillan will once again become strong. Even you have to admit they need help. I can give it to them, Pendragon. I can help all the territories. What's happening here on Quillan isn't unique. Time and again it's been proved that the people of the territories are incapable of guiding their own destinies. All I want to do is help. Is that so bad?"

He said this last with a gleam in his eye that made me want to punch him. I think I would have, if I thought it would do any good.

"Why did you bring me here?" I asked.

The demon walked back to the window and gazed out at the grim city. "I want to see how strong you really are, and the only way to do that is to see you lose."

"I thought the territory was already lost."

"Not the territory, fool!" Saint Dane snapped. "You!" He lost his cool for a second, but quickly regained it. "I'll admit, I'm surprised by how you've disrupted my plans on so many of the other territories. Press said you would be strong, but I had no idea just how resourceful you could be. Bravo! If I were being perfectly honest, I'd have to say I thought you would have given up by now. But that's not the case, is it?"

"No, it isn't," I said.

Saint Dane was actually complimenting me, and admitting his own failures. How weird was that?

"I have a proposition for you," he said. "I know you don't have to compete in the Quillan games. I'm sure you'd find a way to escape from those Veego and LaBerge buffoons. But I'd like you to compete in this extravaganza they call the Grand X."

"Really?" I said sarcastically. "Is that all? Why sure! I'd do anything for you, old pal!"

Saint Dane laughed. "Will it be that simple?"

"In your dreams."

"I thought not." He chuckled.

"Then what's the point?"

"The point is I want you to lose!" he snarled.

The guy's emotions changed on a dime. I never knew when he was going to laugh, or get all angry and try to beat me into jelly. "You've gotten strong, Pendragon," he said through clenched teeth. "Not just in your resolve, but physically. You've become a force that I've grown weary of dealing with."

"And you know you can't beat me," I said, getting cocky. "We found that out in the cavern on Zadaa, didn't we?"

"Perhaps," he said. "But I believe your intensity in battling me was fueled by the emotion you felt over the death of your friend Loor. I'm not so sure you could beat me again."

"Want to find out?" I asked. If this was turning into a macho contest, I didn't want to lose. Saint Dane stared right into my eyes. I didn't blink. For a moment I thought I saw the image of this Mr. Kayto dude waver, as if Saint Dane was losing his grip on the illusion and turning back into his normal self. Was he going to attack me again? I did a quick mental inventory of the room from memory, thinking about what I could grab as a weapon.

"That may happen someday," Saint Dane said, backing off. "But not here. Not now." The moment passed. "I'm offering you a challenge, Pendragon. If you should triumph, which I don't believe you will, then you'll be stronger and more confident than ever. Perhaps as a champion you might even be able to do some good for this miserable territory. Who knows? You have the charisma to do that."

"But if I lose, I might die," I said. "Sorry, the upside isn't worth it."

"Ahhh, but that's where my offer comes in," Saint Dane said. "What is it that you want most, Pendragon? Other than defeating me, of course. What is the one thing you want that would make the risk worthwhile?"

"Something you can't give me," I said.

"Which is?"

I debated about telling him the truth. Why should I expose my deepest feelings to my enemy? It might only give him more ammunition to use against me.

Before I had the chance to say another word, he said, "I'll tell you. You want to see your family again."

That's exactly what I wanted. I suppose I shouldn't have been so surprised that he knew. He was evil, not a dope.

"Can you do that?" I asked, my voice cracking.

"No," he said. "But I can offer you the next best thing."

I couldn't imagine what the next best thing could be, but I wasn't going anywhere until he told me.

"If you compete," he said, "I will reveal to you the true nature of the Travelers."

It felt like the room had suddenly closed in around me. I couldn't breathe. My ears rang and my head got light. Did I hear right? Was Saint Dane offering up the holy grail? The demon slowly walked toward me.

"Certainly you must be wondering why all of this has been happening to you," he said. "I have the answers you're looking for, Pendragon. How far are you willing to go to get them?"

I must have worn the total shock on my face, because Saint Dane laughed.

"Tempting, isn't it?" he said with a chuckle. "Make no mistake, I want you to lose. I want you humiliated. I want you to give up your futile quest and leave me be. I'm admitting that to you. I'm also admitting that I want it so badly, I'm willing to do what Press would have done, but never got the chance."

"Because you killed him," I said.

"Yes, I killed him," Saint Dane said. "But he promised you'd be together again, didn't he? Wouldn't you like to know how that is possible?"

I nearly fell over. Seriously. Saint Dane's words made me dizzy. The idea that he would reveal who I really was and why I was chosen to be a Traveler seemed impossible. Was it worth it? This wasn't just about losing some dumb game. If I played, I could be killed. But if I survived I'd have answers to the questions that had haunted me since the moment I sat on the back of Uncle Press's motorcycle, headed for my first trip through the flume. I had done everything that was asked of me. I had saved territories. I had suffered through the deaths of friends. I'd risked my life more times than I could count. I had done all of that on faith in the idea that it was the way it was meant to be. And now Saint Dane was offering me the chance to discover the one answer that was beyond my grasp. Learning the truth would give me the strength to keep going, and possibly be the final nail in his coffin. The question was, was I willing to risk my life to get it?

"Yeah, it's tempting," I said in a small voice. I couldn't lie.

"Of course it is," Saint Dane said. "I wouldn't believe you if you said otherwise."

"But I can't do it," I said.

Saint Dane didn't react. He must have expected I'd say that. "Yes, you can," he said. "And I believe you will. But not out of curiosity."

"Then why?" I asked.

Saint Dane took a step closer to me and hissed, "Because after all of your success against me, you are starting to believe you can't lose. Admit it. You're beginning to feel invincible, aren't you? Especially after Loor cheated death. That's why I'm making this offer, Pendragon. You *can* lose. You *will* lose. In fact, you've already lost."

"How do you figure that?" I asked.

"Because I've just put you in a no-win situation. If you accept my offer, you will be defeated and quite possibly killed. But if you decline, then you'll show me that your confidence isn't as strong as I suspected. It means you doubt yourself, and that's just as important to me as seeing you beaten at the Quillan games. So you see, either way I win. That's why I'm on Quillan, Pendragon. That's why I lured you here. Now, how are you going to handle this? Hmmm?"

QUILLAN

I didn't get the chance to answer Saint Dane's challenge, because there was a knock on the door.

"I look forward to hearing your decision, Pendragon," Saint Dane said as he brushed some invisible lint off his suit. He walked back to his desk and called out, "Yes, come in!"

The door opened slowly. LaBerge meekly peered in.

"Excuse me, Mr. Kayto, sir," he said nervously. "I don't mean to interrupt you, but is everything all right? I mean, should we leave Challenger Red here with you or bring him back to the compound? Whatever you wish."

"I'm done with him," Saint Dane said. "He should return with you. Thank you for your concern."

LaBerge looked surprised that a trustee was being so polite to him. "Oh, thank you," he said. "I know you're busy. We won't bother you any longer." LaBerge looked at me and cocked his head, as if to say, "Let's go."

After what had just happened and all that I'd heard, I wasn't so sure my legs would hold me. I slowly got to my feet and didn't topple over, I'm happy to report. Saint Dane was sitting at his desk, already engrossed in reading a report of some kind. But I knew it was an act. He wasn't thinking about some blah blah report from Blok. He was thinking about me.

"Not gonna happen," I said to him. "I won't do it."

Saint Dane looked at me and smiled. "Then my life just got much easier because I've proven that you are indeed a coward. Good day."

I walked toward the door, and LaBerge. The confusion on his face was obvious. I didn't say a word; I just walked past him into the corridor.

"Good day, Mr. Kayto," LaBerge said subserviently as he backed out. "I'm sorry to have disturbed you."

"Close the door," Saint Dane barked.

LaBerge quickly closed the door and ran after me. I was already halfway down the hall when he caught up. "What happened back there?" he asked nervously. "You can't talk to a trustee like that!"

"I guess I can," I shot back at him. "You heard me."

"Not while you're a challenger," LaBerge said, trying to be tough. "I will not allow anyone who works for me to be so disrespectful of—"

I grabbed LaBerge by the collar of his goofy green suit and pinned him against the wall.

"Ow!" he complained.

"I don't work for you," I said. "And I am not a challenger. Get yourself another victim."

"You're saying that as if you think you have a choice," he sniveled.

I let the guy go and continued down the hallway toward where I thought the elevator was. I wasn't staying in this building or with these idiot gaming people any longer. I was going to hit the elevator, get outside, and find my way back to the flume. Saint Dane was right. Quillan was history. I didn't want to spend another minute here. I had no doubt that there would be some dados outside, waiting to take me back to the castle. They were going to have their hands full. I wasn't going back there without a fight. The elevator was there, open. I stepped in and turned around just as LaBerge jumped in after me. The doors closed automatically, and we were on the way down.

The guy stared at me. I don't think he wanted to be alone with me in that elevator. I think he knew I was a raw nerve. If he so much as burped I would have, well, I don't know what I would have done, but I was ready for a fight. Saint Dane's words kept rolling through my head. There was too much to make sense out of quickly. All I knew was I wanted out of there and off of Quillan. That's all I could focus on. Escape. I reached into my back pocket and pulled out the blocking diode. I wasn't waiting for Nevva. It was now or never. The little metal clip snapped easily over the loop.

"What is that?" LaBerge asked. "What are you doing?"

As soon as I snapped it over the loop, the light around the center glowed red. I hoped that meant the loop was deactivated.

"You can't do that," LaBerge whined.

"I just did," I growled.

LaBerge took a step toward me, but I shot him a look that made him back off.

"Fine, whatever you say," the weenie agreed, groveling.

The elevator began to slow. I didn't know what was going to be waiting for me outside the doors. I had to be ready.

"You realize this is futile," LaBerge said.

For some reason those words got through to me. It wasn't so much what he said, but how he said them. It was with no emotion, like it was a simple statement of fact. It gave me a second of hesitation, but that's all. I wasn't going back to that castle.

The doors slid open. I put one foot on the back of the elevator and pushed off, propelling myself out of the compartment. I quickly realized that Nevva Winter was right. We were being watched. They were ready for me. I shot myself out of the elevator and into the arms of four security dados. I didn't stand a chance. I was grabbed by the arms and the legs, and lifted onto their shoulders. No amount of struggling mattered. I might have been able to beat one of those guys, or maybe even two. But not four. I was helpless and frustrated. I wanted to shout out, but didn't want to give anybody the satisfaction of seeing me lose it. So I bit my lip and held it in.

Veego was waiting inside the front door of the building.

"Don't injure him" was all she said. "He must be able to compete."

The dados carried me outside and down the steps where a car was waiting. I was vaguely aware that people had stopped to watch from across the street. I'm sure the scene confirmed all their fears about how bad a place the Blok building was. I was thrown roughly into the backseat. Veego and LaBerge jumped in on either side of me and quickly closed the doors. Two dados were in the front seat and the driver hit the accelerator.

"The doors are locked," Veego said calmly. "You cannot get out."

I sat between the two of them, feeling like a helpless child. I wanted to explode.

"Where did you get the blocking diode?" Veego asked.

I didn't answer. The dado drove us quickly along the city streets, weaving in and out of traffic.

"What is wrong with you?" LaBerge asked. "Don't you realize what an honor it is to be in your position? The trustees put their faith in you and you treat them with such disrespect? It's embarrassing is what it is."

They kept talking but I wasn't listening. I was doing all that I could to calm down and plan my next move. It was looking like I couldn't stop them from taking me back to the castle, which meant I was going to have to make my escape from there. I hoped there wouldn't be increased security around me. That would make things even more difficult. But not impossible. One way or another, I was out of there. I needed to regroup. Maybe talk to Loor. I wished I could talk with Gunny or Spader, but that wasn't going to happen. I even thought about coming home to Second Earth to see you guys. I know that Saint Dane has been sniffing around there. A thousand plans raced through my head, all of which were some variation of getting the hell off Quillan. There was no way I was going to risk my life in the Grand X. If that made me a coward in Saint Dane's cycs, fine. It wasn't going to shake my confidence. No, he wasn't going to goad me into the games, no matter how tempting a prize he was offering. As we raced through the busy streets of Rune, I made up my mind. I was going home.

I think it was at that exact moment, the moment when I realized what I needed to do, when everything changed. The car that was traveling directly in front of us slammed on its brakes. It was so sudden and we were traveling so fast that our car slammed into it.

"Ahhh!" screamed LaBerge. "What happened?"

Veego shot a quick look out the rear window.

"Don't stop," she commanded. "Get us out of here!"

On command, the dado spun the wheel and hit the accelerator. With a lurch we shot to the left and launched forward.

"What are you doing?" LaBerge shouted. "That was an accident! We have to stop!"

"Shut up," Veego spat at him.

At that exact instant we were slammed from behind, hit by another car. We rocked forward so violently that my head hit the back of the seat in front of me.

"That was no accident," Veego said calmly. "They're coming after us."

"Who?" LaBerge shouted.

I thought he was going to cry. The dado hit the accelerator again and turned into oncoming traffic.

"Look out!" LaBerge cried.

The dado was good. We were traveling fast, but his robotic reflexes were faster. He dodged the oncoming cars quicker than is humanly possible, which made sense, because he wasn't human. I looked back to see two cars accelerating behind us. A moment later I felt a sharp jab in my side. Veego had jammed one of those golden stun guns into my ribs.

"You will die before I let them get you," she hissed.

She didn't realize how wired I was. She had barely gotten the words out when I jammed my elbow into her biceps. She squealed in pain and let go of the gun.

"What is happening?" LaBerge cried. "Why are they chasing us?" He saw me grab the gun from Veego. "Ahhh!" he squealed.

With one quick move I grabbed the gun, aimed at the front windshield between the two dados, and pulled the trigger.

Fum! The windshield shattered but didn't break away. The dados were driving blind. They either had to stop on their own, or would hit something that would make us stop.

We hit something.

Whatever it was, the force of the impact sent us up on two wheels and flipped the car. LaBerge screamed. The three of us tumbled together in the backseat like we were in a washing machine. A fast-moving washing machine. The car landed on its roof and kept moving. I braced myself for another collision, rolling myself into a ball with my arms wrapped around my head. The next hit came quickly. It stopped our forward movement but sent us spinning. The whole event only took a few seconds, but as it was happening, it felt like a lifetime. The metal of the car screeched and scraped as we spun across the pavement. The side windows exploded under the pressure of the collapsing roof. Luckily, they blew out, not in, or we might have been shredded. I had no idea which way was up. All I could see was a jumble of Veego and LaBerge.

Finally we hit something else and came to a stop. But it wasn't over. No sooner did we stop moving than the car started rolling again. I had no idea what was happening, but it felt as if we were being lifted up into the air. I soon realized we were being flipped back upright, onto our wheels.

"Help! Help!" LaBerge squealed.

With a bone-jarring shudder the car was righted. I heard the sound of wrenching metal. There were people outside using tools to pry open a door. It only took seconds. The door was wrenched open and light poured in.

"We're saved!" LaBerge shouted.

Everything was a blur. Being bounced around and getting my head whacked a few times didn't help. I felt hands groping at me and pulling me out of the wreck. I realized they weren't doing the same for Veego or LaBerge. Or the dados for that matter. It was me they were after. As they yanked me out of the car, I saw several people dressed all in black, with black hoods over their heads to hide their faces. Nothing made sense. Were they commandos? Burglars? Hijackers? Dados? There were enough of them that I understood how the car had been flipped over so quickly. These guys had done it, physically. I was too dizzy to do anything but go along with them. They lifted me up and quickly carried me to a car that I saw had a crushed front grill. This must have been the car that hit us from behind. I was vaguely aware that many people were on the street watching. Nobody came to help. I was bundled into the backseat of the damaged car. Two of the guys got in back with me, another got in front. A few more ran to another car, which must have been the car we hit from behind. There was no question. This was an organized operation. They had come after me. Somewhere in the distance I heard a siren. Was it an ambulance? The fire department? More security dados?

"Go!" shouted one of the guys.

The car lurched forward and I was once again moving. One of the guys pulled a cloth bag over my head. I tried to fight against it, but I was too weak.

"It's all right," a calming voice said. "You're safe. This is just for security."

Security. Right. Wherever we were going, they didn't want me to know. I was too loopy to care anyway. I think I might have passed out. I can't say for sure. We could have been driving for five minutes or five hours. It was all a blur to me. However long it took, we finally screeched to a stop. I didn't move. I was dazed, but not afraid. These guys wanted me alive. Why else would they have pulled me out of the wreck?

"C'mon," one of them said, and helped me out of the car. The urgency was gone, but they didn't take the bag off my head. From the sound of things, we were inside. As we walked, I heard a metal door closing, so it must have been a garage. Without saying another word they led me quickly along, making a few turns and going down several flights of stairs. Wherever they were taking me, it was deep within the bowels of this building. Finally, they had me sit down on a hard chair, where somebody pulled the bag off my head.

I saw that I was in a small, dark room. It looked like a cell. I had seen enough of them to know. There was a bed and a chair, but no windows. Light came from a single overhead bulb. Facing me were three of the kidnappers. They looked pretty imposing with their black outfits and dark hoods. They stood there, legs apart, facing me.

I sat up straight, took a breath, and said, "Well, that was fun."

The commando in the center reached up and pulled off his hood. All I could do was stare. It was a woman, but that's not why I was shocked.

She said, "You are now officially part of the revival."

It was Nevva Winter.

This is where I'm ending my journal. I've been stuck in this cell for nearly a day. I'm not sure if I'm a prisoner or not. Nobody is saying much. Nevva left, but promised to be back quickly to explain what is happening. I'm not going to hold my breath on that one after she left me dangling last time. Still, they're treating me well. They even gave me this paper so I could write. The food isn't as good as at the castle, and neither is my room, but I'll take this any day over being back there and wondering when I'd have to compete in another game. It's given me the chance to write this journal and think about all the things that Saint Dane said to me.

The thing is, I don't know how much of it to believe. I get all that he told me about Blok and how Quillan is such a messed-up territory. I've seen plenty of evidence to know that what he said was the truth, or close to it. What's bothering me more is the challenge he gave to me. I'm trying to get inside his head. Is this really all about him trying to destroy my confidence? Like I wrote to you before, I have to believe that for Saint Dane, a big part of controlling Halla is about beating the Travelers, and me. This may be a weird thing to say, but it feels like Saint Dane is not only trying to push each territory into chaos, but he's also trying to convince me that Halla would be better off under his guidance. How twisted is that? Does he really think I'd buy that?

As much as I know that this is a battle for all of Halla, and it's crucial that we Travelers fight it, part of me is tempted by his offer. I know, it would be idiotic for me to risk my life, but imagine how much stronger we Travelers could be if we understood the nature of our existence. Uncle Press knew, but he died before he could explain it to me. There are so many unanswered questions, and no one has any more answers than I do. Would we have a better chance against Saint Dane if we had a few of those answers? Is it worth risking my life for? Am I being selfish by not taking the chance?

I don't know. My head hurts too much to come up with an answer. Hopefully by the time I write again, the way to go will be much clearer. Until then, I'll sit and wait to find out why I'm sitting in a dark cell that smells like fish, in a deep basement, somewhere on a doomed territory.

It looks like my trip home is going to have to wait.

And so we go.

END OF JOURNAL #25

◔ SECOND EARTH ◔

Courtney had never read one of Bobby's journals alone. It was a strange and not-too-pleasant experience. Whenever she read about the most recent twist in Bobby's adventure, she always had Mark there to help her analyze it. She needed that sounding board. Mark and Courtney were polar opposites. Where Courtney was aggressive and emotional, and shot from the hip, Mark was thoughtful and cautious. Together, they were perfect. Going it alone was difficult for Courtney. It was like Adam without Eve, Lewis without Clark, Itchy without Scratchy. She needed Mark, if only to help her keep from hyperventilating as she learned about each new challenge that Bobby had to deal with. She wondered if Mark had had the same problem when she was away at school and he had to read Bobby's journals from Zadaa on his own.

Mark. Where was Mark? She thought it was lame of him not to call and tell her he wouldn't be coming over after he helped Andy Mitchell clean up his uncle's flower shop. She figured it must have taken a lot longer than expected, but still. He should have called. If anything, it made Courtney feel less guilty about reading Bobby's journals alone. She figured if Mark had a problem with that, she'd throw back at him that he never called. How could he expect her to wait a whole night before reading a new journal?

Mark and Andy's plane to Orlando was leaving early in the morning. She knew there was no way he would come over before that to read the journal. He'd have to get there at four a.m. to have enough time to read the journal and then get to the airport. As much as Mark could do no wrong in the eyes of Courtney's parents, it would be tough to explain why he was dropping by before dawn. Did Mark really think that Courtney would wait until he got back from Florida to read the journal? No way.

Courtney grabbed her cell phone and punched Mark's number again. It went right to his message box. "It's after midnight," she said curtly. "Where are you? I know you won't come over because it's so late and you've got an early flight, so I'm sorry but I'm going to read. There's no way I can wait until you get back from Orlando. What can I say? I'm weak. Buh-bye."

She felt only a little bit guilty about telling that fib. She was going to have to tell Mark she read the journal at some point. At least this way, she figured, it sounded as if she waited until the very last possible moment. She hoped Mark would understand and not be too upset with her.

It was late. It was a school night. She was tired. Courtney delicately inserted Bobby's journal back into its envelope and placed it safely inside her desk drawer. She even locked it, not that her parents ever went in there. Still, she wanted to be safe. She knew there was no way Mark would call this late, so she turned off her phone, changed into her pajamas and T-shirt, and hopped into bed. . . .

And lay there wide awake. For hours. Her body may have been exhausted, but her mind was racing. Her thoughts were full of challengers and video arcades and mechanical spiders and all the other images that Bobby wrote about. She wondered if Nevva Winter was going to be able to help him. She also wondered if Quillan was indeed lost. As horrible as that would be, if it were true, Courtney wanted Bobby to leave that territory immediately and live to fight another day. Taking part in that Grand X in order to learn about the origin of the Travelers from Saint Dane wasn't worth the risk. She wanted him home. Courtney feared for Quillan, but loved the idea of Bobby coming home. Now. She and Mark would tell him about what happened with Saint Dane, and how he took on the identity of a kid named Whitney Wilcox and nearly killed her. Saint Dane was on Second Earth and Courtney wanted Bobby there too.

All these thoughts about Bobby and Quillan kept sleep from coming. But another thought kept tugging at her. Why hadn't Mark called? She had gone from being angry with him to being worried. Mark was nothing if not the most responsible person in the history of responsibility. This wasn't like him. Not one bit. She had to believe it had something to do with Andy Mitchell. She was happy that Andy wasn't bullying him anymore, but if it meant that Andy's jerkyness was rubbing off on Mark, it wasn't worth it. She couldn't wait to hear the explanation. Why hadn't he called?

Somewhere between thinking about Mark not showing, and wondering where Bobby would stay when he came to Second Earth, Courtney fell asleep. As great as it was to be back at school, she hadn't built up her stamina yet. Her sleep was so deep, she didn't dream. She must not have even moved, because the next morning she found herself in the exact same position as when she'd gotten into bed.

What roused her was her mother calling. "Courtney? Courtney! Wake up!"

Courtney had to pull herself out of coma mode. For a second she thought she was back in the Derby Falls hospital, looking forward to another grueling day of physical therapy and soap operas. Seeing her bedside clock was a relief, until she registered that the clock said 6:10 . . . 6:10! Her alarm wasn't set to go off until 6:30; 6:10 was still night. What was her mother doing calling her so early?

"Courtney, come down here, now!"

There was an urgency to her mother's voice that Courtney didn't like. Had she done something wrong? Courtney pulled her creaky body out of bed. Sleeping in the same position may have been restful, but it didn't do much for her healing muscles. She limped across the room and wasn't able to walk without stiffness until she was halfway down the stairs. Blood flow was good. It took away the pain. The TV was on in the living room. Courtney headed that way, but was intercepted by her mother. Mrs. Chetwynde looked bad. She had a wild look in her eyes that Courtney had never seen before.

"What's up, Mom?" she asked.

"Did Mark leave for Florida last night?" she asked tentatively.

Huh? If Courtney wasn't awake before that, she sure was then. By the look on her mother's face, something was definitely up.

"No," she said. "He stayed to help Andy Mitchell clean up his uncle's florist shop. Why?"

Courtney saw the relief in her mother's eyes. "Oh, thank God," she said.

"Why? What's going on?" Courtney asked.

"Come here," Mrs. Chetwynde said. "It's all over the news."

Mrs. Chetwynde headed back for the living room. Courtney followed apprehensively. The term "all over the news" was never a good thing, especially not first thing in the morning. Good news was always expected and usually didn't end up on TV. Bad news came suddenly and spread fast. Courtney saw that her father was staring at the TV. On the screen was a live shot that looked to be taken from a helicopter over the ocean. There was a coast guard ship in the water, and another helicopter flying nearby.

"What happened?" Courtney asked.

"A plane went down," Mr. Chetwynde said. "An airliner. Apparently it had engine trouble over the Carolinas and flew out to sea to dump fuel before landing. It never came back."

"Oh, man," Courtney said. "Did it crash in the ocean?"

"That's what they think," Mr. Chetwynde said. "There's no wreck, but there's no sign of the plane, either. It had to have gone down."

"Such a tragedy," Mrs. Chetwynde said. "All those people."

"How big a plane was it?" Courtney asked.

"Wide-body, fully loaded," Mr. Chetwynde said grimly. "Two hundred and eighty passengers, seven crew members."

Courtney inhaled quickly. It was an involuntary reaction to such horrible news.

"That's why I asked about Mark," Mrs. Chetwynde said. "The flight left last night from JFK around seven o'clock, bound for Orlando."

"Mark didn't make that flight," Courtney said with authority. "He was going to help Andy and then maybe get a later flight or take one early this morning—"

The words froze in Courtney's throat. A realization hit her so suddenly that it felt like a rush of blood in her brain. It made her ears ring. Mrs. Chetwynde saw the look on her daughter's face change suddenly.

"What?" she asked Courtney.

Courtney's thoughts went into hyperdrive, calculating the possibilities. She wanted to come up with an undeniable fact that would prove her fear couldn't be true. She went through everything she'd heard the day before, every option, every scenario, but came up empty.

"What's the matter?" Mrs. Chetwynde asked. "You said he wasn't on that flight."

"He wasn't," Courtney croaked, barely able to get the words out. "But his parents flew out last night."

Mr. Chetwynde pulled his eyes from the TV and shot Courtney a look. The three stood there, frozen, not wanting to believe. Courtney broke the trance first. She ran to the kitchen and called Mark's house. She got the answering machine and a cheery greeting from Mrs. Dimond that said: "Hi there! Leave a message, okay?"

Courtney slammed the phone down. Her parents had followed her and stood together, watching.

Mrs. Chetwynde asked, "How do we find out if they were on that plane?"

Courtney bolted from the kitchen and ran for the stairs. She leaped up, three at a time. The stiffness and pain may still have been there, but she didn't feel them. Courtney blasted into her room and found her cell phone. She was going to call Mark, but when she turned on the phone, she saw that she had a message waiting for her. She wasn't sure if that was good news or bad news. All she could do was play it. Courtney hit the message code, and listened.

The digital voice said, "Message recorded at three thirty a.m." Courtney allowed herself a small breath. The call had come in long after the doomed flight took off. A moment later Mark's voice was heard.

"I . . . It's me," he said.

Courtney was hit with two huge waves of conflicting emotion. Mark was alive. She would have screamed with joy and relief, if not for the tone of his voice. Courtney knew Mark better than most anyone on the territory. She only needed to hear those few words to know that he was hurting. She feared she knew the reason why.

Mark was crying. Courtney could hear him sniffle, then let out a soft, pained whimper. "They're gone," he said.

Courtney's knees went weak. Those two simple words confirmed it. The plane that went down over the dark ocean was carrying Mr. and Mrs. Dimond. Courtney started to cry. Mark's parents were dead. If not for the accident at Andy's uncle's shop, Mark and Andy would have been on that plane too. She wanted to be with Mark to hold him and tell him how everything was okay, though she knew it wasn't. She wanted to know where he was. Probably at the airport, or the police station, or somewhere. Where did people go when they heard that their family was lost at sea and wouldn't be coming back? Who tells you those things? She hated herself for not leaving her phone on the night before.

Courtney knew what she had to do. She would find Mark and bring him back to her house. She wasn't sure what other relatives he had, but she knew that none of them lived in town. He was an only child. Until things could be sorted out, she wanted Mark to stay with them. Maybe even *after* they were sorted out. They would be his new family. Courtney had no doubt that her parents would take him in. After all, he'd saved their daughter's life!

All of these thoughts and plans flashed through Courtney's head in the few seconds after she heard the words that his parents were gone. It may have been a defense mechanism to keep back the pain, but that was Courtney. She was ready to take positive action and provide solutions. What she heard next, though, knocked those thoughts right out of her head.

"Come to the flume," Mark said. *Click*. He hung up. End of message.

Courtney stared at the phone. Had she heard right?

"Did you get him?" Mr. Chetwynde asked.

Courtney whipped around to see both her parents arriving at her door.

"Uhhh . . ." was all Courtney managed to squeak out. Her

brain had maxed out. She couldn't process the information fast enough.

"Did you get Mark?" Mrs. Chetwynde asked. "Are his parents okay?"

Courtney knew she had to get a grip. She closed her eyes, took a breath, and said to herself, *One thing at a time.* She exhaled and said softly, "He left a message. His parents were on the plane."

"Oh, no!" Mrs. Chetwynde cried.

Mr. Chetwynde hugged his wife. Courtney joined them. Her father put his arm around his little girl, and the three stood there, giving one another support and comfort in this sad and shocking moment. It was the kind of support and comfort Courtney knew Mark would never have again with his own family. Courtney stayed in her parents' arms, not wanting the moment to end, because she knew what she had to do next. She feared there was more to this than a tragic accident. For whatever reason, Mark had gone to the flume. She didn't dare speculate as to why. All she could do was hope he was okay. Anything beyond that was too frightening to think about.

◉ SECOND EARTH ◉
(CONTINUED)

Courtney skipped school. The day before, going to school was one of the most important things in her life. It symbolized her return to being normal and healthy. Now, after what happened, school dropped off the list of important things to do. She didn't want to hear the kids talking about the accident. She didn't want to answer questions about whether or not she had talked to Mark. She didn't want to put on a stoic face and pretend there wasn't more going on than anyone knew. Because there was. Courtney had to go to the flume.

She grabbed her backpack and left at the regular time to catch the bus. Her parents wanted her to stay home, but she said she'd rather go. She didn't say where. After hugging her parents good-bye, maybe a little tighter than normal, she left for the bus stop . . . and walked right past it.

The Sherwood house wasn't a far walk through Courtney's suburban neighborhood in Stony Brook. She had been there several times. It was a giant abandoned mansion that had once belonged to a guy who made his fortune raising poultry. He died years ago, and it had been empty ever since while his heirs argued over what to do with the land. Courtney's dad said it would be in court for years because nobody was giving in. The property was too valuable. Courtney had no idea what the issues were. She didn't care. The kids told stories about how the Sherwood house was haunted by the ghost of the chicken guy, who could be heard clucking at midnight. Courtney had told that story herself more than once. But now, she knew the truth about the house, and it was far more amazing than the appearance of a clucking ghost.

In its basement was a flume to the territories. When she and Mark became Bobby's acolytes, they saw it being created. In this basement they jumped into the flume and traveled to Cloral and then Eelong. It was where the Traveler named Seegen died. It was where they saw Saint Dane for the first time, when his long gray hair exploded in flames, leaving him bald and scarred. It was where the demon dropped off the dirty bag that held Gunny's hand, to lure Bobby to Eelong. Now there was going to be another chapter added to the story of the Sherwood house. Mark had gone there after hearing of the death of his parents. Courtney needed to know why.

The estate was surrounded by a high stone wall. The front gates were locked tight with a padlock. That never stopped Mark and Courtney. Along the side of the property a tree grew close enough to the wall that a quick climb got you on top. Courtney went right for the tree, glanced around to make sure nobody was watching, then climbed like a squirrel. Though Courtney was still stiff and sore, climbing wasn't a problem. Getting down on the other side was. There was no tree there. She had to jump. She knew that was going to hurt. Worse, she wasn't sure how her damaged leg would hold up in a jarring fall. Once on top of the wall, she couldn't waste time. If somebody saw her up there, they'd call the police for sure. Courtney quickly threw her legs over the side, and while putting all her weight on her arms, lowered herself down until she was stretched out to her full body length, with only her fingertips holding on to the top of the wall. It was still a four-foot drop to the ground.

Her newly healed left arm felt like it was on fire. Still, she didn't drop right away. What if the impact was too hard? Her left leg would shatter. She made the snap decision that she had to land on her right leg. But landing on one foot from that high wasn't so smart either. If she landed wrong, she could do just as much damage. She might even blow out her knee. In those few seconds Courtney wished she had thought this part through a little better. It was too late, she was losing her grip. She took a breath and slipped off. She dropped the few feet and landed on her right foot, bending her knee and trying to absorb as much of the impact as possible. She hit and fell, landing on her right side. Courtney had heard the term "bone jarring" but it never meant much to her, until then. Her bones had been jarred. She lay there on the patchy grass, breathing hard, doing a mental checklist of body parts. Though the painful burn was intense, nothing seemed to be damaged. Everything moved. She waited for the agony to pass, and after a minute she was able to sit up. As much as the fall hurt, the only real damage was to her lower lip. She had bitten it. She'd live. And walk.

Courtney pulled herself to her feet and took a few tentative steps. So far, so good. The hard part was still to come. Courtney knew the Sherwood house very well. She had been in almost every room. It wasn't as if she had been exploring, though. She and Mark had taken a very quick tour of the house, on the run, while being chased by a vicious pair of rampaging quig-dogs. The quigs hadn't shown themselves since then, but Courtney wasn't taking any chances. She was armed with two canisters of pepper spray, one in each pocket of her jacket, like a gunslinger with a six-shooter on each hip. She knew there was no way she could outrun one of those beasties in her condition. If they were going to attack, she would stand her ground and unload on them with the burning spray.

With one hand on each canister, Courtney walked tentatively to the house. It was a spooky old mansion, even in daylight. Since it was late fall, the yard was gray and bleak, with dead leaves blowing everywhere. It was easy to see why the place had a reputation for being haunted. She climbed the stairs up to the porch and went right for the front door. It was never locked. She figured the people who took care of the place thought the lock on the front gate was enough to keep out intruders. Fools.

Courtney's heart raced. She feared that a quig-dog might attack, but she was also anxious about what she would find at the flume. She hoped it would be Mark. She pushed the door open and peered into the big, empty foyer.

"Here, doggie doggie doggie," she called.

All she heard back was the lonely echo of her own voice. Her confidence rose. Quigs weren't subtle. If they were around and wanted to attack, they would have by now. Still, she kept her hands on the pepper spray just in case.

She closed the door and went right for the stairs that led down to the basement. Now that she was getting close, her anxiety rose. She wanted to know what she would find down there. She picked up the pace as she climbed down the stairs and walked across the vast empty basement to the wooden door that led to the root cellar, and the flume. She stopped outside the door and looked at the star symbol that marked it as a gate. She remembered back to when she and Mark saw it magically burned into the wood by some unseen force. As she stood there, staring at the symbol, she shook her head in wonder. Life was turning out to be a whole lot different than she'd expected.

"Mark?" she called. "You in there?"

No answer. She pulled open the creaky wooden door and stepped into the dank earthen cellar.

Mark wasn't there. The large, rocky tunnel that was the flume was quiet and dark. Courtney's eyes took a second to adjust. She stood at the mouth of the flume, looking into the depths of infinity.

"What did you do, Mark?" she said aloud.

Her biggest fear was that Mark had jumped into the flume, headed for another territory. But only Travelers could use the flumes. They learned that lesson the hard way. It collapsed on Eelong for one reason and one reason only: because Mark and Courtney had traveled. She had trouble believing that Mark would use the flume again knowing how dangerous and wrong it was. But Mark might not have been thinking clearly. She couldn't imagine getting the news that her parents had both been killed. For all she knew, Mark might have lost it. There was no way that anybody could think straight after hearing something like that. The question was, how "off" did his thinking get? Was he so messed up that he didn't worry about the dangers and jumped in? If that happened, where would he go? To find Bobby? But why?

As well as she knew Mark, she couldn't get inside his head to figure out why he would have come here, or asked her to come. She had done what he asked. But coming here didn't answer any questions. It only raised more. With a shrug, she turned to leave.

That's when she saw it. She hadn't noticed at first, because her eyes were still adjusting to the dark. Now she saw something on top of an overturned wooden box a few feet back from the mouth of the flume. It was a manila envelope. A regular old Second Earth envelope. Written in large black letters was a single word: COURTNEY.

Courtney dove at the envelope and quickly picked it up. She

knew it had to be from Mark. That's why she was there, to get this. Without wasting another second, she tore it open, being careful not to damage anything that might be inside. Peering in, she saw a slip of paper, and two smaller envelopes. She pulled the paper out first to see it was a note.

It read: *This is the hardest thing I've ever had to do. Please forgive me. Mark.*

Courtney couldn't catch her breath. What had he done? She was beginning to think he might have jumped into the flume after all. She dropped the note back in the large envelope and pulled out one of the two smaller envelopes. It had weight. Something solid was inside. Written on the outside of the envelope was a series of numbers: #15-224. Courtney knew exactly what it was, an assigned account code. Seeing this, Courtney also knew what she would find inside the small envelope. She tore it open and dumped the contents into her hand. It was a small brass key. Courtney held the account number and the key to the safe-deposit box where Mark stored Bobby's journals at the National Bank of Stony Brook. Bobby had opened the account on First Earth, 1937, and asked them to keep his journals safe there. Mark had dutifully stored every bit of correspondence from Bobby in that bank. Courtney nervously bit her already hurting lip to stop herself from crying. Mark had handed over the responsibility of Bobby's journals to her. But why?

There was one more small envelope in the bigger envelope. Courtney pulled it out to discover this one had some weight as well. She tore it open, looked inside, and this time she couldn't stop herself. She cried. Courtney wasn't somebody who cried much. She barely shed a tear throughout her whole painful ordeal after the accident. But at that moment, tears filled her eyes and she flat out sobbed. She hadn't expected this. It hit her like a speeding truck. The emotion poured out; she couldn't help it. Inside this envelope was something that couldn't be, yet was.

It was Mark's Traveler ring. It was the ring that was given to him so long ago by Loor's mother, Osa, before they even knew that Bobby was missing. Before they heard of things called flumes and territories and Travelers. Before they heard of Saint Dane. This ring had never left Mark from the moment Osa gave it to him, until now. When she saw it, Courtney knew. There was no doubt in her mind. Mark had jumped into the flume and wherever he'd gone, he wasn't coming back.

"Mark, what were you thinking?" she sobbed.

Courtney sat down on the wooden box and let her emotions pour out. There was nothing she could do. Mark left no other clue as to what had happened. Courtney knew that had to be intentional. If Mark had wanted Courtney to know more, he would have told her. Seeing the items he left, it was pretty clear what Mark had in mind for her. He wanted her to receive Bobby's journals and keep them safe. Alone. She would do it, no question. She was prepared. But she wasn't prepared to be without Mark.

She didn't want to be at the flume anymore. It felt like the walls of the basement were closing in on her. She wanted to be outside, in the light, where she could breathe and think. The open mouth of the flume gave her the shivers, as if it were taunting her. There were answers in there, through the tunnel, but they were beyond her reach.

She quickly put the safe-deposit key in her jacket pocket, along with the envelope that had the account number. She folded up Mark's note to her and slipped it inside the same pocket. She was left with the heavy silver ring with the gray stone that was surrounded by carved symbols—one for each territory. She was about to drop it into her pocket, when she stopped. No, she thought, that was wrong. This ring wasn't a "thing" to be carried around. It was a living symbol of Halla. Of Bobby and the Travelers. Of Mark. There was only one way to respectfully possess a Traveler ring. Courtney held the heavy ring in the palm of her left hand. She had held this ring before, many times, but never with such a feeling of importance. Of destiny. Though she and Mark were both acolytes, it was Mark's ring. Osa had given it to him. Whenever she touched it, she always felt a little bit uncomfortable, as if she weren't worthy. But now Mark had given it to her. It was her ring. She was now the sole acolyte from Second Earth. There was only one thing to do. Courtney held the ring up and looked at it with reverence. She wiped away her last tears and said, "Mark, wherever you are, I hope you know what you're doing, you dork." She slipped the silver circle onto the ring finger of her right hand. It fit perfectly

Instantly, as if in response, Courtney heard a crackling, groaning sound. She froze. She knew what that meant. She'd heard it before. She spun around and saw it.

The flume was coming to life.

◎ SECOND EARTH ◎

(CONTINUED)

Courtney jumped back, away from the flume, hitting her back against the stone wall opposite the mouth. She stared in wonder as the tiny light appeared far in the distance, growing larger. Someone was coming in. Courtney had seen this phenomenon before. She had flown through the flume herself, but never had she experienced any of it alone. She found herself holding her hand out to her side, as if to reach for Mark, but Mark wasn't there.

The light grew brighter. She could hear the faint sweet musical notes that always accompanied the Travelers on their journeys through the flumes. The tunnel itself seemed to twist, ever so subtly, as if stretching out and preparing itself to welcome the visitor—whoever it might be.

"Please be Mark," Courtney said to nobody. "Or Bobby."

She didn't have to say who she *didn't* want it to be.

As the light grew brighter, the gray stone walls of the tunnel melted into crystal. Courtney knew it wouldn't be long now. Whoever was coming was almost there. Brilliant light blasted out of the tunnel and threw dancing, sparkling beams all around the root cellar. Courtney squinted and shielded her eyes, but wanted to see it all. Moments later she saw the shadow of a Traveler landing in the mouth of the tunnel.

"Mark?" she shouted over the now-loud music. "Bobby?"

The light didn't disappear after the Traveler arrived. It continued to shine brightly. That was unusual. Courtney had only seen that happen once before. It wasn't a happy memory. If Courtney could have backed herself *through* the stone wall, she would have.

"Hi, Courtney," came a friendly guy's voice. "Long time no see!"

Courtney nearly fainted. She knew that voice. In her mind she was suddenly transported back to a lonely road in the Berkshire mountains. She was lying in a heap, bruised and broken. The headlights of the car that hit her cut through the darkness. The driver of the car stepped in front of the headlights so she could see him. It was the guy who nearly killed her. The guy who *tried* to kill her. The guy she was riding to meet because she had such a mad crush on him. Courtney's head was spinning. This wasn't making sense. That was a memory. A horrible, life-changing memory. Why was she seeing it happen again?

The Traveler stepped out of the flume. He was a cute guy of around seventeen with curly blond hair and a devilish smile. He wore sweats that said: STANSFIELD ACADEMY, and carried a soccer ball. It was a nightmare. It was Whitney Wilcox.

It was Saint Dane.

"Miss me?" he asked brightly as he kneed the soccer ball into the air and caught it. "I'm glad you're feeling better. For a while there I didn't think you'd make it."

Courtney could barely breathe. She stared in wide-eyed shock.

"I—I don't understand," she stammered.

Whitney laughed heartily. "Now *there's* an understatement! What's even funnier is you don't understand how much you don't understand."

Courtney shook her head. It was all she could do.

"I'm sure you and Mark have been fretting over what I've planned for Second Earth. Haven't you?"

Courtney didn't answer. She couldn't.

"I'll bet you were wondering if Pendragon's success on First Earth spared your territory. Be honest, that's what you were hoping for, right?"

Whitney kicked the soccer ball expertly from foot to knee and back to foot, then caught it.

Courtney stood frozen.

"Well, I'm sorry to say you'd be wrong. I've been having fun here on your self-absorbed little territory for quite some time now. Want to see what I've been up to?"

She didn't, but she had to.

Whitney threw the soccer ball into the air, turned, and kicked it back into the light that blasted from the flume. When he turned back to Courtney, he had transformed. He wasn't Whitney Wilcox anymore. He was . . .

"Mitchell!" Courtney screamed.

Standing in the mouth of the flume was Andy Mitchell. He snorted, pushed his greasy hair back, and said cockily, "Yo, Chetwynde, how they hangin'?"

"No . . . ," Courtney said, stunned. "No!"

"Oh yeah," Mitchell said. "Right from the start. We grew up together, Chetwynde!"

He spit out a lougie and laughed. He may have been Saint Dane, but he had all the mannerisms of Andy Mitchell that Courtney knew so well—because he *was* Andy Mitchell!

"My favorite part was when I stole Pendragon's journals," he cackled. "Man, I had you guys squirming. Pretty good how you got out of that one, I'll give you that."

It was too much for Courtney to comprehend. Her whole sense of reality had been turned inside out. "So . . . there never was an Andy Mitchell?" she asked numbly.

"Of course there was," the kid answered. "You're looking at him. Except he wasn't exactly what you thought he was." Mitchell cackled out another laugh and brushed his hair back. "Surprise!"

"Where's Mark?" Courtney asked with a touch of desperation.

"Oh, no," Mitchell said, wagging his finger. "That would be telling. Let's just say our friendship has entered a whole new phase."

As the truth sank in, Courtney was hit with a realization that was so stunning, it rocked her back into complete focus. She was no longer frightened. She was mad.

"You killed the Dimonds, didn't you?" she seethed. "That plane disappeared because of you, Saint Dane."

Andy Mitchell took a deep bow and said, "Just another piece in a very complicated puzzle."

Courtney snapped to attention. That was the single most horrifying thing she had ever heard. Everything that had ever happened with Andy Mitchell, from the moment they met him in kindergarten until the death of Mark's parents, was all a plot. Saint Dane had been working his way into their lives long before they knew about Travelers and flumes and Halla. Whatever his plan for Second Earth was, it had been in the works for years.

"Enjoy your life, Chetwynde," Mitchell said as he turned back toward the flume. "What is it that your Traveler friend says? Oh yeah. Hobey-ho. Let's go!"

He leaped into the flume.

"No!" Courtney shouted.

Courtney didn't think, she acted. She ran at Mitchell, ready to tackle him and keep him from leaving. It was an insane move, but Courtney wasn't in her right mind. She jumped into the flume, but it was too late. Mitchell was gone. Courtney hit the crystal floor, empty handed.

"Saint Dane!" she screamed at nobody. He was gone.

Courtney was on her hands and knees, still bathed in the light of the flume. That's when she felt it. The slight tug. Courtney snapped a look deeper into the tunnel. She saw that the light wasn't disappearing. What was going on? The tug became stronger. Courtney realized with horror that she was being pulled farther in! She got her wits together and crawled backward. At least, she *tried* to crawl. It was like pulling against a tornado. She spun around, sat on her bottom, and dug her heels into the crystal floor. It didn't help. She was being pulled, inch by agonizing inch, deep into the flume. The harder she fought, the more difficult it became. She made one last-ditch attempt to stop herself by flipping over and trying to grab the edge of the tunnel with her fingers. It was too late. Her hands scraped across the coarse crystal, and she was yanked into infinity.

When Courtney spun back to look past her toes, she saw that she was on her way. She was traveling. But to where? She had been through a flume before, so she wasn't terrified. At least she wasn't terrified of the experience. The fact that she was there at all was a different concern. She forced herself to take a few deep breaths and calm down. She had to be prepared for whatever she would find on the far side.

There was one small consolation. Unlike every other time she'd traveled through the flume, the rocky tunnel hadn't cracked. That was what ultimately destroyed the flume on Eelong. Every time she and Mark had traveled, the flume physically cracked a little bit more, until that last fateful trip when it collapsed and Kasha was killed. But when she was sucked into the flume this time, there was no damage. She couldn't begin to guess why, but she was grateful.

As she sped through the crystal tunnel, she gazed out onto the starfield beyond. As Bobby had described, she saw many of the ghostly images from the territories, as if they were being projected in space. She recognized some galloping zenzens from Eelong, along with the miniature helicopter that Bobby and Kasha flew to Black Water. She saw what looked like a vast tribe of primitive people, chanting and singing. She also saw something that she recognized from history books as the LZ-129—the airship *Hindenburg* from First Earth. All the images jumbled into one another, making Courtney feel as if she were traveling through an ocean of time and space, where all the territories existed together.

She had no idea how long she had been flying through the flume. It was long enough that she had calmed down and prepared to face whatever she would find on the far side. At least, she hoped she was ready. She hadn't said the name of a territory when she left. Then again, neither had Saint Dane. There was no way to know where she might end up. Above all else, she hoped she would find Mark or Bobby.

The musical notes grew more frantic, which meant she was about to arrive at her destination. Courtney tensed up. Just before she landed, the last thought she had was that she wished Mark was with her. A moment later her feet touched solid ground. She stood up, having been gently deposited at the end of the line. Brilliant light swirled everywhere, making it impossible to see where she was. It took a few seconds for the light and music to recede back into the flume, and allow her the first look at her new surroundings. She took a quick look around to see . . . she was back in the root cellar under the Sherwood house. She was still on Second Earth!

Courtney had no idea what to make of that. It was the absolute last place she expected to be. On the other hand, it was the *best* place she could be. She was safe at home, though she knew "safe" was a relative word. She was relieved, but frustrated. There was nobody she could go to and ask what had happened. She didn't have Mark to help figure it out. She was about as alone as she had ever been in her life.

She said to herself, *Get used to it, Chetwynde.*

She felt an odd sensation. Her first thought was that she was being pulled back into the flume, so she jumped forward like she was stepping on hot coals. A quick look back showed her that the flume wasn't activating. So what was she feeling?

The answer came a second later. Light sparkled from the ring on her finger. The Traveler ring. Mark's ring. No, her ring. She quickly took it off and put it on the ground in front of the flume. The ring grew and light flashed from the opening. Courtney closed her eyes. She needed a second to catch her breath. She didn't know when she'd get another chance. The musical notes grew louder, and ended just as quickly. When Courtney opened her eyes, the ring was back to normal. On the ground next to it was another envelope just like the last one that had come through. It was Bobby's next journal from Quillan.

The first journal she was solely responsible for.

She said out loud, "And so we go."

QUILLAN

This is the beginning of the end. Or the end of the beginning. I'm not sure which. After you finish reading this journal, guys, you can tell me. In fact, you can tell me in person because I'm coming home. It's time. Ever since Saint Dane made that comment on Zadaa about knowing what's happening with Courtney, I've been worried about what might be going on back there. Maybe I should have already come home, but I made the choice to go to Quillan. I hope that wasn't a mistake.

My experience here on Quillan has been different than on any of the other territories. As I'm writing this, I'm still not a hundred percent sure of what the turning point is. Saint Dane was right about one thing—this territory is a mess. I already told you a lot about it. I've seen so much more. I'll tell you about it in this journal. The big question is, is Quillan already lost? I don't think so.

I've been given a golden opportunity to try to make things better, at least in a small way. It may not be a huge, global turning point, but who knows? Maybe a small positive change can snowball and help put the territory back on its feet. That's hoping for a lot, but what can I say? It's all I've got.

It won't be easy. In fact, it's pretty scary. But that's okay. I'm up for it. I'm writing this journal now, because it's about to begin. When it's over, I believe I will have done as much as I can for the people of Quillan. But there's more to it than that. If I'm successful, and I will be, I think I'll be taking a huge step toward reaching the end of this whole odyssey. Not just here on Quillan, but as a Traveler. Saint Dane is losing, I'm sure of that now. He's desperate. We've lost Travelers along the way, and that is a tragedy, but we're winning. You know how I keep writing about how I'm afraid that we may be winning battles and possibly losing the war? I don't think that's the case anymore. I think we're winning battles and getting close to winning the war, too. Saint Dane's confidence isn't what it used to be. Since I became a Traveler, he has done everything he could to get me to give up, but I'm still here. He tried to get me to join him, but I never considered it, even for a second. On Zadaa he went so far as to beat me up physically to get me to give up the fight. It didn't work. It only made me stronger. Here on Quillan he's trying something new. He's going to fail at that, too. All this tells me is that he's running out of ideas. We're going to beat him, guys. I think what's happening here on Quillan is the beginning of the end. Or the end of the beginning . . . of my life as a Traveler. Of course there are no guarantees. Anything can happen. But for the first time since I left home, I can see the end, and it's good.

To explain what I'm about to do, I have to go back to when I was kidnapped away from Veego and LaBerge by the Traveler from Quillan, Nevva Winter. It turned out that she wasn't at all the person I first thought she was. But more about that later. After the accident I was kept in that cool, wet, fishy-smelling cell for about a day. They tried to make me comfortable, but that wasn't easy considering the bed was a thin mattress and it was so damp that my bones ached. At least it wasn't as bad as that cell on Eelong. Not by a long shot. Compared to that, this was like living large at the Manhattan Tower Hotel.

I wasn't treated badly, though. There was a guy stationed outside my room who actually apologized for having to keep me in that cell. He said I wasn't a prisoner, but that it wouldn't be safe for me to be wandering around. I didn't question him. Safe was good. A few times I asked him where I was and who the others were, but he just shook his head and said it wasn't his place to tell me.

Just once I'd like to meet up with somebody who had all the answers and was willing to spill.

I took the time to write my last journal and collect my thoughts. Of course everything Saint Dane told me about Blok and how it controlled every aspect of everything on Quillan kept rolling around in my head. This was a territory run entirely by a store, and for profit. It was a soulless society that existed only to serve the bottom line of Blok, and to make those who ran the company wealthy. How sick was that?

On top of my worrying about the sad state of Quillan, Saint Dane had dangled a very big carrot that was tearing me apart. He wanted me to compete in the big game called the Grand X. Why? He wanted to see me lose. No, he wanted to see me humiliated. In return he offered to explain the origin of the Travelers. Could I trust him? It was an incredible opportunity. He was offering to unlock everything. Everything! I could discover who I really was and what had happened to my family. But as desperate as I was to learn those truths, I decided that the stakes were too high. With the Quillan games it wasn't so much about winning or losing, it was about staying alive. People died playing these games. It wasn't worth the risk, no matter how tempting the payoff. No way I was going to enter the Grand X.

That's where my head was as I hung out in that cell. I tried to get some sleep and probably nodded out a few times, but it sure wasn't restful. At one point my guard came in with a breakfast of dry bread and overripe fruit. It wasn't exactly gourmet, but I was too hungry to care. I was nearly finished when my cell door opened again, and in stepped the person I wanted most to see. Nevva Winter. Finally! She was dressed all in black, just as she had been the day before when I was kidnapped. She moved quickly, almost nervously. That was her style.

"Good morning!" she said, hurrying in. "I hope you slept well."

"Keep hoping," I said.

Nevva had a black tool that looked like a heavy set of pliers, with sharp teeth. She opened and shut the jaws, saying, "These are impossible to come by. This one was stolen from a security dado."

"What is it?" I asked.

"Hold your left arm out," she commanded.

I did. Nevva slipped one end of the jaws underneath the silver loop on my arm. Excellent! She was going to free me from my electronic leash.

"Hold still," she said. "This might hurt."

"Hurt?" I shouted in surprise. "Why would it—"

The loop squeezed my arm as she clamped the jaws around it. The little needles, or whatever they were that held it tight, dug into my arm.

"Owwww!" I said. "Let go!"

"We've got to get rid of this," she said, grunting with exertion.

"Then hurry!" The loop was cutting off my circulation. If she didn't hurry, it would cut off my whole arm! "Owwww!" I heard a quick, sharp electronic chirp. An instant later the pain was gone. The loop released. Nevva clipped through it, and the vicious cuff fell to the floor. I rubbed my biceps to get the circulation back.

"There," she said triumphantly. "You're free."

"Thanks, I think. Why the special tool?"

"This not only cuts through the metal, it interrupts the power source," she explained. "If you try to cut off a loop without interrupting the power, it will squeeze off your arm."

Yikes.

"I'm glad I didn't know that before you got it off," I said.

"Put these on," she commanded, handing me a black shirt, pants, and jacket like the ones she was wearing. "You can't go around dressed like a challenger."

She turned her back to give me some privacy. I changed quickly, happy to be rid of that challenger shirt.

"I'm sorry you had to spend the night here," she said. "There was nothing I could do. There was an investigation into the accident when we freed you. I had to be there with the security force to report back to the trustees. If I wasn't there, it would have raised suspicions and—"

"Don't worry," I interrupted. "It's cool. I'm just glad you got me away from those guys."

"It was very well planned," Nevva said. "I know, because I planned it. Everything had to work perfectly or people might have gotten hurt. That's why you weren't brought before the trustees sooner. I needed time to organize the operation."

That explained why I had to wait at the castle so long before being brought to Blok.

"Who helped you do all this?" I asked.

"I'll answer your questions later," she replied quickly. "We need to get moving. There is so much to do, and I don't have much time so—"

"Stop!" I said firmly. "Take a breath, all right?"

She was talking so fast it was like she was a wind-up toy with a tight spring.

"You got me out of there, that's great. But I'm not moving until you tell me who the hell you are," I said.

"I did tell you!" she complained. "I'm the Traveler from Quillan."

"Yeah, but that's all you've told me," I said. "I don't know anything else about you. Give me one good reason why I shouldn't bust out of here and jump back into the flume."

Nevva took a breath to calm herself, which didn't look easy for her to do. She always seemed to be in hyperdrive.

"All right," she answered. "Here's your reason to stay. I know how to save Quillan."

Oh.

We stared each other down for a good long moment.

"Okay, good reason," I finally said, trying to sound casual. It was actually a great reason, but I needed to wrestle back some kind of control.

"Now would you please come with me?" she asked.

"No," I answered, and sat down. "I need to know what I've gotten myself into. Or should I say, I need to know what *you've* gotten me into."

Nevva sighed and glanced at her watch. "I suppose we can spare a few minutes," she said as if she guarded her minutes very carefully.

I said, "Start with telling me your story."

Nevva glanced out the cell door to see if anyone was listening. They weren't. She opened the cell door wide to make sure we'd see if anybody happened by. She seemed upset. I didn't know if it was because she didn't want to open up about herself, or because I was throwing off her precious schedule. I didn't care. I needed to know.

"I've always lived here in the city of Rune," she began. "My father was an engineer who specialized in dado repair. My mother was a maintenance worker at the Blok building. That meant she cleaned the offices of the trustees. Both worked for the same wage that is assigned to lower-sector workers, which is to say we were barely getting by. But we did get by. Things would have been fine, if not for the fact that I was, how should I put it, gifted. From the time I was quite young, I tested very high on the intelligence charts. My parents felt I was destined for great things. They didn't want to see me working a job in the lower sector, where it is so difficult to earn a living wage. But to do that, I needed to go to school. And that was a problem."

"Why? Aren't there public schools on Quillan?" I asked.

"I don't know what you mean by 'public', but most children do not go to school. Only the gifted ones, and it is quite expensive. My parents worked two shifts each to pay the fees. They had such high hopes for me, there was nothing they wouldn't have done to give me a better life."

I wondered if Nevva's parents were her biological parents. So many of the Travelers were raised by people who weren't, including me.

"I did well in school," Nevva said. "I was being groomed for a management position within Blok. It was exactly what my parents hoped for. But it was getting more and more difficult for them to earn enough to keep me in school. The higher the grade level I reached, the more expensive it became." Her voice grew solemn. "That's when my father started to wager on the games."

"I'm guessing he didn't do so well," I said.

"At first he did, but it didn't last. It never does. I won't bore you with the tragic details, but my father ended up losing his job and was sent to the tarz. Do you know what that means?"

Unfortunately, I did. I nodded.

"My mother was never the same," Nevva said. "Losing my father was like losing a piece of herself. She became bitter. The idea that my father died trying to educate me so I could work for the very company that sent him to his death was something she could not accept. To this day I'm not entirely sure of what happened, but I believe she did something foolish. She had access to the trustees because of her job. The security police never told me the exact charges, but I believe she tried to somehow harm the trustees. My mother was not a violent person, but she was pushed beyond her emotional limits. There's no saying what people might do when they get to that frightening place. My mother wasn't herself anymore. I'll never forget that morning. She kissed me good-bye and said she loved me. I never saw her again."

Nevva looked to the ground. For a second I thought she was going to cry. I didn't interrupt her. I knew how she felt, sort of. I had lost both my parents too. Though I'm holding on to the hope that I'll see them again. Nevva didn't have that hope.

After a few moments she took a breath and said, "My story isn't unique. Blok creates pain. It feeds on pain. It profits from pain."

"What did you do?" I asked.

"The trustees actually took pity on me," she answered. "At least that's what they called it. I call it payback. They took over my education and created this job for me as special assistant. Though it's more of a sentence than a job. I'm paying for what my mother did to them . . . or tried to do. I may not be laboring in the tarz, but make no mistake, I am their slave. Sometimes I wish they would send me to the tarz, so I don't have to listen to them anymore."

"When did you learn about being a Traveler?" I asked.

"Shortly after my father was sent to the tarz," she said. "A man paid me a visit and said there was something important he needed to show me. He was a stranger, but there was something about him that made me trust him."

"It was Press, wasn't it?" I asked.

For the first time since I'd met her, Nevva smiled.

"He told me all about you," she said. "He told me that one day you would arrive and help me guide the territory out of this horrible time. That was so long ago, I never thought this day would come. In the meantime he took me through the flumes and showed me the wonders of Halla. I saw all three Earth territories and learned of their history. I could relate to how the Milago were treated by the Bedoowan on Denduron, and how badly the gars were treated by the klee of Eelong. I swam underwater on Cloral and jumped into my own fantasy on Veelox. Without those experiences, I never would have believed I was a Traveler."

"Do you know that Press is dead?" I asked.

Nevva nodded. "I understand we have lost many Travelers."

"There's been a boatload of tragedy," I said. "The one thing I hang on to is that I don't believe anybody died in vain. Saint Dane is getting weaker. At one time I thought for sure that Halla would be his, now I'm thinking we've turned the tide. We're going to stop him."

"Do you think he's come to Quillan?" Nevva asked me.

I wasn't sure how to break the news to her. Nevva seemed like somebody who was all about being buttoned up and in control. I didn't want to just blurt out: "You idiot! He's a trustee!" That wouldn't have been cool, so I answered carefully.

"I've seen Saint Dane take many forms," I said. "Sometimes he creates his own character, other times he takes on the life of someone who already exists. Don't ask me how he can do it. Uncle Press never explained it, and I haven't figured it out myself. Let's just say he's got powers, and he uses them to confuse us."

"You're about to tell me he's already here, aren't you?" Nevva asked.

"Mr. Kayto," I answered. "Saint Dane assumed his character."

For a second I thought Nevva was going to faint. She actually seemed to sway, like it was going to be lights-out. I almost jumped up to grab her, but she collected herself and looked right at me.

"For how long?" she asked.

"I don't know," I answered. "He revealed himself to me after I was in front of the trustees. He likes to tell me he's around, just to make me squirm."

"What is he trying to do here?" Nevva asked.

"If he's telling the truth, he's not doing anything to harm Quillan."

"Really?" Nevva asked hopefully.

"That's not good news," I answered. "It's because he thinks Quillan is already doomed. He's just hanging around to pick up the pieces."

"Oh," Nevva said softly.

"There's more," I said. "He wants me to compete in the Grand X, just to see me lose. Humiliated, embarrassed, whatever."

Nevva's eyes lit up. "Are you serious?" she asked. I could have sworn she was happy about that news.

I said, "Why don't you tell me why you put these challenger clothes at the flume."

Nevva jumped to her feet and said, "Quillan can be saved, Pendragon. The time is coming. Change is coming. All we need is one last piece of the puzzle before the revival can begin."

"Revival," I echoed. "That's what you said when I was brought here. What is it?"

"It's the future of Quillan," Nevva answered. "And the past. Quillan is not dead. There's hope. It rests with the revival. That's what I want to show you. I can explain it all, but it's best you see for yourself. You *need* to see."

"Why's that?" I asked.

"The planning has taken a generation," she said. "The revival is ready to erupt; all that's needed is one more element."

"Which is?" I asked.

"You, Pendragon. It's you."

QUILLAN

Nevva made me put the cloth bag back over my head before leaving the cell so I wouldn't be able to see where I was.

"Trust me," she said. "This isn't my choice."

"Yeah?" I said. "Whose choice is it?"

"You'll find out very soon," she said while handing me the bag. I had to trust her. What else could I do? I put the bag over my head, and she led me on what seemed like an elaborate journey up stairs, down corridors, up elevators and down elevators. It felt like we walked for half a mile. Then again, she could have been walking me around in circles. I had no idea. Finally I felt the warmth of the Quillan sun. We were out on the street. When she pulled the bag off my head, I had to squint against the bright light.

"Is it safe?" I asked. "I mean, if a dado sees me, I could get yanked right back to the castle."

"You tell me," she said as she pointed around the corner. I took a peek and was confronted by a sea of people, walking along both sides of the street, jamming the sidewalks. She said, "Without the loop it's easy to get lost."

I felt like a needle about to jump into a haystack. It helped that I wasn't wearing the bright red challenger shirt anymore. As we walked along, I never felt more insignificant. It was like being one of those fish that moved around in a giant school, with everybody turning at the exact same time. No, I take that back. At least fish have interesting things to look at. The city of Rune was nothing but a whole lot of gray, and loaded with zombies. I'd rather be a fish.

Nevva took me on a short tour, proving that everything Saint Dane told me about the territory was true. If anything, it was worse. Who knew? The demon wasn't lying. I guess he didn't fool around when it came to giving bad news. He enjoyed it too much. I told Nevva what Saint Dane had explained to me about Blok. I was hoping she would tell me he was making it all up, and it wasn't as bad as all that. She didn't.

She first brought me to the apartment of a family she knew. It was in one of the tall, gray, featureless buildings that lined the wide avenues. Their home was on the twentieth floor, with no elevator. We had to climb, and that wasn't the worst part. Fifteen people lived in a one-bedroom apartment. Fifteen. It looked barely big enough for two. My first thought was that these people had fallen on hard times and had to make the best of their situation. I was wrong. Nevva told me their living situation was normal. The rents were so expensive that entire families had to live together in order to survive. I thought back to my home on Second Earth, and how Shannon and I used to argue over who was spending too much time in the bathroom—in a house with three bathrooms. It's amazing how easy it is to take something for granted.

The food situation wasn't much better. The family invited us for dinner. I wish they hadn't. We all sat on the floor as a woman handed us each a portion. There wasn't any meat. We got a slice of bread, a hunk of brown something that I think was a potato, and two pieces of a tribbun. That was it. I was hungrier after I ate. It killed me to take food out of the mouths of these people, but they wouldn't take no for an answer. As bad off as they were, they still wanted to share. It told me a lot about them.

As we left the apartment, I asked Nevva, "How can they survive on so little food?"

She answered, "You're beginning to see why these people will grab at any chance to better their lives. Betting on one of the Quillan games might mean an extra slice of bread on everyone's plate. Or something to drink with more calories than water."

"Or it could mean losing it all," I said soberly.

Nevva nodded. We walked several blocks until we came to a large, windowless building. Inside, I saw it was a manu-facturing center. Nevva and I moved along a catwalk that looked down on a huge room holding row after row of people sitting at stations, assembling shoes. I'm serious. They were making shoes. These weren't happy cobbler elves, either. It was a massive assembly line of people, all doing it by hand. It was one of the most depressing things I had ever seen. Nobody spoke or even looked at the person next to them. They worked diligently, hunched over their stations. Some sewed, others dyed, still others cut pieces out of material. The only sound came from the clattering of tools or the cutting of fabric.

"I don't understand," I said. "Quillan isn't a backward territory. Why haven't they built machinery to do this work?"

"They have," Nevva explained. "But machinery is expensive. People aren't. At one time much of what you see being done here was automated. Blok had the machines destroyed."

"But . . . why?" I asked. "It can't be cheaper to have people do the work!"

"It is when you pay them slave wages," Nevva answered. "Machinery must be serviced and repaired. People can be replaced. Besides, as long as these workers rely on Blok for their wages, the company controls their lives."

It was like stepping through the looking glass. Blok was so completely in control of the territory and its people, it was more cost-effective to pay workers slave wages than to automate the manufacturing process. Blok was deliberately holding back the territory from advancing in order to keep control of the people. No, they were forcing the territory into taking a step backward. To the company, the people of Quillan were disposable. It was absolutely diabolical.

A horn sounded. The people stopped working, stood up, and filed out quickly and quietly. As hundreds of people exited to our right, a fresh group of workers entered from our left. The horn sounded, the new people sat down at the stations and picked right up where the other group had left off. The whole process from horn to horn probably took thirty seconds.

"They're like living dados," I said numbly.

"Oh, no," Nevva said. "Dados have it much better. They don't realize how bad off they are."

I didn't want to see anymore and asked to leave. Unfortunately, the worst was yet to come. Nevva took me to a building that from the outside didn't look much different from any of the other buildings in the city. Big, gray, blah. The inside was a different story. It was a giant round space with a colossal domed ceiling. At one time it must have been a pretty fancy place. The walls were made of a light-colored brown brick. The dome itself looked like a stained-glass sculpture. The floor was made of a brilliant white marble. It reminded me of Grand Central Station in New York City. I wasn't far off, because Nevva told me that at one time it had been a busy train station. There were dozens of gates ringing the circle that led to tracks. In the center was a structure that looked like a ticket booth with a golden ceiling. Along one wall was a big board that at one time must have shown the train schedule to travelers. I could imagine this place being a busy station with loads of people hurrying to far-off places.

It wasn't like that anymore. The round structure couldn't even be seen from the street because it was hidden by gray, windowless walls that made it disappear into the rest of the dismal cityscape. Inside, the place had gone grimy. The stained-glass ceiling had been bricked over from above so light wouldn't shine through. The walls were streaked with dark stains. The marble floor was chipped up. The gold roof of the ticket booth was tarnished. It had been a long time since the place was used by travelers. Or at least, used by travelers who were there by choice.

The place was still busy, all right, but not with happy travelers. Nevva and I stood high above the floor, looking down from a window near the ceiling to observe the action below. I saw that the floor was loaded with people who stood in lines that snaked around wooden fences erected to keep them organized and moving. As if these fences weren't enough, security dados wandered through the crowd, making sure there weren't any problems. All the people in line had loops around their arms. I noticed in the street that not everybody had loops. But not in here. Each and every person wore a loop. They were all glowing yellow.

There were men and women of all ages, and some children,

too. It didn't look like the children were with adults either. They all looked to be on their own, and scared. They were pushed along by those in line in front or in back of them, or were prodded by a stern dado if they didn't move fast enough. What made it even worse was that most of the little ones were crying.

The lines led to one of five tall desks. Behind each was a sour-looking person at a computer screen. As the next one in line reached the desk, this person referred to the screen, input something, then sent the traveler on his or her way to one of the gates that led to the trains. If I were on Second Earth, I'd say this looked like a busy train station and the people were checking in or buying tickets for their journey. But this wasn't Second Earth.

I was about to ask Nevva what it all meant, when I heard a scream coming from the floor. A man had just checked in and apparently didn't like what the guy behind the desk had to say, because he turned and ran away. He shouldn't have bothered. The dados were all over him. They tackled the guy, then picked him up and dragged him toward one of the gates to the trains. The guy was screaming and crying the whole way. The reaction from the other people was mixed. Some looked away, but I saw a few women burst into tears. As soon as any kind of emotion was shown, a dado rushed right to that person. They didn't do anything, they just walked alongside them, being all intimidating. I think it was a warning in case they decided to bolt.

"Do I really want to know what's going on here?" I asked nervously.

"You may not want to, but you have to," Nevva said. "These are the losers."

"What do you mean?" I asked.

"Exactly what I said," Nevva countered. "This is where

they bring those who have placed the ultimate bet, and lost. They are processed, categorized, filed, and then shipped off to where they will be needed most. It's all very efficient. My guess is that fellow who ran away was headed for the tarz."

"Whoa, wait," I said. "You're telling me these are all people who bet on the games and lost?"

"Only the ones who made the ultimate bet," Nevva corrected me. "They are here to pay with their lives, or the lives of their loved ones."

I looked down on the crying children. It was too much to believe. People were being treated like cattle.

"They don't all die," she said. "Some only have sentences that last a few quads. Others aren't as lucky, like those sent to the tarz." As she spoke she looked down on the people coldly. There was no emotion in her voice; she was just stating facts. I didn't think it was because she didn't care. After what had happened to her parents, I think she had built up some kind of defense mechanism. But this was all new to me. I didn't know how to deal. I wanted to cry myself.

Nevva added, "I'm sure some of the people are here because they bet against you in Hook and Tock. After all, you were barely known to them."

That rocked me. I had actually played a part in forcing these people to be torn from their families, and their lives, to be slaves of Blok. Worse. Many wouldn't be coming back. I wanted to scream.

A little boy beat me to it. He yelped and ducked under the wooden fence to run away. I found myself silently cheering. I wanted him to run as far away from this insanity as his little legs would carry him. He didn't deserve this. None of these people deserved this. All they were guilty of was being driven to desperation by the greed of Blok. This wasn't their fault. Two dados chased the little guy. I never saw what happened to him, because he ducked into one of the tunnels that led to the trains, with the dados right after him. In my mind I pretended that he had escaped. I knew I was kidding myself, but I needed to believe it was possible to escape from this insanity.

"I gotta get outta here," I said.

Nevva nodded and led me away from the window. I knew I'd never forget the image of the little running boy. My experience of the last few hours left me sad and angry. Saint Dane was right. This territory was lost. How could this have happened? Was it like he said? Was it all because of greed? I couldn't accept that. There had to be more.

"Who is Mr. Pop?" I asked.

"You've heard of him?" Nevva asked with surprise.

"I've heard his name," I said. "Who is he? What part does he play in all this?"

"I've never met him myself," Nevva answered. "But I know many who have. You need to meet those people. They will tell you more."

"Who are they?" I asked.

Nevva answered, "I lead three lives here, Pendragon. I'm the special assistant to the trustees of Blok, that you know. I'm a Traveler. That you know as well. But I'm also a reviver. There are tens of thousands of us, all over Quillan. You look at this territory as being populated by mindless zombies. It isn't. The revivers want to take back our lives, and our territory.

Nevva spoke with an intensity that I hadn't seen before. She was on a mission, though not as a Traveler. She was putting her life on the line to take back her territory. It sounded as if there were others who were just as dedicated. Revivers. We stood looking at each other. I lifted my right hand and grabbed my left biceps. It was the subtle signal that I'd seen the people give to each other who had helped me escape from the security dados.

Nevva smiled and said, "You are full of surprises, Pendragon. So far you have lived up to your reputation."

"Am I going to meet these revivers now?" I asked.

She grabbed her left biceps, returning the salute, and said, "They're waiting."

QUILLAN

We traveled along rooftops. Sky bridges connected many of the tall buildings, making it much easier to move quickly. I was surprised more people didn't use them. At one point we stopped on a rooftop to watch a game that was being broadcast. We were on the same level as one of the giant screens. It was like watching an IMAX movie from the first row. It was big, loud, and exciting.

The match was between the champion, Challenger Green, and Challenger Blue. I recognized Blue from hanging around the castle, and from the two parties I had attended. Of course I also recognized Green. He was *the man,* after all.

The contest looked like an obstacle course. The challengers had to run through the woods, climb fences, swim, tightrope walk—you know, an obstacle course. I won't bore you with the details. I will tell you the one thing about the contest that got my interest. Challenger Green wasn't that good. I mean, he was okay, but the course gave him trouble, and Challenger Blue made it a good race.

"Green might lose," I said as we watched the race.

"It is only a matter of time before he is beaten," Nevva said. "He has been lucky."

The crowd was definitely into it. I looked down to see thousands of people choking the streets, all staring up at the screen. It was like watching one of those massive crowds at a World Cup soccer game. The only difference here was that there was a lot more at stake for the spectators. I wondered how many of them would end up on that grisly line in that old train station after this game was over. If Challenger Blue pulled off the upset, I'd guess there would be a lot. I actually found myself rooting for Challenger Green, if only because he was the favorite and most people had probably bet on him.

"Challenger Green is slow footed," Nevva said. "He's strong, but clumsy. His real strength comes from his attitude. He's ruthless. He never panics. I'm sure that when he is matched up against someone as confident as he is, he'll lose."

"You know a lot about these games," I commented.

"It's part of my job," she said. "I may not like it, but I have to keep up with the games."

"This race doesn't look all that dangerous," I said.

"Compared to many, it isn't," Nevva answered. "Both challengers usually survive, unless they make a wrong move on the course. There are many treacherous obstacles."

The last obstacle of the course consisted of two ropes that spanned a wide pit. The challengers had to grab a rope and make their way across. Falling would hurt. It looked to be around a thirty-foot drop, which was bad enough, but there were no cushy pads down there. The span beneath the ropes was littered by what looked like chunks of sharp metal. Challenger Blue hit the ropes first. He had a comfortable lead. Unless Green could make up the huge gap, he was done, and Blue would triumph. Challenger Blue grabbed one rope and threw his legs up, hooking it with his feet. That was his technique. He moved head first, upside down, pulling himself along with his hands. Having his legs up on the rope took some of the weight off his arms. Smart move. It looked for sure that he was going to win.

Challenger Green wasn't giving up, though it sure seemed like it at first. When he reached the spot where he was supposed to grab the rope, he stopped. The guy looked winded. I thought he was done. The crowd went nuts. They yelled at the screen, as if he could hear them, begging him to keep moving. I could almost feel the anguish rise up from the crowd below. The favorite was about to lose. There was going to be hell to pay, literally.

Challenger Green had other plans. He took a deep breath. I thought he was going to jump up onto the rope. He didn't. He reached down to his ankle, lifted up the bottom of his pants, and from out of his shoe he pulled a knife. It was the same kind of knife we were given during meals. It wasn't a weapon, but it was sharp.

"What's he doing?" I asked. "Is that allowed?"

"Everything is allowed," Nevva answered. "The only rule is to get to the finish line before your opponent. How you do it is your choice."

Challenger Green casually reached up and began sawing through Challenger Blue's rope! The crowd's anguish turned to cheers of delight. They weren't stunned by his cruel tactic, just the opposite. They saw this as a way for him to win, and they yelled for him to hurry. I guess when your life is at stake, sportsmanship doesn't count. Neither does murder. Challenger Blue saw what was happening and tried to speed up. I couldn't believe it. Nevva was right. Challenger Green was ruthless. He didn't have the skill to beat Challenger Blue, so he had to cheat. But then again, if there were no rules, he wasn't really cheating. Many in the crowd below screamed for Blue to hurry. They didn't care that he might get hurt; they wanted him to win.

He didn't.

Challenger Blue was still a few yards away from the end when Green sliced through the rope. The crowd screamed with joy. Challenger Blue just screamed. He dropped straight down, headed for the jagged metal below. The cameras didn't show him hitting, so I didn't know how badly he was hurt. All I saw was Challenger Green looking down at his victim, then casually grabbing the other rope and hoisting himself up. He used the same feet-up technique as Challenger Blue, though he moved slowly and methodically. He was in no hurry. That told me Challenger Blue wasn't going to be climbing out of the pit. As soon as Green touched down on the far side, the screen went blank and the words WINNER—CHALLENGER GREEN! flashed.

There was jubilation in the streets, though the joyous shouts were quickly drowned out by the sound of sirens as the dados arrived to collect the losers. Nevva and I watched the scene below as people scattered. Some went quietly. Others ran and were chased down by the dados.

"This territory is a nightmare," I said.

"It is," she agreed. "But we can change it."

"I want to meet the revivers," I said, gritting my teeth with anger. "Now."

Nevva held up the black bag that had to go over my head, and shrugged. "I'm sorry," she said. "They have survived by living in the shadows. Their trust isn't earned easily. Even I don't know all their secrets."

"Like who Mr. Pop is?" I asked.

"That's a big one," she answered.

"What do you know about him?" I asked. "I heard the challengers toasting him."

"Mr. Pop is a false name, obviously," Nevva said.

I didn't think it was so obvious. I'd heard plenty of wacky names since I left Second Earth. It wasn't like "Nevva" was so common either. But I didn't say anything.

"He is the heart of the revival," she continued. "When the movement begins, he will lead us. But until then, he must live in secrecy, for obvious reasons."

"Do the trustees know about the revivers?" I asked.

"Not exactly," she answered. "They've heard rumors, but they don't take them seriously. The trustees believe their domination of the territory is complete. They aren't far from wrong. But they're arrogant. The idea that there might be a movement of tens of thousands of people with the single goal of bringing down the company is so alien to them, they don't take it seriously. They underestimate the spirit of the people. I believe it will be their undoing."

"So they don't know about Mr. Pop?" I asked.

"There have been many stories about heroes who will rise up and rescue the people from oppression, but none have proved true. Have they heard the name Mr. Pop? Yes, absolutely. But they consider him to be a myth, born of desperation. They have no idea that Mr. Pop is real. The revivers want to keep it that way, until the time is right."

"So how did you hook up with these guys?" I asked. "Isn't it kind of a stretch to be working for the trustees while being part of an underground organization trying to overthrow them?"

Nevva said, "That's the beauty of it! When Press told me of my destiny as a Traveler, I did a lot of soul searching. After visiting the other territories and seeing Quillan from a different perspective, I knew the best way I could help my own territory was to plot against the very people I work for."

"And get revenge for what happened to your parents," I said.

Nevva shot me a stern look. I wished I hadn't said that; it was kind of harsh.

"Sorry," I said. "Sometimes I think out loud."

"It's all right," she said quickly. "I do blame the trustees and Blok for what happened to my parents. But this isn't about me, Pendragon. It's about what Blok has done to the whole territory. My story is one of millions. That's why I sought out the revivers."

"If they're so secretive, how did you find them?" I asked.

Nevva chuckled and said, "I am very resourceful, Pendragon. There isn't much that gets by me. I listened, I asked careful questions, and I eventually found my way through to the leaders. I have to admit, it helped that I work for the trustees. Having someone on their side who is so close to their enemies was too tempting for the revivers to pass up. I've been training with them for nearly twenty quads now—"

"Just for the record, I have no idea how long a quad is," I said.

Nevva didn't know how to answer that. How would you explain to somebody what a year is? Or a month? That's a tough one.

"Twenty quads is long enough for the revivers to accept me. In fact, I've proved to be so valuable they made me a unit leader."

I didn't want to ask her what a unit leader was. That probably would have been just as hard as explaining what a quad was.

"But I still haven't been accepted on the highest levels," she said. "Which is why I haven't met Mr. Pop. With my plan, that will certainly change."

"And that plan is . . . ?"

"It's about you, Pendragon. That's why we must meet them now." She held up the black bag and smiled sheepishly. "Until they learn to trust you, their location must remain secret."

I took the bag reluctantly and asked, "What did you tell them about me? Not the truth, I hope."

"Of course not. I told them you are someone who can help us," she answered. "Nothing more."

I didn't have to put the bag on until we stepped inside the building, and into an elevator. Nevva took me on another long journey down and through the bowels of the city of Rune. I figured we were descending very deep, because the temperature took a big drop. We were definitely going somewhere out of the mainstream. After walking for about twenty minutes, it felt as if we stepped into a large area. I say that because up until then everything sounded close, like we were walking through narrow corridors. The only sound came from our footsteps bouncing back at us from the hard walls. But this new place sounded open. We weren't outside—it was too quiet and cold for that—but it was definitely a much larger area. Like an airplane hangar or a basketball court.

"We're here," Nevva announced, and pulled the bag off my head.

I had to blink twice to make sure what I was seeing was real. I looked around at the large space, trying to make sense of it. Nevva didn't interrupt. She must have seen my confusion.

"It—it's a mall!" I said.

It was a derelict, deserted underground mall. We were standing in a central courtyard. Directly above us was a skylight that was bricked over, like the stained glass of the train station. In front of us was a fountain that hadn't seen water in forever. There seemed to be three levels. We were on the lowest. Four sets of wide marble stairs led up from this courtyard to the level above us. I wasn't sure how you got from that level to the highest. Maybe there were some escalators somewhere. If there were, I guarantee they weren't working. This place had been dead for many years. Or quads, whatever the heck they were. Like the malls at home on Second Earth, there were several storefronts lined up next to one another. Unlike the stores outside on the street that sold "Clothes" and "Food," these stores had unique names like "Razzle," "Storm & Kissner," "Pookie's Place," and "The Bountiful Table." These were stores that sold the kinds of things you'd see at a mall at home. I saw a music shop, flower stands, bookstores, a toy shop, and even a store that sold nothing but candy.

They were all closed. Deserted. Empty. Dead. Their signs were dark, their windows were clouded with grime. The only clues as to what each store once sold were yellowed signs and empty shelves. I was never much of a mall guy. I know, some people hang out at malls with their friends like it's the center of their universe. Other people walk around and look at stuff like it's some kind of museum. I never quite got it, myself. If a mall had a store that sold something I wanted, I'd go. If not, I'd avoid it like the plague. But seeing this deserted ghost mall here on Quillan actually made me sad. It was proof that Quillan had once had free enterprise.

I was beginning to see the signs of a lost civilization. Like digging through the sands of Egypt to uncover ancient cities, the layer of gray cement here in the city of Rune had covered up a city that once had personality. I could only imagine what else had been hidden by Blok's quest to wipe away a society. There was no doubt, Blok had killed Quillan.

"You're late!" came a voice, echoing from somewhere.

I spun around and saw someone standing on the top of the stairs, looking down on us. He wore one of those masks over his head like the people who'd rescued me from Veego and LaBerge. He stood with his legs wide, holding something that looked like a long, heavy black wand. He held it in one hand and tapped it into the palm of his other, menacingly.

"We stopped to watch the competition," Nevva called up to the person. "I thought it was important for him to see."

Another voice boomed from behind us. A quick look showed another person standing on top of the stairs, across from the first. "You know it's difficult for us to all get away during the day," the second person said. "Our time is valuable."

"I know that better than most," Nevva said. She was apologizing, but she wasn't backing down. "I don't believe I wasted a minute of our time. Everything we did was important. I hope you'll trust my judgment on that."

Three more dark figures appeared at the tops of the stairs. We were surrounded by these masked people, each with their own black baton.

I said to Nevva, "Tell me these are the revivers."

"They are the leaders of the revival here in Rune," she said. "Rune has the largest number of—"

"That's enough!" the first person barked.

Nevva fell quiet.

"I'm sorry," she said. "But if he's going to help us, we have to trust him."

The first person started walking down the stairs toward us. The others walked as well. The circle was closing in around us. These were supposed to be the good guys, but they didn't know who I was. If they thought I was a bad guy, it wouldn't matter if they were good guys or bad guys because . . . oh, you get the idea.

"What is your name?" the first person asked.

"Pendragon," I answered. "What's yours?"

Nevva shot me a look as if I were being a little too smart-ass. "Forgive him for that," Nevva said, trying to do damage control.

"Should I also forgive him for being a liar?" the guy asked.

Huh? What did he mean by that? I looked to Nevva. She looked as clueless as I felt. The guy stepped off the stairs directly in front of me and pulled off his mask to reveal . . . he wasn't a he. He was a she. And I knew her. It was the woman on the motorbike who'd helped the guy escape from the dados when I first got to Quillan. That must mean . . .

I looked around as the other people removed their masks as well. Sure enough, one of them was the older guy who'd helped me escape from the dados, and brought me to the garage where I was captured.

"This is Tylee Magna," Nevva said. "She is our leader here in Rune."

"I see your loop is gone," Tylee Magna said to me sarcastically. "Did you remove this one the same as the last one?"

"Wait!" Nevva said, confused. "You've met already?" It was the first time I saw Nevva rattled.

"I was being chased by security dados," I said to Nevva. "They helped me get away, at least for a little while."

This was going to be tricky. I had forgotten the lies I told these people when they helped me escape. If I wanted to gain their trust, I couldn't sound like I was making stuff up back then—which I was.

"You knew our sign," the older guy said, grabbing his left biceps with his right hand.

"Pure luck," I said. "I saw you give that sign to each other when you helped that other guy get away from the dados."

The older guy and Tylee Magna exchanged looks. I didn't know if they were impressed that I was so observant, or angry at themselves for being so obvious about their supersecret spy signals.

"So you tricked us into helping you, then lied to us," Magna said matter-of-factly.

I figured I shouldn't add more lies to my lies so I said, "Yeah, I lied."

"He is from another city," Nevva said. "I gave him the challenger clothes, and the loop."

The older guy with the gray hair said to Nevva, "We've seen him compete. You're right; he is exceptional."

"It doesn't matter," Magna said forcefully. "The risk is too great. There is too much at stake."

Nevva said, "But think of what could happen if we're successful! This could be our defining moment! We have the chance to create the spark that puts the revival into motion. We can't pass up this chance!"

"And if he fails?" the woman asked.

"If he fails then we will be no worse off than we are now," Nevva answered. "I don't see that there is a choice."

"Uh, hello, folks!" I said. "Would somebody mind telling me what's going on?"

Nevva looked at Tylee Magna as if to get the okay to talk. Tylee nodded. Nevva stepped in front of me and said, "We are ready. Throughout all of Quillan there are tens of thousands of people who are prepared to take back their lives."

"Are you talking about a civil war?" I asked.

"In a way, yes," she answered. "We will start with the security dados. They must be destroyed. We have been storing weapons and training to do just that. Once their security force is no longer a threat, the power will be ours. Blok relies on manpower to exist. If the people revolt, Blok will be powerless. Their factories can be shut down, the tarz can be interrupted, water plants can be controlled."

"If it's that easy, why haven't you done it already?" I asked.

Tylee Magna answered, "Because the people don't have the will. Blok not only controls our lives, it controls our minds. After so many generations of living this way, people don't believe there is any other way of life. Blok has stolen the most valuable possession any person can have—imagination. "

The old guy who reminded me of my father added, "The revivers believe we can bring that back. We have been working to show people that there is so much more to life than what they have. It sounds so simple, but to do it on such a large scale is daunting. We have tens of thousands on our side. We need millions."

"How does Mr. Pop fit into this?" I asked.

The revivers shared looks. Nevva leaned toward Magna. She wanted to hear the answer as much as I did.

"Mr. Pop is our spiritual leader," the woman answered. "Once the revival begins, it will be Mr. Pop who will show us all the way. But it is up to us to take the first step."

Nevva added, "That's where you come in, Pendragon. We've been looking for the right person to light the fuse on the revival. I believe it is you." She looked right at me for emphasis and said, "This could be the turning point for Quillan, Pendragon."

Crash!

Shattered glass and pieces of brick rained down on us. The revivers jumped back, looking just as surprised as I was. I covered my eyes and looked up to see dark figures descending from the broken ceiling directly above us. Like giant marauding spiders they quickly slid down on ropes that were dropped from the roof.

"They found us," Tylee Magna gasped.

They weren't giant spiders. They were security dados. They had discovered the lair of the revivers.

QUILLAN

We were under attack.

"How did they find this place?" the old guy said, stunned.

Nobody hung around for an answer. The security dados were coming down right on our heads. It was like being descended on by commandos. They zipped down the lines with military-like precision and skill. There were about eight of them headed down the lines. Who knew how many more were waiting above? We were outnumbered. Worse. They had guns. My first instinct was to run. For all I knew, this was an assassination squad. The others had the same thought. Nobody wanted to stick around and fight these guys.

"Scatter!" Magna commanded. "They can't get us all."

The five revivers scampered off in different directions.

I looked at Nevva. Her eyes were wide and scared. "I'll find you," she said, and took off.

It was time for me to do the same. As the dados slid down their lines, I ran for the stairs up to the next level of the mall, taking them three at a time. I got to the top and took off running down one wide corridor. I was totally winging it because I had no idea where to go. My *hope* was that I'd find a doorway that led out, before the dados hit the ground and could follow. Of course my *fear* was that I'd find a door that led to a dead end and the dados would catch me and bring me back to the castle. Or worse. Running ahead of me was one of the revivers. I made the snap decision to follow him. I figured he had to know where he was going.

Fum! Fum!

Too late. The dados were firing their golden guns before they even reached the ground. The running reviver was nailed by both shots. His head snapped back as he fell forward. I think he was unconscious before he hit the floor. I dove to the ground and slid on my belly across the hard marble floor. I wanted to make as small a target as possible. I looked back quickly to see the dados descending on their lines past the level I was on, down to the bottom, where we had been standing moments before. That meant I had a few seconds before they landed, ran up the stairs, and started shooting again. I spotted the metal wand that the reviver had dropped when he was shot. On instinct I scrambled over and grabbed it. The unconscious reviver had no more use for it. The thing was about six feet long. It was thin, but it had weight. It wasn't as heavy as the wooden stave weapons from Zadaa, but I needed something to protect myself. It would have to do.

I was about to take off running, when it hit me that the unconscious reviver was at the mercy of the security dados. What if this really was an assassination squad? Or what if they captured the guy and made him give up more secrets about the revivers? I couldn't leave the guy there helpless. So I dropped the black wand, grabbed his legs, and pulled him toward one of the empty stores.

Inside I saw row after row of empty racks that spanned from the front of the store all the way to the back. It was once a bookstore. The shelves were barren, except for a few sad and yellowed books. In that split second I imagined these empty rows to be full of colorful books. The idea that the heart and soul of an entire territory could be destroyed, forgotten, and cemented over by a blanket of gray was gut wrenching.

It was also gut wrenching to know that we were being hunted down by killer robots. I didn't have time to hang around getting depressed over the loss of Quillan's books. I grabbed the unconscious reviver guy by one arm and one leg, and awkwardly picked him up in a fireman's carry. The guy was small and fairly light, but I have to admit, I was getting strong. All that work at the training camp on Zadaa had paid off. It also helped that I was scared to death. Like I've always said, adrenaline can be your friend. Once he was up on my shoulders, I knew I could move. At least for a little while. No way I could outrun anybody, but at least I could get the two of us to a safe place where we could hide. I took two steps toward the back of the store, when my big plan shattered . . . along with the front windows of the bookstore.

Fum. Fum. Fum.

Yeah, they saw us. I ducked down behind the first empty book rack as three dados jumped in through the smashed-out windows. I was operating more out of instinct than anything else. With the reviver guy still on my shoulders, I put my back against the book rack and pushed. The long rack fell on top of the attacking dados. I hoped it would slow them down long enough for me to get past them and out of the store. There was nothing more I could do for the unconscious reviver. If I tried to carry him, the dados would get us both. I had to let go of the poor guy and try to escape.

I leaped over the crashed book rack, past the flailing dadoes, through the broken window, and back out into the mall. I braced myself, expecting to feel the shock and shudder of getting shot by one of those stun guns. I told myself to keep moving until it happened. When I got through the window, I saw the metal wand was right where I'd left it. Without hesitation I scooped it up.

Those two seconds were costly. It gave the dados in the bookstore the chance to get their wits back. (Do robots have wits?) No sooner did I straighten up than one leaped at me through the shattered window with his gun drawn. I was done. Running was not an option. This mechanical robot would shoot me for sure at a range that was barely farther than point blank. When I was back on Zadaa, I made the decision that I no longer wanted to be a helpless victim who relied on others to protect himself. I had gone through grueling warrior training for situations just like this one. I now had the skills to defend myself. There was only one thing to do.

Use them.

I figured if I could keep them in close, I could keep them from shooting. Of course it was still three on one, and they were robots, but what the heck. Nothing I could do about that. All I knew for sure was that I did not want to go back to that castle. At least not easily.

The first dado came at me like a defensive back trying to make an open-field tackle. I spun out of the way and slashed at his gun hand with the black wand. The weapon made a nasty *swoosh-crack* sound as it cut through the air and slapped the dado's outstretched hand, knocking the gun out of his grip. I quickly slashed with the other end, cracking the robot on the back of his head, sending him sprawling. I didn't want to think what this simple but lethal weapon would do to flesh and bone.

The dado didn't make a sound. He didn't feel pain. Or if he did, he covered it well. I was about to go for the golden weapon when I saw the other two dados leap at me from the bookstore. I held the long wand out in front of me with both hands, parallel to the ground and my arms locked. I caught both the robots in the gut at the same time. If they had been people, they both would have doubled over in pain. They weren't people. There was no doubling over and no pain. I was on one knee, holding the weapon out, with a dado on either end. The two stood there, looking down at me with their dead doll eyes as if nothing had happened.

I hadn't trained for this. Battling robots wasn't part of Loor's warrior course.

I pulled the black wand into my chest and did a back somersault, landing on my feet. I quickly stood, holding the weapon ready, for what, I didn't know. I could whack away at these machines until doomsday, and they'd still keep coming. But I wasn't going to give up without trying. One dado came at me. His gun was out, ready to fire. I faked a swing of the metal wand, he flinched, I ducked, rolled to my right, and came up swinging on his unsuspecting friend. The second dado didn't see me coming and didn't know what hit him, literally. I knocked the robot off his feet and he crashed to the floor. I sidestepped and jammed the end of the weapon into his back. I wasn't prepared for what happened next. The wand pierced the back of the robot's body! I felt a slight tingle in the weapon, and the dado stopped moving. I had killed him! If I'd stopped to analyze it, I probably would have been grossed out. But this wasn't a person, it was a machine. It wasn't alive. Whatever this metal weapon was, it could pierce the fabric that covered these robots and knock them out of commission.

I was in business.

I realized it wasn't about knocking them down, it was

about getting through the outside layer and damaging the works. These simple weapons were more than just batons to be used like the staves on Zadaa. These were dado killers.

The dados may have been robots, but they weren't dumb. They saw that I had their number, and they became more cautious. The robot I had first knocked to the ground went for his gun on the floor. I lunged at him and plunged the metal rod into his arm before he got to it. The wand was so powerful that it actually jammed itself into the hard floor of the mall as if the surface were loose dirt. It stuck there like I had planted a flag on a mountaintop. Whatever material that thing was made out of, it was awesome. The dado's arm gave a slight shiver and went dead. But the dado was still functioning. His gun was out of reach so he grabbed at me with his other hand. I made sure I was out of reach too.

The next dado attacked. He grabbed my shoulders, pulled me away, and threw me across the floor like a limp doll. If that weren't bad enough, I lost my grip on the dado-killing wand. The dado who'd just tossed me aside didn't go for it. I thought for sure he would pull it out of his buddy's arm to free him, but he didn't. Instead he took his own gun out of its holster and fired at me. *Fum!*

I felt the energy of the charge raise the hair on my neck as it barely missed me. I knew I wouldn't be that lucky again so I scrambled to my feet and ran into a store across the aisle from the empty bookstore. The place was a junkyard of old displays from the mall. Dust covered everything. When I first jumped inside, what I saw made me freeze. It was a sea of people! I thought they were mummies, or maybe inactive dados. It took me a second to realize they were mannequins. There must have been a couple hundred of them in all sizes, colors, and poses. Some had distinct features that made them look real. Others only had the vague shape of a face. It was one of the creepiest things I had ever seen in my life. I probably would have been scared, if it weren't for the fact that I was in the middle of something a lot scarier.

Fum. Fum.

I felt the energy pulses of the stun gun fly past my head, crackling the air. I dove into the rows of mannequins, trying to lose myself amid the lifeless forms.

Fum! A mannequin exploded next to me, covering me with a wash of dummy muck. *Fum!* An arm blew off another one. I crouched down low, hoping to get out of the dado's line of sight. I didn't know how many shots that golden gun had. Six? Ten? A thousand? Several seconds went by. The dado didn't fire. I didn't think he had given up. No way. He was getting smart and listening for me. Somehow I had to make my way back to the front of that store, get outside, and either grab the dado-killing weapon, or the gun that was on the ground. I stayed low and crept forward. My sneakers had soft soles. Soft meant silent. I looked through the tangle of mannequin arms and legs to try to get a glimpse of the dado, but the jumble was too dense. I couldn't see a thing. Maybe that was good. It might mean he couldn't see me, either. I took a few more cautious steps.

Peering through the mannequins, I saw the front of the store. The dado wasn't there. I could only hope that he had gone deeper into the store hunting for me, never thinking I'd double back and go out the exact same way I came in. I peered around a tall mannequin and looked down a long, empty aisle. No dado. Sweet. I was getting closer to the front door, and weapons, with every step.

I crept slow and low down the aisle. Still no dado. I turned to look back over my shoulder . . . and there he was, taking aim! He was right behind me! Without thinking, I launched myself at the robot and drilled him in the chest with my shoulder.

Fum. Fum.

He fired harmlessly at the ceiling, blasting out pieces of tile that shattered and fell down on us. The force of my tackle sent the two of us tumbling into a group of mannequins. We landed in a jumble of arms and legs and hands. It felt as if I were being grabbed at by a dozen different people. That was fine, so long as none of them was the dado. I rolled off the pile, bounced up, and dove over the next row of mannequins.

Fum! The dado had gotten himself back together and was firing away. The time for finesse was over. I had to get out of there. I crashed over a bunch more mannequins, barely keeping my feet under me. With a final leap I landed on the floor, slamming my shoulder into the ground. I had landed in the doorway back out to the mall. Yes! I got right back to my feet and sprinted toward the other dados. One was dead, or whatever you call it when a robot goes belly up. I'll use "dead." The other was still pinned down by the metal rod I had stabbed into his arm. I wondered why he didn't just pull it out. I spotted the golden gun that I had knocked onto the floor, and I sprinted for it.

Fum!

The other dado was out of the store and taking aim. I dove forward, head first, arms stretched out in front. I hit the floor on my belly and continued sliding. Half a second later I scooped up the gun.

Fum! Fum!

I rolled to get out of the line of fire as I fumbled to hold the weapon. I had never fired a gun at anybody in my life. I wasn't even sure of how to aim. I rolled onto my back to see the dado was closing in on me. That was okay. Aim wasn't going to be a problem. I was going to nail this guy, point blank. I brought the pistol up, held it with both hands, and pulled the trigger.

Fum!

There was no kick or recoil. I felt the slight sensation of an electrical charge. I nailed the dado dead on.

But nothing happened. The dado pulled up and stood there, no worse for wear. The charge from the gun had done nothing! The dados were impervious. Now he had me. The robot knew it too. He stood not more then a few yards away, his feet spread apart. Slowly he raised his gun at me. I wasn't afraid. I knew I wasn't about to die. But I was beaten. The dado took aim, making sure I was perfectly in his sights . . . and pulled the trigger.

The gun didn't fire. It was empty.

I had life. Before the dado could react, I rolled toward the other robot whose arm was pinned to the floor. I needed that weapon. I jumped to my feet, grabbed the wand, yanked it out of the floor, and with one quick move I heaved it at the other dado like a spear. The deadly missile nailed him right in the chest. I heard a sharp, crackling electrical sound. A moment later the robot shuddered, and crumpled to the ground like one of those dusty mannequins from the store. Dead. Out of commission. Whatever. I thought it was over.

It wasn't. I had made a critical mistake. When I pulled the wand out of the arm of the other dado, I had freed him. Oops. I sensed him before I saw him. I spun around to see he had gotten the gun from the holster of the first dado I had killed. The weapon was raised and ready to fire . . . at me. I was about to dive out of the way in a desperate attempt to ruin his aim, when the robot made an odd shudder. I heard the electrical *zap* sound again too. The dado's gun hand dropped to his side. What had happened? The robot lurched forward and fell flat on his face. Dead. Sticking out of his back was another wand. Behind him was Nevva Winter.

"That's all of them, I believe," she said matter-of-factly, as if making another efficient report to her bosses.

I heard a single person clapping from somewhere overhead. Looking up I saw the other four revivers looking down on me from the level above. The person clapping was Tylee Magna.

"There's another guy in that store," I said. "I don't think he's hurt, but he was shot."

"He'll be fine," Tylee said. "We saw how you tried to save him."

"Tried," I said. "That's about as far as I got."

Tylee looked to Nevva and said, "Maybe this Pendragon person can help us after all."

I looked to Nevva. She gave me a smile of satisfaction and said, "I never had a doubt."

I had impressed them. Like Nevva, the revivers now believed I could help them. It would have been nice to know what exactly it was they wanted me to do.

I was about to find out.

QUILLAN

We had to get out of that mall. It was explained to me that this was one of the many secret locations the revivers used as a meeting place. Now that the dados had discovered it, it was no longer safe. I feared it was no coincidence that the place had been a total secret, until I showed up. Tylee agreed that my being there probably had something to do with the discovery, but she didn't blame me. I was an escaped challenger, after all. I was being hunted. They figured that someone, somewhere, must have recognized me and alerted the security dados. Luckily, the only causualty of the dado attack was the reviver who had been shot with the stun gun, and he was going to be fine. The other revivers had been able to pick off the rest of the dados, one by one, using those amazing dado-killing wands. Each of the other revivers had been chased by only one dado. Three of them had come after me. There was no question. The raid had been about me. The trustees of Blok wanted me back. Veego and LaBerge wanted me back. Saint Dane wanted me back. I was a popular guy.

We took turns carrying the unconscious reviver through the deserted mall. I didn't ask where we were going. I figured it had to be someplace safe. We came upon two small vehicles that reminded me of golf carts. I got in one with Nevva, Tylee, and the older guy. The rest took the unconscious reviver in the other car. What followed was a fast trip through an incredible underground mall system. The cars gave off a low hum as we sped along. We were quiet and quick. I discovered that the abandoned mall was only one of many malls that were connected by tunnels under the city of Rune. I kept thinking we would reach the end of the line, but with each turn we came upon yet another wide-open mall full of empty stores. I couldn't begin to tell you how many empty storefronts we passed. It was definitely well into the thousands.

Nevva must have read my mind, because she said, "It's sad, isn't it?"

"It's unbelievable," I replied. "How long have these stores been empty?"

Nevva answered, "No one can say for sure; there isn't a person alive with firsthand knowledge of what it was like. But there are stories. The winters are harsh here in Rune. As I've heard it told, these underground shops were built so that people could stay out of the cold and still have access to everything they might need. There are amazing stories of shops that had a variety of different foods, and repair centers for every item in your home. I've heard it said that you could visit your doctor, buy a pair of shoes, eat a meal at a place where they actually cooked it and served it to you, and then see a dramatic theatrical performance, all within walking distance. It all seems so impossible."

Impossible? It sounded pretty much like Second Earth to me.

"Why is it all so empty?" I asked. "I saw the overcrowding in the buildings up top. People could come down here just to get a little breathing room."

"At first it was forbidden," Tylee answered. "But so much time has passed that most don't even know these places exist. There are no entryways. Everything has been sealed and forgotten—by everyone but the revivers."

We traveled for at least half an hour. As we sped into one large mall area, I started seeing signs of life. There were people dressed in the black clothing of the revivers. Several appeared from out of doorways, holding golden guns. Some held the familiar black wands, ready to deal with unwanted visitors.

"Guards," Nevva said, reading my mind.

Question was, what were they guarding? I wondered if we would have to give some kind of password, but once the guards saw Tylee, they gave a quick salute, which meant they grabbed their left biceps. We sped past without incident. These guys looked pretty dangerous, but it didn't seem like there were enough of them to repel an army of dados.

Farther along I saw that in spite of what Tylee had explained, there actually were people living down here in the mall. We passed several families huddled together in storefronts. Some were eating, some sleeping. To be honest, they reminded me of homeless people back on Second Earth.

Tylee said, "We discourage people from living down here. This is where we base our operations, and the more people who come and go, the more chance there is for us to be discovered."

The old guy added, "Some people simply can't be refused. Many of these poor people would be sent to the tarz if we didn't give them sanctuary. Others are unable to provide for their families. It's tough deciding on who can stay and who can't, but we do what we can."

"Guards are stationed throughout," Tylee said. "If a security dado, or even a stranger, should approach, we can disappear into a different section immediately."

"There have been inspections," the older man said. "Security dados have made sweeps. But we have been able to erase any trace of our existence quickly and move on. When the threat is gone, we return. The system has worked for generations."

These people were like guerrilla fighters living in the jungle in the hopes that one day they could free their repressed people. From what they told me, that's exactly what they were planning to do, and soon. The question was, what part did they expect me to play?

Our journey finally ended at the far end of one of the malls. The store we were facing was big. At one time it was probably a department store. The doors were guarded by several armed revivers. They greeted us with the familiar salute, then several took charge of the reviver who had been stunned by the dado. I was happy to see that he was already waking up.

"I'll take care of him," the older guy said. "Welcome, Pendragon."

I nodded, then turned to Nevva and asked, "What now?"

"Come with me," Tylee answered.

She got out of the vehicle and walked quickly into the big store. I shot a look at Nevva and said, "You're coming too, right?"

"Of course. This is my show," she said. Then added, "The way you handled those dados was very impressive. That cemented it."

"Cemented what?" I asked. This was getting frustrating. I had been manipulated from the moment I landed on Quillan. First by the dados, then by Veego and LaBerge, then by Saint Dane, and now by Nevva and the revivers. I felt like I had fallen into a rushing river and had no control over where it swept me. All I could do was keep my head above water and hope that things would slow down.

I was about to find out that things were only going to get faster.

Unlike the thousands of other stores in the malls, this one wasn't empty. It was packed, but not with merchandise for sale. I found myself standing in the center of a huge supply of weapons. There were racks and racks of stun guns. There were rifles as well as pistols. I saw a stand that was loaded with hundreds of the long, black dado-killing wands. It was pretty impressive. There was no doubt, these guys were preparing for action.

"How did you get all this?" I asked Nevva.

"Slowly" was her answer. "Shipments were hijacked. Robberies. Some manufacturers who are sympathetic to the revival passed things along. Getting the weapons wasn't the problem. Getting them slowly, so that Blok security wouldn't realize what was happening, was the bigger challenge. I've seen more than one memo to the trustees warning of random weapon theft. Those reports conveniently found their way into the shredder."

"I guess the revivers are lucky to have somebody on the inside," I said.

"So are the Travelers," Nevva said softly, so that Tylee couldn't hear. She then added, "But luck had nothing to do with it. I've worked very hard to get where I am."

We walked through aisle after aisle of weaponry to the far side of this large room and through a set of double doors. We entered into another large room with a high ceiling that looked like it once had been a theater. There were a few hundred seats all facing a stage. On the stage were a few beaten-up couches, and desks that were stacked with papers. There were maps set up on easels, along with a chalkboard that had a list of names and data that meant nothing to me. If I hadn't known better, I would have thought this was a theater set up for a play about people planning a big operation of some sort. But I knew better. The maps and data on the stage weren't for show. This was real. I was in the war room of the revival.

Tylee went right up onto the stage and quickly looked through some papers. She was like a business person returning to her office. Nevva and I stood by the theater seats below her.

I whispered to her, "Why am I here?"

Nevva gave me a "shhh" sign. Finally Tylee sat on the edge of her desk and looked down on me.

"I was impressed, Pendragon," she said. "I've never seen anyone fight like you. You're strong, you're quick, you're agile. It's almost like you've been trained."

"I was," I said, before realizing I had no idea how to explain that. I could feel Nevva tighten next to me, as if I had said the wrong thing.

"Oh?" Tylee said. "How is that?"

"He comes from a military family," Nevva answered before I had the chance to say anything else stupid. "The tradition of combat was passed down from fathers to sons and daughters for generations."

Tylee gave me a suspicious look and said, "There hasn't been a military presence on Quillan since the dados were put into operation."

"Traditions live on," Nevva answered with authority. "Both sons and daughters are taught to fight, in anticipation of the time their services will once again be needed."

Nevva thought fast and was a very good liar. I guess I shouldn't have been surprised, seeing as she was leading a triple life.

Tylee nodded. She really didn't care about how I got to be such a good fighter.

"Do you believe in a better future for Quillan?" she asked me.

"Absolutely," I said confidently. Finally there was a question I could answer honestly and with conviction.

"Then will you help the revival?" she asked.

I had to choose my words carefully. Of course I wanted to help the revival. From what I'd seen, Blok had destroyed this territory. Whether Saint Dane had a hand in it or not didn't matter. He liked what Quillan had become. I didn't. There needed to be change. Nevva might have been right. This revolution definitely felt like it could be a turning point on the territory, which explained why Saint Dane was here. Maybe there was hope for Quillan yet. Of course, the demon would want the revival to fail. Tylee was offering me the chance to help it succeed. It all seemed so perfect, except for one minor detail.

"I believe in the revival," I said. "I believe that Blok must be put out of business and their grip on the territory broken. But I'm still waiting to hear what you want me to do."

Tylee looked to Nevva. "This is your concept, Nevva," she said. "You should explain it."

"It started with me," Nevva said modestly. "But it has become a group effort. Please, you continue."

Tylee nodded, and paced the stage. It felt a little like a performance, but it was all too real.

"We are on the threshold of a new Quillan," she began. "There are tens of thousands of people who are prepared to rise up and take a stand against Blok and the oppressive society it has forced on us. But tens of thousands aren't enough. We need the hearts and minds of most everyone on Quillan, if we are to succeed. Bringing that many people into the revival has been difficult. The harsh truth is that when the revival begins, life will undoubtedly get worse before it gets better. Right now the water runs, the lights are on, and there is food on the store shelves. If Blok is destroyed, it will take time to pick up the pieces. For a time, people's lives will become more miserable than they are now. There's no avoiding that. We have to re-create an entire society. An entire world. But to do that will mean giving up what little we have now. It's difficult convincing people that they have to fall to the bottom before they can build a better future."

Nevva added, "Blok not only controls every aspect of our physical lives, it has taken away our spirit."

"We believe the first step is to give people hope," Tylee said. "We want to stage a display that shows how the individual can triumph against the odds. We want a symbol. A spark. It doesn't have to be huge, but it must be stirring."

"I get it," I said. "People have been brainwashed into accepting things the way they are, and you're trying to show them they have a choice. Makes sense. What I don't get is how I can help you do that."

"The people need someone they can believe in," Nevva said. "Someone who is just like them, but can demonstrate how it's possible to rise above their inconsequential lives and do something spectacular. Something exciting. Something impossible."

"Something like . . . ?" I asked.

Nevva dropped the bombshell. "Like winning the Grand X."

I stood there, staring at her in disbelief. I never saw that coming. She was asking me to do the exact same thing Saint Dane wanted me to do. My ears rang. All I could squeak out was a soft, "You're kidding, right?"

"Absolutely not!" Nevva shot back. "The Grand X is shown all over Quillan. Everyone watches it, and when I say everyone, I mean *everyone*. There is no bigger stage on Quillan."

Tylee said, "We plan to use the revivers all over Quillan to position you as the champion of the people. The fact that you've won two games has already gotten you noticed. The revivers will build on that. The contest will be built up as the challenge of a lifetime. Challenger Green is hated. The people see him as the champion of Blok. But they wager on him because they know he will win."

I said numbly, "And you want everybody to bet on me?"

"No!" Tylee said. "We don't want people to wager at all. We want them to turn their backs on Challenger Green and the Grand X in a show of defiance. Your winning will then provide an emotional uplift like we could never hope to get any other way. We live in secrecy, Pendragon. We speak in whispers and meet in small groups. We speak of what can be and what needs to be done, but our ability to rally the people is limited. With this one bold stroke we can proclaim to the people of Quillan that the common man can rise up and triumph. We fully believe it will drive people to the revival, and when they come, we'll be waiting for them. Once our numbers swell, we can begin the attacks that will bring Quillan back to life. That's what we want you to do, Pendragon. Provide the spark. The rallying point. The event that will move the people to action."

The two of them stared at me, waiting for an answer. There was only one thing I could think of saying. "What if I lose?"

Nevva said quickly, "You won't. You know that in your heart. You are superior to Challenger Green in every way. You've said it yourself."

"But—"

"I know," she said. "There are no guarantees. Things happen. But the sad truth is that if you should lose, nothing will change. There will be disappointment, yes. Our cause will suffer a huge setback, but in the long run it would only mean that we will have to find some other way to win the minds of the people." She smiled and said, "But if you win, we can start the chain of events that will save Quillan."

I said, "Let's not forget one small detail. If I lose, I die."

"Not necessarily," Nevva said. "The Grand X is not always a match to the death."

"Does Challenger Green know that?" I said quickly. "You told me with that guy, it's all about winning no matter how it happens, right?"

Nevva fell silent. She knew I was right.

Tylee jumped down from the stage and said, "Wait here a moment. I have an idea that might help you decide." She quickly hurried out of the theater, leaving Nevva and me alone. Once I saw that she was out of earshot, I turned on Nevva quickly.

"Are you crazy?" I shouted. "Didn't you hear me before? This is *exactly* what Saint Dane wants! That's why he's on Quillan. He wants me to enter the Grand X and be humiliated!"

"I don't know why he would want that," Nevva said.

"Because this isn't just about Quillan," I said, getting worked up. "It's about all of Halla. If you've learned as much as you say, then you know Saint Dane lures me into these situations. It's like he's testing me. He could probably kill me as easily as he changes personalities, but he doesn't. He keeps me around because I think he can't control Halla until he beats me. Why? I have no idea. But I do know that here on Quillan, he wants me to enter the Grand X and get my ass kicked!"

"But you won't lose, Pendragon," Nevva pleaded. "You know you can beat Challenger Green."

"Yeah," I agreed. "I think I can, but what if something goes wrong? Bye-bye, Bobby."

"You brought Loor back to life," she said flatly.

This rocked me. "How did you know that?" I asked.

"I told you," she said. "I've read journals. Saangi from Zadaa shared Loor's journals with me."

"How did you contact her?" I asked, stunned.

Nevva ignored my question and shot back quickly, "Do you seriously think you're the only Traveler who uses the flumes? I know you feel as if this whole battle with Saint Dane is about you, Pendragon, but there are other Travelers who are just as involved. I've known that Saint Dane would someday come to Quillan. I've been preparing. I believe the revival is the turning point here, and I've set it up so you can do your job. Why is that so hard to accept? You've risked your life many times, I know that, but it's looking like we Travelers might have more powers than we thought possible. Loor was dead. You brought her back. Do you really think that was a fluke? I don't. Whether you choose to accept it or not, the Travelers are more like Saint Dane than we are like the people from our own territories."

Nevva was throwing some truths at me that I hated facing. She added calmly, "If it's true, and Travelers can't die, then what's the risk? The choice should be easy."

"Easy?" I shouted. "You're asking me to put the future of a territory onto my shoulders by playing a game, and you think that's easy?"

"I'm sorry," she said softly. "That was a bad choice of words. All I'm saying is that we have an opportunity here, and we should take it."

"What about Remudi?" I asked. "Did you give him the same pep talk?"

Nevva looked hurt. She walked away from me and stared into the darkness of the theater. When she turned back, I saw that she was crying.

"Yes, in a way I did," she said. "I went to Ibara. Have you been there?"

"No," I admitted.

"I went because I thought Remudi could do exactly what I'm proposing you do. He was an athlete. He was a fighter. Together we came up with this plan."

"But he lost," I said. "And he died. Or did you forget that?"

"He wasn't supposed to compete so soon!" she shouted through her tears. "The trustees pushed Veego and LaBerge to use him. I didn't even know it until the Tato game began! I was supposed to be there. If I had been, I might have been able to save him."

"By bringing him back from the dead?" I asked.

"Yes, if that's what it took!" she shouted.

Man, this was heavy stuff. The idea that the Travelers could bring one another back from the dead was kind of, oh I don't know, staggering.

"It must have been Saint Dane," I said. "He must have known that Remudi was a Traveler. He doesn't miss things like that. I'll bet he put Remudi in quickly to make sure he'd lose."

"But why?" Nevva asked.

"Isn't that obvious?" I said. "To get to me."

Nevva dropped her head, then said softly, "Do you think he knows I'm a Traveler?"

That actually made me laugh. "Are you serious? From the moment you were born," I answered. "Or whatever it is that happens when we show up on our territories."

The door to the theater opened and Tylee strode back in. She must have seen that our emotions were running pretty high, because even though she walked in with authority, she actually downshifted when she saw us.

"I have a proposal," she said.

"Another one?" I asked. "In case you missed it, I'm not so thrilled with your last proposal."

"I understand," she said. "That's why I'd like to bring the two of you on a small trip. Pendragon, we're asking you to risk your life. I don't want you to think we don't understand how enormous a request it is."

"Yeah, so?" I said.

"I want you to see something," she continued. "If afterward you don't want to go through with the Grand X, we will smuggle you out of Rune and away from the trustees. You'll never have to compete again. But I'm hoping that after this trip you will change your mind."

I walked up to Tylee Magna and said boldly, "What could you possibly show me that would make me agree to a death match?"

Tylee looked me straight in the eye and said, "I'm going to introduce you to Mr. Pop."

QUILLAN

The journey to Mr. Pop was a long and complicated one. It probably felt even longer than it was because both Nevva and I had to wear blindfolds. We were told that it was all about security. The more people who knew Mr. Pop and where he was hiding out, the more chance there was of Blok finding him. Tylee explained how devastating that would be. She said that the revival had faced many setbacks and managed to survive. She feared that if the trustees of Blok learned for certain that Mr. Pop was real, and discovered his whereabouts, he would be killed and the revival crushed.

People spoke about him as if he were some kind of mythical being, yet they were cautious not to mention his name too loudly, for fear of making him seem too real. The challengers offered toasts to him. The revivers said he represented the future of Quillan. I couldn't imagine how a single guy could be so powerful and represent so much. Was he a former king? A president? Maybe he was a poet who wrote about freedom, or a visionary leader who knew how to build a new Quillan. Whenever I asked about him, I only got vague, unsatisfying answers. Nothing concrete like, "He's a great military tactician who knows how to destroy the security dados." Or, "He is a wise leader with a vision for a new government." It was always something vague like, "He is our future." Or, "He will be our inspiration and we will follow." It was all very touchy-feely and not very satisfying. I was dying to know how this guy planned to bring Quillan back from the brink.

Nevva was pretty excited too. Or maybe it was nerves. Whatever it was, she didn't say a word for the whole trip. That wasn't like her at all. I figured she was overwhelmed by the concept of finally getting the chance to meet the big guy. The only clue that Tylee gave us about where we were going was that we were leaving the city. She said that in generations past, many people lived outside the city and traveled in and out on trains. She didn't have to explain it any further than that. I knew all about living in the suburbs and taking a train into the city. You guys know how many times we've taken the train from Stony Brook into Manhattan. It seemed as if Mr. Pop was a suburban kind of guy. That was cool. I was too.

We were blindfolded as soon as we left the theater in the mall. They first put us back on those electric carts, where we sped underground for several minutes. Though I couldn't see, I could sense that security was tight. I heard several voices I didn't recognize and they kept changing, as if we were being handed off from team to team. Tylee explained that it was another security measure. The fewer people who knew where we were going, the better. It was all to keep the location of Mr. Pop a secret, even to most of the people of the revival. Once off the electric vehicles, we were put into the backseat of a car. We drove for several minutes, then changed vehicles. For all I knew we were doubling back, and zigzagging, and doing whatever it took to hide our trail. I figured people didn't visit Mr. Pop too often. It took too long.

"You okay?" I finally asked Nevva. I wasn't used to her being so quiet.

"Yes," she said quickly. Short and sweet.

"You don't sound okay," I pressed.

"To be honest, I'm a little scared," she admitted. "This all feels a little like a dream."

I knew what she meant. If I were back home and being taken to meet the president or the pope or somebody big like that, I'd be tense too. Actually, this was bigger than that. We weren't going to see just any old important person. We were going to meet some mythical character that Nevva had only heard stories about. I guess the better analogy would be it was like being taken to meet Santa Claus. Yeah, that would make me kind of nervous.

It felt like we had been traveling for at least a couple of hours when Tylee finally said, "We're here."

I felt Nevva tense up next to me. I probably did the same. We were led out of the car by strong hands and walked for several hundred yards in sunlight. Though I couldn't see, I knew we weren't in the city anymore. The sounds were different. Wherever we were, it was far away from civilization. The only sounds I heard were the crunching of our footsteps on gravel, and birds. Yes, they had birds on Quillan. Hearing them actually raised my spirits. There was life outside the dead city.

Tylee explained, "We are now in what was once an industrial complex, but it has long been abandoned. There are thousands of structures like this spread out beyond the borders of the city. It is the perfect place to go if you want to get lost."

"The dados don't come out here?" I asked.

"There's no need to," Tylee answered. "Blok shut down all the outlying industry. The trains no longer run. With no jobs, people had to move into the city. That's why Rune is so crowded."

Nevva added, "It's another way the company controls people's lives. All over Quillan they've herded the population into cities, where they can monitor our every move."

We stopped, and I heard a heavy metal door being opened. Wherever we were going, it was secure.

"So Mr. Pop lives out here in the middle of nowhere?" I asked.

Nobody answered. I figured I'd be able to ask him myself. We walked inside the building for several minutes. The quick echo of our footsteps made it sound like we were walking down a corridor. Finally the long, mysterious journey came to an end when Tylee announced, "You can remove your blindfolds now."

When I pulled off the cloth, I saw that we were in front of silver steel doors. It was an elevator. Nevva bit her lip. Her eyes darted around nervously.

"It's okay," I said. "This is a good thing."

She nodded, but she was definitely on edge. She took a couple of deep breaths to calm herself. We entered, and had only descended for a short time when the elevator shuddered to a stop. The doors remained closed.

Tylee faced us and said, "Pendragon, Nevva, you two are about to experience something that very few others have. And that's a shame. Hopefully that will soon change. There is a group among the revivers called guardians. I'm one of them. We have been given the single most important task ever conceived of in the history of Quillan. For generations we have been entrusted with the care and protection of Mr. Pop. Guardians have died rather than give up his secrets. I'm not ashamed to admit that some have threatened to reveal his truths and were executed without hesitation. That's the level of importance we give to our task."

"Strong words," I said.

Tylee said, "Once you step through these doors, you'll understand."

"Wait," I said. "You guardians have been protecting Mr. Pop for generations? How old is this guy?"

Tylee smiled and said, "As old as Quillan."

Nevva and I exchanged confused looks.

"Would you like to meet him?" Tylee asked.

We nodded dumbly. Suddenly I was nervous too. Tylee stepped aside and pressed a button on the control panel. The silver doors slid open quietly.

"Nevva, Pendragon," Tylee said, "this is Mr. Pop."

We stepped out of that elevator and into another world. It was a vast underground warehouse. The structure seemed even bigger than the warehouse full of wooden crates that led to the gate and the flume. We're talking immense. But it wasn't the room itself that took my breath away, it was what it contained. The instant the doors opened, I understood everything. I knew why security was so tight. I knew why Mr. Pop was spoken about in hushed tones. I knew how he would guide the people of Quillan into the future. I knew why they didn't want Blok to know he existed. I knew why people died to guard his secrets. I knew why Tylee said protecting him was the single most important job ever conceived of in the history of Quillan, because what we saw in that room *was* the history of Quillan.

Mr. Pop wasn't a person, he was civilization.

I looked to Nevva. Her wide eyes told me she was just as surprised as I was.

"Did you know?" I asked.

All she could do was shake her head. She had no idea.

This huge, impossible vault held the artifacts that defined the history of a territory. Everything that had been wiped out by the juggernaut that was Blok, was here. I'm not sure where to begin telling you about it. I'll just dive in and describe it as it comes to me: There was artwork. Beautiful artwork of all styles—realistic, impressionistic, modern. Paintings and murals and sketches were displayed in one giant section. Next to it was a library. There were many thousands of volumes on shelves stacked nearly to the ceiling. These were the writings and thoughts of the people of Quillan. This is what Blok destroyed—or tried to.

Nevva and I didn't speak; we simply followed Tylee as she led us on a slow stroll through this amazing archive. Music came from one section. It sounded kind of like classical music from Second Earth. There were multiple bins of small disks that contained every piece of music ever composed and recorded on the territory. It was all there.

Another section had hundreds of mannequins, though this wasn't scary and sad like that empty store at the mall. These mannequins wore clothing from all different periods in Quillan's history. There were vibrant colors and colorful patterns and some daring styles that would even turn some heads on Second Earth. There wasn't a single gray, plain suit to be seen anywhere.

I felt as if I were floating through an impossible museum. I can't begin to imagine how Nevva felt. This was her history, a history she never knew. It was Quillan. We passed cars from different eras, models of homes of every sort, examples of furniture and kitchens. There were even artifacts from ancient Quillan cultures. I saw dugout canoes and rudimentary tools. We passed one section that was ringed with hundreds of portraits. Tylee explained how each of these people had been notable in their time. Beneath each portrait was a detailed history of the person's life and his or her contribution to the history of Quillan. There were artists and athletes, politicians and kings, outlaws and scientists. No aspect of Quillan's history had been overlooked, whether it was good or bad. The infamous criminals were given the same treatment as the noted scholars.

Every so often we'd pass someone who was quietly going about the business of caring for the displays. The people all wore dark green smocks that made them look kind of like doctors. Or scientists. Tylee explained that these guardians maintained and cared for everything within these walls. I saw one guy touching up an ancient oil portrait that was starting to fade. Another woman mended a gown that was frayed at the shoulder. Two guys worked on a car. They kicked over the engine and it sputtered to life. The two guys hugged each other as if they had just performed a miracle. I guess in some ways, they had.

We passed sculptures of every kind. Some were realistic depictions of people, others were modern-looking pieces with fascinating shapes and textures. One marble sculpture reached as high as the ceiling. It was a massive, muscular hand, holding a wispy feather. As big as it was, it looked incredibly delicate. We saw vases and hats and flowers and jewelry and poetry and toys and, and, and—I could keep going forever. We toured for an hour and only scratched the surface. It was clear why Tylee brought us here. She wanted us to see what Quillan once was. She wanted *me* to see what Quillan once was.

"So Mr. Pop isn't a person," I finally said.

"We created a name," Tylee answered. "It was a simple way to refer to this collection without raising suspicions as to its true nature."

"The people need to see this," I said.

"Of course they do," Tylee replied. "What you're seeing here isn't just our history, it's our essence. Our very being. This room is filled with tragedy and triumph. There's a library of data where you can look up most every event of note. But this isn't just about grand events. It's about the little things that make up a life. There's creativity in here. There's individuality in here. It's everything we ever were, and lost. No, that's not right. We didn't lose it—it was taken away. You're right, the people desperately need to see this. They need to learn from it. They need to remember what we were and what we can be again. Our goal in preserving this is to have it ready for the time when the people are ready to take back their lives. It will be our guide to help us into the future. Hopefully, we can pick up where we left off, and not make the same mistakes."

"But most people don't know it exists?" I asked, amazed.

"Only in theory," Tylee answered. "People have heard of Mr. Pop and how he will help show us the way. He's a symbol in the form of a man. It gives people hope that there is more out there than the grim future that Blok has created. When the revival begins, and we can be sure that this collection is safe, these items will once again be shared with all the people of Quillan."

Nevva was crying. It must have been pretty emotional to see what your life could have been. I didn't blame her one bit. But I think she was embarrassed by showing such emotion in front of us.

"I need some time," she said, and left Tylee and me alone.

Tylee said, "Nevva has helped the revival in so many ways. She knows that before we can recapture Quillan, we must recapture the minds and the imagination of the people. I truly believe in her idea of creating a hero of the people, who will triumph in the Grand X. It's a brilliant way to charge people's emotions. You've seen what's at stake. But I understand your reluctance. Whatever choice you make, I'll respect it. Now, I'll leave you to explore, and think."

She left me alone. I have to admit, I was rocked. Up until that point, all I had seen was the horror of Quillan. But here, within these walls, I saw hope. Thinking of those masses of zombies walking along the city streets, I couldn't help but wonder what any of those brain-dead people would think if they saw Mr. Pop. It would be like a caveman seeing fire for the first time. I had to believe that learning the truth would change the course of Quillan. As I stood alone in that archive, I truly didn't know what to do.

"Is there something in particular you need?" came a pleasant voice.

It was an elderly woman with long gray hair and warm brown eyes. She wore the same green smock as all the other workers.

"Sure," I answered. "Inspiration."

The old woman looked deep into my eyes for a moment, then said, "Come with me."

I followed her on a winding route through the history of Quillan.

"Is this your first visit to Mr. Pop?" she asked.

I nodded and said, "It's stunning." It was the only word I could think of to describe it.

"The only thing stunning is that it needs to exist at all," she replied.

She led me into another area of portraits that was similar to the first display we'd seen. Only the portraits in this gallery were all of children.

"Who were they?" I asked.

"Ordinary children who faced the same fears we all do," she said. "I hope you find what you're looking for."

She gave me a warm smile and left me alone. I walked into the gallery and stared at the faces in these portraits. There were kids of all ages, from toddlers up to young teens. I quickly scanned the histories that were printed below. These were regular kids who had each done something remarkable. One guy overcame blindness to graduate at the top of his school class. There was a girl who looked about twelve who was a champion swimmer, and a little guy who wrote poetry that was widely published. Some stories were dramatic, like the girl who survived for an impossibly long time in the wilderness. Others were simple, like the guy who raised puppies to be trained for use by the handicapped. One kid designed a simple toy that became very popular; another kid helped his single mother raise his younger brothers and sisters. Most of the stories weren't territory-changing, but they all had one thing in common: They were kids who weren't afraid to try.

I left the gallery in tears, knowing that Quillan didn't have kids like this anymore. Worse, parents gambled away their children in the hopes of finding a better life. It didn't get any worse than that.

I found Nevva and Tylee waiting for me at the elevator. They looked at me as if expecting an answer. I didn't have one. I truly didn't know what to do.

"We should get back" was all I said. I sensed their disappointment, but they didn't say anything.

Tylee had us put our blindfolds back on. As best as I could tell, we retraced the exact same route back to the car and back to Rune. Nobody said a word the whole trip. That was fine by me. I needed to think. I had too many conflicting emotions and concerns. The blindfolds weren't removed until we were back in the center of the city. When we were allowed to see again, we were on a side street somewhere in the heart of the city.

Tylee said, "I know this decision cannot be easy for you, Pendragon. When you have decided what you want to do, Nevva will contact us, and we will go from there."

Tylee nodded to Nevva and left. I wanted more time to think, though I wasn't sure what more thinking would do. The facts weren't changing. It was entirely up to me. Nevva reached for my arm, and was about to lead me away when we heard music boom through the streets. The overhead screens had come to life. We walked out to the corner and gazed up at the nearest screen. All around us the people of Rune did the same.

Loud electronic music blared from the screens, getting everyone's attention. The geometric shapes danced and bobbed on the screen.

"What's going on?" I asked. "Is it another game?"

"No," Nevva answered with certainty. "Unless they've changed the schedule."

The next image we saw on-screen was a familiar one. It was Veego and LaBerge. Veego looked like her normal, intense self, while LaBerge looked like his normal, annoying self. He couldn't keep still as he sang, "Hiding hiding, running scared, maybe under a bed. Your name will bear the mark of shame, the coward Challenger Red!"

Nevva shot me a look. I kept my eyes on the screen. The image changed and was replaced by another familiar face. It was Challenger Green. The crowd cheered. The big guy seemed to be looking right at me as he said, "Stay away, you frightened little boy. Is it because you know you can't beat me? Is that why you ran away? We're laughing at you, Challenger Red. We're all laughing at you. What made you think you could challenge me in the Grand X? I am the greatest champion Blok has ever known. You were nothing before, and you have returned to nothing. Thank you for not wasting my time. Is there anyone else there brave enough to challenge me? The Grand X is nearly here. Who is brave enough to face me? Or maybe I should say, who is stupid enough?" Challenger Green laughed, the crowd roared its approval, and the screen went dark.

I turned to Nevva and said, "I'll do it."

That's where I'm ending this journal. I'm going to enter the Grand X. I know it sounds crazy. I'm doing exactly what Saint Dane wants. But how can I turn my back on these people? Seeing that library they call Mr. Pop was what did it. Quillan had life once. If the revivers are successful, I think the territory can be turned around. Nevva was right, this definitely feels like the turning point for Quillan. I think Saint Dane was lying. Quillan isn't lost. Not yet. There seems to be a moment here where things can turn for the better. It's all about the revivers, and if they think my competing in the Grand X will help them, then I've got to do it. It's what I'm supposed to do. Yes, I think it's the way it was meant to be.

I can't say I'm not nervous about it. I am. But I'm confident, too. I can beat that guy. I know I can. Of course anything can happen, but all things being equal, I know I can take him. Whatever positive effect that will have on the revival is the main reason I want to take him on. But there's another. This guy killed a Traveler. I don't care if it was during a game. He killed a Traveler. I'm tired of being cautious. I'm going to take him apart.

And I haven't forgotten Saint Dane's offer. He told me if I competed in the Grand X, he'd reveal the origin of the Travelers. Do I believe him? Not really. But when I win, I'm going to do all I can to hold him to that. I'm beginning to understand that guy. As much as he's jerked me around, I've been able to get to him, too. If I compete and he doesn't live up to his end of the bargain, I can turn it around on him as proof of his own weakness. He hates that. He wants to beat me. No, he *needs* to beat me. He won't.

That's why I think this can be the beginning of the end. Or the end of the beginning of my life as a Traveler. When I win the Grand X, I'm not only going to be helping the revivers save Quillan, I'll be taking another step toward stopping Saint Dane for good.

But first I've got to stop Challenger Green.

Bring it on.

END JOURNAL #26

◎ SECOND EARTH ◎

Courtney read the entire journal at the Sherwood house.

She couldn't wait. She took the envelope upstairs to the empty living room of the old mansion, sat on the hard floor, and read. Her heart raced the entire time. With each new turn in Bobby's story, she grew more upset. Bobby had announced that he was going to enter the Grand X. She wanted to cry. Bobby was changing. She feared he was becoming too aggressive, too cocky. It scared her to death.

She needed Mark. She *really* needed Mark. But Mark was gone. He had jumped into the flume and traveled to territories unknown. The only people who knew where he went and why were Mark . . . and Saint Dane. Saint Dane. Andy Mitchell was Saint Dane. He had been Saint Dane from the very beginning, which meant back in grade school. Courtney zipped through her memories of the creepy kid with the greasy hair who loved to torment others. The thought was impossible, yet strangely, the more she thought about it, the more it made sense. It didn't make her feel any better, but it made sense.

Courtney put Bobby's pages back into the envelope, hugged her knees, and put her head down to think. Andy

Mitchell had tormented Mark all his life, then suddenly became his best friend. What was the point? To get Mark to like him? Courtney didn't know much about psychology, but she thought about how quickly Mark had accepted Andy as a changed guy. As a friend. Was Mark somehow drawn to Andy Mitchell because the former bully suddenly showed a different, better side? Did that make him more appealing as a friend? Now that she thought about it, the whole thing was so obvious. Mitchell had magically become a science geek. Saint Dane knew that's what Mark would respond to, so that's what he became. Was Saint Dane that smart? Of course he was, she thought. Saint Dane had tricked entire governments into trusting him. He worked his way into the confidences of princes and queens, of bandits and scientists. Saint Dane knew which buttons to push, all right. Mark didn't stand a chance.

Another thought hit Courtney. Saint Dane was Whitney Wilcox. Saint Dane was Andy Mitchell. Whitney Wilcox tried to kill her, but Andy Mitchell helped Mark save her. Why would Saint Dane try to kill her, only to then save her?

"Oh, my God," Courtney said as the truth rushed at her.

Her accident was a setup. A devious, diabolical setup. By helping Mark save her, Andy Mitchell had cemented their relationship. It created a bond. They had saved Courtney. Courtney realized in horror that she'd been a pawn. It was about Mark all along. There was no doubt in her mind, Saint Dane had gone to great lengths to get Mark to trust him. Now Mark's parents were dead. If there was ever a time that Mark needed support from a friend, it was then. And who was there to give it to him? Saint Dane. Courtney wanted to scream. Whatever Saint Dane wanted with Mark, it had to have something to do with his plans for Second Earth. Why else would he bother? She squeezed her hands into fists. They'd been worried for years about what Saint Dane might do on Second Earth, without realizing he was laying the groundwork right under their noses. Worse, they were part of it!

Courtney wanted Bobby home. He needed to know what was going on. They had to find Mark not only to save him, but to stop Saint Dane from using their friend for whatever his plans were for Second Earth. Courtney was faced with a decision. Should she go to Quillan to find Bobby? She felt certain it was wrong for him to enter the Grand X. It was way too risky. And now that Mark needed help, it was all the more reason that he had to come home. For Mark, for Second Earth, and for himself.

Courtney jumped to her feet. She had made up her mind. It was worth the risk of damaging the flume. She grabbed her pack and took a step toward the stairs to the basement . . . when she heard the growl.

Courtney froze. It was coming from the foyer of the mansion. She cautiously slid her hand into her jacket pocket and grasped the canister of pepper spray.

Grrrrr . . .

She knew that growl. There was no mistaking it. Quigs. She glanced over her shoulder to see if there was another way out of this room. A window, a back hallway, anything.

There wasn't. It was too late anyway. The quig sprang.

It was a huge muscled black dog with rows of sharp teeth that were too big for its jaw. It rounded the corner from the foyer and charged her at full speed, its yellow quig eyes focused, its teeth gnashing.

Courtney pulled out the pepper spray, aimed, and waited. She didn't want to miss. It meant she had to let it get dangerously close. The quig charged; Courtney steeled herself. She waited . . . waited . . . waited . . . and pulled the trigger.

Fum!

A burst of energy blasted out of the bottle and hit the quig, knocking it backward. It hit the ground, rolled, and lay there unconscious.

"Ahhh!" Courtney screamed and dropped the bottle. It was an unconscious act. Whatever had just shot out of the bottle, it wasn't pepper spray. Pepper spray didn't knock out a charging quig. Or anything else for that matter. Yet the demon-dog was out cold. Courtney slowly knelt down and retrieved the canister. She looked at it as if it were something alien, because it was. Looking closely, she realized that it wasn't her pepper spray. It was the same size and weight, but the canister was metallic silver with no markings. Her pepper spray was plastic with writing that said very clearly, PEPPER SPRAY. This wasn't it. Courtney reached into her left pocket to check the other canister of spray. It was the exact same as the first. It wasn't hers. She had no idea when or how they were changed.

Courtney didn't want to be there anymore. She abandoned the idea of jumping into the flume, at least for the time being. She jammed the silver canisters into her pockets, picked up the envelope holding Bobby's journal pages, put it into her backpack, and ran out of the Sherwood house. All she wanted was to get home. Too much was happening and none of it was good. She made it back over the wall surrounding the Sherwood property with no problem, and down the tree to the sidewalk. With her head down, she walked quickly along, wanting more than anything else to be someplace safe and sane.

A car horn sounded behind her, making her jump and scream, "Ahhh!"

She turned to see her father pulling up behind her in their Volvo wagon.

"Sorry," he said. "Didn't mean to do that."

Courtney tried to catch her breath.

"You want to tell me why you're not in school?" Mr. Chetwynde asked.

Oh. Right. School.

"I couldn't," she said, truthfully. "I wanted to go, but there's just too much to deal with. I can't stop thinking about the Dimonds. I want to go home."

"I don't blame you," Mr. Chetwynde said. "Hop in."

Courtney wanted to kiss her dad. He always made things better. She wished she could confide in him all that was happening. It was tough not being able to turn to him when she needed him most. She clutched her backpack to her chest and slipped into the passenger seat.

"Any more news on the plane?" she asked, wiping away the tears.

"No," Mr. Chetwynde said. "But no news is bad news. They're analyzing radar data but there isn't much hope. They're looking for survivors now. Man, what a tragedy. You see stuff like that on the news all the time, but you never think it'll happen to somebody you know."

Courtney loved her father. He was her protector. Her champion. He always seemed to know how to make things better. It bothered her to know that she knew so much more about the true perils of the world, and of Halla, than he did.

Mr. Chetwynde added, "They officially released the passenger list."

"And?"

Mr. Chetwynde gently shook his head and said, "Mr. and Mrs. Dimond were on board."

Hearing those words made Courtney wince, though it didn't come as any real surprise. She knew they were gone. It fit too perfectly into Saint Dane's plans to get close to Mark. Courtney didn't want to talk any more about airplanes or tragedies. She closed her eyes and settled into the seat for the short ride home. She had grown to hate riding in that old car. The long, painful drive home from the hospital was still a vivid memory. She was glad that their house was only a few blocks away. There wasn't enough time for her to get sore from the old seat. But no sooner did she close her eyes than she felt a strange sensation. She didn't understand what it was at first. She looked at her ring. It wasn't activating. Still, something felt odd. It took a few moments for her to realize what it might be.

"Did you get new car seats?" she asked.

"No, why?"

"This seat is really comfortable all of a sudden. I mean, really comfortable, like an easy chair."

Mr. Chetwynde chuckled. "That's an odd thing to think of at a time like this!"

Courtney wiggled her back into the seat. The seat moved in response!

Courtney looked to her dad and said, "C'mon! I rode in this seat for three hours when I got out of the hospital, remember? I felt every bump in the road between here and Derby Falls. This is definitely not the same seat."

"I don't know what to say," Mr. Chetwynde said. "Maybe it's because you're feeling better."

Courtney shifted her butt again. The seat seemed to take on a subtly new shape, giving her perfect support. Whichever way she moved, the seat compensated and cradled her like a down cushion. Courtney figured her dad was either hiding the fact that he spent a bunch of money on fancy new seats and didn't want her mom to know, or she was imagining things. She was about to challenge him again when they arrived at their house. Mr. Chetwynde stopped at the curb, kissed his daughter good-bye, and continued on toward work. As she walked up the path to the house, Courtney had a vague sense of unease. Something felt off, but she couldn't put her finger on it.

"Mom? Mom!" she yelled when she got into the house.

There was no answer. Courtney realized it was already past nine. Her mother always left for work by eight.

"Dinner's ready for defrosting, sweetheart," came her mother's voice from the living room.

"You're still home?" Courtney yelled back with surprise.

Courtney's mom called, "Throw it in the microwave for me?"

"Now?" Courtney yelled back. "It's too early!"

Courtney's mom called out again, "I'll be working late tonight, so don't wait for me, okay?"

Huh? Courtney walked into the living room saying, "What are you talking about?"

When she entered the room, she looked around for her mom . . . and froze. There was something on the desk that wasn't there when she'd left earlier. It was the desk where they normally kept their ancient computer. The computer was still there, but it wasn't ancient. It was a wide high-tech screen showing the image of Courtney's mother.

The image said, "When I got to work, I saw there was a late meeting scheduled. Sorry. Let me know as soon as you get this message. I hope school wasn't too rough. Such a tragedy about the Dimonds. I love you."

The screen went blank.

Courtney didn't move. She knew that computer screen was not there when she left a few hours before. Even if it were, how was her mother able to leave a video message? From work! That was impossible. Stranger still, how did it know enough to play itself when she came into the house? Courtney wouldn't normally be home until after three. What was going on?

Courtney felt her cat, Winston, rub against her legs. Courtney looked down . . . and screamed. It was a cat all right, but it wasn't Winston. Winston was a short-haired tortoiseshell. This cat was black, with yellow eyes and a little tuft of white on its chest. Courtney dove onto the couch. Instantly the image of her mother appeared again, as if Courtney's scream had triggered it.

"Dinner's ready for defrosting, sweetheart. Throw it in the microwave for me?"

Courtney looked at the strange cat who was sitting on the floor staring at her.

"How did you get in here?" she yelled at the animal.

The cat purred and said in a strangely metallic voice, "I live here!"

Courtney screamed.

"Dinner's ready for defrosting, sweetheart. Throw it in the microwave for me?"

Courtney jumped up and ran out of the room, headed for the stairs and the safety of her bedroom. She'd only made it up halfway when the ring on her finger came to life.

"No!" she shouted, as if it would make a difference.

She yanked the ring off and threw it on the floor near the front door. She plunked down on the stairs, hugging herself, watching the ring grow, the lights flash, and the music play. Compared to everything else that had happened that day, this magical event was run of the mill. Courtney closed her eyes for the final, bright moment. When the lights were gone, she looked to see that Bobby's next journal had arrived. This one looked like the last few. It was a brown envelope that she knew would contain the small gray pages with Bobby's handwriting.

Courtney dragged herself down the stairs and approached the journal slowly. She wasn't entirely sure if she wanted to read it. She didn't think she could take any more. But she had to. It was her job. She was an acolyte. She took a breath, bent down, picked up the envelope, and . . .

The doorbell rang.

Courtney jumped and yelped. She had no idea if somebody

could get a heart attack from being surprised too often, but if it was possible, she figured she was due. She quickly picked up her ring and hid the envelope in her backpack with Bobby's previous journal. The doorbell rang again. She looked out the window next to the door to see who it was and saw a young guy she didn't recognize. He looked about her age, with longish, unkempt brown hair and a yellow sweatshirt that looked too small for him. It wasn't because he was fat, either. If anything, he looked pretty built. She wondered why he would wear a sweatshirt that was so ugly and way too small. She went to the door and called, "Can I help you?"

"Is Courtney home?" the guy asked.

"Who wants to know?" Courtney asked.

"She's expecting me," the guy answered.

"I am?" Courtney said, and opened the door.

The first thing that hit her was how handsome the guy was, in a rugged kind of way. The next thing that hit her was that the ugly yellow sweatshirt had the words COOL DUDE printed on the front in red seventies-looking cheesy lettering. She knew that sweatshirt! It was the shirt Mark always kept at the flume in case a Traveler came to Second Earth. That meant this handsome guy was a Traveler, but who could it—

She looked more closely at the guy. She hadn't seen him in over a year. He had changed. He had grown up. He wasn't a little kid anymore.

"What's with the stunned face?" the guy said. "I told you I was coming home."

"Bobby!" Courtney shouted and threw herself into his arms.

The two stood there, holding on to each other. Courtney cried. They were tears of joy and pain and loss and love and pure emotional release. Bobby was home. Things would be better.

"Don't want the neighbors talking," Bobby said as he

maneuvered Courtney back into the house. "I hope your parents are at work."

"They are," Courtney said, tearing herself away from him and wiping her eyes. "You've changed," she said.

"In a good way or a bad way?" he asked.

"Oh, good," she said. "Mostly. But you look tired."

"Yeah, that's one word for it," Bobby said.

"What happened on Quillan?" Courtney asked. "With the Grand X?"

Bobby frowned. "Didn't you guys read my last journal?"

Courtney grabbed her backpack and pulled out the envelope. "I just got it like five seconds ago!" she said.

Bobby shook his head in wonder. "Amazing. I sent it ages ago."

"I don't get the whole relative time thing between territories," Courtney said.

"Join the club," Bobby said.

"So what happened?"

The expression on Bobby's face turned dark. "It's all coming apart, Courtney. Everything. I want you to read the pages, then we'll talk."

"I will," she said. "Come in, sit down."

She pulled Bobby into the living room. The two sat on the couch, facing each other. Bobby looked around the room and smiled. "This house is exactly like I remember it. It's good to know some things don't change." He pointed to the big computer screen and said, "Other than that bad boy. That's a little high-tech for your dad, isn't it?"

Courtney didn't know how to answer. She was as clueless as Bobby.

Bobby spotted something else and said, "Hey! Who's that? What happened to Winston?"

Sitting in the doorway was the cute black cat, staring at

them. It stood up and said, "My name is Doogie." With a flick of its tail, it turned and strutted off.

Bobby and Courtney sat staring at the animal for a good thirty seconds before Bobby said, "Now that's something you don't see every day."

"Something's happened, Bobby," Courtney said nervously. "Something odd. I don't even know how to explain it. That's not our cat."

"Yeah," Bobby said. "And it talked. That's like...not right."

"That's not the half of it," Courtney said. "There's so much to tell you I don't know where to begin!"

"Where's Mark?" Bobby asked. "Doesn't he usually have the ring?"

Courtney wanted to cry, but didn't want to show weakness in front of Bobby. She closed her eyes and took a deep breath to get a grip.

"I guess that would be the other half of it," she answered. "I don't know where he is."

Bobby looked at Courtney for a good long time. He finally said, "Don't take this the wrong way, but you look like you've been through some stuff."

Courtney chuckled at the understatement.

"I've got a lot to tell you," she said calmly. "About Mark. About me. But first I want to know what happened on Quillan."

Bobby nodded and said, "Read the pages. I don't have the energy to explain it all. After that, we'll talk."

Courtney reached for the backpack and pulled out the envelope that had just arrived.

Bobby stood up and said, "Can I raid your fridge? Right now I'm dying for anything Second Earth."

"Go for it," Courtney said.

Bobby headed for the kitchen. Courtney watched him go. She was amazed at how powerful he looked. He wasn't a huge guy or anything. He might have stood just under six feet, but all the training he had done had put a layer of muscle on him that couldn't be missed.

"Bobby?" she called.

Bobby stopped and turned back to her.

"It's a good thing you're here," she said.

Bobby nodded and continued on to the kitchen. Courtney curled her feet up under her on the couch, and read.

QUILLAN

It's over. I'm alive.

Mark, Courtney, there's no need to worry about me, at least as far as the Grand X goes. I survived, but I guess that's obvious. The question now becomes, will Quillan? I'm going to get right to it and describe the events that happened to me from the time I decided to compete in the Grand X until now. When I'm done with this journal, I'm going to come home. I need to see familiar faces. Let me say that another way. I need to see the familiar faces of *friends*. There's so much we need to talk about, not just about what's happened here on Quillan, but about what the future might hold. For me, for you guys, for Second Earth, and for Halla.

When I told Nevva that I would enter the Grand X, I thought she would be all sorts of excited. She wasn't. At least not at first. We stood on that street corner after having heard the taunts thrown at me by Challenger Green, and I gave her the news that I'd compete. Instead of being all happy and relieved, she gave me this odd look.

"What?" I asked. "Isn't that what you want??"

"It is," she said, but it sure didn't sound like she meant it.

"Look, you made your case," I said. "I know what you're going for. On Second Earth a big game or race or fight can capture people's imaginations. It's like the whole world stops to watch and cheer. We have Super Bowls, World Series, prize fights, Kentucky Derbies, Olympics, NASCAR races, and tons more. People root like crazy, even though there really isn't anything at stake for them. Some people make bets, sure, but mostly they just want their favorite to win because it's fun to root. But here, people *do* have something at stake. Seeing Mr. Pop made that clear. If you guys can get the people behind me the way I've seen fans at home believe in their favorite team, then I think it can launch something big. It all comes down to the revivers taking advantage of the emotion that comes from my winning."

Nevva still didn't say anything. She looked troubled.

"This is weird," I said. "I feel like I'm convincing you. This was your idea, remember?"

"Yes," she said, shaking off whatever was bothering her. "You're absolutely right. You've made the right choice. We have a lot of work to do. Let's tell the others."

She was back in hyperefficient mode, but I was left with an odd feeling. I knew I had made the right decision, but for that brief moment Nevva looked like she had second thoughts.

"Wait," I said. "Something's bugging you."

"I'm sorry," she said. "It's just that, I still have this image of Remudi falling from the Tato platform."

"Don't worry about me," I said. "I've been through a lot worse than anything Green boy can throw at me."

"I know," she said, smiling. Whatever doubts she had were gone. "This is the way it was meant to be."

She walked down the street, headed for the underground. This time Nevva didn't ask me to wear the hood over my head. I guess I had passed whatever test needed to be passed in order to be accepted by the revivers. She led me into a building, down an elevator, through some subterranean corridors, and generally on a twisting, confusing route that I don't think I'd be able to tell anybody about even if I wanted to. We eventually found ourselves at a cement wall that looked as if a hole had been blasted through it.

"This is one of the entry points to the underground that the revivers opened up," she explained.

I felt like I was entering an ancient tomb that had been unsealed by archeologists. Beyond the hole were more corridors that eventually led us through a steel door and into one of the underground malls. Waiting there for us was another electric-powered cart. Or maybe it was a tarz-powered cart. With Nevva at the wheel we drove another several minutes through the deserted malls until we found ourselves back at the department store that was the base of the revivers.

"So what do we do now?" I asked.

"We prepare you" was Nevva's answer.

It seemed like she had been planning this for a long time. There was no question she'd thought the whole thing through. That was Nevva. Her mind was like a computer, calculating every possibility and planning for every contingency. I guess you had to be organized like that in order to juggle three different lives.

The first phase of her plan was to prepare me for the Grand X. That meant a lot of things. For one, the revivers trained me. They worked me over pretty good, too. It wasn't like the grueling training at Mooraj that Loor put me through, but it was tough. We worked on strength with weights, and agility. We did tons of cardio to build up my breathing and stamina. I ran for miles through the deserted malls beneath the city of Rune. I also did sprints. Many, many sprints. I was already in pretty good shape, but after the time I spent in the underground, I had to admit, I was rocking.

Nevva wasn't there very much. She had to deal with her job as assistant to the trustees. Every few days she'd come to the underground with news about what was happening with them. The hunt for me was still on. They wanted me for the Grand X. Or maybe I should say, Saint Dane wanted me for the Grand X. He wouldn't let them give up on me. I think he must have known all along that I would compete. I hated that he was right.

Tylee Magna reported back to me on how the word had gone out to revivers all over Quillan about the upcoming event. I was being talked about as a champion of the people. The buzz was building. Only time would tell if it would get big enough to have the effect the revivers wanted. It was a weird feeling to know that I was being promoted like this. Up until this point, everything I had done as a Traveler was pretty anonymous. That was about to change. Here on Quillan my face would be known to every person on the territory. You'd think I'd be intimidated by the whole thing. I wasn't. I don't know why. Maybe it was because I was so confident.

My training with the revivers had a lot to do with that. Nevva had gathered a boatload of information about Challenger Green. She studied the replays of his matches and put together a report on his strengths and weaknesses. His biggest strength by far was his attitude. He was ruthless. I won't go so far as to say he enjoyed killing off his opponents, but he definitely didn't mind it. He was smart, too. He adapted to situations quickly. I saw that in the replay of the Tato match where he smashed open the dome, then held on to the opening as he threw the platform off balance, killing Remudi. That was a snap decision and a smart one. I couldn't count on him making mistakes. He was also strong. He was bigger than me, and I was sure if it came down to a show of pure strength, I'd be in trouble.

But the guy had weaknesses. He wasn't agile. He could easily be thrown off balance. And he was slow. Running both distance and sprints. There's a big difference between being fast in the forty-yard dash and being fast in a two-yard dash. From what I'd seen, I was better than Green in both. It made me feel confident that even if things went sour and I got in trouble, I could get away from him. As an added bonus, Nevva told me that the vision in Challenger Green's left eye was weak as the result of a childhood accident. That was a great thing to know.

But what gave me the most confidence was the fact that I was a trained fighter. Me. Bobby Pendragon. Hard to believe, isn't it? I never even got in a dumb wrestling match back at home, let alone a fistfight. But that was a lifetime ago. I had recently been hardened by the tough physical regime that Loor and Alder put me through, and by fighting for my life more times than I like to think about. Challenger Green had no such training. The fighting skills I had would help me in so many phases of the Grand X, there was no way Challenger Green could compete with me. I was sure of that.

Nevva walked me through many of the possible events. There were hundreds to choose from—far too many for her to cover all of them, but I got a pretty good overview. The Grand X wasn't just one game, or battle, or race. It was a series of five contests. Nobody knew what the actual games would be until the day of the event. They were chosen by Veego and LaBerge. Nevva explained that sometimes the Grand X was a huge spectacle, with each event a team sport that pitted several challengers against one another. But usually there were two challengers who battled head-to-head. It was important to win each event, because the loser would be given a handicap for the next stage, or the winner an advantage.

Here was the kicker; the Grand X ended if either of the challengers was killed, or injured so badly that he or she couldn't go on. Nevva told me that many Grand X's never got past the first event. That was a grim thought. I had no doubt that Challenger Green would not only try to beat me, but once he realized how good I was, he'd try to hurt or kill me. So the Grand X was not only about winning, it was about staying in one piece.

"So how do you win?" I asked Nevva.

"The champion is the challenger who wins the most events. Which means the Grand X might only last for three events if one challenger wins them all."

"So it's possible to lose the Grand X and still survive?" I asked.

Nevva hesitated.

"Tell me the truth," I said.

"Yes, of course it's possible, but only if you lose the Grand X within the first four events."

"Why's that?" I asked.

"Because if it goes to the fifth event, the tiebreaker, it's usually a game where, to win, you must kill your opponent."

Oh. That gave new meaning to the phrase "sudden death overtime."

I won't go into the details of the possible events, because I'll describe the actual events to you when I write about the competition, but I will say this much: After spending roughly three weeks training in the catacombs of Rune, I was ready. Mentally and physically. As we got closer to the Grand X, I felt that my biggest problem would be overconfidence.

There is something else I need to mention. An odd thing happened during my time with the revivers. I slept in a small room that wasn't much better than a cell. But it was comfortable, so I didn't complain. One night while I was sleeping, I had a visitor. At first I thought it was a dream, but then I recognized her as the old woman I had met on my trip to see Mr. Pop. The one who showed me the children's portrait gallery for inspiration. Remember her? She knelt down by my bed and woke me up by stroking my hair. You'd think I would have jumped in surprise, but I didn't. There was nothing frightening about her. Just the opposite. She had this calm air that made me feel as relaxed as if I were still sleeping.

"You are a very brave young boy," she said softly. "We are all very proud of you."

"Thank you," I whispered.

"You said you were looking for inspiration?" she said, and held up a dark necklace made of stone beads. It wasn't fancy, the only unique thing about it was a single gold bead that was slightly larger than the rest. I'd say it was about the size of a large pea. "This once belonged to someone who sacrificed everything for what he believed in. I wish you would wear it. For luck."

I reached for the beads, but the woman gently pushed my hands aside and put it around my neck herself.

"Who was it?" I asked.

The old woman put her hands over my eyes to close them. She didn't answer, and I fell asleep. When I woke up the next morning, I thought for sure it was a dream. But when I touched my throat, the necklace was there. I had no idea who that old woman was, or whose necklace this was, but I had no intention of taking it off. I needed all the luck I could get.

Finally, after so many weeks of hard work, the day came to take the next step. I had just finished a megalong run through the mall, when I got back to the department store to see Nevva and Tylee waiting for me. They looked tense. I didn't have to ask why.

"It's time, isn't it?" I asked.

Nevva was carrying a sack. She reached inside and pulled out something I hadn't seen in quite a while. I hoped I would never see it again, but as things turned out, that wasn't meant to be.

It was a red shirt with five black diagonal stripes—the jersey of Challenger Red. My uniform.

"Get dressed," Tylee said.

Soon afterward I was in the back of a car being driven through the streets of Rune. The older man whose name I hadn't learned was driving. Tylee was in the passenger seat. Nevva was next to me.

"The campaign has been incredible," Nevva said. It sounded like she was talking about my run for class president or something. "The anticipation is huge. Everybody wants to know when you'll reappear. The mystery has only helped build excitement."

"It's going to work, Pendragon," Tylee said. "We've positioned you as being the first challenger to compete on your own terms. You've stood up to Blok, and now you're going back voluntarily. That's never happened before. I almost want to say that it doesn't matter what happens with the Grand X. You're already being spoken about in awe, all over Quillan."

"So what you're saying is we're in a no-lose situation. Depending on what happens I'll either be a hero . . . or a martyr."

Tylee looked at me, debating about how to answer. She knew she had to be honest with me. I was too smart. "We'd much prefer you to be a hero."

I smiled. "Good answer."

"I'll be there the day of the Grand X," Nevva said. "In case . . ."

She didn't finish. I knew what she meant. She was going to be there in case I was killed. She would do all she could, as a Traveler, to bring me back.

"It won't come to that," I said defiantly.

Nevva nodded.

I added with a smile, "But try to be there."

"I will," she said.

"So when does this big doo-da begin?" I asked.

"Soon," Nevva said. "I'm sure Veego and LaBerge are going to want to show you off a little and whip up some excitement. They have no idea that the entire territory is already primed and waiting."

"Are they expecting me?" I asked.

"No, of course not," Nevva answered quickly. "But the trustees have promised them that they would bring you back. Or should I say, Mr. Kayto made that promise."

Nevva and I exchanged looks. Saint Dane knew I'd be back. He knew I'd compete. I hated his confidence. I just hoped he was ready to live up to his end of the bargain.

"We're almost there," Tylee said. "Get out quickly. We don't want to be seen."

"Got it," I said. "Just slow down enough so I don't break my leg. How stupid would that be?"

The old man said, "We're proud of you, Pendragon. And more grateful than words can say."

"Good luck," Tylee said. "I'd say we'll be watching, but that's a pretty big understatement. Millions will be watching right along with us."

"Good thing I'm not camera shy," I said.

Nevva touched my arm in a show of support. I winked and said, "I'm doing this for Remudi, too."

She smiled and nodded.

The car slowed and Tylee shouted, "Go!"

I threw open the door and jumped out. My feet barely hit the road when the old man hit the throttle and sped off. As I watched the car disappear into traffic, I felt very much alone. For a quick moment I wondered if I was doing the right thing. I had the sudden urge to take off into the city and disappear into the crowds. It didn't last. I knew I was in the right place. Slowly I turned to see that I had been deposited exactly where I needed to be. I was standing directly in front of the big, ornate golden gates that led into the garden of Veego and LaBerge. I stood there with my hands on my hips, not entirely sure what to do. Ten seconds later the big metal gates slowly swung open with an eerie *creeaaaaaaak*. I stood watching until they had opened the whole way and stopped with a loud *clang*!

I was headed back into the fire.

QUILLAN

"I never thought we'd see you again!" LaBerge said, all bubbly and happy as I walked up the marble stairs toward the front door of the castle. Behind me were the two security dados that had met me as soon as I set foot back inside the front gate. "This is just incredible! Do you know how much excitement is building for the Grand X? It's impossible! It's phenomenal! It's—"

"Yeah, I get it," I said.

"Oh," LaBerge said, looking all pouty. "Just wanted to let you know how happy we are to see you back."

He turned with a huff and stormed into the castle. Veego stood at the top of the stairs, staring at me with those cold, calculating eyes.

"Miss me?" I said, faking a smile.

"They told me you'd be back," she said coldly. "I didn't believe them. Yet here you are. I must admit, I don't understand."

I walked right up to her and said, "I'm here to win your dumb little contest. Is that a problem?"

Veego said, "Absolutely not. This is going to be the most widely seen Grand X in the history of the games. Your running away has only raised the interest. And now that you've come back on your own, well, let's just say we expect the wagering to be very high."

"Then we're all good," I said. "I want to compete and you want to look good to your bosses. Everybody's happy." I was being kind of obnoxious, but couldn't help myself.

Veego continued to stare at me suspiciously. "Don't push your luck, Challenger Red," she said. "We aren't as dumb as you seem to think."

"Really? How dumb are you?" I asked.

Veego didn't fight back. "Your quarters haven't been touched," she said. "Settle in and we'll begin the preparations."

"Terrific," I said, and walked past her, headed into the castle.

The woman grabbed me by the arm and said, "Just one more thing."

Before I realized what was happening, she deftly slipped something over my hand and pushed it all the way up my arm. I instantly felt the tight grip of the loop as it grasped my biceps.

"Welcome back, Challenger Red," she said with a sneer.

I didn't give her the satisfaction of reacting, though the feeling of being constrained again by one of their leashes made my skin crawl. I continued on into the castle, where someone was waiting for me in the grand entryway.

"Hello, Challenger Red," Fourteen said formally. "I'll bring you to your room."

"Hi, Fourteen," I said. "Or maybe by now you're Fifteen." My robot friend didn't even crack a smile.

"Never mind," I said. "I'm glad to see you." I really was.

He had been pretty decent to me. I was glad that he was going to be my personal dado again. The two of us walked up the staircase toward my room.

"I wish I could say the same to you, Pendragon," Fourteen said. "Why did you return?"

"For the Grand X," I said. "I'm gonna win."

Fourteen didn't answer. If a robot could look worried, he looked worried.

"What?" I asked. "Don't you think I can?"

"You certainly have the ability," the dado said. "But Challenger Green does not win on ability alone."

"I know, he's a rotten cheat," I said. "Don't worry. I'm ready for him."

"I do not think that is possible," Fourteen said. "At least for you. I cannot see you lowering yourself to compete with his type of tactics."

"Don't worry," I said. "I've got some tactics of my own, but thanks for your concern."

Fourteen led me to my room and left me alone. When the door closed behind me, I looked around at the familiar space. I got the same feeling as when I'd jumped out of the car a while before. What had I gotten myself into? Why did I come back to this horror house? Up until that moment it had all felt like theory. Seeing the castle and this room made it real.

The Grand X didn't happen right away. Nevva was right. Veego and LaBerge wanted to whip up as much excitement as they could. When I did my training, there was always a dado there with a small handheld camera. They were beaming my image all over Quillan so that everybody got to know Challenger Red. I didn't see Challenger Green much, but the few times I caught a glimpse of him outside lifting weights, or doing exercises, I saw that there was a camera on him, too. I guess it was like showing those "up close and personal" videos of athletes during the Olympics on Second Earth.

Of course, there was no way that Veego and LaBerge could know that all this publicity was playing right into the hands of the revivers. Up until then, all anybody had actually seen of me were the Hook and Tock matches. Now they were seeing hours of me. I imagined my picture being shown on hundreds of screens lining the streets of Rune. It was kind of intimidating, to be honest. I found myself getting nervous. Not about the Grand X. I was more worried that I might not come off as the big "champion" that the revivers were building me up to be. I mean, I was still me. What if nobody was impressed? It would all be for nothing. I found myself trying extra hard during training to look worthy. I ran a little faster and did my best to impress during agility drills. I really wanted to do my part to build up the myth. I figured that was just as important as the actual training.

I had no idea if it was doing any good, until one day when I got an interesting opportunity. Fourteen brought me to the platform where the Tato competitions were held. Waiting there for me were Veego, LaBerge, and Challenger Green. I had no idea what was going on, but tried to act cool.

"Is this it?" I asked. "Are we starting?"

"No!" LaBerge said with excitement as he scampered up to me. "Veego and I thought it would be wonderful if you two could say a few words to the people of Quillan. You know, to let them know how you feel, and how it's going to be such a fabulous Grand X and all."

"It was my idea actually," said Nevva Winter as she stepped up onto the platform. "What better way to let the people of Quillan know who they will be wagering on than to hear from the challengers themselves?"

As Nevva said this, she looked me square in the eye, as if she were trying to tell me something.

"We can say whatever we want?" I asked.

Veego chimed in, "So long as it doesn't embarrass us, or Blok."

"Oh, no," I said sarcastically. "Wouldn't want to do that!"

Nevva said, "Just tell them what you're about, and why it's important for you to win the Grand X."

Nevva again looked right at me. I realized that she had set this up as a golden opportunity for me to tell the people why I was competing. Every person on Quillan would see this. I had to find the exact right words.

Challenger Green laughed and said, "You mean, there are other reasons for winning besides not getting killed?"

LaBerge was the only one who laughed. When he saw that nobody else did, he stopped. Idiot.

"Let Challenger Green go first," I said. "He is the champion, he should have the honor."

Actually, I wanted more time to think about what I was going to say.

"All right," Green said. "Let's do this."

Veego and LaBerge stood together. A service dado appeared with a small camera and pointed it at them.

"Let us know when we are online," Veego said to the dado.

Nevva stood next to me and spoke quietly, while looking at Veego and LaBerge.

"How are you?" she asked.

"Ready" was my answer.

"You know this is an incredible opportunity," she said. "The right words will put you over the top."

"Yeah," I said. "And the wrong words might bury me. Stop talking and let me think."

The service dado nodded and signaled for the two to begin.

LaBerge put on his biggest smile and sang, "The time is growing near, the games are almost here; the challengers are ready, and now their words you'll hear!"

Veego added, "This will be one of the most difficult choices you will ever face. Who best to place your wager on? We've done our best to educate you about the two challengers, now it's time to hear from them, in their own words. First we will hear from the champion, Challenger Green."

The service dado panned over to Challenger Green, who stood with his hands on his hips.

"You know me," he said brusquely. "You know I don't lose. I've been watching the games my whole life. Blok has never seen a champion as powerful as me. I'm going to be the first challenger to retire undefeated, and then tour Quillan to promote the games for Blok. When you think of Blok, you think of power and you think of me."

He turned and jumped down off the platform. The service dado quickly panned back to Veego and LaBerge, who seemed surprised by Challenger Green's quick exit. I couldn't have been happier about what he said. Nevva looked as if she were holding back a smile.

"That's perfect," she said. "He has totally aligned himself with Blok."

Veego said to the camera, "And now we will hear from Challenger Red, the only challenger in history who is so confident, he actually asked to compete against Challenger Green. I give you . . . Challenger Red."

The service dado whipped the camera to me as Nevva stepped aside. It's a strange feeling to know that your image is being broadcast to millions of people. It was the biggest stage possible. I needed to make the most of it. I folded my hands in front of me and said, "You don't know me as well as Challenger Green, but there's something important you should understand. I didn't come back to compete in the Grand X for myself. I could have disappeared and nobody would ever have seen me again. But I came here as a tribute to the people of Quillan."

Out of the corner of my eye, I saw Veego and LaBerge give each other concerned looks.

"I'm here to prove that you don't have to be big and powerful to triumph. I believe in myself, and I believe in the people of Quillan. And even though I know I will win the Grand X, I am asking each and every one of you to be brave, and as a protest against these brutal games, do not wager on the Grand X. Either on me or on Challenger Green. It's the best way you can show Blok that you aren't going to live by their rules any longer."

"What?" LaBerge screamed.

Veego walked quickly to the service dado and pushed the camera off me.

"End this transmission," she hissed at the dado. "Now!"

The dado hurried off the platform with the camera.

"How could you say that?" Nevva asked, faking surprise. "That was not authorized! The trustees will be very angry! I'm going to have to bring this up with them at once."

Nevva hurried off the platform. Before she stepped down, she stole a quick look back at me, and winked. I had just kicked some serious Blok butt. Veego stood there, glaring at me, while LaBerge paced nervously.

"This is bad," he clucked. "Very bad. We'll be blamed, you know. How are we going to control this? Do you think the people will listen to him? What are we going to do?"

"We're not going to do anything," Veego said without taking her eyes off me. "Challenger Red will no longer be allowed to address the public. Beyond that, we will do nothing."

LaBerge hurried off the platform, shaking his head fretfully and muttering, "This is bad; this is very bad."

Veego took a step closer to me and said, "What are you doing, Challenger Red?"

"Just trying to get a little excitement going," I said innocently. "That should get people talking, don't you think?"

Veego stared at me for another moment, then turned and left. I wasn't sure if I had gone too far. I didn't think for a second that they would cancel the Grand X after all the buildup, but I couldn't be sure.

There was one more event planned before the Grand X, and it was a big one. Challenger Green and I were to be paraded through the streets of Rune on the backs of two cars. The idea was for the people to see us in the flesh so they'd get all sorts of whipped up and excited . . . and of course make big wagers. Mark, Courtney, what happened that day was something I could only dream of. Up until that point, the idea of the people of Quillan seeing me and learning about me and believing in me as a symbol of their freedom was only a concept. It wasn't real. I had to take what the revivers had said on faith. Though I had fully bought into the plan, somewhere in the back of my mind I wondered if the people were going to really care. What happened that afternoon shot those doubts to pieces. No, it vaporized them.

There were three cars in the parade. The first held Veego and LaBerge, I was on the second, and bringing up the rear was Challenger Green. We stood up through an opening in the roof so we could be seen by all. A line of security dados marched alongside the procession in case somebody did something silly and tried to get at us. I figured that was a good idea, because the streets of Rune were pretty crowded.

At the very least, the security dados would be able to clear a path for the cars to get through.

What happened was bedlam. I can only liken it to one of those ticker-tape parades they have in New York City for sports champions and astronauts and whatnot. It was absolutely, positively nuts. People were everywhere. They were packed on the sidewalks, hanging out of windows, and perched on top of buildings. They were screaming, too. As the parade turned off the side street and onto the main parade route, it was like being hit with a wall of noise from a thousand jet engines. It was such a mad sea of faces, it was hard to pick out any one person, but the thing that struck me most about the people was that they were smiling. I saw joy in their faces. It was something I hadn't seen at all on Quillan, except for maybe the lucky few who had won a wager on a game. These people were ecstatic.

There wasn't any ticker tape falling, but there was something else even better. I can't say that every person had one—that would be impossible to judge. But thousands did. Wherever I looked, I saw old men and young kids and women and every type of person you could imagine waving a solid red flag. Maybe I'm a little slow, or maybe I was just too stunned by the whole scene to realize what that meant right away. It wasn't until I heard the chant that it came together. It was tough to make out at first, because it was like white noise, but soon enough I understood what they were chanting: "Red! Red! Red!" These people were chanting for me! The red flags they were waving were for me! To say this was unbelievable is too simple a statement. It was impossible.

Ahead of me LaBerge beamed and waved like he had just won the World Series. I don't think anybody cared. Veego stood stock still, with a tight smile on her face. I don't know what she was thinking. If I were to guess, she was calculating how much these fools would wager on the underdog, me, and how much her enterprise would benefit. So I guess she was happy.

Turning around, I saw that Challenger Green was probably the only sour-looking person in sight. He stood with his hands gripping the roof of his car. I wouldn't have been surprised to see the metal twisting in his fingers. Besides that, he was glaring at me. As they say, if looks could kill . . . there wouldn't have been a Grand X. I would have been history right then and there.

I turned to face front. This was my moment and I wanted to enjoy it. If what was happening here in Rune was any indication, the revivers had done their job. The people were on my side. What remained to be seen was if they would take the next step and not wager on the Grand X. I suppose that didn't matter much. This wasn't about the betting. This was about creating a display that fired the people into action.

As great as the day was turning out to be, the best was yet to come.

The parade ended at the big, imposing Blok building. There was a wide balcony below the giant BLOK sign that looked down onto the street. We were quickly brought up there for a final event. On the balcony were me, Challenger Green, Veego, LaBerge, and a few of the trustees. Mr. Kayto wasn't one of them, though I felt sure that Saint Dane was watching from somewhere. There were speeches and presentations and lots of blah blah blah about how exciting the event was going to be and how Quillan had never seen the likes of this and may never again and . . . who cared.

I looked down on a sea of people. That's no exaggeration. It was a sea. The streets were packed solid. I'm sure that only the people up front could actually see us, but our images were projected on the screens up and down the street. As I stood there, trying not to listen to the speeches, a strange feeling came over me.

I wasn't nervous, or intimidated. Of course I had played many basketball games in front of big crowds, but a big crowd for Stony Brook Junior High was about a thousand, and that was for a championship. Here I was being watched and scrutinized by millions. Literally, millions. I wondered why it didn't freak me out. I guess it had something to do with the confidence I had in our mission. I looked at these people and knew that their lives would soon be better. Strangely enough, it seemed as if they felt it too. What I saw on those people's faces that day was hope. Yeah, it was hope that I'd win the Grand X. Maybe I was making too much of it, but if these people had the ability to hope, then they had the ability to change their lives. It felt like they were beginning to realize that.

Of course, all of that had even greater implications. If I could help turn the course of events on Quillan, then Saint Dane would be done. I was sure of that. His goal of having me compete in the Grand X was to have me humiliated. Instead, I stood on that balcony being cheered by millions. I figured that Saint Dane must have been seething mad. It seemed like bringing me to Quillan had backfired. Before I got there, Quillan was lost. But my being there and competing in the games looked as if it would spark a revolution that would put the brakes on and bring Quillan back from the brink. The best part about it? Saint Dane had invited me. His quest to destroy me was going to lead to the salvation of a territory, and his own undoing. It was all pretty sweet. I looked out over those hopeful people and imagined all the many faces of Halla. The faces of all places and times. It was good. I had no doubt in my mind.

We were going to save Halla.

Challenger Green and I were not allowed to speak. I think my little speech a few days before might have had something to do with that. Still, we were both introduced and asked to step forward. First Veego introduced Challenger Green. I'm not going to say the guy was booed off the balcony—he wasn't. There were a lot of cheers. After all, he was the champion and people had won bets on him. I didn't hear a single "boo." I wasn't sure if that was because they still liked him, or they didn't know the concept of booing.

On the other hand, what happened next was electric. I was introduced and the place went berserk. It was so loud, I thought the glass in the windows would shatter. The crowd became a sea of red as thousands of people waved their flags. I wasn't sure what to do. Should I wave back? Should I clasp my hands over my head in the classic "champion" gesture? Or should I hold my arms out like you see royal people do? As I stood there, buffeted by the tornado of sound, an idea came to me. I wasn't sure if it was a smart thing to do, or totally idiotic. I didn't take the time to analyze it, I just went for it. I stepped forward on the small platform so the crowd could see me better. That small movement made them scream even more. I looked up and saw my image projected hundreds of times on screens along the avenue. The setting was perfect, so I did it.

I lifted my right hand and grasped my left biceps in the salute of the revival.

The reaction was so strong and so sudden, I thought the building was going to collapse. The whole place shook. I swear, this huge building made of black rock shook like a house of cards. It felt like an earthquake hit the street, that's how strong the reaction was. The pounding of thousands of people jumping up and down made the foundation rock. I remember being in Yankee Stadium when the place was full and the people were rocking. The whole place moved. That's what this felt like. The screams became so loud, it was painful. But it was perfect. There was no denying it now. The people knew exactly where I stood, and they were with me. I wished I could take that moment and bottle it. For a brief instant I saw my image on all the screens with my hand clasped on my biceps. Suddenly, all the screens went blank and I was pulled roughly off the platform by security dados. I was quickly brought into the building, but the crowd wouldn't stop. The building was still shaking. I thought they might tear it down with their bare hands.

"Get them out of here," Veego commanded the dados.

Challenger Green and I were hurried into separate elevators and taken down to the basement, where we were put in different cars and quickly driven underground away from the building. Even underground I could hear the chaos above. I could feel it. The dead city had returned to life. As I sat in the back of that car, alone, I had to smile. It was working. The revivers had succeeded. That image of me giving the reviver salute was icing on the cake. It had just been broadcast all over Quillan. The message was there. Change was coming.

Now all I had to do was win.

Oh, that.

I was driven back to the castle, where Fourteen met me and brought me right to my room.

"Did you enjoy your day?" he asked as we walked.

"Yeah," I said casually. "It was okay."

When I stepped into my room, I saw that Veego was there, waiting for me. I couldn't tell if she was happy about what had happened, or totally pissed.

"Some show, huh?" I said cockily.

"You think you're in control here, don't you . . . Pendragon?"

Whoa. Talk about a buzz killer. The party was over. How

did she know my name? The look on my face must have told her how surprised I was.

"Yes, I know your name, Bobby Pendragon," she said. "Aja Killian told me all about you."

My knees went weak. Did I hear right? Had she said Aja Killian?

"I—I don't understand" was all I was able to get out.

"Let's drop the pretense," she said. "I don't know what you're hoping to accomplish here, but I've worked too long and too hard to build up this operation to let you tear it down. I didn't leave one disaster to step into another one."

"I don't know what you're talking about," I said. I wasn't covering, I really didn't know.

"Stop feigning ignorance, Pendragon!" she snapped at me. "LaBerge and I know the truth. We aren't from Quillan either."

"Really? Where are you from?" I spoke weakly but my mind was racing.

"I know you," she said, wagging her finger at me like a stern teacher. "I remember seeing you. You nearly destroyed Lifelight. I will not let you do the same here on Quillan."

I wanted to scream. What was happening? "You're from Veelox?" I shouted. "But . . . that's impossible."

"Apparently it isn't, because here we are," she said.

"But . . . how?" was all I could ask.

Veego paced while staring at me with hatred. I truly had no idea what was going on. Was she Saint Dane? Was LaBerge? No, they couldn't be. Saint Dane can do a lot of things but he can't split himself in two. They had both been in the chambers of the trustees together with Mr. Kayto. Kayto was Saint Dane. Who was this woman?

"LaBerge and I were phaders on Veelox," she finally said. "We monitored the Lifelight jumps. Aja Killian was our supervisor."

My mind was reeling. I tried to keep up with what this could mean, but it was impossible.

"LaBerge and I entered into the fantasies of many people," she said. "That's where we came up with the ideas for the games. You really didn't think LaBerge was that creative, did you? He's an imbecile. I'd have gotten rid of him long ago if he weren't my brother."

Her brother. That explained a lot, but there was a long way to go.

"We found the ideas for the games from a thousand sources. A thousand fantasies. Between us we had access to the collective imagination of Veelox . . . and beyond."

"Beyond?" I croaked. "Beyond what?"

"Wippen," she answered. "We found that game on Eelong. It isn't quite as exciting with horses as with zenzens, but it will do."

"You've been to Eelong?" I shouted. I was reeling.

"Interesting place," she answered. "I wouldn't have minded staying longer, if it weren't for the fact that those cat creatures thought we were food."

"But . . . are you Travelers?"

"I don't understand the question," she said.

"Yes you do!" I shouted. "You have to! Only Travelers can use the flumes. If you're not Travelers, then you would have destroyed them. Saint Dane must have told you that!"

"You mentioned that name before," she said. "Who is this Saint Dane person?"

"Don't lie to me!" I shouted. "You have to know Saint Dane. That's who sent me the invitation to come here!"

"I'm sorry. I never heard the name. Is he from Veelox as well?"

This was maddening. Veego and LaBerge couldn't be from

Veelox or they would have destroyed the flumes when they traveled.

"I don't believe you," I said. "If you're really from a different territory, and you're not Travelers, when you jumped into the flume you would have destroyed it. End of story."

"I do seem to remember something about that," she said calmly. The tide had turned. Veego was back in charge and I was groping again. My brief moment of control was long gone. The feeling I had while standing before the multitudes of Rune was less than a memory.

"Mr. Kayto explained it," she said. "He said that as long as we went through the flume with him, there would be no trouble. Obviously he was right, because there wasn't any. Marvelous devices, those flumes. Though I must admit, I don't fully understand how they work or what the difference is between territories. Maybe you can explain that to me."

"Mr. Kayto," I said. "The trustee. He's the one who brought you here?"

"He came to Veelox in search of talent to resurrect the gaming business here on Quillan," she answered. "And found us. Veelox is in shambles, in case you didn't know. Lifelight is failing. There is no one left who cares. Everyone has chosen to stay in their own fantasies . . . and they are dying there. People are starving. Power plants are failing. There is no food. Even the gloid plants are shuttered. It's a nightmare. When Mr. Kayto offered us an alternative, we jumped at it, so to speak."

"What about Aja?" I asked.

"She's fighting a losing battle," Veego said. "She's very noble, trying to keep those poor souls alive. But it's impossible. Which is why I'm here talking to you."

That was it. That was the connection. Saint Dane went to Veelox in the form of Mr. Kayto. Veego and LaBerge didn't know his true identity. That's how Saint Dane got the invitation to send to me. Everything was falling into place . . . and falling apart.

Veego continued, "Now, I've told you what I'm doing here, what are *you* doing here?"

How could I answer that question simply? This woman had no clue about Travelers and Halla and what Saint Dane's true goal was. I didn't think for a second it would do any good to try to explain it to her. Not her. Not to someone who used people as pawns to serve her own selfish purposes.

"I—I think I'm here to compete in the Grand X," I said. That was the honest truth.

"You think?" she asked.

"Yeah, I think. That's the best I can do for you. Sorry." I suddenly felt very tired.

"I don't know who you really are, Pendragon, or where you're from or what Travelers are, but I did see what you tried to do on Veelox. You wanted to destroy Lifelight, and you almost succeeded. For all I know, that may have been a good thing. I don't care anymore. All I care about are my games and my life here on Quillan. LaBerge and I plan on being here a good long time, and we will not let you destroy something that is so perfect."

"What are you going to do?" I asked. "Cancel the games? Pull me out? You saw how popular I am. Blok would get rid of you so fast your brother wouldn't have time to pack up his little clown dolls."

For the first time since I'd met her, Veego looked unsure of herself. She bit her lip.

"No," she finally said. "You will compete. I don't care if you win or you lose. I don't care if you die or become the greatest challenger of all time. All I care about is that you compete."

"Then we're on the same page," I said. "That's all I want

too. I want to compete and I want to win. You have my word on that."

Veego looked at me and nodded. "We'll take it one step at a time. After the Grand X, if you're still alive, we'll decide what to do from there."

"Agreed," I said.

Veego stood up straight. The cool, calm woman was back. She walked to the door, saying, "Get a good night's sleep, Challenger Red. The Grand X is tomorrow." She yanked the door open, walked through, and slammed it shut.

I sat there for a good long time, trying to make sense of what she'd told me. She and LaBerge were from Veelox. I believed that. There was no other way she could know those things. But they weren't Travelers, which opened up a whole new, scary chapter in this already twisted story. Ordinary people could travel safely, so long as they were with a Traveler. They had no idea that Mr. Kayto was really a demon named Saint Dane, which meant they had no clue as to his plans for the destruction of Halla.

The thought of what this all meant was horrifying. The Travelers weren't supposed to mix the territories. I was told that again and again by Uncle Press. I'd learned it myself more times than I could count. Territories had to play out their own destinies, without contamination from other worlds and cultures and times. Travelers were able to intercede, but they always had to work within the defined ways of a territory. That was the way it had to work. The Travelers had always tried to abide by that rule.

And now Saint Dane was flaunting it. He had tried to tip the natural balance of every territory he'd visited. He'd found the turning point on each territory and worked his evil to push events the wrong way. Now it seemed as if he were taking the next step by deliberately intermingling worlds. Was this his ultimate plan? Was he going to create chaos by having cultures and people collide? Was this how he intended to crush Halla? I didn't pretend to understand the natural balance of all existence, and what might happen when that's thrown off, but Saint Dane seemed to.

I'd thought that for Saint Dane, Quillan was about setting me up to get beaten. I learned there was a whole lot more to it when I met the revivers and saw their plans to take back the territory. But now it looked like Saint Dane had shifted into another gear. He was trying to blow Quillan apart by bringing in ordinary people and unique ideas from other territories. I couldn't even begin to guess what that would lead to, for Quillan and Halla.

My head was exploding. I needed to talk to Nevva. She had to work her influence with the trustees to get rid of Veego and LaBerge. The games had to be shut down. We needed to get those two back to Veelox where they belonged. Quillan needed to be put back on its natural course. This had gotten bigger than Blok. This was about the future of Halla. I ran to the door. It was locked. My door was never locked. I threw my shoulder against it. It didn't budge. I was a prisoner. A second later the door flew open. Standing there were three security dados.

"Is there something we can get for you?" one asked.

I slammed the door. I was trapped. Veego was going to keep a very close watch on Challenger Red.

Challenger Red. That's right. The realization hit me. There was no way out of it. Tomorrow was the Grand X. I had to put these conflicting thoughts out of my head and focus. If I didn't, I feared it might truly be the beginning of the end . . . not for just Quillan, but for Halla.

The only thing left for me to do was win.

QUILLAN

Compared to the excitement of the day before, the Grand X was kind of a letdown, at least as a spectacle. This wasn't like a big sporting event with cheering crowds and cheerleaders and bands playing and whatnot. It was actually the reverse of what I was used to. With most sports you practice day after day with your team and your coaches, alone. Nobody watches. Nobody cheers. The payoff comes on game day when the crowds come out, everybody gets ramped up, and the excitement kicks in. With the Grand X, all the excitement was the day before with the parade through Rune and the rally at the Blok building. For the actual event nobody was there to watch and cheer. There were a bunch of dados keeping an eye on things, Veego and LaBerge, who told us what to do, Challenger Green, and me. That was it.

Of course I knew there were cameras everywhere that saw our every move and sent the images all over Quillan to be watched by millions. I had seen the crowds in the streets, their gazes riveted on the giant screens. I knew people would be watching and cheering, probably in numbers greater than ever before. But I didn't see any of that. It was just me, Challenger Green, and the future of all existence.

Did I have butterflies? Oh yeah.

Fourteen came to my room as soon as the sun was up. I was dressed and ready.

"Is there anything I can do for you before the competition begins?" he asked.

"Yes," I said. "Tell Miss Winter that I need to speak with her as soon as possible."

If anything happened to me, Nevva needed to know what was going on with Veego and LaBerge. She needed to know that Saint Dane had brought them from Veelox and that they were importing items and ideas from other territories. As dramatic as everything else was that was happening on Quillan, Veego and LaBerge's operation spelled the biggest trouble for all of Halla.

"Of course," Fourteen said.

The two of us walked silently from my room, down through the castle, and out into the forest. The whole time I worked on staying focused on the games. As confident as I was, all that Veego revealed to me the night before had me rattled. If there were ever a time that I needed to keep my head on straight and not let anything distract me, it was then. But it was tough. I hoped that once the competition began, I'd be locked into the moment and all the other worries would go away. If they didn't, I'd be in trouble.

Fourteen led me along a windy path until we came to a grassy clearing that was roughly the size of a tennis court. There was nothing special about the place. There were no markings or apparatus. Standing across from me on the far side was Challenger Green, along with his service dado, who looked just like Fourteen. I gave Green a slight nod. He scowled at me. He didn't like that I had stolen his thunder. I hoped I could use his anger to my advantage. If we were going to be playing with emotion, I had to be cool. Anger led to mistakes. My confidence rose. . . .

Until I saw what the first game was going to be. Any hope I had of putting aside my worries about what impact this would have on the rest of Halla was shot to pieces. First off, this wasn't a game that Nevva had prepped me for. But that was okay. I had played this game before many times. I was good at it. But that was also the bad news. I had played this game before . . . on the territory of Zadaa. As soon as I saw the equipment, I knew that Veego and LaBerge had been to Zadaa. It was another case of worlds being mingled.

I had to force that worry out of my head as Fourteen helped me on with the gear. He gave me stretchy bands that fit above my biceps and above my knees. Each of these bands had a round red peg attached on one end that was about ten inches long and stuck out like red horns. He also gave me a lightweight helmet with the same kind of peg sticking up from the top. I knew what the final piece would be before seeing it. It was a heavy wooden stave about six feet long. When Fourteen handed it to me, I felt its weight and thought it was a pretty good replica of the weapons they had on Zadaa. For all I knew, it had actually come from Zadaa.

"Good luck, Pendragon," Fourteen said.

"Piece of cake," I said, and winked at him. I had grown to really like Fourteen. Unlike everything and everyone else I encountered on Quillan, there was no mystery about him.

Veego and LaBerge appeared out of the forest, dressed for the big event. Veego had on her purple jumpsuit, but this one was trimmed in gold. LaBerge was much more flamboyant, with a multicolored robe that made him look like the king of Gumdrop Mountain. Neither looked happy. Even LaBerge wasn't his normal, bubbly, annoying self. Veego motioned for her brother to go to the center of the clearing while she came to me. I didn't like the look in her eyes. I couldn't tell if it was anger or fear. Whatever it was, she was trying her best to keep her emotions in check.

"Nice day for a beating, don't you think?" I asked cheerily.

"It won't work," she said through clenched teeth.

"What won't work?" I asked.

"You won't destroy these games," she snarled.

"What's your problem?" I said innocently. "I'm here, aren't I? I'm ready to compete."

"There has been next to no wagering . . . on either of you!" she said as her head started to shake with pent-up rage. Tears of anger formed in her eyes. But she stayed in control. "This is the Grand X! Wagering is normally tripled. It seems as if you're insidious little speech had some effect."

It took a lot for me not to smile. It wasn't my speech alone that had done it. It was the revivers. They turned the Grand X into a contest that was about showing Blok they were ready to take back control of their lives. My confidence rose again. There was a real chance that the people of Quillan could turn things around. I decided not to say that to Veego.

"I don't know what to tell you," I said. "Maybe they're waiting for later in the competition. You know, to see how things are going."

"You had better be right!" she snapped as she turned and walked toward LaBerge.

Fourteen said, "I have never seen her so angry."

"Stick around," I said. "It's early."

When she got to the center of the field, Veego motioned for Challenger Green and me to join her and LaBerge. The two of us strode to the center of the grassy playing field from opposite sides. I saw that, like me, Green had his wooden pegs on. They were, of course, green. Duh. His eyes were locked on mine. He was doing his best to psyche me. I kept my face blank.

"I will explain the rules," Veego said.

"Don't bother," I said. "I know how to play."

I saw Green stiffen slightly. Oops. Maybe I had been too cocky. I didn't want to tip my hand.

He snarled, "I know too. Let's go."

"Very well," Veego said. "Begin on the horn."

Veego and LaBerge walked away, but as they left, LaBerge stopped and gave me a confused look. "How do you know this game?" he asked.

"Didn't you know? I'm an honorary Batu," I said.

"You are?" LaBerge said with shock. He looked quickly to Veego for a reaction. She didn't give any. Obviously LaBerge didn't remember me from Veelox, and Veego didn't bother to remind him.

I focused on Challenger Green. The guy had no idea what he was in for. I almost felt sorry for him. Almost. I had seen the Batu warriors of Zadaa play this game many times. I had watched Loor triumph. When she put me through training at the Mooraj camp, we played this game constantly. You know the rules. The idea is to use your wooden stave to knock the wooden pegs off your opponent. The first one to knock off all the pegs wins. Simple as that.

Green and I locked eyes. He said, "You shouldn't have come back."

"Why?" I asked. "Are you afraid of losing?"

I saw his eyes widen. I had touched a nerve. This was going to be fun. I clutched my stave and bent my legs slightly. I felt totally comfortable. It was like riding a bike.

The horn sounded, and Green charged me so hard and fast that I didn't have time to react. He drilled his head into my chest and knocked me flat on my back, hammering the air out of my lungs. Green tossed aside his stave and wrestled me to get at the pegs. I guess I could say that he wasn't playing fair, but I didn't think there was any such thing as fair in these games. If I didn't do something fast, this fight would be over before it even got started. He had already pulled off two pegs and was going for the third, when I drilled my elbow into his jaw. He wasn't expecting that and rolled off. I rolled the other way and scrambled to get back to my feet.

Green didn't give me time to recover. He charged again, without his stave. This guy wasn't about finesse. His plan was to use brute force to beat me. He was like an angry charging bull. I bent over as if trying to get my breath, but I was waiting for him. He screamed as he lunged. I drove my stave forward and caught him in the gut.

"Oooph," he grunted in pain.

I pulled my stave back and expertly spun it left, then right, knocking off both his arm pegs. It was pretty clear how this fight would go. It was style versus strength. Green wisely backed away or it would have been over right there. He clutched at his gut and looked at me with fiery eyes.

"You use that weapon like you've been trained," he said.

"You think?" I shot back.

Green scooped up his stave and came at me, more cautiously this time. He held the stave low, pointing one end at me like he was going to poke me with it. I almost laughed. The guy didn't have a clue. He jabbed at me a few times, but I flicked his attacks away easily. I was getting my breath back now. All I had to do was wait for him to make a mistake, which he did pretty quickly. He took a few steps back, then threw the stave at me like a spear. He followed right behind it, charging at me while screaming out a horrifying war cry. Yeah, right. Nice try.

I knocked the spear away easily. When he lunged at me, I faked a swing, which made him falter. I then jammed the end of the stave between his knees and pushed. Green's legs got tangled and he hit the grass hard. Before he had the chance to get up, I flicked away both pegs from his legs. All he had left was the peg on his head. He was about to roll and get up, when I jammed the end of the stave into his neck, pinning him to the ground.

"It's done," I said. "Drop the last peg and I won't hurt you."

It was like I had thrown acid on him. He let out an angry scream and pushed to get up. Too little, too late. I held the stave to his throat and kicked the final peg off his helmet.

A horn sounded. The match was over. Winner— Challenger Red!

I backed away from him, still holding the stave ready in case he tried coming after me. He lay there for a second, breathing hard. When he sat up, he gasped, "This will just make my victory even sweeter."

"Yeah, whatever," I said as I backed away. I didn't dare turn my back on him. I walked backward all the way until I got to Fourteen.

"That was very good," he said with no emotion.

"You think he's mad?" I asked with a chuckle.

Fourteen said, "That was the first time Challenger Green has been defeated. Ever. I would say yes, he is angry."

Green got up and stormed off the field toward his own dado. Round one went to me. I was happy that it was a fight I was familiar with, but the idea that it was brought there from Zadaa was disturbing.

Round two proved to be just as disturbing. We were brought in separate carts deep into the forest. When we finally broke out of the trees, I saw that we had come upon a giant round aboveground water tank. The thing was huge. It had to be three stories high and fifty yards in diameter. I knew it was a water tank because the sides were clear.

"What's this?" I asked Fourteen. "A swimming race?'

"Not exactly," he said. He led me to an open elevator that brought us up to the top. I was feeling nervous because, once again, Nevva hadn't told me about any games that had to do with a giant tank of water.

"Have you spoken to Nevva Winter?" I asked Fourteen.

"I am afraid not," he answered. "I have been with you the whole time."

Oh. Right. As we rose higher in the air, I looked around to see if I could catch sight of Nevva. She was supposed to be here in case the worst happened. I figured she was nearby, watching closely, ready to jump in if things went south.

The elevator reached the top, where a bridge led to a platform in the dead center of the tank. Waiting for me there were Veego, LaBerge, and Challenger Green.

"Find Miss Winter," I said to Fourteen. "Now."

I walked across the bridge to meet my opponent while Fourteen went back down in the elevator. The three watched me with sour expressions. We had only finished one event, and I was already proving to be a pain. I liked that.

"Kind of a SeaWorld thing you got going on here," I said.

Nobody reacted. I wasn't surprised.

"This is a timed contest," Veego explained to me, and probably to the rest of Quillan at the same time. "Whoever remains on top the longest is the winner."

I figured this would be some kind of fight on the platform where we had to try to dunk our opponent.

It wasn't.

LaBerge produced two clear globes that were very familiar to me, unfortunately.

"Where did you get those?" I asked with surprise.

They didn't answer. They didn't have to. I knew the answer. They were air globes from Cloral. This was even more disturbing than the game from Zadaa. You guys know how these air globes work. The material is created from minerals on Cloral. When you put it over your head, it becomes soft and formfitting, with an airtight seal. The silver device attached to the top is a breathing apparatus that converts carbon dioxide into oxygen. With these air globes you can breathe and communicate underwater. Having them on Quillan meant that Veego and LaBerge weren't only bringing in ideas from other territories, they were introducing technology and material. These things shouldn't exist on Quillan.

It got worse.

Veego said, "Since he won the first game, Challenger Red will be given a ten-click time advantage."

Yay me.

Challenger Green wanted to get going right away. He didn't like being behind. Without being instructed, he angrily grabbed one of the air globes and stuck his head through the hole. The globe melted and formed around him. My stomach turned. This was wrong. I couldn't imagine what might happen to a territory if alien minerals were introduced.

"What exactly are we supposed to do?" I asked.

"You don't know? " Veego said smugly. "You have to ride a spinney fish."

I gritted my teeth in anger. Spinney fish were from Cloral too! They were bringing in creatures from other territories! I didn't want to think what would happen to the habitat of one territory if organisms were introduced from another. This could be an ecological catastrophe in the making.

As for the game, I knew it. Spader called it "Spinney-do." Remember? The fish were long and thin, like skinny dolphins. You had to sneak up on one, grab the ridges that ran across its back, throw your leg over, and ride the fish like a bucking bronco. The trick was that once you grabbed a spinney, they swelled up like big blow fish, making it that much harder to hang on. The worst part was, I was terrible at Spinney-do.

Challenger Green jumped in the water feet first. There was a big screen on the far side of the tank that allowed us to see him. I figured it was the same image that was being broadcast throughout Quillan. Above the screen was a digital clock showing two zeroes. I watched as Green dove down and swam strongly to the bottom of the tank. There were several spinney fish there, grazing on the bottom. They were big, slow creatures. It wasn't hard to grab one. The tough part came when they felt threatened.

Challenger Green maneuvered himself around, hovering just above one of the big fish. He got as close as he could without touching it, then quickly grabbed the ridge on its back and clamped his legs around it. The fish instantly blew up to three times its size and started bucking. Green gripped the ridge with both hands. He may not have been agile, but he was strong. As soon as the fish started to move, the clock did too. I didn't know how long a "click" was—it seemed to be around a second. Green held on with both hands as the clock moved to 5. Then 10. One of Green's hands flew off, but he held on with the other. He wouldn't last much longer. Finally, with a quick snap of its back, the fish threw Green off and scooted away. The final time: 22 clicks.

There was no way I could match that.

"What about the penalty?" I asked.

I looked at the clock to see the number 22 disappear. It was replaced by the number 10—my bonus for winning the first contest. Big deal. It didn't matter. Even with the extra 10 clicks there was no way I could hang on long enough to beat

Green's time. But it had been a long time since I'd played Spinney-do. I was a bigger, stronger guy. I had to hope I'd do better.

As Green climbed out of the water, LaBerge handed me an air globe. I put my head through the hole and felt the familiar sensation as the clear helmet molded to me. Challenger Green looked up at his time and punched his fist into the air shouting a jubilant, "Yes!"

I wanted this over as quickly as possible, so without another word I jumped into the water and swam toward the bottom.

Three spinney fish were waiting for me. Such odd creatures. You'd think they'd take off once they sensed someone coming. Maybe they were blind. Or just plain stupid. I didn't know. All that mattered was that I grab one and stay on for 13 clicks. I picked one that looked to be the smallest of the group and lowered myself toward it. The strange fish had no idea I was there. I took a breath, reached out with both hands, and grabbed the ridge.

It was almost over before it began. The fish moved so fast it nearly yanked itself out of my grip. My left hand flailed in the water. If I didn't grab on with both hands, fast, I wouldn't last for 3 clicks, let alone 13. I was able to bring my left hand down and hold on, just as the fish bloated. It threw my legs out wide, which made it even harder to hang on. It got so fat I had trouble gripping with my legs. I knew this ride wasn't going to last long. The spinney twisted and bucked, then swam upside down! I was head down, but I wouldn't let go. When I managed to hang on even though I was upside down, I had a faint glimmer of hope. I knew it wouldn't be a long trip, but maybe it would be long enough. I only had to hang on for 13 clicks.

The fish spun me upright, then quickly spun back in the

other direction. That did it. I had shifted all my weight one way to counter that first twist. As soon as it went the other way, I was gone. With a flap of its tail the fish squirted away from me and shot to the bottom. All that was left was for me to surface and check my time. I was confident. I felt there was a really good chance that I had hung on long enough.

When I surfaced, I saw that my time—including my head start of 10 clicks—was 20. Missed it by 3 clicks, however long that was. As I climbed onto the platform, I imagined the screens all over Quillan flashing: WINNER—CHALLENGER GREEN! What a depressing thought. When I pulled off my globe, I saw that Veego was smiling. She may have said she didn't care, but she did. She wanted me to lose.

"That's one event each," she announced. "There is one more event before the rest period."

After we took the elevator down and walked a fair distance through the parklike compound, we all stood on the edge of a dense forest of pine trees. There were so many trees, it looked unnatural. The branches began about ten feet off the ground, so I was looking at a sea of tree trunks. From where I stood, there only looked to be a few yards between each of them. The forest looked about a hundred yards wide. I couldn't tell how deep it was. I figured that was part of the game.

Veego and LaBerge stood with their backs to the trees, facing Challenger Green and me.

LaBerge looked giddy. "This is my favorite game," he said. "Hidden in this maze of trees are six flags. Three green, three red. The goal is to enter the forest, find each of your flags, and make your way to the far side, where we will be waiting. The first to arrive with all three flags is the winner!"

He clapped his hands and giggled. I couldn't imagine why this would be his favorite game. There wasn't much to it. On the other hand, it was another game that Nevva didn't tell me about. I figured there were hundreds of Quillan games, so there was no way she could have covered them all. I just wished she had guessed right on one of them.

But the game didn't seem so hard. It was all about finding the flags. They could have been anywhere, so the winner would be the one who was lucky enough to find them. Not a lot of skill involved, or danger for that matter. It all seemed so random, I didn't think the 10-click advantage would mean anything.

Veego said, "Since Challenger Green won the last contest, he will get a ten-click head start."

"Everybody ready?" LaBerge asked. "Go on the horn. Challenger Red, wait until we release you."

The two stepped aside, the horn sounded, and Challenger Green sprinted toward the trees and disappeared.

"This is your favorite game?" I asked LaBerge. "I don't get it."

"You will," he said slyly.

I didn't like the way he said that.

"Ready, Challenger Red?" Veego asked.

"Just give me the go," I said.

She counted down for me, "Three, two, one, go!"

Fum!

My left arm went numb. It was like I'd been shot by one of those dado guns, but it only affected my arm. I couldn't lift it.

"Don't worry," Veego said. "The effects are temporary. Try not to get shot in the legs."

Shot? Who was shooting? A flash of movement caught my eye. I looked at the forest and saw something skitter through the trees at ground level. Whatever it was, it was colorful. I thought I saw a flash of bright yellow and red. Was it an animal? What kind of animal was colored so strangely? And shot a tranquilizer gun? I wondered what territory Veego and LaBerge had taken such a strange creature from.

"Better get moving, Challenger Red," LaBerge warned. "They're very quick."

I looked back into the forest and saw it. In that one sickening moment I realized why this was LaBerge's favorite game. The flash I saw wasn't an animal. It wasn't from another territory, either. These things were homegrown. Peering out from behind a tree, no more than a foot high, was a mechanical doll. After seeing the quig-spiders at the gate, I had no doubt that this thing would be trouble. It could run, it could hide, and it could shoot. There was one more thing about it that gave me a cold shot of dread.

It was a clown.

Have I told you how much I hate clowns?

QUILLAN

They were sneaky-little-dado-clown-creeps. I didn't stop to ask how they worked. If they could make life-size dados, it followed they could make small ones too. But dressed like clowns? LaBerge was a sick puppy.

"Run, Challenger Red!" LaBerge shouted with glee.

Freak.

I took off for the trees with my arm hanging dead at my side. If one of those clowns shot my leg, I'd be done. I hoped they were after Challenger Green, too. The clown who shot at me tossed his gun down and ran at me. He was quick, too. I sprinted through trees, desperate to keep ahead of that little monster. I was already getting feeling back in my arm. The effects were definitely temporary. It must have had something to do with the fact that the guns were so small.

I had no idea where to go. At least my legs were longer than the clown's, so I put some distance between us. I reached a large tree, rounded it, and put my back to it, listening to hear the sound of his little red clown shoes pitter-pattering on the ground. It was quiet. I had lost him. Or he had lost me. Whatever. I turned to get my bearings, and saw another mini-clown sitting on a branch just above my head with a golden gun aimed at me. His face was white and his eyes and mouth were red with clown paint. It was a nightmare. The thing grinned at me and fired.

Fum!

I dodged around the tree and heard the little bolt of energy crackle against the trunk. The little beast ran along the branch and got right in front of me. I had nowhere to hide. I was done. But he didn't shoot. He dropped the gun and leaped at me! The fiend sailed down and landed on my shoulder. He grabbed me around the neck and started to bite! Yeow! I wrestled the thing off and tossed him against a tree, hard. The thing hit and fell to the ground. A second later he was back on his feet like nothing had happened, and he started after me again.

I ran. There were two things I learned about these monsters. One was that it seemed they only had one shot with their guns. That was good. But the other thing was, they liked to bite. That was freakin' gruesome. I hated clowns now more than ever.

I ran wildly through the woods, always alert for little flashes of color that would mean I was about to be ambushed. All I could think about was getting away from those bozos. It was hard to run fast and dodge trees at the same time. I wasn't even thinking about the game when I rounded one tree and saw a red flag. Yes! It was the size of a bandanna and tacked to a tree. I grabbed it, jammed it in my pants, and continued running. It didn't matter which way I went. I had no way to know where I was, or where the next flag might be.

Fum!

I heard it first, then I felt it. My left leg went numb. I fell to my knee, my good knee, and turned to see a little clown in a striped suit with big blue buttons charging at me, screaming like a banshee. I couldn't run; I had to fight him. The little gremlin leaped at me, his sharp teeth gnashing. I caught him and threw him at another tree. The clown hit, landed on the ground, and instantly jumped up and attacked me again. I couldn't stop these things. It was like they were made of rubber. Except for their teeth. The teeth were sharp.

Without a gun the thing wasn't going to hurt me badly, but he was making my life miserable. Until the feeling in my leg came back I was going to have to deal with being semi-lame. He leaped at me again, I caught him, and rather than throwing him against a tree, I threw him as far as I could. I got lucky and the little banshee sailed between trees, screaming the whole way. As soon as I let him fly, I furiously rubbed my leg to get the circulation going and get rid of the effect of the stun gun. I grabbed a tree and pulled myself up, stomping my foot to get the blood flowing. . . .

And got jumped by two more dolls. I lost my balance and crashed to the ground as they clawed at me and viciously bit my shoulders. I pulled them both off and jammed them together. In their frenzy, they started biting each other! Idiot clowns. I turned and heaved them as far as I could. By then I had gotten enough feeling back in my leg that I could start limping. I had gotten a few yards when I saw the next red flag! Unbelievable! I pushed myself forward, dragging my leg behind me. I hadn't heard any horns go off so I had to believe Challenger Green was having as much trouble as I was. Hopefully more. I was still in the race.

I got closer to the flag. No clowns were in my way. I reached out, and was about to grab it when I got a faceful of fist. Challenger Green had returned. He'd been hiding behind the tree with the flag on it, waiting for me. I never had a chance to defend myself. He hit me so hard that I was knocked off my feet, though I suppose that wasn't so hard, since one of my legs was almost useless. The guy leaped on me, jammed a knee into my chest, and stuck his nose right in my face.

"I'll kill you before I let you win," he snarled.

He pulled out the same knife I'd seen him use to saw the rope and kill his last opponent. He held it to my throat. "Or maybe I'll just kill you now and be done with it," he said, his spittle spraying me.

"We're not alone," I said. "All of Quillan is watching. Is this how you want to win? Kill me like this and everybody will know you only did it because you knew you couldn't beat me. Is that how the great Challenger Green wants to be known? Not good enough to win, but good enough to murder?"

I saw his confusion. He may have been ruthless, but he had an ego. He liked being champion. He pulled the knife away and jammed it back in his boot. He then stood up and grabbed my red flag off the tree.

"You want to win?" he taunted. "Then you've got to get this from me."

He laughed and took off into the trees. I sat up, rubbing my throat. That was too close. I had no doubt he would follow through if he got another chance to kill me. This wasn't a real competition. This was survival of the fittest. Or the most ruthless. Or craziest. I cautiously stood up and tested my leg. I was okay. But the game was over. I had no chance. The only thing left for me to do was keep away from those clowns until Challenger Green made it to the far side with his flags. I started walking in the general direction of where I thought the far side was. Maybe the clowns knew I had given up, because they didn't bother me anymore. I actually found the next red flag, too. I was going to leave it, but took it anyway. Just because.

A few minutes later I heard the horn that signaled the end of the game. Winner—Challenger Green. Good for him. The rest period was coming up. I needed it. And I needed to talk to Nevva.

Fourteen was waiting for me when I finally made it to the far side. We got in the electric cart, and he drove me back toward the castle.

"It is two games to one," he said. "What's important is that you are still competing."

"Yeah, I feel really great about that," I said sarcastically. "Did you find Nevva Winter?"

"She isn't here," Fourteen said.

"What do you mean?" I said with surprise. "She said she would be here for the competition."

"I inquired with Blok," Fourteen said. "They told me that she was observing the Grand X with the trustees in the city."

I stared straight ahead, trying to compute what that meant. She was supposed to be there! She promised me she would be there! Something must have happened that she couldn't get away. Was she all right? Was she revealed as a member of the revivers? Nevva was a Traveler. She knew how serious this was. Then again, she wasn't there when Remudi competed, and that turned out about as badly as possible. Things were coming to a head here on Quillan, on all fronts. I wondered if her triple life had finally caught up with her. There had to be a good reason why she wasn't there, but I couldn't come up with one. I decided not to let it freak me out. It didn't change what I had to do. I was down. Two games to one. Challenger Green had the upper hand. I had to keep my head in the game. Or the games. Or whatever.

When we arrived back at the castle, Fourteen led me back up to my room and stopped at my door.

"I will try to learn more about Miss Winter," he said. "It seems to be of great importance to you."

"Thank you," I said. "You've been a real friend."

"Friend," he said. "No one has ever referred to me as a friend."

"Yeah, well, you are. How much time do I have?"

"I do not know," he replied. "I will return shortly to let you know. Please try and get some rest."

I was beat. Not tired. Beat. It's not like I wanted to lie down and go to sleep or anything. I just needed to catch my breath, and my thoughts. I dragged myself over to the bed and lay down on my back. I actually hoped this rest period wouldn't be too long. I didn't want to stiffen up or lose my psyche.

Be careful what you wish for.

No sooner did I settle in and focus up at the ceiling, than my bed fell through the floor! A trapdoor had opened and swallowed up my bed, with me in it! I looked up to see the door close above me, cutting out all the light. I was falling in pitch darkness. I quickly grabbed on to either end of the bed, not knowing when I'd hit bottom. The fall only lasted a few seconds, and it turned out that it was more of a controlled fall than I thought. The bed had actually been lowered quickly. I landed with only a minor thump.

I didn't move. There was nothing to see. Absolutely nothing. I was in total darkness. The room sounded big, though.

"Are you ready, Challenger Red?" came a teasing voice that echoed through the emptiness. It was LaBerge. His voice was amplified.

"Ready for what?"

LaBerge laughed and said, "Ahhh, that's your penalty for losing in the Clown Forest."

"Clown Forest." That's what he called that game? What a geek.

"What do you mean? What's my penalty?" I called out.

"Your penalty is . . . we're not going to tell you the rules to this next game." He chuckled. "Good luck."

There was no rest period. Game number four had already begun.

QUILLAN

I had been here before. I knew what it was like to be in the dark and vulnerable. Loor had trained me in the dark. She taught me how to use my other senses. To listen and feel. I knew what to do. I lay flat on the bed and kept my breathing shallow. If Challenger Green was out there, I would feel him before he got close enough to attack.

I heard nothing. I felt nothing. It was like I was floating in limbo. But I didn't panic. Moving would be a mistake.

I heard a sound. It wasn't a living thing, it was . . . something. Something quick. It sounded like it flashed by overhead. It couldn't have lasted for more than a second. Whatever it was, it gave off a high-pitched ring as it sped by. I heard another one. It came from a different direction. The sound flew over me and disappeared quickly. There was no question, something was flying above me in the dark. Another one flew by, this one was barely over my head. I felt the slight ripple of air as it sped past. Whatever it was, it was moving fast. I didn't want to get hit, so I stayed on my back, listening.

I heard a few more passes, some close, some distant. All fast. What was it? Though I wasn't told the rules for this game, something didn't make sense. I was in total darkness. How could the rest of Quillan see what was going on if there was no light?

As if in answer, the world suddenly came alive. White light filled the room. It was so bright that I was just as blind as when it was dark. At the same time, music started playing. It was loud, upbeat, electronic music like they played at the challenger parties. It was so loud that I could no longer hear the thing flying around the room. This was worse than darkness. I now had two senses taken away. I forced myself to stay on my back. Looking around, my eyes adjusted enough that I could make out shapes. The room itself was totally white. Floor, walls, ceiling, everything. The bright lights were on the high ceiling, and they were moving in time to the music. There were hundreds of them, all flashing in different directions. They were painting the room with light, making it impossible to see.

I saw a flash of silver a few feet above my head. It had to be what was making the sound, though I couldn't hear it over the music. I lost it in the lights. What was it? I started feeling a little too vulnerable by lying on the bed like that, so I quickly rolled off onto the floor, but crouched down low, using the bed for protection. I peeked my head up over the mattress in time to see another silver flash. This one I locked on to. It was headed in my direction, about five feet over my head. I followed it as it shot over me, continued on, then stuck into a wall only a few yards away. What was it? I was close enough to that wall that I felt confident enough to crawl to it. I got down on my belly and crawled, commando style, across the floor to the wall. Looking up, I saw what was making the sound . . . and my heart sank. It was a silver disk. It didn't look much different from a CD. But it was embedded an inch into the wall. CDs weren't sharp like that. I realized that the sound I was hearing wasn't from a single source. Whatever the game was in this white, noisy room, to play it meant you had to dodge sharp, lethal Frisbees that were randomly fired in all directions.

Suddenly, rampaging clown dolls didn't seem so bad.

Chunk! Another disk embedded itself in the wall over my head. There was no fooling around. These things were deadly. Veego and LaBerge had upped the stakes. The question now was, what was the game? I kept my back to the wall and squinted to get a look at the room. My eyes had adjusted enough that I could make out some detail. The room was giant. The ceiling was high. You could fit eight basketball courts inside, with room left over for a running track. It wasn't empty. There looked to be several mountains scattered around. I'm serious. There were craggy mounds all over the place that had to be thirty or forty feet high. They were just as white as the rest of the room, looking like giant icebergs. I could see little glints of silver where the killer disks had embedded themselves at various places. Still, I had no clue as to what the game could be, besides avoiding decapitation, that is.

My eye caught movement. It was dark against all the bright white. It was Challenger Green. He was climbing one of the mounds. If my penalty for losing the clown game was to not learn the rules, that meant Challenger Green *did* know the rules. I watched him for a clue. He climbed the mound easily. There were several places for foot- and handholds. It looked like climbing was the easy part. The hard part was avoiding the speeding disks. I saw one disk fly toward him and stick into the side of the mound, next to his leg. He never saw it coming, but dove back in surprise when it hit. He nearly fell off the mound. That meant he didn't know when to expect these things. Which meant I wouldn't know either. Swell.

The top of this minimountain came to a peak. Challenger Green quickly scampered to the summit, did something I couldn't see, then hurried back down. Whatever he did up there, I figured I had to do it too. That was the deal. We had to climb these mountains. At least I had a goal now, besides avoiding being sliced in half, that is.

I decided that safety was more important than speed, so I stayed on the floor and crawled along on my belly. My plan was to get to the mountain closest to me. I hadn't seen any of the disks flying that low, so I figured I'd be okay until I had to climb.

I was wrong.

I had gotten about halfway there when the floor in front of me suddenly moved! A whole section of floor quickly slid to the right, opening up a cavern. It seemed as if the room were built on air! Or at least, over a chasm. The opening was dark, so there was no way to tell how deep it might have been, but I didn't want to jump down to find out. No way. I caught a glimpse of movement to my left. My bed was hurtling toward me! I quickly realized it wasn't just the bed, it was the floor below it that was moving. The bed shot across the floor, then suddenly tipped on end and fell into another hole that had opened up in front of it. I quickly crawled over and looked down. The bed was long gone. The chasm below was deep.

I had learned the next wrinkle to this game. The floor was a constantly shifting puzzle. Holes opened up quickly and randomly. If you were in the wrong spot, buh-bye. But you couldn't stand up and leap from spot to spot or you might get sliced by the flying disks. The trick was to stay alive and get to the top of those mountains to do . . . whatever. At least my penalty had been erased. I understood the game. I kind of wished I didn't.

I was still looking down into the hole where my bed had disappeared, with my fingers curled over the edge, when a section of floor flew toward me. I saw it coming at the last second and pulled my hands away as the pieces of flooring slammed together with a *chunk!* The hole had closed so fast and so violently that my fingers would have been crushed for sure.

I scrambled back toward the first mountain. I felt a few disks flying overhead, but I was more worried about the floor suddenly opening up and swallowing me. I reached the base of the mound, took a breath, and quickly climbed. There was no problem getting up, thankfully. At least that gave me a fighting chance to dodge the disks. I leaped up, climbing from ledge to ledge while scanning back and forth for any flashes of silver headed my way. A few stuck into the mound on either side of me, but neither came close enough to be scary. There was one good thing—it didn't seem like they were being aimed. I wasn't being shot at. If I got hit by one of those things, it meant I was in the wrong place at the wrong time.

I reached the pinnacle and saw what I had to do. It was simple. There were six round, flat lights about three inches in diameter that were built into a plateau on top of the mound. Three red, three green. One of the green lights was glowing. I took a guess and touched one of the red lights. It lit up. That was the game. You had to climb three mountains and light all your lights . . . without getting killed, of course.

The race was on. I turned and looked down at the room from a bird's-eye vantage point. It was so white and the lights were so bright, the whole place glowed. From high up on top, the floor looked like a checkerboard with squares about five feet across. The squares were constantly moving, opening up pieces and filling in others. There didn't seem to be any pattern to it. That was bad. There was no way to guess where a hole might open up. I also saw the flashes of silver as the sharp disks flew across the room. Winning this game was about being lucky and keeping your head. Literally.

I saw Challenger Green down on the floor, hopping from square to square. He landed on one just as it moved. It was so fast that it threw him off balance. He had to throw himself backward or he would have been dumped into the hole.

A flash of silver sped by me, very close. It got my attention. I had to get moving. I leaped down the mountain faster than I should have. But Green was ahead of me. I needed to make up time. I was lucky I didn't take a tumble. That would have been weak. When I hit the floor, I crouched down low to make a smaller target and started running for the next closest mountain. I only got a few steps when I saw a silver disk headed for me at head level. I threw myself to the side and it sailed past, but I was falling right toward a section of floor that was opening up! I had to contort my body to change my direction in midfall. I hit the section of floor right next to the new opening. Too close. I rolled to my right just as the section of floor beneath me started to move. It was so fast, it spun me into a barrel roll. I had to fight against my own momentum and stop myself from rolling off the edge. I ended up on my belly, with my left arm dangling over the side of the chasm. I took a second to catch my breath, then realized I was in a bad spot. I quickly pulled my arm out a second before a piece of floor slammed into place, nearly cutting off my limb.

As frantic as I was, I couldn't stay still. No place was safe. I got on my knees and crawled toward the next mountain. The loud music picked up the pace. I wished it would just stop. It made a difficult game nearly impossible. I made it to the base of the next mound and started my climb when I felt a sharp, hot pain in my right leg. Looking down I saw that a disk had clipped my right thigh. It made a neat cut through my black pants and stuck in the side of the mound. I didn't want to know how deep the cut was. There was nothing I could do about it anyway. So I climbed. If it hurt, I didn't know it. My adrenaline was pumping too hard to notice. I got to the top of the mound to see that there were still only one red and one green light lit. I quickly hit the next red light. I was in the lead!

I turned to head down just as a second green light turned on. I looked out over the room to see Challenger Green on top of another mound. It was dead even. I hurried down the mound, even more recklessly than last time. It was going to be close. I hit the floor and scanned to see which mound I should climb next. Challenger Green was doing the same thing. We were maybe twenty yards apart. I saw the mound that was closest to me. Unfortunately, it was the same mound that was closest to Challenger Green. It was decision time. Did I go for the closest mound and possibly have to fight Challenger Green to get to the summit? Or risk running for a mound that was farther away?

The two of us made quick eye contact. We both knew what we had to do. We ran for the same mound. We both chose to fight each other rather than make a suicide run across that deadly, random gauntlet.

I was halfway to the mound when I saw two disks flying at me from different directions. I dove to the ground as they hit above me and shattered. Pieces of metal rained down, nicking my arms like stinging bees. Challenger Green saw this and laughed. My dive cost me precious seconds. Green was almost at the mound. I was going to lose.

That's when the floor opened up beneath Challenger

Green. He fell. Not to the floor—he fell into the hole. He never saw it coming. He screamed, but kept his wits. He caught the edge of the opening with his arms. His arms and shoulders were above the floor, the rest of his body dangled below. But he was trapped. I saw him kicking to try to get a leg up, but he couldn't get leverage. He wasn't going to fall, but he wasn't getting up, either.

I realized with horror that he may not have been in danger of falling, but in seconds he was going to be cut in half. As soon as that piece of floor jammed back into place, he'd be history. It was almost over. I was seconds away from winning the Grand X.

The reality of the situation hit me hard. This guy was about to die. I would be the champion, but at what cost? Another gruesome death? In those few vital seconds I realized there was an opportunity here. Which would have more impact on the people of Quillan? My victory in the Grand X? Or a selfless act that would demonstrate yet again how things were going to be different? I could win the competition and let Challenger Green die, or I could save him and be a hero. Even if I ended up losing the Grand X, I would have made my point. The choice was easy.

I quickly crawled across the floor and grabbed Challenger Green by the arms.

"What are you doing?" he growled.

The floor piece started moving. I pulled back hard, but the guy was heavy. He quickly realized I was trying to save him.

"Pull! Pull!" he commanded.

He got one leg up onto the edge, and had nearly brought up the other when I heard the crunch.

"Ahhhhhh!" he screamed as the flooring slammed home, crushing his foot.

I heard the cracking sound, even above the music. It was horrible. The poor guy lay on his back, his foot jammed between pieces of floor, trapped. I tried to force open the pieces of floor, but they wouldn't budge. Challenger Green screamed in agony. There was nothing I could do to help him . . . except to win. When the game was over, I had to believe he would be released. It couldn't have been a better situation. I not only saved his life, but the game was mine to win. I quickly left him and climbed up the mound. The silver disks seemed to be coming from every angle. I didn't bother ducking or dodging. I was either going to be lucky or I wasn't. I got to the top of the mound and saw the lights. All I had to do was press the final red light and it would be over. My finger hovered over it. The game was mine. But I didn't push it. I suddenly remembered what Nevva said. If the competition was tied going into the last round, the final game was always a match to the death. If I pressed that button, the competition would be tied. By saving Challenger Green and winning the game, I might have set myself up to die.

I kind of wished I had remembered that a few seconds before.

I looked down at Challenger Green, who was clutching at his shattered foot. The guy was in a lot of pain. Whatever the next competition was, I was going to have a pretty big advantage. I wondered if I had just saved Challenger Green from a random death, only to be put in a position where I might have to kill him myself? I had never killed anyone in my life and didn't want to start. Had I made a huge blunder?

There was only one thing to do. I pressed the red light.

QUILLAN

Fourteen worked to seal up the slice in my leg. The cut was clean, and luckily not very deep. He used a device that spit out a gluelike substance that sealed the wound and deadened it so I felt no pain. I was good to go, but I still didn't know for what.

We were in the dining hall of the castle. I refused to go back to my room, or anywhere else in the castle. I didn't want to be surprised by any more trapdoors or falling beds or killer clowns leaping out to bite me. Whatever was going to happen next, I wanted to see it coming.

"You saved Challenger Green," Fourteen said. "Why? By letting him die you would have won the Grand X."

"Lots of reasons," I said. "I think mostly it's because I'm not cut out for this warrior business."

"But you are fantastic," Fourteen said. "I have never seen anyone like you."

"Thanks. I've got the tools, but I don't have the killer instinct. I don't even like putting lobsters into boiling water."

"I do not understand that," the dado said.

"What I mean is, I'm not cold enough for this."

Fourteen nodded and said, "You are not like the others. I knew that from the moment I saw you. I believe if there were more like you, Quillan would be a better place."

"There *are* more like me," I said, putting on my pants. "You're going to see that pretty soon."

Veego entered the dining hall, followed by two security dados.

"You have succeeded," she said coldly.

"At what?" I asked. "I thought it was all tied up."

"You have succeeded in destroying us," she said bitterly. "Wagering is nonexistent. People are taking to the streets, demonstrating against the games. Against Blok. Crowds have broken into Blok stores to ransack them. Several of our gaming arcades have been overrun and destroyed. You have somehow . . . inspired them to insurrection."

I sat down on the dining table to get off my leg and said, "This was going to happen whether I was here or not. If it wasn't me, it would have been somebody else. People can't live like this. Fear works for only so long. Blok became powerful out of greed, but you can't build a civilization on that."

"But they did," Veego countered.

"No, they didn't," I said quickly. "They tried to destroy one. And they almost did. But you can't crush people's spirits. At least not forever. It may have taken a long time, but the people of Quillan are going to take back their territory. Ending your games is just the first step."

Veego shook her head as if she couldn't believe it could be true. Her world was crumbling.

"It can't be happening again," she said. "First Veelox, now here."

"No, there's a difference," I said. "The people of Veelox

did it to themselves. Every last one. Nobody forced anyone to stay in Lifelight. But here on Quillan there's only one enemy. Blok. Blok took control of their lives, and now they're fighting back."

"But none of this was our doing!" she said. "We were just doing our job and filling a need."

"Yeah, well, that need is about to go away," I said. "And don't act all innocent. You kidnapped people and set them up to kill one another. For profit. That's not a job, that's a crime. It doesn't matter if it was your idea or not. You made it happen. And you know what else . . ."

I walked toward her. The two dados straightened up so I didn't get too close.

"Maybe you didn't know what you were doing, but taking things from other territories and bringing them here could lead to a catastrophe. You've brought in raw materials and animals and ideas that don't belong here. They're not natural to this place. I suppose you can't really be blamed, because you just don't get it, but trust me, what you've done is a crime against humanity. Unless we can figure a way to purge everything you've brought here, you might have started a chain reaction that will make what happened on Veelox look like a party."

Veego looked shaken. I was glad. She was a criminal. So was her goofy brother. I supposed they couldn't totally be blamed for mingling the territories, because they didn't know better, but still. When Blok was brought down and these guys put out of business, I sure hoped they would meet some kind of justice.

"LaBerge and I have been called to meet with the trustees first thing tomorrow," she said. "I have no doubt we will be relieved of our responsibilities and the games taken away."

"Don't worry about it," I said. "I don't think the games are going to be around much longer anyway. You'll be lucky to get out before it comes down around you, and the people start storming the castle the way they're tearing apart your arcades."

Veego shot me a frightened look. She hadn't thought of that.

"Well," she said curtly. "At least there is one bit of consolation I can take from all of this."

"What's that?" I asked. "Do you get to keep your silly outfits? I'm sure that's all LaBerge cares about anyway."

"No," she said, suddenly sounding cold. "You're forgetting, Pendragon. The Grand X isn't over. There's a tie. And when there's a tie, we have one last competition."

"No way," I said, scoffing. "Challenger Green's foot was crushed. He's out of it."

"But he isn't," she said. "He's quite resilient. He wants one more chance at you, and I'm going to give it to him."

I didn't like where this was going.

"We always choose the games," Veego said, enjoying the moment. "We try to pick competitions that will provide fairly matched and exciting contests. But not in this case. You may have been successful in bringing me down, but at least I can keep you from enjoying your victory. That's why I picked a game that Challenger Green is most competent in. It plays to every one of his strengths. I have no doubt that he will triumph . . . and you will die."

"And that game is?" I asked.

"Tato, Pendragon," she said with delight. "I don't know what will happen with these exuberant crowds that you have inspired, but one thing I can say for certain, they will soon watch you fall to your death." She smiled and added, "This may be my last game on Quillan, but it will be the most satisfying." She turned and headed toward the door. "Bring him now!" she commanded to her dados.

I looked at Fourteen. He was about as stunned as a robot can be, which isn't very much. "Find Nevva Winter," I barked at him. "Do what you can to get her here."

I left Fourteen and walked quickly toward the exit. I knew the way. The dados followed right behind to make sure I went where I was supposed to. I guess I knew it would come to this. This is how Remudi died. It was fitting that I'd get the chance to avenge him in the same arena. What I didn't get was how Challenger Green was going to compete. His foot was crushed. I saw it. I'm sorry to say that I heard it too. If this guy was hurt even a little bit, I'd have a huge advantage on that Tato platform. There was no way after an injury like that, that he'd have the kind of balance to fight me, let alone maneuver on that surface if it started to tilt.

Part of me was totally confident. Another part knew it couldn't be that easy. Challenger Green was sly. He could very well have some things planned that I wouldn't expect. I had to treat this event as if he were whole and I had no advantage. To do anything else would be suicide.

I had to hope that since it had come to this, a tiebreaker to the death, that Nevva would do everything in her power to be there. Especially after what happened with Remudi. If she didn't make it, I'd know something happened to her. I couldn't stress about it though. I had to focus all my energy on beating Challenger Green in a competition that he was the all-time champion in. It was like challenging Lance Armstrong to a bike race. The only difference was, when you lost a bike race, you didn't die.

I walked the familiar route back through the forest to where I knew the Tato dome was. When I arrived, Challenger Green was already there, standing in his square on the platform. He stood straight, on both feet. I had no way of knowing how badly he was hurt.

I walked to the edge of the platform and called out, "How's the foot?"

"You're a fool," he said. "You had me beaten. No, I had beaten myself. If the situation were reversed, I would have let you die."

"I did it for lots of reasons," I said. "But mostly because I'm not you."

"For what you did, I will give you one piece of advice," he said.

"Really? What's that?"

"Don't think for a second that I will show you mercy for having saved me."

I waited a second, expecting more. There wasn't. "That's it?" I asked. "That's your big advice? Gee, thanks. That'll help a bunch."

I stepped onto the Tato platform and looked it over. It was the same as I remembered from watching the match when Challenger Green killed Remudi. The five smoky glass domes were intact. I wondered what weapons were hidden below each. I hoped I wouldn't find out, because breaking them would make the platform unstable.

I pushed my foot down to discover the surface was soft and spongy, kind of like a wrestling pad at school. It had some spring to it. I tried to slide the sole of my boot across the surface. It gripped tight. That was good. There would be no slipping on this surface. I stood in the center to get a feel of how far it was to either side. It felt pretty big, but I knew it would seem to shrink the moment we got into the air. Amazing how that happens. The whole time I inspected the platform, Challenger Green kept his eyes on me. He didn't move, the same as before his match with Remudi.

As I stepped into the square outline opposite Challenger Green, LaBerge and Veego entered the clearing. The two stood on the edge of the forest and gave each other a hug. It was the first sign of affection I had seen between this brother and sister. I would have been touched, if they weren't sadistic monsters. One of them was a sadistic monster in a clown suit. You don't get much worse than that. I expected them to both come up onto the platform, the way they had before the match between Green and Remudi, but only LaBerge climbed aboard. Veego stayed back, her arms at her side. Just as well, I didn't want to hear any more of her obnoxious comments.

LaBerge went up to Challenger Green. He whispered a few words to him, which I'm sure were along the lines of, "Good luck. Kill him." He handed Green the short, metal rod that could either be used as a weapon, or to break the domes. He then came to me. His eyes were red. He had been crying. He reluctantly handed me my steel weapon and said, "I hope this hurts."

"Thanks!" I said. "I love you too, clowny."

The guy didn't even look me in the eye. Wimp. He started to walk away when I asked, "Hey, don't I get an advantage because I won the last game?"

LaBerge said, "It's tied. There are no advantages in a tie."

I said, "I'll bet you just made that up."

He didn't answer. The guy hated me for ruining his fun.

He walked to the center of the Tato platform and stood there quietly, his eyes closed. What was he doing? A few moments passed. He opened his eyes and glanced over to his sister, who stood on the edge of the clearing. She gave him a slight nod. LaBerge nodded back. He took a deep breath and stood up tall, puffing out his chest. In seconds he transformed himself from the broken, sorry clown whose world was about to crumble, to the outgoing ringmaster I had first seen on the screen above the city of Rune. This was his last dance, and he was going to play it for all it was worth. He dramatically raised one hand. It was a signal. Music blasted through the forest. It was the same loud, thumping electronic music I'd heard before the last Tato match. I could only imagine what was happening on the streets of Rune and the rest of Quillan as they watched the spectacle.

LaBerge put on a big smile, threw his arms out, and sang, "Place your bets, the time is near; the greatest games on Quillan are here!"

He stalked around the platform, spinning, sliding, and gesturing wildly. "This has been a match for the ages! The greatest Grand X in the history of Quillan. What better way to end it than here, in the Tato dome." He paused, probably for the crowd to cheer, but there was no way to know if that was happening. I have to admit, he was good. It's gotta be hard playing to a crowd you can't see or hear.

"Introducing for the last time, undefeated in an unprecedented *seven* Tato matches, and ready to retire after one last crushing victory, your champion, Challenger Green!"

Challenger Green didn't move. It was like watching a statue. He kept his eyes on me.

"And his opponent, a challenger who has done surprisingly well in this Grand X. A new favorite who hopes to last as long as he can before falling to a painful death, Challenger Red!"

Wow, I guess there was no mystery about who he thought would win. It wasn't until that moment that it finally hit me: This fight was really going to happen. I had to get my game face on, fast.

"Good luck to you both!" sang LaBerge. "The betting is closed. The game will begin!"

He skipped to the end of the platform and jumped off. I bent my legs. I knew what was coming next. With a slight jolt, the platform began to rise. I kept my eyes on Challenger

Green, trying not to think about how high we were going. It was hard to miss, since behind him, I saw the trees seemingly sinking down as we rose into the air. I imagined hearing the multiple thousands of people in the streets chanting "Taaaaaaaaato!" as we ascended. A few seconds later we cleared the tops of the trees to reveal a breathtaking sight. Literally. I had to catch my breath. I could look over the sea of treetops to see the buildings of the gray city far beyond. I felt the platform sway slightly. We were way the heck up there.

The platform stopped with a lurch. This was it. The final stage of the Grand X, the last chapter of my mission here on Quillan, and maybe my last act as a Traveler.

I heard LaBerge's amplified voice shouting, "Four . . . three . . . two . . . one . . . TATO!"

And it was on.

QUILLAN

Challenger Green moved instantly. He had a plan. He dropped to one knee and used his metal weapon to smash open one of the glass domes. I could instantly feel the platform wobble. He knew he was at a disadvantage with his bad foot, so he had to pull out every possible trick to beat me. That was good, I thought. He was already desperate. He reached into the dome and pulled out a weapon that looked familiar. It was a three-pronged knife. I knew I had seen it someplace before, but couldn't remember where.

Challenger Green held it up and said, "They call this a tang. I use it for fights in close. Are you ready for a fight in close?"

A tang, of course. It was a weapon made from the three claws of a tang beast on Eelong. Seeing it didn't even bother me. It wasn't the time to be worrying about mixing the territories. Challenger Green held the knife low. It looked like he knew how to use it. He started to circle to his right. I knew why. He had a bad left eye. If he was going to attack, it would be to his right. I circled away. I wanted to keep on his left side. The platform wobbled, but not dangerously. That wasn't a factor. At least not yet.

"You knew we would end up here, didn't you, Red?" he growled. "This is what I wanted, you know. I could have won all those games, but I wanted us here, on the Tato."

"Yeah, sure you could have," I said. "That's why I had to save your life."

Green jumped up and slammed down hard on the platform, making it tilt. It wasn't much, but it surprised me, and my arms flew out to get my balance.

Green laughed. "Wait until we start to rock! It's all about balance," he said, shifting weight from one foot to the other. "I know everything about this platform. I know where it's tight and where it dips. When you hit the wrong spot, look out. You'll go down."

I was surprised to see that his foot didn't seem to bother him. Either he had an incredible tolerance for pain, or he had it strapped up tight in a cast under his pants. Or took painkillers. Or something. Whatever it was, I realized that it wasn't going to be a factor in this fight. Unfortunately. Green continued circling.

I circled away and said, "You know that either way, the games are done."

"Then I'll retire as the only undefeated challenger," he said proudly. "You think that bothers me?"

Green had a temper. I wanted him to fight angry. If he lost control, it would take away the advantage he had of knowing this game and the platform.

"No," I said. "I think it bothers you that nobody cares about you anymore. I'm the favorite now."

"Until you lose," he said. "People like winners."

"Yeah," I said. "And people like to win. This is way bigger

than two fools in bright shirts trying to kill each other. The people know that now. They're looking for something better, and after I beat you, they'll get it."

Green frowned. I hoped I was throwing him off, if only a little. I didn't think he cared at all about the future of Quillan. He had a huge ego and wanted to be the champion. His concerns began and ended there.

"I *am* going to beat you," I added. "Sorry."

"Let's see about that," he snarled, and came after me.

He didn't charge; he was still in control. He had the tang-claw knife in one hand and the metal rod in the other. I only had the metal rod. He led with the rod, making short, tight swings, testing me out. But he had the tang claw in his other hand, cocked tight to his hip, ready to lash out. That's what I had to look out for. I ducked his swings easily. I was more worried that he would try to steer me close to the edge of the platform. When I ducked, I made sure to reset myself near the center.

Nevva was right. He was clumsy. He was an amateur, too. I knew that he'd soon get frustrated and attack. That's when I would make my move.

"Tired yet?" I taunted. "This fight has already gone longer than what you're used to. You gonna make it?"

That got him. He lunged at me with the metal rod, but I knew it was a fake. I ducked it, ready for the tang claw to come. It did. He lashed out with it and I was ready. I blocked it with both my arms and brought my knee up hard, crushing his wrist between my arms and my knee.

"Ahhh!" Green shouted and dropped the tang.

I quickly kicked it away. I wanted to knock it off the platform, but it skittered across the soft floor and stopped just beyond one of the glass domes. Green recovered quickly and rammed his metal weapon into my ribs. He caught me hard and I doubled over. He followed with a punch that sent me sprawling backward. As I fell, all I could think of was how close I was to the edge. I landed hard on my back, but it was a relief. At least I landed.

Green charged and leaped at me. I rolled out of the way and jumped back to my feet. We were both closer to the edge of the platform, and I could feel it dip slightly. Without thinking, I ran back toward the center. I didn't want to be anywhere near that edge. Green spun back to me and laughed. He was still on his knees.

"You're more afraid of falling than you are of me!" he shouted. "All right, then let's play that way!"

He smashed another dome. The platform dipped. I'll admit it. I was scared. I scrambled closer to center. With every move I made, I could feel the platform change subtly. Green was totally confident. He jumped up and started running around to try to scare me. He was doing a good job.

"Look out!" he taunted. "Whoa! It's going over!"

He was all about trying to make it tilt. I tried to stay opposite him to balance us out. What else could I do? Charge at the guy? Wrestle him down, and then what? Try to push him over? He was in charge. This was his show. All I could do was react.

"Not scary enough for you?" Green shouted. "Let's try another!"

"No!" I screamed. "This is crazy! "We'll both fall!"

"Is that so?" he laughed. "Let's see!"

He knelt down and smashed the third dome. I knew what was going to happen and quickly knelt down too. The platform became totally unstable.

This was as far as it got with Remudi. With that match, Challenger Green deliberately threw off the balance of the platform by throwing his legs over the side. He then grabbed on to the rim of the smashed dome for safety. Remudi wasn't ready. The platform tilted over and he fell to his death. I had to be prepared if Green tried that same move. If he did, I was going to make the exact opposite move and keep us balanced . . . or fall trying.

He must have known I was ready, because Green didn't go for it. We held steady, balanced on opposite sides of the platform. It was like being on a seesaw. It felt like every breath I took threw the balance off a hair. I was on my knees, just inside one of the domes that was still intact. I put my foot on the glass to try to get a little more stability. It seemed hopeless. I didn't see how this could end well, for either of us.

It got worse. Green looked into the dome he had just smashed and let out a jubilant, "Yes!" He reached inside and pulled out the ultimate prize of a weapon. It was a golden dado gun. He held it up triumphantly, shouting, "This is too easy!"

He took aim at me. I was history. One shot and I'd be out. I had no doubt that once I was unconscious, he'd find a way to tip the platform so that he'd be safe and I'd roll off. At least I wouldn't know I was falling.

Green put me in his sights and said, "Now let's see who the real champion is."

He pulled the trigger.

Fum!

I rolled to my right. The shot missed me, but it hit the dome I had been pushing against. *Smash!* The dome exploded. The platform was now totally loose and tipped down toward me. I scrambled to get back to the center, digging my fingernails into the soft floor, desperate to get a grip. It was like being on the deck of a boat in rolling seas.

Green had no fear. He laughed, aimed his gun, and shot out the last dome! The platform was free-floating. I fell flat on my belly, dug my toes in, and pressed my palms flat on the floor. It was the only thing I could think of to get some kind of traction to stop from slipping toward the edge. But the angle was too steep and I started to slide. Gravity was winning. Green tried to run up to the opposite side, but this time even he lost his balance. He pinwheeled his arms and fell on his back. When he hit, he scrambled for something to grab on to but found nothing. His luck had finally run out. We were both moments from going over.

Something caught my eye. It was rolling toward me, picking up speed on its way down. It was the tang knife. It was about to roll past me when I lunged out and grabbed it. I was seconds from going over the edge. This was my only chance. I grabbed the handle of the sharp knife and stabbed it into the soft foam padding of the platform. It held! I felt like one of those guys who climb frozen waterfalls with an ice ax. The only thing keeping me from sliding to the edge was this knife made of claws that was barely stuck into the padding. The platform had stopped tilting, but it was at an incredibly steep angle. A few more degrees and it would be fully perpendicular to the ground. I heard the knife tear through the padding. It wasn't going to last. I had to get a better grip. I did something dangerous, but it was the only chance I had. I pulled myself up farther, grabbed the handle with both hands, and yanked it out. Instantly I started sliding down. Using the power of both of my arms, I jammed the three-pronged knife as hard as I could back into the padding.

I felt the tip hit something hard underneath. It held firm. I stopped sliding. I had embedded the point into something more solid than just the pad. I was secure. Or at least more secure than before. I had no idea how long it would last. I stole a cautious look down. With the platform nearly on its side, I could see down to the ground. I have to tell you, we were way high. I could barely make out the figures of Veego and LaBerge on the ground. They looked like tiny toys. My feet were only a few feet from the end of the platform. If the knife pulled out, there was nothing else to grab on to. My hands started to shake. Looking down wasn't a good thing, so I turned my face back to the platform.

I didn't know what had happened to Challenger Green. Had he fallen? No, that couldn't be or the competition would be over. I cautiously turned my head to the left. He wasn't there. I slowly turned my head the other way and saw him.

Challenger Green was hanging on to the rim of a shattered dome, just as he had when he killed Remudi. But this time the platform was at a much steeper angle. He was hanging there with his feet dangling in space. His hands were bloody from grabbing on to the sharp edges of the shattered dome. For the first time, I saw fear in his eyes. He had never been in this position. He was terrified. I realized it was only a matter of time. Either he was going to lose his grip, or my knife was going to pull out.

"Tell me, Red. Do you like it?" he shouted up at me, spittle flying from his mouth. His eyes were wild. "Do you like killing?"

"Give up," I shouted. "I'm not going anywhere. Tell them you give up, and it'll be over. They won't let you die if you give up!"

Challenger Green moved his hands around to get a better grip. The sharp edges dug into his flesh. He was only hanging on by his fingers. I knew there was no way he could last much longer. He looked down, then back up at me.

"Only one problem with that," he shouted.

"What?" I shouted back.

"I don't like to lose!"

And he fell. I didn't know if it was because he couldn't

hold on any longer, or he gave up. It didn't matter. He fell. He would rather die than live with defeat. I couldn't watch. I turned my face to the platform and closed my eyes. The guy didn't even scream. Challenger Green was gone. Beaten at last. Though he went to his death silently, his final question kept playing in my head. He wanted to know if I liked killing. Was that true? Had I become a killer? As I hung there on that knife, the only thing I could do was press my forehead into the platform, and cry.

A moment later I felt the platform lurch. The knife slipped. What was happening? Was Veego was so angry I'd won that she was going to kill me anyway? Why not? She didn't have anything to lose. I got a tighter grip on the knife, though I didn't know what good that would do. I felt an odd sensation. It was like the platform was pressing into my body. At first I didn't understand what was happening, but soon realized the machinery had kicked in and the platform was being returned to level. In moments I was no longer hanging, I was lying on my stomach. I didn't let go of the knife though. I couldn't.

I felt the platform descend. It was over. I had survived. My crying turned to laughter. There was absolutely nothing funny about what had happened, but I was so full of emotion, I didn't know what I was doing. It just flew out of me. I didn't have a say in the matter. I felt the final jolt that told me the platform was back on the ground. I was still flat on my stomach, clutching the knife. I sensed that somebody had stepped up on the platform next to me. I didn't want to deal with Veego and LaBerge. I was too drained. When I looked up, I had to laugh again. This time it was genuine. Standing there was the only person I cared about seeing. Mostly because I think he was the only person who cared about me.

It was Fourteen.

"Congratulations, Pendragon," he said. "Look."

He pointed up. I looked to see one of those big screens in the trees. Flashing brightly were the words: GRAND X CHAMPION—CHALLENGER RED!

I looked back to Fourteen and, I swear, the robot smiled.

QUILLAN

There was no sign of Challenger Green's body. I assumed some security dados had removed it. They never showed the true result of a game to the people. They kept it all sanitized. Neat and clean. No bodies, no blood. Also missing were Veego and LaBerge. I figured they had run back to the castle and were packing for a quick getaway. I had a brief worry that they would try to jump into the flume on their own to get away from the wrath of the trustees. If what Veego told me was correct, the only safe way for non-Travelers to use the flumes was with a Traveler. I couldn't imagine that Saint Dane would be willing to escort them back home. If Veego and LaBerge jumped into a flume, well, I didn't want to think about what might happen. The idea of being trapped on Quillan was beyond horrible. There was nothing I could do about it just then anyway, so I tried not to stress about it.

Fourteen and I headed back to the castle. My plan was to get out of there, find Nevva, and get back with the revivers. After going through the hell of the Grand X, I wasn't in any shape to fight my way out of there through some security dados. But if I had to, I would.

When we arrived back at the castle, we stepped into something I never expected.

The whole time I had been competing in the Grand X, the only clues I had as to what was happening outside in the city were the few angry comments that Veego had made. She told me that people were storming Blok stores and had trashed their gaming arcades. She told me that wagering on the competition was nonexistent. That was definitely good news, but I hadn't seen it for myself. I had to take her word for it. What I found in the next few hours was that it was all true. In fact, Veego had underestimated the impact of the Grand X.

First we were greeted at the castle by the rest of the challengers. They treated me like a conquering hero. They enthusiastically clapped me on the back and congratulated me and said how I'd saved their lives. Unlike the false friendliness of the parties I had been to, this felt sincere. They were genuinely happy that I had won. Better still, there wasn't a security dado in sight. I was told that before the Tato game had even begun, the security dados left the castle. They took every last vehicle, piled in, and took off. The challengers showed me that their loops were no longer active. Sure enough, I was able to pull mine off. This happy reunion wasn't only about my victory over Challenger Green, it was a celebration of our new freedom. They were all itching to get out of there and back to their homes and their loved ones. But they stayed long enough to thank me.

Amid the celebration Fourteen approached me, put a gentle hand on my shoulder, and said, "Pendragon, you should come with me."

"Why? What's up?" I asked. I didn't want to leave the party.

"You should see for yourself" was his answer.

I gave the challengers a final good-bye and quickly ran up the wide steps after Fourteen. He led me up to the second floor of the castle to a spot I hadn't been before. It was a balcony over the main entrance, that looked down on the courtyard below.

"Why are we here?" I asked.

A familiar voice answered, "To protect you from your fans."

I spun to see Nevva Winter standing just outside the doorway.

"Nevva!" I yelled. "I knew you'd be here!"

"I wasn't the whole time," she said. "I'm sorry. The trustees gathered to watch the Grand X together and they demanded I be there. I couldn't get away until just now."

I didn't care. It was okay. I survived on my own.

"Is it true?" I asked. "Has the revival begun?"

"It's incredible," she said. "Everything is going exactly according to plan. Better. All the people needed was a little inspiration, and you gave it to them, Pendragon. They've taken up arms. This is the turning point for Quillan, and it's all because of you."

"It's all because of the revivers," I said. "I just lit the fuse."

"You're being modest," she said. "Without you, none of this would be possible."

It was an incredible feeling to know the fate of Quillan was about to change, and that I had a direct hand in making it happen.

"I want to see it," I said. "I'm feeling kind of removed from the whole thing."

Nevva chuckled and said, "You won't be for long."

Fourteen added, "They're almost here."

"Who?" I asked.

Nevva pointed out beyond the wall that surrounded the castle. I looked to see an impossible sight. Thousands of people streamed along the road through the forest, headed for the castle.

Nevva said, "They were watching the Grand X from beyond the gate. When you won, they couldn't be stopped. The dados didn't even try."

I now understood why the dados had taken off. There was no way they could contain this many people.

"They want to see you, Pendragon," Nevva said with a smile. "You're going to have to say something to them."

"What? I don't know what to say to all those people!"

"You'll think of something," Nevva said.

The three of us stood there and watched as the huge crowd moved up the road, through the wall, and into the courtyard. This wasn't an angry mob; they were happy and singing. They had begun the long process of taking back their lives, and they were starting with the castle, a symbol of the games. The courtyard filled quickly, though the multitude stretched back all the way into the woods. You'd think I'd be nervous about talking to a crowd like this, but I wasn't. I was on top of the world. Fourteen set some kind of microphone in front of me. I'd never done anything like this before, but I was ready to give it a try.

I raised up my two hands, and the people cheered. What a feeling! They wouldn't stop. I looked down on the people who were right below us and saw them looking up at me with joy. It was the single most incredible moment of my life.

After a few minutes I waved my arms for them to quiet down. It took a few minutes more, but they finally did. It was odd to be looking out over so many people and have it go absolutely quiet.

I leaned into the microphone. When I spoke, I heard my voice boom. "I've never spoken to so many people like this, so forgive me if I'm not very good at it," I began. "Today is a day you will never forget. Not because I won the Grand X, but because when the history of Quillan is written, this day will be remembered as the day the fight began to win independence, and freedom."

The people went nuts. Many waved red flags in honor of me. I wondered if this would become the new flag of Quillan. I quieted the crowd again and said, "There is a long road ahead. This is only the first step. But you will be able to tell your grandchildren that this was the day a new Quillan was born, and you were all part of it. The revival is here. It has begun. Take back your lives!"

The place went absolutely stupid. I raised my hands and waved, firing them up even more. Man, what a rush. I never thought I'd do anything even close to this, and I have to admit, I kind of liked it.

Nevva leaned into me and whispered, "We'd better go. There are people you have to see."

I didn't want to leave. Who would? I had thousands of people cheering for me like I was the greatest hero of all time. What the heck? I'd never gotten any credit for saving all those other territories. I deserved a little applause.

Nevva gently pulled me inside, but the crowd didn't stop cheering. I was so excited I couldn't talk fast enough.

"Did you see that?" I said. "They're going nuts out there! It worked! They're really going to do it! Quillan is going to be okay!"

While I blathered on, Nevva kept leading me away. "Yes, it is incredible, but if we don't get out of here now, you'll be crushed by all these well-wishers."

Fourteen led us down into the bowels of the castle,

where there was an underground tunnel, and a car waiting for us. Nevva got behind the wheel, and I got in on the passenger side.

"Come on!" I said to Fourteen. "You're part of this too!"

"No," he said. "My place is here."

I got out of the car and stood by him. "There is no here anymore. You're free."

"There is no such thing as free to a dado," Fourteen said. "I will remain with the other service dados."

"Come on, Pendragon," Nevva coaxed.

I gave Fourteen a hug. He wasn't expecting that. He definitely didn't know what to do.

"Thanks, man," I said. "I wouldn't have made it without you."

He awkwardly patted me on the back. "Yes, you would have," he said. "I am proud to have served you."

It was weird being so emotional over a machine, but Fourteen had been the only voice of sanity I had to cling to at the castle. I was going to miss him.

"I hope we'll see each other again," I said. "Wear something different so I'll recognize you. You guys kind of look the same."

"I will remember that," he said. "Good-bye, Pendragon. Good luck."

I nodded and jumped in the car. Nevva hit the throttle, and we were on our way. We traveled through the tunnel for so long I knew we had to be outside the gates of the castle. The whole time I pumped Nevva for information. I wanted to know what was happening in Rune, and with the trustees and all over Quillan. The revival was under way and I wanted to hear what the game plan was. Nevva laughed and said I should wait for the official briefing. That was okay with me. I wanted to hear it from Tylee Magna anyway.

Nevva had done her part. Together, we Travelers had sparked the revival. The rest was up to Tylee and the revivers.

We didn't talk much the rest of the trip. I just sat there, replaying the incredible day in my head, from every game of the Grand X to the screaming masses. It was too amazing to believe. I didn't want to forget a single detail.

The tunnel led us inside a building that looked to be an abandoned factory of some sort. Nevva knew exactly where she was going. We drove outside and onto the streets of Quillan. After a short distance Nevva sped us into a garage that led to yet another subterranean tunnel. It was incredible how there was a whole separate world below Rune. Finally we arrived at a large garage that seemed to be the former parking area for one of the abandoned malls, complete with faded white lines to designate parking spaces. Nevva led me through the empty space, into a building, and finally into an elevator. She didn't join me.

"Aren't you coming?" I asked.

"No," she said. "The trustees don't even know I'm gone. I'm not going to give up that job just yet. This is only the beginning of the revival. There's a very long way to go."

"Okay, but be careful," I said. "And hurry."

"Pendragon," she said, "you were incredible. For a while there, I was afraid you weren't going to pull it off."

"Only for a while?" I asked. "I wasn't so sure the whole time."

"I had more faith in you than that," she said. "I knew you would win. That's the way it was meant to be."

I nodded and said, "Hurry, okay."

Nevva waved and the doors closed. The elevator started moving. I figured it must know where I was going because there weren't any buttons inside. Without any little lights, I couldn't tell if I was going up or down. I couldn't wait to talk to Tylee and the others. I knew the revival had just begun, but my part in it was done. To me, this was a victory lap. A well-earned victory lap.

The elevator came to a stop, and the doors opened. With a big smile on my face I stepped out . . . and froze. I was in a bare room with a double door across from the elevator. To either side of the door were big silver letters that spelled out BLOK. I stopped smiling. What the hell was going on? I wasn't with the revivers. This was the courtroom of the trustees of Blok.

The doors opposite me opened. I saw the room where I had been introduced to the trustees. It was empty. Eerily empty. Except for one person.

"I thought you'd never make it," came a voice from inside. "But I guess you had to bask in the glory of your adoring public."

I knew that voice. But it made no sense. It couldn't be . . .

But it was. Stepping from the shadows of the darkened trustee room was a ghost. I knew it was a ghost because I saw him die. Yet there he stood . . . Challenger Green. I blinked. He didn't go away. I blinked again. He smiled. He wasn't a ghost. He had somehow survived the fall. He didn't even look injured.

"I thought for sure you would have put it together when I wasn't bothered by my injury," he said, stomping his left foot hard on the ground. "But then again, you never were a very good detective."

My ears rang. My palms started to sweat. I started to shake. I actually started to shake.

"No," I said softly. "No way."

"Oh, yes," Green said. "Once again you have failed to grasp the obvious. You are right about one thing though.

Things are indeed going exactly as planned. It's just that the plans are a little different than you thought."

Challenger Green started to melt and morph. I closed my eyes. I didn't want to see it. I didn't have to. I knew what was happening.

"Open your eyes, Pendragon," Saint Dane said. "It's time for you to see the new Quillan . . . the territory you helped create."

QUILLAN

When I opened my eyes, I saw Saint Dane standing there in his normal form. You know it. He was well over six feet tall and wore a dark suit that buttoned right to his neck. He was completely bald, with his pale skin marked by red scars across his head that looked like jagged lightning bolts. What always stood out the most, though, were his eyes. His blue-white intense eyes that glowed with a hint of insanity.

I ducked back into the elevator, but with no controls, I didn't know what to do.

Saint Dane chuckled. "Where are you going? Do you want to run and announce to Quillan that Challenger Green wasn't who they thought he was? Maybe you could tell that to your reviver friends." He grabbed his left biceps in a mock salute. "I liked that touch when you did this to the crowd, by the way," he said. "Very theatrical. Very effective."

"Tell me what's going on," I demanded.

"Oh, I will," Saint Dane said. "I've been looking forward to this."

"But . . . you wanted me to compete and lose!" I shouted. "And I beat you!"

"You didn't beat me, Pendragon," Saint Dane said. "I wanted you to win. I *let* you win! The only reason I let the competition get that close was to build the drama. People love drama."

I leaned against the back of the elevator for support.

"Actually," he continued, "the Grand X was the icing on the cake, as they say on Second Earth. You lost the territory long before that."

I was having trouble breathing. My heart raced. Nothing he was saying made sense.

"You see, Pendragon," he said, taking a step toward me, "everything you've heard is correct. The people of Quillan are ready to take back their territory. The stage was set by the revivers. All they needed was the last piece. The inspiration. And you gave it to them. It worked! You've seen the result. People are massing by the thousands and marching on the city. It's happening all over the territory. You've given them hope and they are running with it. Anarchy rules!"

"But you let me win!" I shouted. "That means you wanted it to happen this way."

Saint Dane chuckled. I hated it when he chuckled.

"Hope is a fragile emotion, my friend. It isn't real." He tapped his bald head. "It exists only in the imagination. If you believe there is hope, there is hope. If you don't believe there is hope, there isn't."

"Just tell me," I demanded.

"Defeat is always devastating," he said. "But it is never more crushing than when it comes after you believe you have won."

He turned and walked into the trustee courtroom. I didn't want to follow. Nothing he was going to tell me in there would be good. If there were buttons on the elevator, I would have pushed them. Or maybe I wouldn't have. As bad as I knew this was going to be, I had to know. I followed him.

Inside the courtroom, the two big screens where they had shown the replay of my Hook competition were in place. Saint Dane held the remote control.

"I didn't lie to you, Pendragon," Saint Dane said. "At least not entirely. I had nothing to do with the creation of Blok. Or of the games."

"But you brought Veego and LaBerge from Veelox," I said.

"Ahh, you discovered that," he said. "Those two are such annoying little cretins. Don't you agree?"

"You know you're not supposed to mix the territories," I said.

"No, Pendragon, *you* are not supposed to mix the territories! I'm the bad guy, remember? At least from your perspective. You have this illusion that the territories must remain separate and evolve along their own paths. I don't share that philosophy. I believe we won't reach our full potential until the walls are broken down and Halla becomes one."

"But that would be chaos," I said.

"Oh? What do you think is happening out in the streets of Quillan right now? A tea party? You knew that once the revival was under way it would create havoc."

"Yes, but it's the only way they can topple Blok," I argued. "They're willing to suffer to create a better life."

"Exactly!" Saint Dane exclaimed. "Before my vision for Halla is complete, I have to break down the old ways and, yes, create chaos. From that, a new Halla will emerge. Is that so different from what you knew would happen on Quillan?"

"It all depends on what your final vision is," I said.

Saint Dane didn't respond to that right away. Instead he gave me a slight smile. "Well said," he countered.

"You said that if I competed, you would reveal to me the nature of the Travelers," I said. "Was that another lie?"

Saint Dane looked at me, then put down the remote.

"I don't think you truly want to know, Pendragon," he said. "You would rather believe what you want to believe. Your version of reality is so much more . . . comfortable."

"Don't tell me what I think. I want to know," I said.

"Very well, then," Saint Dane said.

My heart hammered in my chest. Was this it? Was the truth finally going to be revealed? Saint Dane looked at me. This may sound strange, but for a moment I actually thought I saw his eyes soften. The evil madness had been replaced by . . . what? Kindness? Sympathy? Compassion?

"You aren't real, Pendragon," he said softly. "You're an illusion. As am I. As are all the Travelers. It's how we're able to travel through time and space with little concern for the physical rules that restrict the inhabitants of the territories."

I wasn't buying that.

"Maybe you're not real, but I sure am," I said. "I can't turn myself into other beings. I feel pain just like everybody else. I was born, I'm getting older, I'm a normal physical person like everybody else on Second Earth."

"To an extent," he said. "It's true, you don't have my abilities, and you may never evolve that far, but make no mistake—the Travelers defy the physical laws of their territories. You feel pain, but think of how quickly you heal. I killed Loor but you brought her back from the dead. Does that seem 'normal' to you?"

"What about Uncle Press? And Osa? And all the others who died?" I said quickly.

"It was their choice," Saint Dane said. "You didn't want Loor to die, so she didn't. That was your choice."

My mind was going in a million different directions. He

was telling me everything, and nothing. "So if it's true, where did we come from? How did we come to exist? Where do *you* come from?"

Saint Dane sat down on a chair. It was strange. He no longer seemed like the monster demon who was bent on destroying Halla. He came across as a kindly, concerned adult. Okay, a kindly concerned adult with lightning bolts blazed into his head, but still.

"I'm afraid the answer to that question is at the very heart of our conflict, Pendragon," he said. "I will be honest with you and say I cannot reveal the answer because it would put me at a disadvantage. I will not do that. But I will say this: You have an opportunity. We are not as different as you think. Join me. We can build a new Halla . . . together."

He looked at me with kindness and sincerity. I wanted to believe him. I wanted to put an end to this battle and have everything be all right. I wanted to learn the truth. All of it. It would have been so easy.

But the memories came roaring back. All of them. He was a murderer. He caused more pain and suffering than I can even remember. I saw it all. He took joy in it. How could that possibly be the way it was supposed to be? If that was his vision of Halla, then there was no way I could let it happen.

"No," I said. "I can never be like you. Whatever your vision for Halla is, I can't accept that it includes bringing out the worst in humanity."

His eyes changed. The kindness evaporated. The evil had returned.

"The worst in humanity?" he said, seething. "You mean like arrogance and vanity and the thirst for power and revenge?" He stood up and walked toward me, backing me off. "Look at yourself, Pendragon. You hold yourself up to be the model of righteous deeds, but what happened here on

Quillan? You believed you couldn't be beaten—that's how I was able to lure you into the games. Your pride was your undoing. I killed a Traveler to see how you would respond. What did you do? You vowed revenge! You cling to the precious words of your uncle, who told you the territories cannot be mixed, yet you intercede time and time again with the natural order of a territory. You're aghast at the fact that I'll bring an animal from Cloral or a weapon from Eelong, yet you are quick to bring something that is far more intrusive. You bring ideas, Pendragon! You were raised on Second Earth, and you are all too quick to impose what you feel are the higher morals of that territory on all others. How is that any different from what I have done? Your arrogance astounds me! You stood facing thousands of adoring people who saw you as a savior, and you reveled in it, didn't you? You loved the feeling of power. Don't lie to yourself, Pendragon. You aren't driven by nobility alone. You are as flawed as anyone. That is the truth, whether you choose to believe it or not."

"You're twisting it," I said.

"Am I?" he shot back. "Let me ask you again, Red. Do you like killing?"

"What? No!"

"You think you are unable to kill, but let me remind you how much blood is on your hands. People died when the tak mine exploded on Denduron. How many died when the *Hindenburg* crashed? But that is nothing compared to our battle, Pendragon. If you didn't exist, I wouldn't exist. Everything I've done is because of you! How many more will die before you give up this foolish quest?"

"No," I said. "No way. You can't blame me for what you've done."

"We're both responsible, Pendragon," he said. "When the Convergence comes, you will play as big a role as I."

"The what?" I asked. "What is the Convergence?"

"It's our future, Pendragon," he said. "The future of Halla."

He spun away from me and picked up the remote control. "Do you need more convincing? Let me show you what your arrogance has brought to Quillan. This territory was on the verge of a revolution. The revivers brought together thousands, convincing them that their road to happiness would be to overthrow Blok. Blok knew it was coming, but it wasn't the revivers they feared. No. What Blok feared more than anything else was the past. They had done all they could to destroy anything that would make people want to return to the old ways. It took them generations to wipe out an entire way of life and replace it with their own. They broke down the territory physically, and the people emotionally. They had total control because the people simply didn't know any other way. They had completely purged history. The only true threat to them would be if enough people learned of the past. But it wasn't a real problem because the past no longer existed. Or did it?"

Saint Dane pointed the remote control at the screens. They both came to life with images that made me want to get down on my knees and cry. On each screen was a wide shot of the inside of the secret library that contained all the relics of Quillan's past.

"What's their special secret name for it?" Saint Dane asked. "Oh, yes, Mr. Pop. How very . . . cute. You see, the revivers did an exceptional job of keeping it secret. The trustees heard rumors of its existence, but could never prove that it was real, let alone find it. Well, Pendragon, they've found it . . . thanks to you."

What happened next was nothing less than Armageddon. I first saw images of the green-smocked curators running through the aisles in fear. Some tried to grab items, others simply fled. It was futile. Following right behind them was a legion of dados. The first wave came with golden rifles, shooting up everything they saw. Glass shattered; shelves fell over, spilling books and manuscripts; sculptures were pulverized. Bits and pieces of Quillan's past exploded into bits of debris. The next wave of dados brought flame-throwers. Long, hideous jets of fire streaked across the room. Paintings sizzled, books burned, clothing turned to ash. The flames were so intense that even metal burned. I saw the giant hand holding the feather turn black. The room had become a huge incinerator, with the dados in the middle of it, oblivious to the heat, and the sorrow.

They were methodical and thorough. The two screens kept changing views, so I could see it all. I didn't want to, but I had to. Once the room was completely engulfed in flames, the dados retreated and were replaced with a handful of other dados who carried items that looked like small barrels. They moved quickly through the inferno and placed them in various sections throughout the immense space. They quickly retreated. I feared what would happen next.

The barrels exploded. One after the other, they erupted with a powerful fury that rocked the structure itself. I saw heavy beams falling from overhead and walls collapsing. A long beam hit the giant hand, shearing off the feather and toppling the sculpture. More barrels exploded. The last one finally destroyed the cameras that were recording the carnage. Mercifully, the spectacle was over. I had witnessed the complete annihilation of Quillan's past. What had taken eons to create, and generations to collect and hide, had been destroyed in a few violent minutes.

The screen went black, and Saint Dane turned to me. "As I said, truly devastating defeat can only come at the moment of victory. Those images were shown all over Quillan. I wanted you to win the Grand X, Pendragon. I wanted you to be the champion of the people. I wanted them to think they actually had a chance, because now they know it is truly hopeless. Blok will survive. This pathetic territory will continue on its sad little course. The select few will prosper; the masses will suffer. This was the turning point on Quillan, Pendragon. The destruction of their history. And it's all thanks to you."

I was stunned senseless. Every devious twist of Saint Dane's plan had finally been revealed. But with all that had happened, there was still one thing I didn't understand.

"How?" I said. "How did I reveal the location of Mr. Pop? I didn't know where it was. I still don't."

I heard another voice say, "Neither did I."

I spun around quickly to see another person had entered the room. It was almost as confusing to me as when Challenger Green showed up. Maybe more so, because the implications were far more disturbing.

It was Nevva Winter.

"I couldn't get them to bring me there, no matter how much I begged," she said. "It wasn't until they needed to convince you to put your life on the line for their cause. I told them that one look at Mr. Pop would convince you to compete. Of course, it was my idea, so it was only fair that I tag along. Before we left, I dropped off one of these."

She held up one finger. Around it was a loop.

QUILLAN

I stood staring at Nevva with my mouth open.

"I . . . I . . . don't understand," I said.

"It's very simple," she said. "They tracked the loop."

"No!" I shouted. "You're a Traveler! How could you do this?"

Nevva walked farther into the room and stood next to Saint Dane. My mind wasn't accepting what I was seeing. It was impossible.

"I'm sorry I had to deceive you, Pendragon," she said. "I'm not your enemy. But we needed you to compete, and to help us find Mr. Pop."

My mind flashed back to the time I spent with her. Was it all a lie? Did she really read journals from the acolytes, or did she just listen to Saint Dane?

"Remudi!" I said. "How did you get him to compete?"

"The same way," Nevva said. "We told him he would be the inspiration for the revival, but that was never the plan. He was there to lure you into the competition."

I couldn't believe what I was hearing. "You knew he would die," I said. "You caused a Traveler to die."

"It was necessary," she said. "I'm not proud of what I did, but I'm very proud of the result."

"You're no better than Saint Dane!" I shouted.

"I've been all over Halla, Pendragon," she said. "What I saw time and again was hypocrisy. People everywhere fight and die for what they believe in. The trouble is, so few believe in the same thing, which pits them against one another. It's all so . . . futile. Saint Dane has convinced me that his vision can bring about a unified Halla with a single purpose."

"But what is that purpose?" I said, trying to keep from screaming. "He's a monster, Nevva! He may want to unify Halla, but into what? He has no conscience. He has no compassion. He doesn't have the ability to love."

Saint Dane said, "Ahhh, love. Love is at the root of every conflict. To say I am incapable of love is a compliment."

"How did he do it, Nevva? How did he get to you?"

"I lost my parents, Pendragon. I was angry. Then Press told me I was a Traveler. He showed me so much of Halla, but as much as he told me how things were the way they were meant to be, I couldn't accept it. Not after what happened to my parents. I knew there had to be a better way, and Saint Dane showed me. When the Convergence comes, I plan on being by his side."

"What is the Convergence?" I screamed. "Tell me!"

Saint Dane said, "You are barely beginning to evolve as a Traveler. I have taught Nevva many things. I can teach you as well."

Nevva said, "The battle will soon be over. You can make it so much simpler for everyone by giving in to the inevitable."

The impossible had happened. Saint Dane had turned a Traveler. I now had two enemies.

"What's next?" I asked. "Second Earth? Third Earth? What is this Convergence?"

Nevva said, "After what's happened here on Quillan, I don't think it would be wise for me to be here any longer. Ibara no longer has a Traveler. I might just take Remudi's place."

"It's done, Pendragon," Saint Dane said. "Save yourself and the lives of thousands. Do the right thing and take the advice you gave me on the Tato platform. Give up."

Boom!

The double doors leading into the trustee courtroom blasted open. We were under attack, but from whom? I dove down between some seats and looked up to see several people pouring into the room who looked like commandos. They were dressed all in black with black hoods, and carrying golden rifles. I knew them. It was the revivers.

Saint Dane and Nevva took off running. They sprinted out of the courtroom and down the corridor to the office of Mr. Kayto. Of Saint Dane. One of the revivers ran up and said, "Pendragon!"

"It was her!" I shouted. "Nevva! She's the one who gave away Mr. Pop!"

The guy motioned for the others to chase Nevva and Saint Dane. They quickly blasted out of the room. I don't know why I bothered telling them that. It was too late. The guy next to me took off his hood. It was the older guy who'd helped me when I first came to Quillan.

"What are you doing here?" he asked.

"They brought me here," I said. "What are *you* doing here?"

He sat down, looking tired.

"Making a useless gesture," he said. "With all the confusion after what happened to Mr. Pop, we thought we might get to the trustees to . . . I don't know what. The building's been evacuated. We didn't see anyone, until just now." The guy looked like he was going to cry. "It's over. It's done. Everything is . . . gone."

I knew how he felt. I wanted to cry too.

"I don't even know your name," I said.

"It's Sander," he said. "You were amazing, Pendragon. Everything was coming together. The revival had begun. And then . . ." He couldn't finish.

"Let's go see what the others have found," I said.

We left the courtroom. In the corridor there was a reviver standing outside the door to the office Saint Dane had used as Mr. Kayto. We hurried to meet him.

"Are they in there?" Sander asked.

"N-No," the guy said, sounding shaken. "Look."

We entered the office and saw the other revivers standing by the large floor-to-ceiling window—or what was left of it. The window had been smashed out.

"They jumped," one of the revivers said.

Sander looked cautiously out the window and down to the ground. I knew there would be nothing to see. They were gone. The grim reality hit me that I now faced two enemies with the same powers.

"Come on," Sander said. "It won't be long before the dados return. We're not safe here."

Sander brought me back to the underground. Though Nevva had revealed the location of the malls, there were still several safe places where the revivers could gather. Or what was left of them. The revival was dead. Destroying Mr. Pop had the exact effect that Saint Dane wanted: It destroyed the people's will to resist. Their hope was gone. In a short few moments the people had gone from the heights of enthusiasm to the depths of despair. The movement would not recover from it. Mr. Pop was more than a symbol—it was the last physical evidence of their past civilization, and it was gone.

I spent the next few weeks living with the remains of the revivers, trying to make sense of what had happened. They accepted me because I had given my all to help them, as futile as it may have been. I had earned their respect and their thanks. The whole time I spent with them, I didn't say much. I listened. I didn't like what I heard. These people were the heart of the revival, and they had given up. The destruction of Mr. Pop was too much for them to handle. Saint Dane was right. Hope is a fragile emotion that's easily lost. These people had lost all hope.

I knew how they felt, but my own loss of hope went far beyond the territory of Quillan. I felt as if we had reached another turning point. The turning point of Halla. I feared it had gone the wrong way. Knowing that I was partly to blame was hard to take. Saint Dane played me. So did Nevva. They built up my ego and made me think I was invincible. For all I knew, this was Saint Dane's plan all along. We Travelers have had a lot of success. I've had a lot of success. When Saint Dane physically attacked me on Zadaa, it pushed me into becoming a fighter. I was good at it. I may not have had the full-on killer instinct, but I was good. It now looked as if everything was designed to put me in this position, and cause the loss of another territory. And Halla.

My shame became complete when I was walking on the street several days after the Grand X. The screens on top of the buildings came to life. Who appeared? Veego and LaBerge. They were back in business. If that weren't bad enough, they were there to introduce a new Quillan game.

The contestants were the new Challenger Red and Challenger Green.

The new Challenger Green was . . . Tylee Magna. They had captured her shortly after Mr. Pop was destroyed. None of the revivers knew what had happened to her until that moment. The revivers had not only failed, their leader was being forced to play the Quillan games. I didn't watch the match. I couldn't.

I spent much of my time alone, writing this journal. This is the hardest journal I have had to write so far, because I feel as if I'm writing the final chapter. I don't know what to do next. Go to Ibara and track down Nevva Winter? But what of Saint Dane? Where was he headed next? He mentioned something called the Convergence. Is that a territory? An event? I have no way of knowing.

I think one of the reasons I wasn't quick to leave Quillan was because I didn't want to accept total defeat. I wanted to believe there was some seed, some person, some slight burning ember that was dug out of the ruin of Mr. Pop that would tell me all wasn't lost. But the longer I spent here, the more I realized I was dreaming. Quillan was dead. I helped kill it.

I almost ended the journal here. I was about to send it off to you guys when Sander paid me a visit in my little cell room.

"There's someone here who wants to see you," he said.

"Who is it?" I asked.

"I don't know," Sander answered. "She says she knows you."

I had no idea who it might be. Could another Traveler have shown up? Was it Loor? Or Aja? I followed Sander out to the common area that was an abandoned barbershop. Sitting in the ancient unused barber chair was an elderly woman. I didn't recognize her until she spoke.

"Hello," she said. "Do you remember me?"

"Yes!" I said. "I met you when I visited Mr. Pop. You gave me this for luck." I still had on the dark beaded necklace with the single gold bead. "You probably should have kept it yourself," I said, taking it off to give back to her.

"I don't want it," she said brusquely, almost in anger.

"Oh, okay," I said. "I'm glad you're okay."

"I barely escaped ahead of the attack," she said.

We both fell silent for a moment, remembering the carnage.

"Is there something I can do for you?" I asked.

"Maybe," she said. "And maybe there's something I can do for you. A while back I was given a gift. At the time I couldn't accept it. My life was falling apart and I didn't have the strength to deal with much of anything. I'm not proud of that, but at the time I did what I thought was right. I went into seclusion. I left behind everything I knew and dedicated myself to the revival, and to caring for the archives. For Mr. Pop."

"I'm sorry," I said.

"Not as much as I," she said. "If I hadn't done what I did, the library might still be safe. I'll have to live with that for the rest of my life."

"I don't get it," I said. "How could dedicating your life to Mr. Pop lead to its being destroyed?"

The woman took a deep tired breath, then said, "My name is Elli. Elli Winter. Nevva is my daughter."

My head felt light. I had to sit in the other barber chair.

"Did she tell you about me?" she asked.

"Yes," I said. "She thinks you tried to assassinate the trustees and that's why you disappeared."

Elli scoffed and said, "Maybe that would have been the smarter thing to do, as things turned out. Did you know my husband died in the tarz?"

"Yes," I said.

"He loved Nevva. She was his world."

"Excuse me," I interrupted. "You said she's your daughter?"

"Yes. We adopted her. She was always a precocious child. She challenged everything and questioned everyone. I wasn't surprised when I found out she'd gone to work for the trustees of Blok, but I was never more proud than when I heard she had joined the revivers. I was able to keep up with her through word of mouth, but never wanted her to know where I was."

"Why didn't you tell her you were okay?" I asked.

"At first it was because of what happened to my husband. I was devastated. I truly couldn't face the world, even Nevva. And then I was given some news that confused me even further. Instead of trying to understand, I ran away. Time went on and I found peace, but I didn't know how to tell Nevva what I had done. I was so ashamed. That's why I chose to live in the library. It was the most secret place I could find. Nobody came there. I was in a place where I could be alone to think and try to understand all that had happened."

"So what was the news you got?" I asked.

Elli was wearing a dark cloak. She reached into the folds. "I told you that I received a gift. It was shortly after my husband died. I think you might know what this is." She pulled her hand out of the cloak, clutching something tightly. She held it out and opened her hand to reveal . . . a Traveler ring.

"I was supposed to be the Traveler from Quillan, Pendragon. Your uncle Press brought me this ring and told me of my destiny. He said that I would be the Traveler until Nevva was ready, then I would pass the responsibility on to her." Tears welled up in Elli's eyes. "But I couldn't do it. I was frightened. Hearing stories of flumes and territories and

Halla and Saint Dane and *you*—it was all too much for me. So I ran away. Press was understanding, he told me that Nevva would take my place right away, but asked me to keep the ring. Now I find that my daughter has turned her back on everyone. She betrayed her people, and she betrayed the Travelers. If I'd been stronger, if I had been a better mother and faced my responsibilities, none of this would have happened."

Elli was in tears. I put my arms around her and held her tight. She clutched at my shoulder.

"Why did she do it? What was she thinking? Is my daughter evil?"

"I'm not going to defend her," I said. "But I will say that Saint Dane is a powerful influence. He's got her twisted into believing that to follow him is the best way to save Halla. Nevva is brilliant, maybe that's why she was vulnerable. Saint Dane somehow appealed to her intellect, and won her over."

Elli pulled away from me and wiped her eyes. "I promised myself I wouldn't do that."

"It's okay," I said.

"No, it's not," she said with authority. "I'm not the same person I was. This may sound strange coming from an old woman, but I've grown up. I'm ready."

"For what?" I asked.

Elli took a deep breath and announced, "I'm ready to be the Traveler from Quillan."

After all that had happened. After the devastation and betrayal and crushed ideals and total despair that had marked my stay on Quillan, I finally found it: In this simple old woman I found a small glimmer of hope. Would it be enough to resurrect a territory? Or save Halla? It's way too soon to tell. But when you get as low as I had gotten, and this territory had gotten, having someone willing to take on the fight goes a long way. Saint Dane was right. Hope is a fragile thing. It's easy to lose, but it's possible to get it back.

And I got it back.

I'm ending the journal here and sending it to you guys. I'm going to spend a few weeks with Elli, filling her in as best I can on all things about the Travelers. That's pretty funny. How can I be the one to explain what it means to be a Traveler, when I barely know myself? I can't help but run Saint Dane's words over in my head. He said we weren't real, that we were illusions. I don't believe him. We are very real. We have saved territories. We have made mistakes, but we have made a difference. Mostly it's been good. I'm not ready to give up the fight yet. I was, but Elli changed my thinking. If she's willing to give it another go, so am I.

But right now I need to see a familiar face. I need to see people I know I can trust. I need to see you guys. Having Nevva turn on us has really set me back. It makes me wonder what reality really is, and where this is all going to lead. If there's one thing I've gotten from Quillan, it's that the battle with Saint Dane is a lot more complex than I thought. There's good. There's evil. And there's a sea of confusion in between. I can only hope that at some point I'll be able to sort it out.

And so we go. I'll see you guys soon.

END JOURNAL #27

◉ SECOND EARTH ◉

"I'm sorry," Courtney said as she put the pages down.

Bobby was lying on the floor. He wasn't used to sitting on soft furniture anymore. "Don't be," he said. "I only have myself to blame for what happened."

"I'm not so sure about that," Courtney said. "But what I meant was, I'm sorry for what I'm about to do."

"What's that?" Bobby asked.

"You need a break. I'm not going to give it to you. I've got to tell you what's been happening here. It's only going to make it worse."

Courtney spent the next hour telling Bobby all that had happened since they left each other as the flume collapsed on Eelong. She didn't leave out a single detail, telling him how no time had passed while they were on Eelong; about the depression she went into after learning of Kasha's death; about her recovery at summer school, and of course, about Whitney Wilcox. She told him the whole story of Andy Mitchell and how he joined Mark's science club, and how they became friends and ultimately how he helped Mark save her life. She told Bobby all about the science project that he and Mark had worked on and how Mark's parents were killed in the plane tragedy.

The hardest part of all was telling Bobby how Andy Mitchell was Saint Dane all along. From the time they were kids. She ended by telling Bobby that after learning of the tragic death of his parents, Mark jumped into the flume with Andy Mitchell. With Saint Dane. Where? She didn't know.

Bobby listened to the whole story without saying a word. Courtney saw him wince a few times, but he never interrupted. She ended her story by explaining how, after she had been pulled into the flume and dumped back on Second Earth, strange things had appeared, like the talking cat and the impossible computer and the pepper spray that wasn't pepper spray. When she finished, she sat back on the couch, exhausted. The two sat there for the longest time, not saying a word. Courtney knew that Bobby needed time to digest all that she had told him.

Finally Courtney said, "I know you came home to get away, but I don't think a place exists to get away anymore."

Bobby nodded. Courtney could tell he was rolling all the events around in his head.

"Let's take this slowly," he said. "We first need to confirm some things. Are you with me?"

"You know I am," Courtney said.

The first order of business was to get Bobby better clothes. Courtney's dad was roughly Bobby's size, so she raided his room. She got Bobby better jeans and a shirt that fit him. It was cold out, so she also grabbed a Polarfleece jacket that her dad wore hiking. She thought that Bobby looked way better, and more importantly, wouldn't get a second glance from anybody. The mystery of what had happened to Bobby and the Pendragons was still out there. People didn't talk about it every day anymore, but the police investigation was still ongoing. It wouldn't be a good thing for him to be recognized. But Bobby had grown so much that Courtney was pretty sure nobody would recognize him. Just to be safe, she grabbed a pair of her dad's sunglasses. The illusion was complete. No way did he look like the fourteen-year-old Bobby who had disappeared three years earlier.

Even though both of them were old enough, neither had gotten their driver's licenses. Courtney had been dealing with too many issues to take the time, and there weren't any driver's ed classes being taught on Eelong, Zadaa, or Quillan. That meant to get around they had to ride bikes. Courtney rode hers and Bobby borrowed her dad's.

"Hey," Bobby said as they started to pedal. "It's just like riding a bike."

Courtney laughed. For that one instant she felt as if things were back to normal. Bobby was making dumb jokes and they were riding bikes through Stony Brook. Courtney allowed herself to pretend life hadn't changed, if only for a few precious minutes.

Their first stop was at the florist shop that was run by Andy Mitchell's uncle. It was gone. There was an empty lot where the building once stood. Neither Bobby nor Courtney said a word. Neither was surprised. The next stop was Glenville School, the grammar school where Bobby, Courtney, Mark, and Andy Mitchell had all gone. Bobby waited outside while Courtney went in to the office and spoke to the secretary, explaining how Andy Mitchell was going to some big science fair in Orlando, and she was doing a piece on him for the high school paper and could she please look through some of the old records for pictures and whatnot of Andy? The secretary said she couldn't give out official records, but she'd look to see what she could find.

Fifteen minutes later she returned with strange news that wasn't strange to Courtney at all. There was no record of Andy Mitchell. Nothing. Zero. The secretary didn't understand, because she remembered Andy very well. She'd caught him smoking in the boys' room more than once. The woman wanted to keep talking, but Courtney had heard enough. She thanked the woman and left.

Bobby and Courtney rode to Stony Brook Avenue, where they bought a couple of boxes of golden fries and cans of Coke from Garden Poultry Deli. The sun had warmed the day up enough so they could sit in the pocket park near the deli and enjoy their greasy-delicious lunch while they talked.

"So it's true," Bobby said. "Saint Dane was Andy Mitchell the whole time. I always hated that guy. He was such a tool to Mark."

"It's scary to think he was watching us our whole lives," Courtney said. "He's been plotting this for years."

"What was that science project they were working on again?" Bobby asked.

"They called it 'Forge.' It looked like a hunk of Play-Doh, but it was voice activated. You told it what shape you wanted it to be, and it turned into it. It was pretty incredible. Do you think that's significant?"

"I think everything is significant," Bobby said. "Do you still have that pepper spray?"

Courtney reached into her pack and took out a silver canister.

"That is *not* the same thing I put in my pocket when I left this morning," she said.

Bobby looked around to see if anybody was watching. He pointed the canister at a sculpture of an owl that was carved out of wood, and pressed the trigger.

Fum!

The owl was knocked off its perch.

"I've never seen anything like it," Courtney said.

Bobby handed her back the canister and said, "I have. On Quillan. That's the same kind of weapon the dados used."

Courtney looked at the canister like it was an alien creature—because it was.

"How did it get here?" she said in awe. "And how did it get in my pocket?"

"Something happened when you went through the flume," Bobby said. "That's the only thing I can think of."

"But I didn't do anything!" Courtney said.

"Somebody did," Bobby said. "You came back at the exact same time you left, but things were different. Somehow, technology has changed."

"But nobody else notices!" Courtney exclaimed. "That car seat was definitely not the same, but my father didn't know it. And my mother doesn't even know how to turn on the computer, let alone send video messages from work."

"That's because things haven't changed, for them," Bobby said. "But you weren't here for it. You were in the flume."

"Huh? What does that mean?"

"It means somebody's been messing with the past," Bobby said. "Let's go."

They got on their bikes and went right to the National Bank of Stony Brook, where Courtney put Bobby's journals in the safe-deposit box with all the others. With that done, their plan was to go back to Courtney's house, but Bobby wanted to take a quick detour. He wanted to ride by the spot where his house used to be. The house he grew up in. The house that disappeared when he left home. Courtney tried to talk him out of it, but Bobby's mind was made up.

When they got to 2 Linden Place, Bobby saw why Courtney didn't want him to come back. Someone had taken over the property. A house was being built. It was a modern-looking building, nothing like the classic old farmhouse where Bobby had lived with his family for the first fourteen years of his life. Bobby stood across the street, staring at the place that was so familiar, and so wrong.

"You okay?" Courtney asked.

"He said I was an illusion," Bobby said softly. "Maybe he was right."

"You're not an illusion, Bobby Pendragon!" Courtney scolded as she grabbed his arm. "I can touch you. I can hear you. Everything you do has an effect on physical reality. That doesn't sound like an illusion to me."

"No?" Bobby asked. "Then what am I?"

Courtney started to answer, but stopped. The truth was, she didn't know.

They pedaled back to Courtney's house silently. Once inside, Bobby examined the strange new computer that had appeared in the living room.

"I'm not a computer geek," he said. "But I've never seen anything like this."

"I'm less freaked about the computer than I am about the cat," Courtney said.

Bobby spotted the black cat lying on a windowsill, sunning itself. They both walked over to it. Bobby tentatively reached out and rubbed his hand across the cat's belly. The cat purred.

"Nice," the cat said dreamily.

Bobby whipped his hand back.

"That's just creepy," he said. He reached out again and rubbed the cat's belly again. He didn't so much stroke the cat, as examine it. After a few seconds he announced, "It's not real. I mean, it's not a living thing. Feel."

"No thanks," Courtney said.

"Go ahead, I won't bite," the cat said.

Courtney shot Bobby a look, then cautiously reached out and stroked the cat's belly. "It's not soft. It feels . . . stiff."

"It's mechanical," Bobby said.

Courtney said, "I don't know what's weirder, a talking cat or a mechanical cat."

"There's no mystery," Bobby said. "I've seen this. That pepper-spray weapon and this cat—they're technology from Quillan."

"Is that it?" Courtney said with surprise. "Has Saint Dane somehow brought Quillan technology to Second Earth?"

"I believe it," Bobby said, pacing. "He's trying to break down the barriers between territories. Whatever happened here, the natural evolution of Second Earth has been altered. Every time something new is introduced, a shift is bound to happen. This is nothing. What happens when he stumbles on something that causes a catastrophic change? He might create some mutant strain of disease, or natural disaster. One territory could effect the next and the next until—"

"The Convergence," Courtney said.

"Yeah," Bobby said. "The Convergence."

"What could it be?" Courtney asked.

"I don't know," Bobby said. "But Saint Dane and Nevva were pretty sure that it was inevitable."

The two fell silent.

Courtney had been standing with her hand on the cat's belly. Suddenly she yelped and pulled her hand away.

"What?" Bobby asked.

"I must have hit something," she said. "Look."

A panel had ejected from the cat's belly, like a drawer. It was a flat white panel with writing on it.

"What is it?" Bobby asked.

Courtney leaned down and took a close look. The cat continued to purr, oblivious.

"Man, this is strange," she said. "It's product information. There's care instructions, it says where to call for service, and—"

Courtney stopped talking. Bobby watched her, waiting for her to continue. She didn't.

"What?" Bobby finally asked.

Courtney spoke slowly, saying, "There's a trademark. It has the name of the company that built this thing."

"Yeah? What is it?" Bobby asked impatiently.

Courtney's voice was quivering. "Maybe it's a coincidence."

"Tell me!" Bobby insisted.

"The name of the company that made this cat is the Dimond Alpha Digital Organization."

"Dimond?" Bobby repeated. "Spelled like—"

"Yeah, spelled like Mark," she said.

Bobby paced nervously. "It could be a coincidence," he said hopefully. "Dimond's not a hugely common name, but it's not unheard of, either."

"Are you not getting it?" Courtney complained.

"Yeah, I'm getting it!" Bobby said. "Dimond, Mark Dimond. We can't jump to the conclusion that Mark had anything to do with this."

"Bobby!" Courtney yelled with frustration. "Maybe Mark had something to do with this and maybe he didn't. But look at the name of the company."

Bobby leaned down to the cat and read the trademark. "Yeah, I heard you, Dimond Alpha—" Bobby cut himself off. He looked at Courtney.

Courtney finished the thought, "Digital Organization. D-A-D-O. Dado."

The two stared at each other for several seconds, then Bobby said, "I'm going to the flume."

"To go where?" Courtney asked.

"To find Mark," he said.

"I'm going with you," Courtney said.

"You can't!" Bobby argued.

"Yes I can!" Courtney shot back. "I read what Saint Dane said. I can use the flume as long as I'm with a Traveler. That's you."

"Courtney, first off, I don't want to put you in danger."

"I'm already in danger!" she countered. "I spent a whole lot of months in the hospital, remember?"

"And you're still recovering."

"I'm fine."

"Your place is here, on Second Earth," Bobby argued.

"It's not just about Second Earth anymore, Bobby!" Courtney shouted. "It's all coming together. I know what you're thinking. Whatever Saint Dane did with Mark, they somehow altered the course of events on Second Earth. That's why things are different. If I'm going to help you protect Second Earth, we've got to find Mark, and Mark . . . isn't . . . here."

"If you went with me, I'd be no better than Saint Dane," Bobby said. "I'd be mixing the territories too."

"They're already mixed!" Courtney shouted. "This freakin' robocat is proof of that. And I hate to say that Saint Dane's right, but every time you go to a territory, you're kind of mixing things up yourself, aren't you?"

Bobby stared at Courtney. Her words were harsh, but hit him. "Is that true?" he said. "Did I do exactly what Uncle Press told me not to do?"

"I don't know, Bobby—"

"But if we can't do anything, what's the purpose of the Travelers?"

"To stop Saint Dane," Courtney said. "Any way you can. Any way *we* can."

Bobby paced nervously and said, "Is it really possible that he convinced Mark to join him?"

"I don't know," Courtney said. "But I don't think it's that simple. Mark was vulnerable. His parents were killed. I can't imagine where my head would be if I suddenly lost my parents."

"Nevva lost her parents," Bobby said. "It's one of the things that drove her to Saint Dane."

"We've got to find him, Bobby," Courtney said. "You can't go alone. I read how tough it was for you to be alone. Don't do it again."

Bobby rubbed his eyes angrily. He looked to Courtney like he wanted to scream.

"He's my friend too, " Courtney said.

Shortly after, Courtney sat at her kitchen table with a pen and paper to write the impossible. She had to say "good-bye" to her parents. As she sat staring at the blank notepad, she had no idea how to put what she felt into words.

"We should go," Bobby said.

Courtney wiped away her tears, gripped the pen, and simply wrote: "I love you both more than I can say. Try not to worry about me. I'll see you soon. Courtney." She folded the paper in two, placed it on the kitchen table where it was sure to be seen, and looked around the room. She wondered if she would ever see it again. Or her family.

"Second thoughts?" Bobby asked.

"Let's go," Courtney said.

Half an hour later the two were standing at the mouth of the flume, staring into infinity.

"How do you feel?" Bobby asked. "I mean, physically. You've been through hell."

Courtney took a second to answer, as if she were doing a mental inventory of her injuries. "You know what I feel like?" she asked.

"Tell me."

"I feel like all the work I did to heal was getting me ready for this," she said with confidence. "I am so ready."

Bobby smiled. That was pure Courtney.

"How is this gonna work?" Courtney asked.

"I don't know," Bobby said. "I guess we should just hold hands."

Bobby held out his hand.

Courtney took it and laughed. "Remember when we all went to the movies after that inter-city Little League game?"

"You mean the game I hit the homer off of you?" Bobby replied.

"And I struck you out three times," Courtney shot back.

"Yeah, I remember."

"I worked it so that I could sit next to you in the theater because I was going to try and hold your hand," Courtney confessed.

"But you didn't."

"I was scared."

"You? Scared?" Bobby said jokingly. "I'll bet that was the last time."

Courtney laughed too, then got serious and said, "It wasn't the last time. I'm scared right now. I'm going to do my best, Bobby, but I'll never be like Loor."

"Don't worry about it," Bobby said. "Neither will I."

They both chuckled at that.

"Do you really think Mark is on First Earth?" Courtney asked.

"Maybe," Bobby said. "It would fit. But I wouldn't know where to start looking for him, especially with Gunny gone. I think we're doing the right thing, at least to start."

"Me too," Courtney said. "I'm scared, and totally excited."

"Then let's go," Bobby said. He looked into the flume. "Ready?" he asked.

Courtney nodded.

Bobby called out, *"Third Earth!"*

The flume came to life. Both tensed up, fearing that the tunnel would crack the way it did the last time Courtney traveled. The light appeared from far in the distance and grew quickly. The jumble of sweet notes grew louder. The gray walls melted to crystal. . . .

And the tunnel didn't crack.

Courtney stepped closer to Bobby and put her arms around him.

"I want to see the future," she said.

"Good thing," Bobby said. "You're about to."

The light engulfed them. Courtney squeezed Bobby tighter and said, "Hobey-ho. Let's go."

The light flashed white, and a moment later they were gone.

To Be Continued

Here's a glimpse at PENDRAGON #8: THE PILGRIMS OF RAYNE

FIRST EARTH

The future isn't what it used to be.

I know that makes no sense. What else is new? There isn't a whole lot that has made sense since I left home three years ago to try and stop a shape-shifting demon who is bent on destroying all humanity. At least I think it was three years ago. It's hard to tell when you're out of your mind. And space. And time. My name is Bobby Pendragon. I'm a Traveler. The lead Traveler, in fact. The Travelers' job is to stop this guy named Saint Dane from changing the natural destiny of the ten territories of Halla and plunging them into chaos.

Do I have your attention yet? Stick around. It gets worse.

The Travelers' mission is to protect Halla. Halla is everything. The normal and the exceptional, the common and the impossible. Halla is all that ever was and all that will be. I know, sounds like a bad sci-fi movie. I'd think so too if I weren't living it. Every day. When I left home I was an ordinary fourteen-year-old guy whose biggest worry was whether or not Courtney Chetwynde liked me . . . and if she'd notice the zit that erupted in the middle of my forehead like some third freakin' eye. Now I'm seventeen and the leader of a group that must protect the well-being of eternity. The future is in my hands. The past is in my hands. There's nobody else who can stop Saint Dane.

Kind of makes the whole zit-on-the-forehead thing seem kind of lame, doesn't it?

Why Saint Dane calls himself "Saint" is a mystery to me. He is anything but. He isn't even human. At first I thought he was pure evil, just for evil's sake. But the more I learn about him, the more I realize there's something else that drives him. It's hard to explain because I don't understand it myself, but I've come to think that for some twisted reason, Saint Dane believes what he's doing is right. I know, how can a guy who is pushing societies toward cataclysmic disaster possibly believe what he's doing could be *justified*? When I find that answer, I'll unravel the entire mystery of what has happened to me. Why was I chosen to be a Traveler? What happened to my family? Where did Saint Dane come from? Why does he have these incredible shape-shifting powers? What did he mean when he said all the Travelers were illusions? (I've lost sleep over that one.) What is this all leading to?

Saint Dane talks about something called the "Convergence." I have no idea what it is, and I'm not entirely sure I want to. But I have to. Is it something Saint Dane is creating or was it destined to happen anyway? No clue. The only thing I know is that it's up to the Travelers to make sure whatever the Convergence is, it won't come out the way Saint Dane wants it to. It's the only way to be sure that Halla will continue to exist the way we know it. The way it was supposed to be.

I write these journals for two reasons. One is to document what has happened to me for the ages. You know, history and all that. A thousand—no, a million years from now I believe it will be important for people to know what happened. The other reason is to let my best friends from back home know what's going on with me. Mark Dimond and Courtney Chetwynde are the only people from Second Earth who know the truth.

But things have changed. Mark is missing. Worse, I'm afraid he started a chain reaction that caused serious damage throughout Halla. The cultures of the territories are not supposed to be mixed. I've learned that the hard way more than once. Okay, a lot more than once. Territories have their own distinct destinies that must be played out. Mixing the territories creates havoc. Saint Dane likes havoc. He's mixed the territories at every opportunity, and I believe he has gotten Mark to unwittingly help him do it again. At least I hope it's been unwitting. The alternative is unthinkable. I wish I had never gotten my friend involved in all this by sending him my journals.

As for Courtney Chetwynde, she's with me now. Together we've got to find Mark and try to undo the damage. Courtney and I have come a long way since we were childhood rivals. She is my acolyte and she is one of my best friends. Same as with Mark, I wish she weren't involved in any of this. She's been through hell. But we can't look back. We've got to keep moving ahead, which in some ways means looking back. Don't worry, that will make sense as you keep reading. I think.

With Mark missing and Courtney with me, I have no one to send these journals to. But I have to keep writing. For history's sake, as well as my own. Yes, there's a third reason why I write them. They help keep me sane. They allow me to look back and try to make sense of it all. The whole "making sense" part hasn't worked so well, but the keeping me sane part is a good thing.

I don't know who you are, reader, or how my journal

ended up in your hands. I hope that you've already seen my earlier journals, because I'm not going to repeat everything that has happened. Those early journals, starting with #1 (duh), contain the whole story. If you haven't seen them, go to the National Bank of Stony Brook in Stony Brook, Connecticut. Second Earth. My hometown. There's a safe-deposit box there registered to Bobby Pendragon. That's where my journals are kept. Find a way to get them and guard them with your life. They contain a story that, when complete, will tell of the events leading up to the destruction or the salvation of all that exists. Of Halla. It's a real page-turner, if I do say so myself.

As I write this, Courtney and I have traveled to Third Earth. Our home world in the year 5010. That's three thousand years in the future from the time when we were born. This is where we hope to find answers. This is where we hope to find Mark. After being here for only a short time, we've quickly discovered a scary fact.

The future isn't what it used to be.

This is where the next chapter in my adventure begins.

And so we go.

FIRST EARTH

I hope I haven't made a huge mistake by leaving Second Earth with Courtney Chetwynde.

She isn't a Traveler. Only Travelers are supposed to use the flumes—the highways between territories. I learned that lesson when Mark and Courtney traveled to Eelong on their own. The flume there collapsed, trapping the Travelers Spader and Gunny and killing the Traveler Kasha. Since then I learned that as long as someone uses the flume with a Traveler, nothing bad will happen. At least, nothing bad to the flume. What happens to the future of a territory once a non-Traveler gets there is a whole nother issue. Like I wrote, territories are not supposed to be mixed.

Which is exactly why Saint Dane has been doing it.

He's deliberately brought people and technology and even animals from one territory to another. I don't know if that has been his plan all along, but he's definitely going for it now, and things are getting whacked. When he won Quillan, I'm afraid he tipped the balance of the war for Halla. He's winning. I feel it. It's not that I'm getting desperate, but it's time to level the playing field. Maybe I've waited too long already. Why do the good guys always have to play by the rules while the bad guy does whatever he wants? Where is that written? It's not like I want to start messing with the territories randomly. No way. But if I can gain an advantage over Saint Dane by bringing an element from one territory to another, I'm going to do it.

Right now, that element is Courtney Chetwynde.

Things have gone strange on Second Earth. History has changed. Technology has changed. Whatever caused it has something to do with Saint Dane's plan for our home territory. Courtney is the one person who can help unravel the mystery of what happened. Together we're going to learn the truth and try to make things right. The future of Halla is at stake. The future of Second Earth is at stake.

The future of Mark Dimond is at stake.

Am I making a mistake by bringing her? I don't know. Uncle Press always warned me about mixing the territories, but he isn't here anymore. Is it the right choice? I won't know until the ultimate battle is over and the Travelers have won.

Or lost.

During the journey, Courtney and I floated next to each other on the magical cushion of air that sped us through the flume. We both wore jeans, low hikers, and T-shirts. You know, your basic Second Earth uniform. I had to admit, Courtney never looked better. She'd grown up since I saw her last. I guess we all have. Her incredibly long brown hair was tied back in a practical braid. Her big gray eyes sparkled, reflecting the light from the stars beyond the crystal walls of the flume. I remembered the very first time I saw her. It was at recess the first day of kindergarten. I decided to pick up the dodgeball she had been playing with. She decided to punch me in the head.

"Don't touch my stuff," she scolded, and grabbed the ball back.

I should have been ticked, but something about her playful smile told me she wasn't your typical playground bully. I held back my tears, smiled, and said, "Don't start a fight you can't win." I grabbed the ball and ran away. She took off after me and chased me through the busy playground for the next ten minutes. By the time we stopped, exhausted, we were laughing. That began a love-hate relationship that has lasted to this day. We were always friendly rivals, trying to outdo each other in sports. Sometimes she'd win, other times it would be me. Neither of us really felt superior, but that didn't stop us from trying. The strange thing was that over those years our rivalry turned into serious affection. The night I left home with Uncle Press to become a Traveler, Courtney and I kissed for the first time.

So much had happened since that night. We were different people. As we floated through the flume, I saw it in her eyes—she was older. But "older" didn't really cover it. We'd both seen things that no kid should have to. No adult, either. The fourteen-year-old kids who kissed that night were long gone. We were the keepers of Halla now.

Courtney explained to me what happened when she followed Mark's instructions and went to the flume in the basement of the Sherwood house. Mark had left his Traveler ring for her. When she saw it, she realized the frightening truth. Mark had jumped into the flume. But where had he gone? And why? Mark no longer wanted to be an acolyte, that much was clear, because he left his ring. The flume wasn't damaged, which meant he'd left with a Traveler. But who? Could it have been Saint Dane? Not knowing what else to do, Courtney put on the ring. The flume sprang to life. Seconds later Saint Dane himself blasted out of the tunnel between territories and added yet another twist to the mystery by revealing a disturbing truth.

He had been with us on Second Earth our entire lives.

"It's so strange," Courtney said as we flew along. "Can you believe Saint Dane was Andy Mitchell from the beginning?"

"Yes," I replied flatly.

"Well, it surprised the hell out of me. He's been watching us our whole lives, Bobby. How creepy is that? He's been setting us up."

"No," I corrected. "He's been setting Mark up."

The cruel truth of what Saint Dane had been doing on Second Earth was finally revealed. Sort of. He became a person named Andy Mitchell, a low-life bully who harassed Mark for years. After I left home to become a Traveler, Andy Mitchell showed Mark another side of his personality. He turned out to be smart. Incredibly smart. He joined Mark's science club, which at first freaked Mark out. Courtney told me how it seemed impossible that a nimrod like Andy could suddenly become brilliant. But Mark believed. Soon the victim was drawn to the tormentor.

"That's how he works," I reminded Courtney. "He pretends to be a friend and lures you into doing things you think are right, but lead to disaster. He takes pride in that. He says that whatever happens isn't his doing. He believes the people of the territories make their own decisions."

"That's so bogus," Courtney snapped. "How can people make their own decisions when he's pushing them the wrong way?"

"Exactly. On Second Earth, he pushed Mark."

Andy Mitchell and Mark worked on a science project they named "Forge." It was a small, plastic ball with a computer-driven skeleton that would change shapes when given verbal commands. They were about to fly to Florida to enter a national science contest when Andy asked Mark to stay behind to help him clean out his uncle's florist shop that had been wrecked in a flood. Mark's parents flew to Florida without them.

Mr. and Mrs. Dimond never made it. Their plane disappeared over the Atlantic. Everyone on board was lost. Saint Dane had a hand in that tragedy. No doubt. He killed Mark's parents.

Courtney continued, "Saving First Earth didn't change things, Bobby. Saint Dane is coming after Second Earth. And Third Earth."

"I figured that."

"Whatever he's planning has to do with Mark," Courtney added. "He said their relationship had entered a whole new phase. What was that supposed to mean?"

"I don't know," I answered honestly. "But I think there's a pretty good clue in what happened next."

Second Earth changed. That's the simple way of putting it. It changed. Saint Dane jumped into the flume and Courtney got pulled in after him. Rather than being swept to another territory, Courtney was dumped right back in the cellar of the Sherwood house, where she'd started. But it wasn't the same place she had left only moments before. Second Earth had changed. Courtney quickly recognized strange differences, mostly to do with technology. She returned home to find a computer that was way more elaborate than anything she'd ever seen, and a robotic talking cat that nearly sent her off the deep end. Kinda freaked me out when I saw it too. We discovered it was manufactured by a company called the Dimond Alpha Digital Organization. DADO. It may have been a coincidence, but the robots on Quillan were called dados. That, along with the fact that the company that made the mechanical cat shared the same name as Mark, meant the coincidences were piling up a little too high to be coincidences anymore.

"I think when you did a boomerang through the flume, the history of Second Earth was changed," I concluded. "And since you were in the flume, you weren't changed along with it. You still remembered what the old Second Earth was like."

"Probably because Saint Dane wanted me to remember."

"Probably," I agreed. "I think Saint Dane used Mark to help create a new technology that is somehow going to lead to the turning point of Second Earth. Killing the Dimonds made Mark emotionally vulnerable. Who knows what Saint Dane told him to get him to leave Second Earth?"

"Still," Courtney countered. "I can't believe Mark would leave Second Earth with that monster, no matter how badly he felt about his parents."

"I know," I said softly.

"We've got to find him," Courtney concluded soberly.

The jumble of sweet musical notes that always accompanied a trip through the flume grew louder and more frequent. We were nearing our destination—Third Earth. It was where we would start our investigation. Patrick, the Traveler there, would be able to research the incredible computer databases of Earth in the year 5010 to trace how the Dimond Alpha Digital Organization came to be, and what may have happened to Mark. We were about to step into the future to try and piece together the past. But when we hit Third Earth . . .

Third Earth hit back.

D. J. MacHale's new trilogy,

MORPHEUS ROAD,

will make you want to sleep with the lights on.

Here's a sneak peek at how it all begins in Book One:

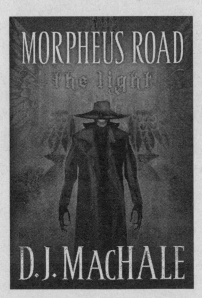

I believe in ghosts.

Simple as that. I believe in ghosts.

Maybe that doesn't come across as very dramatic. After all, lots of people believe in ghosts. You always hear stories about some guy who felt a "presence" or glimpsed a fleeting, unexplainable phenomenon. There are mediums who claim they can make contact with the great beyond and receive messages to let the living know that all is well. Or not. Then there are those people who operate on a more philosophical level . . . the spiritual types who believe that the energy of the human soul is so powerful, it must continue on after death to some other plane of existence. Of course, there are millions of people who love getting scared by ghost stories. They may not believe, but they sure have fun pretending.

I'm not like any of those people. At least not anymore. A little over a week ago you could have put me in the category of somebody who didn't necessarily believe in anything supernatural, though I did like horror movies. But that was then. Before last week. A week is like . . . nothing. How many particular weeks can anybody really remember? A week can fly by like any other. Or it can change your life. You tend to remember those weeks.

I remember last week.

It was the week the haunting began.

Or maybe I should call it the hunting because that's what it was. I was being hunted. And haunted. It wasn't a good week.

My name is Marshall Seaver. People call me Marsh. I live in a small town in Connecticut called Stony Brook. It's a suburb of New York City where moms drive oversize silver trucks to Starbucks and most kids play soccer whether they want to or not. It's the kind of place where kids are trained from birth to compete. In everything. School, sports, friendships, clothes . . . you know, everything. I'm not sure what the point is other than to win bragging rights. Luckily, my parents didn't buy into that program. They said I should set my own priorities. I liked that. Though it puts pressure on me to figure out what those priorities are.

I guess you'd call us middle class. We've only got one car and it's almost as old as I am. I can't believe it's still running, because we drove it into the ground. My parents liked to travel. That was one of *their* priorities. Whenever they had two days off, we'd hit the road, headed for some national monument or backwater town that served awesome gumbo or had historical significance or maybe just sounded different. I complained a lot about how boring it was, but to be honest, I didn't hate it. Bumping around in the back of a car wasn't great, but the adventure of it all made it worthwhile.

It's kind of cool to see things for real instead of on TV. I miss those trips.

Other than that, my life is pretty usual. Unlike a lot of people in this town, I've never been inside a country club. Most of my clothes come from Target. I ride my bike to school. We don't live in a monster-size house, but it's plenty big enough for the three of us.

That is, when there were still three of us.

Things have changed. Not that long ago I thought I had a pretty good handle on what normal was. I was wrong. Nothing about my life is normal anymore. The events that unfolded over the last week weren't just about me, either. Many lives were touched and not all for the better. As I look back, I can't help but wonder what might have happened if different decisions had been made. Different paths taken. So many innocent choices added to a butterfly effect that fed the nightmare. Or created it. I guess it goes without saying that I'm still alive. Not everyone was so lucky. That's the harsh thing about ghost stories. Somebody has to die. No death, no ghost. I survived the week and that gives me a feeling of guilt I'll carry forever. Or at least for as long as I live. I hope that's a good long time, but there are no guarantees because this story isn't done.

The hunt is still on.

My story may sound like a fantasy, and maybe some of it is. But many things happened over that week that can't be ignored or explained away as having sprung from an overly imaginative mind. People died. Lives were changed. That was no dream. After what I saw and experienced, there's one other bit of reality I have to accept.

I believe in ghosts.

After you hear my story, I think you will too.

PLAY!
Live the Game
Read the Adventure

Imagine the Unimagined

Log on to **DJMacHaleBooks.com**.
Answer the clue to unlock the secret
code! How good are you?

**What is the name of
the robot who is Bobby's
servant and companion
in the castle?**

There is a game for each
book and a code to match. Be sure
to use the answer to this clue as
the code to Game #7!

Keep reading Pendragon books
for more codes!

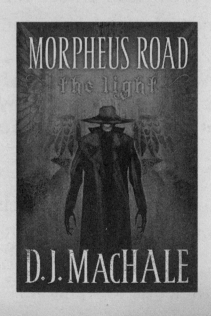